JAKOB'S STAR

JAKOB'S STAR

THE THIRD VOLUME OF THE JAKOB'S STAR TRILOGY

BY
RICHARD BARNARD
AND SAM HERTOGS

LOUIS HUBBARD
PUBLISHING

© 1999 by Sam Hertogs and Richard Barnard
Published by Louis Hubbard Publishing
1350 South Frontage Road
Hastings, Minnesota 55033-2426

Edited by Barbara Field

ISBN: 0-9644751-5-4

First Printing March 2000

10 9 8 7 6 5 4 3 2 1

Cover artwork by John Keely

Cover design by Richard Barnard

Printed in U.S.A.

PREFACE

WHAT I SEE FOR THEM IS NOT YET, WHAT I BEHOLD
WILL NOT BE SOON, A STAR RISES FOR JAKOB. A
METEOR COMES FORTH FROM ISRAEL

—Numbers
"Chapter 24, verse 17

The Jakob's Star Trilogy is a work of historical fiction.
Fictional events and characters have been interwoven with
the factual historical period from the end of the First World
War through the end of the 1980s. Names, characters,
places, and incidents in the fictional scenarios are either
products of the authors' imaginations or are used fictitious-
ly. Any resemblance of those fictional persons and situations
to actual events or persons, living or dead, is entirely coinci-
dental. Due to the extensive number of characters, we have
included a list at the back of the book indicating which
characters are fictional and which are based on actual people. Sam Hertogs and I have made efforts, through extensive research, to produce an accurate historical background,
but we have also taken license with historically ambiguous
episodes based on popular conjecture of that time.

The story of Israel is an incredibly complex history of
clashing religions and cultures all focused on an area of little more than 8,000 square miles, about the same size as the
state of Massachusetts.

Teshuva is a Hebrew word, a distinct part of the Jewish
religion which means "to return." It's part of the two-fold
concept of "Averah", the sin, and "Teshuva", the return
from that sin. It could be equated with the Christian vision
of sin and grace although the Jewish version requires action
on part of the individual, an atonement for the sin. Many
Jewish people see the founding of Israel as a return of the
Jewish people to the home of their ancestors. Some on the
extreme say Israel was denied to them for 2,000 years
because of the shortcomings of the Jewish people. Their
enemies say their claim is invalid either because it's only
based on 2,000 years of history or because 2,000 years is too
long for the claim to be valid. It's this sort of flip-flopping
that has precluded a meaningful dialogue between Israel

and her neighbors in terms of peace for the better part of half a century. How do you discuss peace when an enemy says you don't even have the basic right to exist?

Why is this little strip of land on the shores of the Mediterranean the focus of such a disproportionate amount of attention throughout the world? Perhaps because it was founded on a political consensus of the United Nations, or maybe because it's a modern state based on a unique combination of democratic precepts and a strong religious foundation. It seems obvious that a state claiming freedom and equality for all its citizens in the name of God would be held up to a higher ethical standard. And further, in an historical context, the people of Israel represent a human version of the Phoenix; a race risen from the ashes, suffering an incredible torture and then surviving. Perhaps many want Israel to prosper on that basis. Perhaps we expect something more of Israel because we assume they would seek to be the antithesis of the people that tried to destroy them. In our search for moral clarity, we'd like to view the victims as good and the oppressors as bad and carrying that to a logical conclusion, the survivors would be good as they went on to live their lives after their oppressors were beaten. We would simply like to view this nation's survival as the extension of an archetypal battle between good and evil. But, of course, the world doesn't exist in those terms. Good is never completely good, bad is never completely bad, and the past is no predictor of the future. The lesson learned by victims most often is not to live an exemplary and pious life, but rather that they must be sure that they will never be victimized again. The paradox then would be that in their drive to insure security, would they perpetrate the same kinds of acts as their former oppressors?

The fictional Jakob Stein Metzdorf is an exploration of this moral ambiguity. Jakob is a snowflake in the blizzard of existence, part of all that forms us and all that will follow, one of the lines that makes up this particular caricature of humanity.

RICHARD BARNARD
MINNEAPOLIS, MINNESOTA
NOVEMBER 1999

ACKNOWLEDGMENTS

We gratefully acknowledge the assistance of the following institutions and individuals:

The staff of the archives of the City of Munich, Germany
The staff of the archives of the City of Berlin, Germany
The staff of the National Archives of the
United States of America
The staff of the United States National Holocaust Memorial

Mr. and Mrs. Ralph and Ruth Jacobus
Frau Brigitte Schmidt
Mr. and Mrs. Wilhelm Schwartz
Mr. and Mrs. Gottfried Loescher
Mr. Ludwig Hirsekorn
Mrs. Kathy Murphy
Ms. Jean Weissenberger
Ms. Myra Dinnerstein
Mrs. Zemta Fields
Professor Herbert Jonas
Rabbi David Nussbaum of Salzburg, Austria
Mrs. Bobbie Jean Tervo
Ms. Dorothy Fritze
Ms. Jaci McNamara
Ms. Jeri Parkin
Mr. Brett Zabel
Mrs. Tamara Winn
Mr. Noah Anderson
Ms. Misha Dille
Ms. Michelle Russell
Mr. Nathaniel Edward Olson

The Jakob's Star Trilogy
is dedicated
to the innocent victims
of racial hatred.

CONTENTS

CHAPTER 1

The history of Central Europe has kept mapmakers busy for generations. Hungary, in particular, just in the first half of the twentieth century, was chopped up as part of the punitive actions inflicted by the Allies on the defeated Austro-Hungarian empire. Part of Hungary went to the newly formed nation of Yugoslavia, which was created of a panoply of former medieval kingdoms such as Croatia and Serbia. Another part of Hungary went to the newly formed independent republic of Czechoslovakia, which was a union of Slovenia, Moravia, Bohemia, and Ruthenia.

The loss of territory through the Treaty of Trianon at the end of the First World War was part of the reason Hungary allied itself with Germany early in the Second World War. Hitler had made overtures to Admiral Horthy, the Hungarian regent, suggesting that Hungary would regain its lost territory if they supported Germany. Hitler kept his word, allowing Hungary to take parts of Czechoslovakia and Romania. He also offered up territory from Yugoslavia when Hungary aided German forces in an attack on that country in April 1941, thus entering the war.

When Germany's fortunes changed in 1943 with the dramatic defeat in February of the German Sixth Army at the hands of the Russians in the siege of Stalingrad and the loss of North Africa in May, the Hungarian government began to reconsider its alliance in the face of the Russian advance. Hitler began to worry about Hungary's

1

allegiance for the same reasons and no longer considered the Hungarian government a reliable ally. German troops occupied the country in March 1944, and Horthy was placed under arrest in October, when a government friendly to the Nazis was installed.

Much the same as in Italy, the Hungarian government, as an ally of Germany, had not pursued Germany's genocidal policies against the Jews with any conviction. And also as in Italy, once Hungary's allegiance was in question and German troops occupied the country, Jewish deportations began shortly thereafter.

By the time Germany occupied Hungary, the Jewish community in Palestine knew about the German death camps from various reports across Europe. Despite the millions and millions of people who claimed they had no knowledge of the death camps, a number of firsthand accounts describing the camps had been published in newspapers around the world. Details of the death camps were given to intelligence agents who were assigned to debrief refugees from the German-occupied territories in Eastern Europe, and that information was forwarded to heads of state and government officials.

In Palestine, a plan was launched by the Jewish community under the auspices of the British government as part of the British mandate. Under the plan, volunteer Jewish commandos were dropped by parachute behind enemy lines to warn the Hungarian Jews of the impending disaster. The impending disaster, however, would also consume those sent to sound the alarm.

"WHY IS TONIGHT . . . ," Istvan Bartalan began, but then he realized he had said it wrong. Not wrong necessarily, but not the way his father preferred it, and so he looked up sheepishly toward the head of the table, where his father held the second cup of wine for the seder, and corrected himself: "I mean 'How does this night differ from all other nights?'"

Mikhalis Bartalan looked at his son, smiling gently. Istvan wanted to do well asking the questions at his family's Passover seder to please his father.

Istvan went on to ask the other questions. "Why on this night do we eat only bitter herbs?"

The words stuck in Mikhalis's mind as Istvan kept reading: ". . . Bitter herbs."

It had been six weeks since the leader of Hungary, Admiral Miklós Horthy, was summoned to Germany to meet with Adolf Hitler in his Obersalzberg retreat. Hungary had allied with Germany back in 1941, but now there were rumors that the Hungarian government was considering the prospect of capitulating to the Allies, just as Italy had done in early September of the previous year. Hitler was calling Horthy on the carpet and accusing him of betraying Germany in her hour of need.

The next day German troops entered Hungary.

While the Hungarians had cooperated with Germany in many ways, including thousands of soldiers joining the Hungarian divisions of the Waffen SS and fighting on the eastern front against the Russians, the Hungarians had not participated in the roundup and deportation of Jews in their country.

Mikhalis had been thinking about it for some time now. How could they possibly get out of the country?

The Russians to the east, Austria to the north . . . Yugoslavia had been occupied since 1941, with the murderous Catholic-supported Ustashi and the German SS decimating the Jewish and Serbian populations there. Romania and Bulgaria were sending troops to occupy Hungary in conjunction with the German forces.

". . . Why on this night must we all recline?"

After Istvan finished reading and the response was given, his mother uncovered the matzot, the unleavened bread, and gave the Hamatzoi blessing. Mikhalis stared past the faces of his loved ones: his wife, eleven-year-old son, and eighteen-year-old daughter, Galia. He stared into the future and saw a terrifying sight, a smoldering prophecy and barren humanity.

"We were all slaves to Pharaoh in Egypt," he finally said in an ominous, distant voice. "And the Lord our God delivered us from there . . ." Istvan thought he saw a tear forming in his father's eye, something he had never seen before. Maybe he had just never noticed it before, and now at eleven years old he was starting to see things around him. ". . . with a mighty hand and an outstretched arm."

Mikhalis's family Passover was taking place just as Jakob Metzdorf and his comrades were returning to Prague from Switzerland.

JAKOB, PETR, AND the others split up as they neared the Czech capital. They couldn't just walk back into their old lives in Prague. First they would have to go underground as they assessed the situation. They didn't know what had happened in the weeks since their departure, and they weren't going to walk blindly into some trap.

Jakob knew it wouldn't be a good idea to meet with any of his previous contacts. Surely word of the ambush in the Alps had gotten back, and even though they wouldn't be expecting him to return to Prague, they would have circulated his picture and were likely keeping an eye on any known associates. He decided to look up a young woman he had known from the university. Her brother had been killed as part of the retaliation for the Heydrich assassination, and he thought she might put him in contact with someone in the underground. He was very careful when the two of them went to meet Ondra.

Ondra wasn't what Jakob was expecting at all. He was a middle-aged, mousy little man with a severely receding hairline and exceptionally bad teeth, which made his speech difficult to understand at times. Ondra had a young man with him who produced a gun as Ondra dismissed Jakob's friend. She told him not to worry, that everything would be fine, and she quickly left.

Ondra needed to make sure Jakob wasn't a German agent sent to infiltrate the underground. They spent several hours going over Jakob's past. The only thing that saved Jakob, however, was the fact that Ondra had once worked with Petr Hrmeni and knew that Petr was back in Prague. Ondra had no doubts about Petr, so he left Sasha, the young man with the gun, to keep guard while he went to talk with Petr and verify the story.

Not long after that, Ondra had Sasha take Jakob to

a hiding place on the outskirts of Prague. Sasha left him there on his own in a little cottage, where he was to keep out of sight. No one contacted him for a week, and he tried hard to relax. He was eager to get back into the fight. When he had dealt with the German Abwehr in the person of Admiral Wilhelm Canaris a year or so earlier, he had gone by the name "Anton," and so when he returned to Czechoslovakia to once again fight with the partisans, he decided to use the same name in its informal Czech form: "Tonda."

When Sasha returned to the cottage, he couldn't find Tonda, but Sasha had a sixth sense, an asset that had saved him and some of his comrades on numerous occasions, and that sense told him that Tonda was nearby and watching him.

Sasha was only eighteen years old, compared to Jakob's twenty-seven, but his serious nature made him seem older than Jakob. Jakob, on the other hand, was playing a game of war. He would never have said that or even allowed himself to think it, but it was true. He had left Rebecca, Thomas, and the others in Switzerland to make their own way, never doubting that they would make it safely to Palestine, because it was what he wanted to believe. He would then be unencumbered by any family living in harm's way as he returned to the wonderfully exciting game of hide and seek.

Before long he was involved in a number of sabotage missions and raids on German positions to get weapons and ammunition. Within just a few weeks Ondra received word through other contacts that the Gestapo had targeted three people and were going to arrest them. Jakob was one of the three, along with Sáša and another young man named Jan.

Ondra soon came up with a plan to get his three comrades out of harm's way. He had a friend who worked in one of the German munitions factories in the area of Prague, a Sudeten German who had kept his anti-Nazi sentiments to himself and was considered infinitely loyal to the German cause, one of the thousands of German nationals liberated by the German army when Hitler sent his troops into Prague as part of the overture to the Second World War. This friend, Eugen Spengler, was a nondescript man in his midfifties, shorter than average, with a pleasant face, but certainly not the sort of man who would stand out in a crowd. Eugen had let Ondra know in general terms that he was not too fond of the Nazis and said that if there was ever a really desperate situation, he would do what he could to help. He wasn't volunteering to fight in the resistance or anything like that; he just wanted his friend to know that when it came down to it, he would stand against the Nazis rather than with them.

Ondra's plan came to fruition when Eugen asked Ondra for a favor. Eugen was assigned to drive a truck to Bratislava in Slovakia, replacing a man in his forties who had been called up for the army soon after Germany revised conscription age limits upward as their need for troops became more desperate. The trucks in a convoy always had two men, and the man with whom Eugen was slated to drive was a friend of Eugen's who was also sure to be called up for army service in short order. This friend had a young child and his wife wasn't well, so he didn't want to leave them. He wanted to go into hiding, but he didn't know how to go about it. Eugen advised his friend to wait before doing something stupid, saying that he might know someone who could help.

Eugen came to discuss the problem with Ondra just as Ondra was considering what to do about the imminent Gestapo arrests. The answer came to Ondra in a flash. If Jakob took the place of Eugen's friend, he could get all the way to Bratislava. Eugen's friend could use the time that Jakob and Eugen were on the road to slip away with his wife and child, and even when Eugen reported the man as missing, it would be in Bratislava, not Prague.

"Do all the drivers know each other? Could another driver slip in?" Ondra asked.

"They rotate the drivers. There are quite a few new ones now. If he keeps low . . ."

"Is there any way two boys could slip into the truck?" Ondra asked Eugen as he worked his way through laying out a plan.

Eugen was surprised as things began to develop much differently, more elaborately, than he had thought, and he stuttered a little as he answered. "I . . . I guess so . . . If there are two of us in the cab and we get away with that. We could hide two . . . but there are checkpoints. They would have to . . ."

"They would have to be in crates," Ondra said, finishing Eugen's thought.

"How could you do that?" Eugen asked.

"When do you leave?" Ondra countered, ignoring Eugen's question.

"The day after tomorrow at daybreak. Can you do it?"

Ondra just smiled.

The following night the trucks were loaded and ready. It wasn't a matter of getting Sasha and Jan into a crate on the truck. It was only a matter of getting an empty crate loaded onto the truck that Eugen and Jakob would be driving. At that point, if something were discovered as Eugen and Jakob started out, it could still be claimed that a simple mistake had been made and the plan could be aborted. The step after that was to get their truck at the end of the line of six trucks. Sasha and Jan would then rendezvous with the truck near a point where resistance men would get the trucks to stop for only a minute, long enough for Sasha and Jan to jump into the back of the truck but not long enough to draw suspicion from the escort at the head of the convoy.

"You look nervous," Jakob said to Eugen two days later as the truck lurched forward into the morning haze.

"I am nervous."

"It's fine to be nervous. Just don't look like you're nervous."

"What if they discover you?"

"You said there are a couple of new men on this run. Why would I stand out?"

Eugen glanced over for a closer look at Jakob as he drove. "I guess you don't. Are you Czech?"

"German. Born in Munich."

"When did you come to Prague?"

"I don't mean to be rude, but it doesn't pay to answer too many questions . . . or to ask too many."

"Of course. Just one more. When will we stop?"

out of the city. We may not even notice it."

"What if they have trouble?"

"We just keep going. If they get on, good for them, but if something goes wrong, we just go on as though we knew nothing about them. They'll have to make other arrangements."

"You're a cold one," Eugen said with an edge to his voice, as though Jakob were talking about abandoning his friends.

"Cold? No, that's just the way it has to be. Sometimes we have to improvise when things go wrong. It wouldn't do any good for us to get hooked if something goes wrong for them."

"I suppose you're right. So we won't even know if they're with us until we get to Bratislava?"

"They'll give us a couple of knocks on the wall of the truck box when we get going after they're on board, but we won't hear a sound out of them after that."

Eugen and Jakob didn't say much after that. They were just waiting for the rendezvous and hoping all went well. Jakob began looking at his watch after about ten minutes, checking almost every minute after that.

"You're making me nervous," Eugen said after Jakob checked his watch for the fifth time, but Jakob ignored the comment. Just then they heard the lead truck honking its horn, and soon the short column of trucks came to a stop.

"What is it?" Eugen asked.

"Could be the diversion," Jakob said. A moment later he felt a slight shake of the truck body. "That's it," Jakob said in response to Eugen's questioning look. Not long after the convoy started up again, they heard three soft knocks on the body of the truck.

The trip to Bratislava was slow, since all such convoys traveled at a constant forty kilometers per hour to conserve gas. The plan was to drive straight through, some eleven or twelve hours, with brief stops every two or three hours to change drivers and stretch. Whenever they stopped, a guard detachment would quickly file out of one of the trucks in front to stand watch for partisans or saboteurs.

It was a hard ride for Sasha and Jan, but they knew there wasn't any choice. Their only other option would have been to go into hiding until the war ended, and neither of them wanted that. The only things they brought with them were coats, their papers, and what money Ondra could spare for them. When they first climbed into the crate, they were grateful for the warmth after sitting out in the cold for an hour, but once the sun came up, it started getting too warm.

They had fasted the night before, knowing they couldn't eat or drink, because once in the crate they wouldn't be able to relieve themselves. There was danger with the heat that they might become dehydrated, so they took along a canteen, but only to use in an emergency. They also knew they could only sleep while the truck was moving. They had to be sure they were awake at all the stops, because snoring or even loud breathing could be a death warrant.

"They're slowing down," Jakob said as he put on the brakes.

"We're probably just stopping for food."

"You must be right. It's about time."

They pulled in close behind the other trucks, waved into place by one of the soldiers who was already posted to guard the trucks. Several of the other drivers and soldiers had started going into a nearby building that had once been a public house for the little village but had been taken over by the German army and now served as a stopover point for small convoys and soldiers in transit. It had the feel of a barracks inside, although there was a dining area on one side of the building, apart from the sleeping area with its wooden bunks stacked up in neat rows. There looked to be room enough for forty or fifty soldiers. The place was totally unmolested by partisans because it had no value in and of itself. There was no weapons stockpile, and the location was of no strategic importance. The only way it might become important would be if someone were to find out when a particular shipment of something valuable was passing through, but there would be much better places to attack such a convoy than this little hole in the wall out in the countryside, so it was a safe place to stop for a rest.

Eugen and Jakob joined the line of men picking up trays of food at a window to the kitchen and then sat down on a wooden bench at one of the long tables, apart from the others. The food was plain but filling, noodles with a bit of meat and a heavy gravy and surprisingly good, fresh bread, along with bitter ersatz coffee.

They were almost done eating when one of the other drivers walked over to Eugen. "Good bread," he said as he stuffed a piece in his mouth.

"Better than my wife makes," Eugen grumbled with a smile.

"How is Alva?" the other driver asked as he put out his hand to shake Eugen's.

"She's fine. How have you been, Heinrich?"

"Not bad, not too bad. Where's . . . ?" Heinrich started to ask, wondering where the regular driver was who traveled with Eugen. Suddenly a strange look came over Eugen's face, and Jakob looked up at Heinrich but then quickly turned away.

Jakob got up as casually as he could and quickly made his way to the door.

"So the son of a bitch did it," Heinrich continued as he watched Jakob leave.

"Heinrich, don't . . ."

"Aach," Heinrich said as he gave Eugen a slap on the shoulder, "it's not my business." Heinrich then just walked away.

Eugen was shaking. He knew he had to control himself. He couldn't run out after Jakob. He had to be calm and not draw attention. He got up and stretched and then started slowly toward the door.

"Hey you!" someone shouted.

Eugen froze in his tracks and looked behind him to see who was shouting at who. It was one of the soldiers, and he was looking directly at Eugen.

"Me?" Eugen asked innocently.

"Yes, you," the soldier said sternly. "What are you up to?"

"Up to?" Eugen repeated as he tried to swallow. "I was just . . ."

"Get back here! We're not your damn maids. Take

your tray to the dishroom!"

Eugen looked back at his and Jakob's food trays on the table. "Sorry," he said as he gathered them up and carried them to the kitchen.

"That's all you slobs ever say," the soldier added under his breath, now addressing the others as well.

Jakob hesitated when he got outside. He moved toward a stand of trees beside the building, but he didn't know what to do next. Should he run? Should he kill the soldier guarding the trucks and try to get Jan and Sasha out?

He stood there only a moment, a few indecisive seconds, but it seemed like forever. He finally made up his mind to try to get Jan and Sasha out, but just as he moved toward the truck he noticed someone coming out of the barracks. They must be on to him. He had to run. He took a couple of steps, watching the door as he moved, but then realized it was Eugen and stopped.

When he was sure Eugen was alone, he walked over to meet him. "What happened?" he asked quietly as he pulled out a cigarette and offered one to Eugen.

"N-n-nothing," Eugen answered.

"Then what's wrong?"

"Just nervous," Eugen said as he took a long puff from the cigarette Jakob had just lit for him. "I don't mind telling you that scared the hell out of me."

"But what about that other driver?"

"He just said it was none of his business and walked away," Eugen said with a relieved smile.

"Do you think he meant it? Are you sure he won't say anything?"

"I'm pretty sure. I've known Heinrich for some time."

"But are you positive?"

"Positive? No, not positive."

"I was thinking we could make a run for it from here."

"From here?" Eugen said questioningly. "What about the guard?"

"I'd have to kill him."

"What about me? If you kill the guard and I'm still..."

"You'd have to come with us."

"With you? Are you crazy? I'm not going to . . ."

Just then the other drivers started coming out of the barracks.

"Too late now," Jakob said as he watched the others, trying to see if there was anything unusual. This would be the time when he would have to leave Jan and Sasha behind. He would have to run by himself if they came for him.

"Let's just walk to the truck," Eugen said as he took Jakob's arm.

Some would say Jakob had an overactive imagination, or just that he always expected the worst, but in his mind's eye he suddenly had a vision of Eugen holding his arm, preventing him from drawing his pistol as the soldiers drew down on him. "Let go!" he said loudly as he shook off Eugen's hand. A couple of the soldiers and several of the drivers looked up for an instant, and that was all it took for Jakob to realize he was overreacting and that nothing was wrong. With that he turned and headed back for the truck.

Not long after they got back on the road, it began to rain. There was a heavy downfall at first that virtually blinded the drivers, but that only lasted about ten minutes before turning into a light rain.

"Good news for Jan and Sasha," Jakob said, breaking the silence that had filled the cab since they left the previous stop. "This will cool it off in there a bit."

"How do you think they're doing?" Eugen asked, feeling a bit guilty at the thought of the boys back there without food or water while he had just finished a relatively pleasant dinner.

"I'm sure they're not doing well."

"Not doing well?"

"They're sleeping in a coffin back there. Two bodies next to each other in a closed box produce a lot of heat. We'll be lucky if they don't suffocate."

"Suffocate?" Eugen repeated with alarm. "You don't mean that."

"They knew what they were in for. The box was supposed to have air holes, but I don't know if it was done. Hopefully the rain will give them some relief."

"It doesn't sound like you give a damn either way."

Jakob looked at Eugen. "That's the second time you've said that."

Eugen just glared back at him. Jakob was giving Eugen a chance to recant, but Eugen had meant what he said and let the words stand.

"You think I'm a monster? Well, I've seen too much, done too much to—"

"To care about those boys in the back of the truck?"

"No. To care too much about things I can't

change. I have to concentrate on the things I can do something about. You take a big chance with your life when you let yourself get distracted."

"Uh-huh," Eugen grunted. "Sure."

Jakob just turned back to the road. He didn't care what Eugen thought of him. He didn't know Eugen, and he'd never see him again once they got to Bratislava. Eugen didn't know what it was like to fight. You had to be . . . cold. Yes, that was it. Just like Eugen said. You had to protect yourself from losing your friends by remaining detached. You couldn't trust anyone. Betrayal was a constant threat for the partisans. It could be a villager turning you over to the Germans to save his friends and family, a fellow partisan talking after being captured, some "super-Nazi" civilian hearing a rumor and reporting it, or any number of things. The Gestapo was always willing to work on even the slightest of leads. They were more than willing to make an example of innocent bystanders because any mistake, even if they didn't get the man they were after, would still have the desired effect. Many a Czech, and indeed many a citizen in any German-occupied country, would refuse to help and might even report resistance fighters to authorities, justifying their actions by saying, "If this is what the Germans do to innocent people, there's no telling what they would do to those who actually helped the partisans."

It was a long road to Bratislava. Jakob found himself getting edgy, watching for signs of trouble. He carried a small bag with some canned food and some poorly forged papers that Ondra had gotten at the last minute. Jakob knew the papers weren't very good, but there wasn't anything he could do about it. Ondra had met him on Thursday night and told him he was leaving Friday morning, and that was it. That was how it had always been with Ondra. He felt any advantage gained by giving his contacts advance notice of upcoming actions was far outweighed by the danger of someone getting caught and compromising the whole group.

It was still raining lightly as they neared Bratislava. It was late in the afternoon, and the sun, which had just begun peeking through the clouds, hung low in the sky. They were running behind schedule, but that worked to the advantage of Jakob and the others. They could get out with the last bit of daylight and then disappear into the darkness. And by the time Eugen arrived in Bratislava without them and reported Jakob missing, it would be completely dark.

"There's supposed to be a stretch of winding road coming up here soon," Jakob said as he checked a map. "All you need to do is slow down a little as you take the corners so there's a minute or so when the truck ahead of us can't see you."

"Can't see me? What are you going to do?"

"I'm going to jump."

"Jump? What about the ones in back?"

Jakob reached out the window and pounded on the body of the truck three times.

"And what's that supposed to do?" Eugen queried.

Jakob didn't respond. He just waited a few seconds and pounded again. After a few minutes—the time it took for Jan and Sàsa to open the lid of the crate—there was a responding knock from the back of the truck. Jakob then gave one last knock to acknowledge their response.

"They know the plan," Jakob finally said defiantly. "I jump first, and then they bail out at the next turn."

"If they can."

"Right. If they can," Jakob cut in, no longer trying to mask his anger. "You heard them knock . . . and if they can't jump, I go on alone. That's the way it is. That's the plan. If you've got a better idea, let's hear it."

Eugen said nothing.

"I don't know what you thought this was about, but this is how it is. It's dangerous and unpleasant, and it's not fair. Now, are you ready?"

"Just slow down around the next two corners?" Eugen repeated nervously.

"That's it. And then when you get to Bratislava in about twenty minutes, you start honking and yelling that I jumped out of the truck and ran."

"Right," Eugen said as he stared straight ahead. "There's the first corner coming up."

"Good luck," Jakob said as he grabbed his small bag and pulled the door handle, releasing the latch but holding the door closed. "And Eugen?"

Eugen looked Jakob in the eye.

"Thanks."

Eugen just shook his head. *What an ass,* he thought to himself.

Suddenly the truck ahead of them was out of sight. Eugen let up on the gas pedal and Jakob opened the door enough to step partway out, crouching on the running board and waiting until the last possible instant before the truck turned the corner and Eugen sped up. Jakob then rolled off the running board, tucking himself into a ball as he landed in the clay on the shoulder of the road, which had been made soft and slippery by the afternoon's rain. It couldn't have gone better.

As soon as they had heard Jakob knock on the side of the truck, Jan and Sasha had started getting out of the crate. It had gotten so hot that they were both soaked in sweat, but Jakob had been right about the rain. It had cooled things off enough to make it bearable. When they had gotten into the crate, they had pulled the lid shut behind them with ropes, tying them off to a couple of nails inside the box. Now they worked feverishly to get the crate open so they would be ready to jump in time. But they hadn't accounted for the incredible leg and arm cramps they were experiencing after lying in the same position through the cold and then the intense heat. They felt as though they had been beaten with ax handles as they got out of the crate and worked their way to the back of the truck. Jan cleared the canvas flap just as Jakob landed in the mud on the shoulder of the road.

"This is it!" Jan shouted as he straddled the tailgate with one foot on the bumper.

"Remember to roll!" Sasha shouted back as they felt the truck jerk slightly when Eugen let up on the gas pedal. There was another slight jerk as Eugen floored it to catch up with the trucks ahead of him, and that was their cue. They rolled off the bumper and across the shoulder of the road just as Jakob had done.

Jakob, running to catch up with Jan and Sasha, rounded the corner as the trucks all disappeared from sight and the sound of their laboring engines began to fade. Just as he got close enough to see his comrades, he heard another vehicle coming down the road behind him.

"Someone's coming!" he shouted. "Get into the woods!"

"What?" Sasha shouted back.

Jakob panicked. "A truck's coming!" he shouted again as he started running for cover.

"Come on," Sasha said to Jan, but when Jan tried to get up he screamed in pain and fell back. "Damn! I've broken my shoulder!"

"We don't have time for that," Sasha said as he grabbed Jan and lifted him up by the other arm, all but carrying him into the woods alongside the road. They made it just as the truck rolled by. Jakob watched in amazement as a German light-armored personnel carrier rumbled by, and just when he thought that was the last of it, another two trucks full of German soldiers came by. He knew they must have been a follow squad for the convoy, but he'd had no idea that they were there. They hadn't stopped with the convoy at any of the stops, and they had never gotten close enough for Jakob to see them.

Once the car passed out of sight, Jakob stood up and, unaware that Jan was hurt, shouted to Jan and Sasha, "Did you see that? I didn't even know we had a follow squad."

"Good, Tonda! Now would you get over here? Jan's hurt."

"We were lucky we didn't wait another minute. They would've—"

"Quiet!" came a voice from somewhere in the woods, cutting Jakob off in mid-sentence.

Jakob instantly dropped to the ground and pulled out his pistol as Jan and Sasha did the same.

"Who are you?" the voice boomed again.

"Who are *you?*" Jakob shouted back.

"We're not going to get very far this way," the voice answered.

Jakob scrambled over to Jan and Sasha. The voice said nothing, so apparently it, or they, weren't threatened by this move. "They must have more men than we do," Jakob said, "or they would have tried to stop me."

"Maybe they're unarmed," Jan offered.

"I doubt that. They wouldn't have said anything if they were afraid of us."

"A funny thing about these woods," the voice boomed out again, "sound travels well. We can hear everything you say."

"Well . . . ," Jakob said in a conversational tone as he sat up, crossing his legs and resting his pistol on his lap, "am I right?"

"You're very good. We saw you get out of the truck... Just a group of vagabonds catching a ride?"

"No . . . we just had to get a ride out of town."

"Munich?"

"No, Prague. Why would you say Munich?"

"You've still got that Bavarian accent. Not a good idea when you're alone in the woods outside Bratislava."

"Some Sudetendeutscheren fight the Nazis," said

Jakob.

"I've also heard stories of unicorns and dragons, but I've never actually seen one."

"That's not a Slovakian accent you have," Sasha interrupted. "Where are you from?"

"We're from Hungary," the voice answered, "but I've seen enough of these woods when I was a boy."

"My mother and I moved to Austria after my father's death, and we got out just before the *Anschluss*," Jakob started in again. "We were in Prague when the Nazis took over."

"You're a Jew!"

"Why do you say that?"

"Who else would keep running a step ahead of the Nazis? Are you saying you're not?"

"No, you're right. I just wondered why you said it. So, how long are we going to keep talking like this?"

"I'll tell you what . . . why don't you throw out those pistols and we'll come down and make sure you're telling us the truth?"

Jakob looked at Sasha and then at Jan. Jan arched his eyebrows and nodded his head, and Sasha agreed that they might as well. They tossed their pistols a few feet away, and as soon as they did, a dozen men in peasant clothes with rifles and a couple of submachine guns seemed to appear out of nowhere, quickly closing in on them.

"Is his shoulder broken?" the voice asked, but now it belonged to a tall, thin man carrying one of the submachine guns.

"I haven't had a chance to look," Sasha answered.

"Lorencz, check him out," the voice ordered as he waved his gun in Jan's direction. The largest man among them, a heavyset man who looked like a wrestler, handed his rifle to one of the others, obeying his commander. "I hate to sound like the Nazis," the voice continued, "but do you have some papers we could see?"

The three of them fished out their forged papers and handed them over as Lorencz inspected Jan's shoulder. "Not broken . . . dislocated," Lorencz pronounced, and suddenly Jan screamed out in pain as Lorencz put him in a scissor lock and pulled his arm firmly, setting it back in place with a loud pop. Jan passed out from the pain.

"My name is Izsak," the voice announced as he handed back their papers. "Where are you going?"

"We just needed to get out of Prague. It was getting too hot. They had our names."

"Bratislava?"

"It just happened to be convenient. It was a ride."

"You cost us a lot of ammunition," Izsak declared, referring to the convoy.

"So that's why you're here," Jakob said thoughtfully, "and we ruined your plans."

"Just as well. We must have been betrayed," Izsak added, as his face broke into a wry smile. "You see . . . we didn't know they had a follow squad either."

"So, we're not such bad luck after all."

"Where are you going now?"

"We don't know much about the area. We were hoping to blend in and make contact with partisans in the area."

"We're heading south."

"South? Hungary? I don't know the language," Jakob said as he looked at Sasha, who shrugged his shoulders, indicating he didn't know much if any Hungarian either.

"Most of us know Slovak. You could get by. We hold a good piece of territory now in the north."

"What?" Sasha asked with surprise. "Partisans hold territory?"

"We're not like most partisans," Izsak responded proudly. "We're going to meet the Soviets at out borders. Hungary will be free."

"That sounds like a good fight, but what about our friend here?"

"He'll be fine," Lorencz answered. "Just needs a sling for a few days."

"Can he travel?"

"Of course," Lorencz scoffed. "I've traveled with a broken arm and broken leg."

"Don't be so hard on them, Lorencz," Izsak admonished. "They may not be as strong as you."

Lorencz just grunted, intolerant of these mere mortals.

"I can make it," Jan growled as he forced himself to stand up with Sasha's help.

"What now?" Jakob asked Izsak.

"We came for weapons and ammunition."

"And you can't go home empty handed."

"No," Izsak agreed humorlessly.

"Even though they were waiting for you?"

"Even so."

Jakob shook his head.

"Let's go," Izsak called out to his men, and as they all started to move, Izsak turned to Jakob. "You three go first."

"But we don't know where you're going," Sasha

pointed out angrily.

"You start walking that way," Izsak said with a wave of his hand, "and if we're still behind you, then you'll know you're going in the right direction."

Izsak looked over the identification papers Jakob and the others had handed him. The papers were obviously forged, but he would expect that regardless of whether the three men were truly partisans or Gestapo agents trying to infiltrate the group. The thing that struck Izsak is that the papers were bad forgeries. The Gestapo knew what forged documents looked like, and when Izsak had heard about agents trying to infiltrate other groups, the Gestapo papers were good forgeries with only the most subtle discrepancies that would indicate forgery. Perhaps they were too proud to make a bad forgery. *Or maybe,* Izsak thought to himself, *I'm thinking too much.*

"Terrible forgeries," Izsak said as he tossed the papers at Jakob's feet just before mounting his horse.

"We only found out we were leaving yesterday. It was the best we could get on short notice."

Izsak shrugged noncommittally, the sort of acknowledgment someone makes when they don't believe you but aren't ready to call you a liar to your face. He then pointed the way and Jakob started walking.

They slept in the forest that night. Izsak's men made a small fire, but only enough to cook some food, and then they put it out. Even though the days were getting warmer as spring awakened the sleeping land, the nights were still terribly cold. Jakob and his cohorts didn't have blankets or bedrolls, and

Izsak and his men didn't offer any. Jakob finally said something to Izsak, and two dirty wool blankets were thrown in a pile at their feet.

Izsak's men were not happy to give up any of what little they had for food and other supplies. Jakob and the others were intruders. They were not expected, not welcome, and perhaps most of all, not trusted. The three of them slept close, like children sharing the same bed, as they tried to get the most out of the worn blankets.

Jakob awoke with a start the next morning. He was disoriented by his strange surroundings, a dreamlike world of pine trees floating in a strangely colored cloud, a fog that lay all about them and picked up the varied hues of the approaching dawn. Close to the ground the fog was so thick that he could barely make out the forms of Jan and Sasha beside him, while he couldn't see any of the other men at all. He wondered if they had left them there, but then he heard the horses stirring nearby.

"It will dissipate soon," Izsak's voice declared from somewhere behind Jakob, and Jakob turned to look just as a little flame came to life off in the same direction.

"What?"

"The fog. It will burn off soon. When the sun gets a little higher."

"Oh . . . And where are we going today?"

"You're much too curious. It's a bad habit."

"I assume we will be leading the way again?"

"Of course," Izsak replied as he started to cook a pot of weak coffee, which would serve as breakfast.

The others were soon up, and in less then half an

hour they were on the move again. Jakob assumed that Izsak must have had another target in mind long before they found out that the convoy was a trap, since there had been no conferences or discussions about where they were going. They knew where they were going, even in the fog. After a while the terrain became more difficult, with large rocks and fallen trees littering the forest.

Jakob, Jan and Sasha were kept out in front of the group once again, but Izsak was now giving directions from his throne on horseback. Whether it was a casual wave of the hand or a grunt and nod of the head, at least Jakob and the others had some idea of which way to go.

They kept going for several hours until Izsak suddenly pulled up in front of the group and slid down off his horse. The fog had thinned to a ghostly haze instead of the thick white blanket from earlier. They could see about five meters ahead of them now.

"Are you sure they won't know about this one?" Jakob asked as he sidled up to Izsak, who was patting his horse.

"This one?" Izsak asked without looking at Jakob.

"Secondary target," Jakob declared. "Standard procedure."

"We have no 'standard procedure' here."

"Most commando operations have more than one objective, so that—"

"I'm well aware of what others do," Izsak interrupted, moving to the side of his horse where he began to adjust the straps on the saddle. "We prefer to be . . . a little more unpredictable."

"Are we heading back to Yugoslavia, then?"

"I told you before," Izsak answered, looking Jakob squarely in the eye, "you ask too many questions."

"I was thinking...," Jakob began slowly, "maybe we, the three of us... should just go on to Bratislava by ourselves like we planned."

"Bratislava is no good," Izsak pronounced.

"Not for you, but we might—"

"No, I think you will stay with us."

"But I was thinking—"

"No," Izsak said firmly. "It would be best if you stay with us for a while."

Jakob pursed his lips and turned away, walking over to Jan and Sasha, who were resting beside a tree.

"Trouble," he said as he sat down next to them. "We can't leave."

"We could try to shoot our way out," Jan offered.

"Not very good odds," Sasha answered. "They'll expect that. The fact that they haven't taken our pistols away says they're not too worried about us."

"I suppose . . . ," Jakob agreed.

"What do they want?" Jan asked.

"I don't know—" Jakob began to answer, but cut himself short as Lorencz lumbered up to the group.

"Time to go," Lorencz grunted as Izsak followed behind.

Izsak nodded at them. "You three will—"

"Lead," Jakob interrupted. "Yes, we know."

"You will be going in first."

"In first?"

"Over that next hill is an ammunition dump. We will still have cover from the fog . . . and a mortar with a dozen rounds of ammunition."

"A frontal assault? With just our pistols?"

"It has to be a frontal assault. There are minefields and obstacles all around the camp. We'll be right behind you."

"How far behind us?"

"This is your chance to prove yourselves."

"This is our chance to commit suicide."

"What about him?" Jakob asked, pointing at Jan with his arm in a sling. "You can't expect him to—"

"You all go. Either that or you all die here."

Sasha instinctively reached for the pistol in his belt.

"That would not be wise," Izsak cautioned.

Jakob motioned for Sasha to stop. "How many men are guarding the dump?"

"A dozen. It's well camouflaged and out of the way . . . a relatively small cache for whatever reason. We don't know why it's there. We only know it is."

"One-to-one odds."

"But we have the fog and the element of surprise."

Jakob looked at Jan and Sasha and then back at Izsak. "We'll do it. We'd better get going before we lose any more fog cover."

"Good, good," Izsak said as he solemnly put a hand on Jakob's shoulder. "Show us you'll fight and we will be there. It's up to you."

"Let's not pretend," Jakob replied as he brushed off Izsak's hand. "I think we stand a better chance with the Germans, that's all. Now, how far away is it and what's the terrain like?"

Izsak knelt down and took out a knife, using it to draw a diagram in the dirt. "There's a ravine that cuts around it, behind like this and to the right, almost like a natural moat on two sides of the dump. They've put land mines in the field on the left side here. Barracks here . . . ammunition dump here."

"How accurate are your mortars?"

"They're good."

"Even when they can't see through the fog?"

"We know the positions. We'll set down as many rounds as we can, and then you rush in while they're confused."

Jakob looked at Izsak without saying a word.

"It will work," Iszak assured him.

"How many men did you start out with on this mission?"

"What?"

"With tactics like these, you must lose a lot of fighters."

"Is that a joke?" Izsak asked accusingly. "Never joke with me about such things."

"Then it must be something else," Jakob countered, accusing Izsak in return. "Apparently you just consider us . . . ah . . . expendable."

"Let's go," Izsak commanded, ignoring Jakob as he turned for his horse.

"What do we do?" Sasha asked Jakob when Izsak was out of earshot.

"We're going to have to play it by ear. Maybe it will be easy to take the camp."

"And if it's not?" Jan asked.

"We could always take cover in the camp and sneak out later. Izsak and the others will think we're dead, and when they've left . . . we sneak out of the camp."

"Damn!" Jan answered with exasperation. "You can't believe—"

"We don't have a lot of choices!" Jakob whispered back hoarsely. "Let's go!"

It was only a moment before the squad was moving again, quicker now than they had been before. It was anticipation that urged them ahead faster, as adrenaline began to pump. Before they knew it, Izsak was stopping again, dismounting and using hand signals to order the other men to do the same. The men quickly unloaded the mortar and ammunition, along with their rifles, and were once again on the move, all on foot now.

Jakob was amazed at how quietly they moved, how everyone knew what to do. He almost got caught up in a sense of . . . of envy . . . of admiration.

And then they were there.

"This is the road," Izsak whispered to Jakob's trio. "It's only about ten meters that way until you'll come to the gate. We've got wire cutters for each of you. Don't try the gate itself. No electricity in the fence, so you can break in anywhere you want, but keep an eye out for the tower at the right corner of the yard. We'll send the first couple of mortar rounds into the minefield and hope we set off some of the mines. That should get their attention. We'll start in . . . Any of you have a watch?"

"Yes," Jakob answered, "I do."

"We'll start in three minutes."

"Make it five," Jakob countered. "If they don't see us, we can get a start on cutting the fence. If there's a guard at the gate, we'll wait for the mortar."

Izsak looked Jakob in the eye for an instant. "Go."

Jakob checked his watch and took a breath, letting it out in a quiet, nervous cough as the adrenaline began to pulse, and then he took off, waving for Jan and Sasha to follow. He found himself counting off the seconds as they ran so he would have a rough idea of the timing. He cast his eyes about nervously as he strained to see anything through the fog—the fence, the gate, a German soldier pointing a gun at them . . . Suddenly the gate came into view, and the three of them veered off to the right with surprisingly perfect coordination. They went about three meters along the fence until they couldn't see the gate on the left or the tower on the right.

Jakob motioned for Jan to stand watch with his pistol while he and Sasha cut the fence. Sasha made the first cut, and once he broke the thick wire, the release of tension caused a sudden, loud rattle. The three of them froze, waiting for the camp to erupt in machine-gun fire, but there was nothing. Jakob checked his watch. It was only a minute before the mortar was supposed to open fire, so he signaled Jan and Sasha to stop and wait for it. They held their breath. Jakob fully expected a couple of soldiers to find them there at any instant, as they checked the perimeter after hearing the noise from the wire, but no one came. Jakob could hear his heart pumping loudly in his ears as they knelt at the fence, waiting for the explosions and confusion that would cover their break-in.

Just then Jakob's fears were realized as a young German soldier, obviously still in his teens, appeared out of the mist and raised his machine gun. Everything seemed to be happening in slow motion, and Jakob could clearly see the boy's eyes widen as the realization swept over him that he had come upon three partisans cutting through the fence. The boy raised the muzzle of the submachine gun to fire at them, but as his hand started to jerk back on the trigger, he suddenly stiffened up and began falling backward. The roar of a mortar round covered the sound of Jan's pistol as he fired three rounds at the boy's face, hitting him solidly and killing him instantly. There were two more nearly simultaneous explosions. It must have been mines going off, since the partisans couldn't have sent off mortar rounds that fast.

Jakob had to force himself back into action, and he and Sasha began frantically cutting at the fence wire, soon opening a hole big enough for them to crawl through. As soon as they made it through the fence, they started running blindly through the fog and the smoke from the explosions. Seconds later, Jan collided with a German soldier, the two of them tumbling into the dirt as another mortar shell hit.

Normally, the impact of the collision wouldn't have been enough to stop Jan, but he took the force of the blow on the shoulder that had been dislocated the day before. The soldier didn't know what had hit him and was scrambling around in the dirt, trying to recover his KAR 98, when Sasha looked over his shoulder and saw what was going on. He turned and shot the soldier in the back just as he was about to shoot Jan. Sasha then ran back and grabbed Jan, pulling him up by his good shoulder. Jan was in so much pain from the trauma of aggravating his injury that he was on the verge of passing out. They were moving as fast as they could to catch up with Jakob when a parked truck became visible through the mist.

They made their way to the truck, thinking it would make good cover as they tried to find Jakob, but as soon as Jan fell against the truck to rest for a moment, a head popped up over the dashboard on the driver's side. Sasha instinctively drew up his pistol and fired with a speed that surprised even him.

"God damn you!" Jakob roared fiercely. "You could have killed me!"

Sasha's knees nearly buckled as he realized it was Jakob.

"Get in!" Jakob shouted as the truck engine cranked over and started.

"What are you doing?" Sasha asked as he pushed Jan into the cab and jumped in after him.

"It's loaded," Jakob shouted as he ground the truck into gear and they lurched forward. "This should be enough for those bastards. Hold on! We're crashing the gate."

Another mortar shell came in, landing so close that clots of dirt flew in through the truck window, but they managed to keep moving. Within moments they could see the gate in the distance. Jakob cranked the steering wheel hard to the right, causing Jan to cry out in pain again as the inertia forced him to slam against Jakob with his bad shoulder. That was when they heard heavy machine-gun fire from the tower. The tower guard couldn't see the gate, but he could hear the truck and assumed someone was breaking in, not trying to get out, so he opened fire in the general direction of the gate.

Jakob was afraid that it would only take one lucky shot to set off everything in the back of the truck, so he pushed the accelerator all the way down and cranked the wheel for a hard left as they approached the gate. Jan and Sasha were thrown to the other side of the truck, and the passenger door suddenly flew open as all of Sasha's and Jan's weight pressed against it. Sasha found himself hanging onto the edge of the seat for dear life as the truck nearly rolled over.

"For the love of God, Tonda!" Sasha shouted as his voice broke.

"Just hold on," Jakob shouted back. "We're almost there."

That was when they heard rifle fire coming from the other side of the camp as the partisans opened up and the Germans returned fire. The truck was so far off balance that even though the wheels on Jakob's side hadn't actually left the road, once he straightened it out, the weight came back down hard on that side, making it feel like the truck was landing.

Jakob upshifted, and they raced out of harm's way as fast as the truck would go. But of course, Izsak and his men didn't know it was them.

"They're shooting at us!" Sasha shouted at the same moment a rifle bullet came whistling through the windshield, shattering it on the passenger side and cutting a hole in the back window.

Jakob let up on the gas and turned away from what he judged to be the origin of the rifle fire. The truck was suddenly off the road, lurching crazily down a hill overgrown with brush. When they finally came to a stop, Sasha brought his knees up to his face and kicked out the remaining glass in the windshield, then scrambled out of the cab, shouting, "It's us! Stop shooting, you fools! It's us!"

Jakob was still in the truck with Jan lying on top of him after having been thrown around the cab on the final descent of their flight.

"You're not *trying* to kill me," Jan groaned, writhing in pain from his injured shoulder. "I mean, Christ . . . at least pretend you're not *trying* to kill me."

"What the hell do you want from me?" Jakob growled back, as he struggled to get out from under Jan while simultaneously pushing the injured man up toward the broken window through which Sasha had escaped. By the time they were about to climb out, Sasha had returned with Ferko, the youngest of the partisans—the one who had shot at them—and the two of them began helping Jan out of the cab.

Jakob sat on the ground alongside the others for a moment before noticing that everything was quiet. "What happened to the others?" he asked Ferko.

"They're in the camp."

"In the camp? It's all over?"

"Of course," Ferko answered, as though the outcome had never been in question. "We have done this many times. It goes very quickly."

"Why were you shooting at us?" Sasha asked.

"How could I know it was you? We have to kill everyone so they won't know where we are. It will be hours before the Germans find out what has happened here. If a truck were to get out and they got word—"

"The truck is loaded," Jakob interrupted.

"With what?"

"It looks like small arms ammunition. I didn't have time to look it over very closely."

"We should get Izsak. He tells us what to take."

"You two stay here," Jakob said as he left with Ferko to find Izsak.

Ferko entered the camp as though there was nothing to fear, even though he hadn't been close enough to actually see what had happened. For all he knew, the Germans could have slaughtered the partisans, but the thought never occurred to him as he strode confidently past the gate, casually carrying his bolt-action rifle by the stock with one hand. Jakob wasn't quite as confident, though, and he dropped back a bit as he followed Ferko, his pistol at the ready as he moved from one point of cover to the next.

"Ferko!" came a shout from near one of the tents.

Ferko was startled and immediately fell to the ground, pulling up his rifle to fire, but Jakob was already aiming at the large man standing next to one of the camp tents.

"Damn it, Ferko!" Lorencz shouted as he lumbered toward the boy. "You *never* come in like that. How do you know who might be waiting for you?"

"Why worry about them when you're the one who will kill me by scaring me to death?" he grumbled as he got up and dusted himself off.

Lorencz looked at Jakob, who was still pointing his pistol at him. "Are you going to shoot me?" he asked defiantly. Jakob lowered his gun. "The others are dead?" Lorencz continued without emotion, just curiosity, as he asked about Jan and Sasha.

"No," Jakob answered curtly, annoyed with Lorencz's obvious contempt for these mere mortals. "They're down the road a few meters waiting by the truck. Where is Izsak?"

"There," Lorencz answered, pointing to a supply shack.

When Jakob entered the shack, Izsak was talking to one of the others as he opened a crate. "This is excellent," Izsak said with the satisfaction of a craftsman who had just found the perfect set of tools with which to work. "It couldn't have been better if we had placed an order with their quartermaster. Just the right ammunition and guns for a commando group. My God, they even have Panzerfaust! We can take on tanks with these!"

"Why would they have all this here under such a small guard?" Jakob asked, surprising Izsak, who hadn't noticed him come in.

"A calculated risk . . . out here in the forest. A secret fallback position."

"But the Russians are—"

"The Russians? What about the Hungarians? The Germans thought Hungary might surrender to the Russians. Suddenly that means the Russians are at the door. This is only one of many temporary ammunition dumps in anticipation of having to fortify the Hungarian border."

"But how did you know that?"

Izsak frowned and clucked his tongue like an impatient schoolmaster. "I warned you before about all those questions. Now help us load what we can take with us."

"And blow up the rest?"

"You sound like a boy asking his father if he can set off fireworks," Izsak answered with a smile. "No, we'll just throw the rest into the ravine. We don't want an explosion that could draw attention. We've already made too much noise with the mortars."

Jakob was about to go through the door when two of the men brushed past him and started carrying crates. He went out to find everyone busily at work. The horses had been brought into the camp and were being loaded with ammunition. The men were also loading a truck that had come through the attack undamaged.

"You're taking the truck?" Jakob asked Ferko, who was helping to load. "How will you get petrol? What about roadblocks?"

"We'll take it as far as we can. Maybe we'll get through with it, maybe not. We don't have that far to go from here."

"It's worth the risk," Izsak said as he came up behind them.

"The other truck can't be fixed," Sasha said as he carried a box up to the truck.

"How is Jan?" Jakob asked.

"He'll be all right if he can rest."

"Can he ride in the truck?" Jakob asked Izsak.

"Yes, of course. You've done well. You'll ride in front with Ferko, and your friends will ride in back. Now it's time to go."

Jakob almost thanked Izsak until he realized that once again they were to be used as forward observers, the first to draw fire if they ran into German troops or a roadblock. Soon everyone else was on horseback and ready to go, with Ferko driving the truck.

"Are we leading?" Jakob shouted to Izsak as Ferko started up the truck.

"Of course."

"How are you going to keep up with us?"

Izsak just smiled. It didn't take long before Jakob realized that the treacherous road would slow them down enough so that the men on horseback could easily keep up as they cut through the woods.

"How far are we going?" Jakob asked Ferko, as they bumped along through the ruts of the dirt road.

"We have a checkpoint coming up soon."

"A checkpoint? And we're just going to—"

"We've done this many times," Ferko said absentmindedly, trying to navigate the road as they came to an area that had been eroded away by recent rains.

They rode along in silence save for the rattle and bumping of their cargo rising above the engine noise and the continuous grind of the transmission. Jakob nervously anticipated the checkpoint ahead. Was this another of Izsak's ploys to use Jakob and the others as clay pigeons, to draw fire before the partisans came in to help?

They soon found themselves on a slight downgrade, and when they rounded a ninety-degree bend in the road, there it was—the German checkpoint. Jakob reflexively put his foot to the floorboard, as though he were the one driving. Ferko did the same, but much more subtly. He wasn't trying to stop. He just wanted to slow down.

"We're early," Ferko said under his breath, but

Jakob heard him nonetheless.

"Early?" Jakob repeated in a panic. "What the hell do you mean, early? What are we supposed to do now?"

"We just—" Ferko began, but before he could finish the sentence, the partisans began pouring into the road at the checkpoint. Not a shot was fired as they came up behind the four soldiers at the checkpoint while they were distracted by the approaching truck. The partisans used knives, and it was so well done—so well choreographed—that it looked surreal. Jakob watched as Lorencz came up behind one of the German soldiers and wrapped him in a bear hug, drawing his hand, which held a polished knife that flashed in the sunlight, across the soldier's throat and then letting him slip slowly to the ground. It all happened in front of Ferko and Jakob as though it were a play staged for their benefit, and then all the partisans disappeared into the woods again by the time the truck rumbled up to the checkpoint shack. Only Izsak was still visible at the edge of the woods, and he just gave Ferko a quick wave, which Ferko returned enthusiastically as Izsak rode away. Jakob didn't notice Izsak because he was busy staring at one of the dead soldiers as they drove by, a man close to his own age with the most acute look of surprise in his unblinking eyes.

The condition of the road didn't change much from there, but Ferko was noticeably more relaxed, which lulled Jakob into a sense of security, and he found himself falling asleep between bone-jarring encounters with bad stretches of road.

Jakob awoke with a start after one particularly long

nap, when he realized the truck had stopped. He looked over and saw Ferko smiling at him. Ferko thought it funny how Jakob snapped awake so suddenly.

"What is it?" Jakob asked as he shook himself awake.

"Time to get out."

"What?"

"We leave the truck."

"Leave it? Are the others here?"

"Yes."

Jakob climbed out of the truck and found that they were on the edge of a camp in the forest. It was soon obvious that this was a large partisan camp, a meeting place where different groups would rendezvous to divide up the spoils of the raid. Jakob went to the back of the truck to check on Jan and Sasha, only to find that they had already gotten out and were heading toward a couple of blankets that had been spread out on the ground. On top of them were some apples, a few loaves of bread, and some bags of goat cheese. It was a rare "community feed," a sort of celebration of their success. Jakob started to follow his comrades toward the food but then stopped in his tracks when he spotted a woman in British khaki. It wouldn't be unusual to see someone in a khaki shirt or khaki pants, but not both . . . she matched too well. It was obviously a military uniform. Just then Ferko walked up beside him.

"Who is that?" Jakob asked.

"Don't know," Ferko answered. "Never seen her before. I'll find out."

Jakob hardly took his eyes off her, mostly out of

curiosity, as Sasha handed him some bread and cheese.

Ferko made his way through the crowd, talking to one man and then another, a handshake here and a slap on the back there, and eventually made his way back to Jakob, or more accurately, to the food, grabbing an apple and a canteen of water.

"They say she's a British commando," Ferko said between bites. "She's to be a spy or something in Budapest."

"No," Jakob countered. "They're putting you on. A spy?"

"You don't think a girl can be a spy? I think they might make betters spies. They talk all the time. They're nosy by nature, always asking questions . . ."

"Don't you like girls?" Jakob interrupted.

"Sure I like girls," Ferko said as he took another bite of apple, "but my best friend since we were little has six sisters, and he told me what they're like."

"Six sisters?"

"Six! And worst of all . . . he was the youngest child. He told me all the things they did. Always got him into trouble. Once he told me that he—"

"But what about this spy?' Jakob interrupted. "What's she doing here?"

"Someone's taking her to Hungary. She just came from Yugoslavia. Oh, and you'll never guess what else."

"What . . . she's rich?"

"No, not about her. The Allies landed in France yesterday."

"What? Where in France?"

"In the north. Across the English Channel. The

war won't go on much longer."

"The landings went that well? How far are they?"

"I don't know, but if they've landed in France, it shouldn't take much longer, should it?"

Jakob just shook his head and shrugged his shoulders, not feeling nearly as optimistic as Ferko. He then walked over to meet the woman.

"Hello."

"Hello," she answered back firmly, but at the same time taking a small step backward as she took Jakob in warily.

"My name is Tonda," Jakob said, offering his hand.

"Janka," the woman answered. It was odd that they were both using cover names, but not unusual in partisan groups. The woman's real name was Hannah. Hannah Senesh.

"You're going to Budapest?"

"Someone's been talking . . ."

"I don't think that's a problem here. Not within the group."

"I suppose you're right, but it doesn't pay to take chances."

"You have an escort to Budapest?"

"Yes. Why? Are you offering?"

"Me? No, I don't speak Hungarian very well."

"I noticed—"

"Watch out for that one," Izsak said, interrupting them as he walked up. "He's some crazy Jew we found outside of Bratislava. You know how the Jews are . . . But this one is a good fighter."

"Imagine that," Hannah said wryly.

"Well, Tonda," Izsak continued, "we've decided

you can come with us."

"Where?"

"Yugoslavia."

"Why are you going to—?"

Izsak put a finger up to Jakob's mouth. "How many times must I tell you?"

"Too many questions," Jakob answered, and Izsak nodded with a half smile.

It wasn't long before the various groups began leaving. Soon the area was cleared and "manicured" so thoroughly that no one would have suspected that over five dozen partisans had just made camp there. One of the other groups took the truck because they could make better use of it than Izsak's group, giving up a wagon and horses in exchange, which meant that Jakob, Jan, and Sasha wouldn't be on foot.

"You!" Izsak called out to Jan as the squad with the truck was about to pull out. "Over here."

Jan looked over at Jakob and Sasha as if to ask if they knew what Izsak wanted. When he saw nothing in their faces, he walked over to Izsak.

"You will ride in the truck."

"The truck?"

"Yes."

"But aren't they going—"

"They're going south."

"You're not."

"No."

"Jakob and Sasha?"

"There isn't room for them. They'll come with us."

"And I'm supposed to go with these people that I

don't even know?"

"You can't fight like this. If you go with these people, they will hide you while you get better."

"And then what?"

Jakob was curious what Izsak and Jan were talking about and walked over just in time to hear Izsak say, "And then you live."

"What's this about?" Jakob asked as Sasha joined them.

"He says I should go with them," Jan said, nodding toward the truck.

"What about us?"

"You will come with us into the mountains. He would not have an easy time of it. If he goes with the others, they will hide him until he gets better."

The driver started the truck, and a pale cloud of exhaust rose about their feet before quickly dissipating.

"Now," Izsak said. "You must go now. There is no more time for talk."

Jan looked at Jakob and then at Sasha, then started to climb into the truck. Sasha hurried over to help him in. "We'll come for you in a couple of weeks," Sasha said as he offered a hand.

It was obvious from Jan's expression that he didn't believe him. "Take care of yourself, Sasha."

"Are you sure about this?" Jakob asked.

Jan gave him a strange, accusatory look, as though somehow it was all Jakob's fault. "This is best," Jan finally said.

Jakob offered his hand and Jan shook it. "We'll come for you," Jakob said as Izsak pounded on the side of the truck to signal the driver to go and the truck lurched forward. They watched as the truck drove away.

"It's time for us to go," Izsak announced

Just then it occurred to Jakob that he was expected to ride a horse. He had never ridden a horse before, and when he had been told there was a horse for him, he just put it in the back of his mind. But now he found himself standing in front of a tall Arabian gelding with big brown eyes that looked back at him with the same expression of concern that he had. Jakob watched as the others mounted their horses, particularly Sasha, hoping to see the same trepidation, so that he wouldn't be alone in his anxiety. But Sasha had ridden many times in his life and mounted his horse with a casual grace.

It finally came down to Jakob being the only one who hadn't mounted up. The last thing he wanted was for Izsak to say something, so he decided to give it a try. Positioning himself on the left side of the horse, he gave the animal a couple of long strokes on the neck. "You be good to me and I'll be good to you," he said quietly as he raised his foot to the stirrup. As he lifted himself up, putting all his weight on the stirrup, the horse began turning to the left, walking around in a circle. Jakob let himself down and took the reins tightly to steady the horse. "I thought we had an agreement . . . ," he said under his breath.

He didn't dare look around to see if the others were watching. He *knew* they were, but at least no one was laughing... yet. He realized his mistake was hesitating and tried again, and this time when he raised up in the stirrup, he simultaneously threw his right leg over the horse's back and was pleased to find himself seated squarely in the saddle. He couldn't restrain a self-satisfied smile. The horse hadn't moved, and he patted him on the neck gratefully. "Thank you, Liebchen," he whispered in the horse's ear. He reached for the reins, which he had looped over the saddle horn, and the left rein slid out of his hand. He stared in disbelief at the leather strap dangling down to the ground. The horse turned its head to look at him. "Don't look at me," he said, trying to decide if he could get hold of it without getting off the horse. He was relieved to look up and find Sasha riding up beside him, grabbing the loose rein and handing it to him.

"Thanks," he said gratefully but casually. He didn't want to give himself away as a fraud, a non-equestrian.

"Have you ever ridden a horse before?"

"Not very often . . . not many . . . ," he stuttered before letting out a sigh. "No."

"It'll be all right. He'll stay with the rest of us for the most part. Don't try to overcontrol him. Just hold the reins loosely like this," Sasha instructed as he demonstrated the proper technique. "Pull in the direction you want him to turn and pull back gently when you want him to stop. Talk to him. And don't pull back too hard when you want to stop, or he'll rear back and throw you."

"That's something to look forward to."

"Believe me, it's not," Sasha said with a smile.

They rode for hours, heading south and southwest until the sun began to set. This was a new kind of war for Jakob. He had always lived in cities, and this horseback guerrilla war was terribly foreign to him. And the people were foreign too. These partisans had not lived under the kind of German occupation that Prague had known. Hungary had been allowed to labor under the illusion of independence until the Germans drove in during March of 1944. That occupation was an awakening to the partisans. There was no longer any hope of working within Hungary to save the nation. It was no longer a matter of having a right-wing government in power that might be replaced. Hungary was now just another zone of German occupation.

These partisans had no way of knowing about the eyewitness accounts that had reached the West about what was happening near the town of Oswiecim, Poland, in the German work camp called Birkenau and the adjoining extermination camp called Auschwitz. That was what brought Hannah Senesh to Hungary. She was part of a group of Jewish commandos in Palestine, trained by the British and operating within the British army as a member of "His Majesty's Jewish Brigade." She and others were parachuted into Yugoslavia, part of their mission being to warn Hungarian Jews of their impending fate, now that they were in the hands of the Nazis. Of course, the British felt that the warning and organization of Hungarian Jewry, the attempt to rescue them, was a secondary or even tertiary priority of the commando missions, but the Jewish commandos knew it to be their primary mission. Hannah, unfortunately, didn't make it very far. She was arrested and imprisoned in Budapest soon after she entered Hungary, when she was caught with her transmitter.

The Palestinian commandos weren't the only ones who tried to save Hungary's Jews, of course.

Many Jewish families in Hungary tried to get to the embassies of neutral countries in hopes of getting provisional passes that would exempt them from anti-Jewish measures and eventual deportation. There was one young man, in particular, from the Swedish embassy in Budapest named Per Anger who helped hundreds of Jews obtain these passes. The embassy was soon overwhelmed by thousands more requests, and embassy officials were forced to ask for additional staff from the Swedish diplomatic corps. Their request was answered in June of 1944 with the arrival of the energetic and compassionate heir of a famous Swedish family. Raoul Wallenberg had been appointed first secretary at the Swedish legation in Budapest and was specifically charged with starting a rescue mission for the Jews of Hungary.

But the far more common response to the plight of the Jews was either complacency or complicity. In northern Yugoslavia, a young man named Kurt Waldheim was following orders as a lieutenant in the Austrian division of the Waffen SS as they hunted down partisans led by Josef Brodz Tito. The forces with which Waldheim served followed the basic practice of German forces throughout Europe. One soldier killed by partisan activity would be paid for with the deaths of a hundred civilians, whereas a wounded soldier would only cost the lives of fifty civilians—all taken at random, of course. It was such pure logic, so obvious to those in charge, especially since they were just following orders.

"We're going to hit them outside of Siklós," Izsak said as he lit the remains of a crumpled cigarette and sat on the ground beside the small campfire with the others. Lorencz gave Izsak a strange look that told Jakob this might not be a good thing.

"Siklós? Where is it?" Jakob asked.

"Croatian border," Lorencz grunted. "Yugoslavia... Tito."

"Tito?"

"We're going to come in from one side while Tito's fighters come in from the other," Izsak explained. "It's a Wehrmacht Jagder group. They're about to start a drive into the mountains looking for partisans. They go in and burn villages and kill men, women, and children in retaliation for partisan attacks."

"So we're going to hit them first?" Jakob asked, trying to follow the logic of it. "Won't they take it out on the civilians?"

"Of course they will," Izsak growled, angry with Jakob for insinuating that he would be the cause of the deaths of innocents. "They're going to kill old women and children and . . ."

"They kill them anyway," Lorencz added. "We just try to slow them down."

"It's a war of the mind," Izsak explained. "They want us to believe that they are everywhere and will kill everyone we love, and we want them to believe that we can kill them anytime we want. It's not so important that we kill every German soldier. It *is* important that every German soldier fear us. That is our greatest weapon."

Jakob almost smiled, but Izsak was so serious. He could imagine a German SS officer making the same statement to justify the actions of his men as they burned a village.

The ride to Siklós took an entire day as the partisans made their way through the countryside, careful to avoid detection. The journey became more precarious as they got closer to Siklós, because the terrain became a flat patchwork of farm fields with numerous areas virtually devoid of cover. Once in the area, some ten kilometers to the east of the German bivouac site, they set up a sparse camp, ready to move on at a moment's notice. Izsak then rode out alone to rendezvous with the Yugoslavian group, which was supposed to be only a couple of kilometers away by then.

The mood in the camp was one of uneasiness as they waited for Izsak to return. The partisans weren't used to being so far from the wooded hills they called home.

"They're nervous," Sasha said as he moved in close beside Jakob.

"They've got good reason," Jakob replied.

"Don't you think we'll make it?"

"Better keep your head down. They're not afraid . . . just unsure. They might not have time to look after us. We'll have to watch out for ourselves."

"I can take care of myself," Sasha growled under his breath, as though Jakob were questioning his manhood.

"In Prague," Jakob countered. "This is different. You've never trained as a soldier, never fought on horseback. You've never been part of an army facing another army. As a matter of fact, of all the men here, I'd say the Germans are the only ones properly trained for this."

Izsak returned to the camp about two hours later.

He gathered everyone around to tell them of the plan laid out by the Yugoslavians. "We follow them tomorrow. We won't go in until they get to the foothills. We'll hit them twice, and then as they get into the mountains, other groups will continue."

"And we . . . ?" Ferko began to ask.

"We go home," Izsak answered.

Izsak's pronouncement brought a smile to Ferko's face and a relieved laugh from some of the others, but most of the men were still solemn as they thought about the fight to come.

Jakob was impressed by the atmosphere of the camp that night. It was surrealistic in its silence. No campfire, no hot food or coffee, a minimum of spoken words. They posted four men on sentry duty instead of one. They were too close to the German camp to take a chance on being discovered by a German patrol. If they had any confrontation—if there was gunfire—the Germans would be able to send overwhelming reinforcements in very short order and catch them out in the open, so the order for the night was to lay low and avoid discovery. Miraculously, even Lorencz's snoring was silenced that night.

They awoke to a dark, blustery morning. Just as they had the evening before, everyone worked in silence as they broke camp and prepared to ride. Jakob watched as the gray figures of men on horseback slowly formed a column and rode out of camp, dark and somber, the horses' breath turning to steam as a misty, cold rain began to fall and his sense of foreboding grew.

Half the day was gone by the time they reached

the Yugoslavians, for they had also been moving after the Germans, and it was up to Izsak's men to overtake them.

The Yugoslavians knew of their arrival well in advance. The meeting of the two groups was uneventful. Izsak's men were not welcomed; they were barely even acknowledged. The Yugoslavians were always suspicious of strangers, and this convenient and temporary alliance was to be no exception. The Hungarians were seen merely as a tool to help them, not fighting men of the same caliber or conviction.

They continued to ride, now some sixty men strong, after the German column, following them to the foothills of the Slavon mountain range. They spent another night in a fireless, silent camp, followed by another dark and rainy morning, a morning set for their first attack.

They started out before sunrise to get ahead of the column, planning to let most of it go by as they hid among the trees and large rocks that lined the road at a predetermined spot, and then they would open fire on the tail end of the column with small arms and mortars for exactly ten minutes before disappearing into the cover of the countryside. They would then meet at another point some fifteen kilometers ahead, where they were to hit the column again.

Jakob and Sasha stayed together, taking cover at the outermost position of the group, where they would be at the very end of the line as the Germans passed. Izsak took notice of them there, but completely out of character, he didn't bother to relocate them. That made Jakob even more nervous.

"Get ready to move," he whispered to Sasha.

"What?" Sasha whispered back in confusion, not sure that he had heard Jakob right.

"Just be ready. If I say 'run,' we head for the horses and beat the hell out of here."

"There!" Sasha interrupted as he saw the first German soldiers making their way up the road.

It took some time for the Germans to pass by, but finally Izsak raised his hand to signal that they were ready to fire. That was when Sasha caught a glimpse of something off to their left. The world erupted in gunfire as the partisans fired everything they had, but the Germans in front of them immediately disappeared into the woods, so quickly in fact that one might think they knew what was about to happen.

Jakob was startled as Sasha suddenly began pulling at his sleeve. The noise was overwhelming, and Sasha had to shout to be heard as he pointed toward some nearby rocks and yelled "Look!" Jakob strained to make out anything unusual among the trees beside them, and then he saw that a squad of Germans was getting into position to outflank the partisans. They couldn't possibly have gotten up there that fast unless they had known in advance of the attack.

"Run!" Jakob shouted at Sasha, knowing full well that the partisans might shoot them in the back, but if what he thought was about to happen actually happened, they didn't have much choice but to run.

It was only out of the corner of his eye that Izsak caught sight of Jakob and Sasha running, but as he turned to shout for the others to stop them, the

Germans opened fire, not just from the left flank where Jakob and Sasha were, but also from behind. Bullets were coming from everywhere. Jakob looked back for an instant as he ran, just in time to see Izsak fall. He felt like stopping, turning back to help Izsak, but he knew it wouldn't do any good. It would only get him killed, too.

They soon reached the horses and frantically mounted. Jakob jerked furiously at the reins of his horse to turn him away, and as he did, he ran into Sasha's horse just as Sasha was hit by a machine-gun burst that seemed to come out of nowhere. Sasha fell across Jakob's lap, and Jakob wrestled him across the neck of his horse and then desperately kicked at the horse's belly to get him going. The horse reared up in pain, almost throwing Jakob and Sasha off, but somehow Jakob managed to hold them on as the horse bolted through an open path in the forest. Jakob thought they might make it as the sound of gunfire began to fade a bit, overtaken by the thundering beating of his heart as it pulsed in his ears, but then he heard one final shot, a little "crack" quite separate and distinct from all the other sounds of warfare he had just left behind him, and the next thing he knew he was falling. He didn't know how or why—it didn't make any sense at all—but he was falling . . . and then there was nothing.

The night was so dark that he couldn't see his own hand in front of his face. He couldn't see a tree or a rock or a star above him. He felt as though he was somehow floating, or maybe he was flying. Perhaps he was dead. He closed his eyes and tried to think, tried to understand what was happening to him, and then suddenly there was a bright light, the kind of light that's so harsh it wakes you up even when your eyes are closed. He forced himself to open his eyes even though it hurt. Everything was blurry and misshapen, so he closed his eyes tightly again, and then it was all darkness again. He tried once more to open his eyes, and when it was all blurry and bright, he blinked rapidly and squinted, managing to raise his hand with great difficulty so he could shade his eyes.

"So . . . you're awake," a deep voice grumbled from behind him.

Jakob turned quickly to see who it was, and suddenly an intense wave of pain swept through his body and he cried out, "Oh, dear God!"

"Sit still!" the voice commanded. "You're hurt."

"What? . . . Where am . . ."

"Where are you? You're safe. Better than I can say for the rest of them. Gone . . . all gone, poor bastards. All of them mowed down . . . betrayed."

Jakob had once again shut his eyes tightly as he winced from the pain, but as it eased up a bit, he looked more closely at the figure hunched in front of him holding a canteen of water. When the face finally came into focus, he was surprised to find it was Lorencz tending to his wound.

"What? Sasha?"

"Dead. He was on your horse. They shot you in the leg, hitting the horse at the same time, and the damn thing fell on your other leg and broke it up pretty bad."

"I must have passed out for a couple of hours?"

"Hours?" Lorencz laughed. "You've been in and

out for five days. This the first time you've made any sense. You come to for a bit and talk crazy, then pass out again. I thought you might be dead soon."

"Am I going to die?"

"I don't think so. I had time to clean up the wound and set the leg. Bad break. Bone stickin' outta the skin. I know a place where I think you can stay to get better. A farmer near here. He's good with sick animals . . . should be able to take care of your leg and keep you 'til you can walk."

We're back in Hungary?"

"Yes. We had to move slow to make sure we weren't caught. They came looking for the wounded . . . to kill everybody. Lucky you was passed out most of the time."

Lorencz paused for a moment as he gathered his thoughts. "Once when you woke up, I had to kill a boy who found us," he admitted with a strange mixture of shame and matter-of-factness. "Didn't look more than sixteen years old, but he would've turned us in and gotten us killed."

"You didn't have a choice," Jakob agreed, seeing that Lorencz felt bad about the young soldier.

"No," Lorencz said as he looked down at the ground and mumbled to himself. "He would've got us killed."

There was an awkward pause as they ran out of things to say, and then Lorencz got up and went over to his horse, packing up a few items.

"Are we going again?" Jakob asked.

"Two more hours to the farm."

Lorencz walked over to Jakob. "I been throwing you across the saddle when you was passed out. You want to ride like that, or see if I can get you sitting up?"

"I'd rather ride sitting up if I can."

It was a difficult process getting Jakob back up on the horse, and the pain was excruciating, but finally they got themselves arranged, with Lorencz in the saddle and Jakob behind him, arms wrapped around the big man. They started to ride off, but the pain soon became too much for Jakob as his wounded legs bounced against the horse's flanks, and he passed out, almost falling off the horse. Lorencz managed to catch him and stopped for a few minutes, using some rope to tie Jakob's arms and shoulders around himself, as though the wounded man were a rucksack. That was how they finished the ride to the farm of Joska and Elga Gazsi.

Joska was cautious as he came out of the little farmhouse when he heard the rider approaching. They didn't get many visitors, except for a couple of neighbors who came by now and again, but Joska recognized something in the sound of this rider, the way the animals reacted and the cadence of the horse, that told him this was someone else. He stood at the corner of the barn as the rider came closer, so that he could see who it was before the rider saw him. It was an instinctive move, without much real value.

"Lorencz?" he asked with quiet surprise as he recognized the rider.

"Hello, Joska," Lorencz said casually, having known all along that the farmer was watching him ride in.

"Lorencz! We haven't seen you for—"

"Long time," Lorencz interrupted with characteristic understatement.

"Who is this?" Joska asked as Lorencz climbed down from his horse, bringing Jakob, who was still unconscious, down with him.

"Coward. Got shot. Broke his leg."

"Coward? What happened?"

"Someone betrayed us. Germans all around. Everyone killed. He ran."

Everyone killed?" Joska asked, his voice cracking. "Ferko?"

"Yes. Ferko too."

"My son . . . ," Joska choked out as tears filled his eyes and he tried to keep his composure. "Did he kill them?"

"Ferko . . . damn good boy," Lorencz said sadly. "He killed lots of Germans before they got him . . . Damn good boy."

Lorencz untied Jakob and laid him on the ground.

"What are you going to do with him?"

"Leave him here."

"Here?"

"He can't ride. Can't take pain . . . keeps passing out. He needs a place to stay while he heals."

"You said he was a coward. Was he the one who betrayed you? Did he get Ferko killed?"

"No," Lorencz said as he looked down at Jakob. "He just got scared. Everybody runs sometime. He saw all the Germans around us and got scared. I think it was the first time he got caught in a fight like that. Just human." Lorencz used the word *human* as an epithet, to denote those who were something less than Lorencz.

"How did you get out?" Joska asked.

"It's not so easy to kill Lorencz," the big man declared with a rare smile.

"Izsak?"

"Izsak was the first to die. They knew he was the leader. Somebody knew. They killed him first. Damn Yugoslavs. They ask for help and get us killed. Izsak thought too much of the rest of the world. We should have just stayed home . . ."

"What are you going to do?"

"There are others. I'll go with them. Kill Germans."

"The war can't go on forever," Joska said.

"It will for Izsak . . . and Ferko . . ."

"My brother died in the last war. He fought with the Germans then. It's all so strange. I always see him as a boy. I suppose that's how it will be with Ferko now. How am I going to tell his mother?"

"Do you want me to tell her?" Lorencz asked as he nodded toward the house.

Joska glanced at the house and saw his wife Elga looking at them through the kitchen window. "I suppose she's already guessed, or she would have come out by now. A mother knows. They know when their children . . ."

"Where do you want this one?"

"Him? I don't know if we can—"

"There isn't any place else. He's got to rest. I don't think he can survive another long ride."

Joska heaved a deep sigh and shook his head as he stood looking at Jakob lying on the ground in front of him. "I suppose we could put him in the hayloft . . ."

Joska then turned to the house. "Aliz!" he shouted. "Bring out some bedding."

Aliz showed up in the small loft just as Lorencz laid Jakob out on a bed of hay. "Who is it?" she asked as she rolled out a thin mattress and shook out a sheet and blanket.

"One of the partisans," Joska answered. "He's been wounded. He'll stay with us for a while."

"Well, pick him up again and let me get the mattress and sheet under him."

Lorencz grunted, annoyed at having to lift Jakob again, but he did as Aliz said and held Jakob while she quickly laid out the bedding. "My God!" Aliz said as she started to put a blanket on Jakob after Lorencz had laid him on the bed. "How long has it been since he bathed?"

"We've been riding for days. Hiding from the Germans. Not much time for flowers and baths."

"Well, it's time now. We have to get him out of these clothes and cleaned up. Papa, you must look at these wounds. They're dirty, but I don't think they're infected."

"Will they be looking for him?" Joska asked Lorencz.

"I don't think they will look for him here. The fight was a long ways from here. Best to keep him out of sight, though."

"You look tired yourself, and I bet you could use a good meal."

Lorencz agreed to stay and help Aliz clean up Jakob while Joska went in to tell his wife about the death of their son. The sound of Elga's cries could be heard all the way out to the barn. The dinner was a somber event, as the reality of their son's death filled the room. Joska tried to make conversation, but Lorencz was never much of one for small talk, and Elga couldn't bring herself to say anything.

Lorencz couldn't be tempted by the thought of a warm bed for the night and left soon after dinner, while there were still a few hours of daylight left for traveling.

Joska checked out Jakob's wounds and found that Lorencz had done a remarkable job of setting Jakob's leg. It was a very bad break, which along with the gunshot wound, would take months to heal completely.

In the days that followed, Aliz quickly took over Jakob's care, since Joska had enough to do with the farm. Not that Aliz didn't have her share of chores to do, but she wasn't averse to taking care of Jakob. She was drawn to the brave, handsome partisan who had given so much in his fight against the Nazis.

Jakob awoke in the middle of the night, finding himself alone in a strange place. He was a bit confused, having no idea where he was, but he felt safe in the loft with just the sound of the animals in the barn below, and fell back to sleep.

The next morning he awoke to find a beautiful dark-haired girl with big brown eyes patting his hand, trying to wake him up for breakfast. "Are you awake?" Aliz asked.

"Yeah . . . Where am I? Who are you?"

"You're at our farm, and I'm Aliz."

"How did I get here?"

"A friend of yours brought you. You were wounded."

"Sasha?" Jakob asked with a note of desperation.

"Sasha? No . . . it was Lorencz."

"Was Sasha with him?" Jakob pressed.

"No, he was alone. He didn't mention anyone else."

Jakob was crestfallen. "Then it wasn't just a dream . . . or hallucination . . ."

"Hallucination?"

"Sasha is dead," he announced.

"He was a friend of yours?"

"I should have taken care of him."

"Maybe there was nothing you could do," Aliz offered empathetically.

Jakob shook his head. It was all he could do to hold back tears. He had been pretty cavalier about the whole arrangement when they left Prague, but now he felt responsible for Sasha, as though he should have done something to protect him. He had hoped the picture in his mind of Sasha falling into his arms had just been a dream, but now it was all too clear.

"We're going to take care of you now," Aliz said as she set down the bowl of hot cereal and bread and then brushed the hair out of Jakob's eyes.

Jakob felt embarrassed. He hated that this girl he didn't even know had seen him in a moment of weakness, but at the same time he felt overcome with emotion.

Aliz could sense that Jakob was uncomfortable and thought it best to leave. "Just shout if you need anything. I'll check on you after I feed the chickens," she said with a smile, "and finish baking bread."

After he finished eating, Jakob decided that it was the pain from his wounds that had made him so maudlin. He told himself he wouldn't let Aliz see him like that again. His mind started wandering as he lay in bed. He began thinking of jokes he had heard about country girls and city boys and laughed to himself. It wasn't long before the smell of fresh-baked bread came wafting in on a gentle breeze. It was like heaven. It was something he had taken for granted for so long. Not bread, but peace and quiet. Everyday life. He thought about his history in the war, his mother and the others in Theresienstadt, Rebecca and Thomas. He thought most of all about Rebecca and Thomas. He was beginning to wish he hadn't left them in Switzerland. He was beginning to wish a lot of things.

"How are you doing?" Aliz asked as she climbed up into the loft.

"I feel better."

"Do you need anything?"

"I could use something to read. Do you have any books?"

"Oh yes, Papa reads all kinds of books. Mostly old, but different languages and lots of different subjects. I'll pick out a few for you."

"Good. How long am I supposed to be like this?"

"Well, Papa says he can make up a plaster cast for your leg tomorrow so we can get rid of the splint. The bullet wound is clean and went right through the leg. You should be able to move around in about three weeks, but it will be some time before the cast comes off. You'll be here for a while."

That was it then. The war was over for him. This

was as good a time as any to start thinking about the future. He should think about how he was going to make it to Palestine. Palestine . . . It seemed like a pretty God-forsaken place to him. *God-forsaken*, he thought to himself, laughing again. He was a Jew. Palestine should be the only place that he didn't consider forsaken by God. But all he could think of was a barren desert thousands of miles from his home. He still considered Munich his home, even after all that had happened. In the back of his mind he had always thought that everything would get back to normal after the war, and he could return and life would be . . . Now *that* was a dream.

The days began to fade one into another. For the most part, it was Aliz who tended to his needs, but Elga was also a frequent visitor to the loft. Jakob could tell Elga wanted something from him, but he didn't know what. It might have been some words of comfort about her son Ferko, or perhaps she just needed to be near Jakob as some sort of connection to Ferko. Whatever it was, Ferko's mother never spoke of it; perhaps she couldn't have put it into words even if she had tried.

The days became an endless stream of books for Jakob. He knew he needed rest and relaxation, but he was starting to get restless. He had to get up and start moving around.

"It's hot up here," Aliz said one morning as she came up with breakfast.

"And it's still morning," Jakob agreed.

"We should try to get you outside."

"I was thinking the same thing."

"I think Papa has some crutches ready. I'll go ask

him. Oh, by the way . . . Happy birthday!"

"Birthday? It's not my birthday."

"No, it's mine!"

"Oh, well, congratulations. How old are you?"

"Nineteen."

"Nineteen? So young . . ."

"Not so young. How old are you?"

"Twenty-seven."

"Oh, I see," Aliz said with a giggle. "Just because you're old, you think I'm too young."

"Twenty-seven is not old," Jakob called out after her as she quickly fluttered down the steps. Suddenly he flashed on a time long before. Ten years before when he and Rebecca first met. The girl next door.

It was July, and after a difficult descent down the narrow steps from the loft, Jakob found himself outside in the beauty of the Hungarian countryside. It was as if the war had ended. In the weeks he had been there, he hadn't heard a word about the war. Joska thought it best and suggested to his wife and daughter that they not bring up the subject. It might only serve to upset their convalescing patient.

Jakob hobbled around on his new crutches as the family dog ran circles around him, barking playfully at Aliz and the stranger.

"You're doing very well," Aliz said, referring to Jakob's competence with the crutches.

"Am I?"

"You'll be ready to leave in no time."

"No time?"

"Another few weeks."

"That doesn't sound like 'no time.'"

"Maybe it's just me then. The past three weeks seem to have flown by. Summer always goes so quickly here. It's not like . . ." Aliz stopped suddenly, as though she had said something she shouldn't have.

"Not like what?" Jakob asked as he stopped walking and turned to face her.

"Uh, like the city."

"Oh. Have you been to the city often?"

"Well . . . I . . . ," she stuttered.

"What is it?"

"Can I tell you a secret?"

"Of course," Jakob said emphatically.

"Don't tell Mamma and Papa that I've told you."

"No. Absolutely not."

"Now you're just making fun. This is serious," she insisted.

"Right. What is it."

"I'm not really their daughter."

"Not their daughter? What do you mean? Are you adopted?"

"No. I'm Jewish and they're hiding me."

"Oh, my," Jakob said as he put his hand to his mouth in a mocking, effeminate manner.

"Oh, you!" Aliz said loudly, pretending to be angry as she hit Jakob on the arm.

"Well, didn't you want me to be shocked?"

"And I suppose you knew all along."

"No, but it isn't a terrible secret. You're very lucky that Joska and Elga took you in."

"I know. A lot of people in the country don't like Jews," Aliz said thoughtfully and then paused a moment before asking, "How do you feel about Jews?"

"Aliz, I'm Jewish too."

"You are? But you don't . . ."

"Don't look Jewish?" Jakob said, finishing her sentence with a smirk, which prompted a return smile from her. "My father wasn't Jewish, so I guess it depends who you talk to. I wasn't raised to be Jewish, but the Jews say that since my mother was Jewish, I'm Jewish. The Nazis say I'm something called a 'Mischling,' which means I'm half Jewish."

"My parents are Orthodox Jews from Budapest. It's been quite a change living here. There's a lot of freedom."

"Freedom?"

"My father was very strict. He arranged a marriage for me, but with the war everything changed. It's much harder to keep kosher here, and I don't want to make things hard for Elga. At home all my time was planned from the time I got up until I went to bed, whether it was by my father or chores for mother, but here when I finish my chores, the rest of the day is mine. And then there are Joska's books. I never could have read such books if I were at home. Sometimes I worry about what Father would say, but then I think that these are extraordinary times and I should take advantage of it."

"Extraordinary times? That's a good way to look at it," Jakob agreed. "You never know what tomorrow will bring. It's best to live in today."

"I wouldn't have expected you to say that."

"Why not?"

"You seem like . . . ," she began, but then turned away from him, not fully sure how to express what she was thinking.

"Like what?" Jakob pressed, hoping for a word of encouragement.

"Like a lost soul," she answered.

"What do you mean by that?" Jakob asked with a note of agitation.

"I don't know," Aliz countered defensively. "It seems like you don't know what you want."

"And you do?" he accused.

"I want to be with someone who loves me."

"Love is a myth," Jakob pronounced.

"No. It's—"

"It's a lie," he interrupted. "Life isn't a fairy tale."

"I know. I know too much. But that doesn't mean there's no such thing as love. Sometimes it's how bad life is that proves what love can be . . ." Aliz's voice trailed off into silence as she remembered saying good-bye to her brothers and parents as they separated, she being sent to live with the Gazsis while her brother was sent off to live with another family.

Jakob was silent too. They walked a little farther until Jakob suggested it might be time to turn back, and they returned to the barn.

"Let me help you up," Aliz said as they came to the narrow steps. Jakob put his arm around her shoulder and they made their way up to the loft. There was an old chair up in the loft, which Joska had stored with the intention of fixing it some day, but now it became part of Jakob's "bedroom set," and he fell into it after the exertion of climbing the stairs.

Aliz stood in front of him silently. Jakob knew she had something to say.

"What? What's wrong?"

"I just didn't want you to think . . . What I said out there. I didn't want you to think I was being mean."

"I never thought—"

"Because I want you to know that it means a lot to me . . . You . . . you mean a lot to me. I was feeling so lonely and—"

"I wanted to thank you for taking care of me," Jakob interrupted.

"I love you," Aliz blurted out, catching Jakob off guard, leaving him speechless as she rushed out of the loft.

He sat there for a moment thinking about what she said. He then picked up a book and started reading again, but soon the book drifted down to his lap and he found himself staring off into space.

CHAPTER 2

The last year of the war in Europe was the bloodiest. Massive armies would meet in desperate open battle as the Allies closed the jaws of a bloody vise on Germany.

The Allied air war was being driven home relentlessly against Germany in the final year of the war. It was Germany's Air Marshall, Hermann Göring, who changed from bombing military targets during the Battle of Britain in 1940 to bombing civilian population centers in what became known as the "London Blitz." Other British cities were similarly bombed, and it was these actions that prompted the British Air Marshall, Arthur "Bomber" Harris, to issue a statement saying that Germany had "sown the wind and now they shall reap the whirlwind." It was not an empty threat. American and British bombers would soon head for Germany in formations that would eventually consist of thousands of planes. No major German city would be left untouched by Allied bombs.

On the eastern front, it was a relentless push by Soviet forces, whose commanders thought nothing of suffering staggering losses as they sent their troops into headlong charges against the German lines. It was a tactic born of Joseph Stalin's policy of executing his officers when they failed in battle. It was simply a question of whether a commander sacrificed the lives of his men or his own life.

On the western front, the Americans and British were encouraged by the liberation of France and the low countries after the long fight inland from the beaches of Normandy, but once they reached the German border, the advance slowed to a standstill. There was still a common belief among the Allied troops, however, that they could mount a concerted effort, pushing into Germany and ending the war by Christmas of 1944. The entire picture changed in mid-December, however, when the Germans launched a dramatic counteroffensive through the poorly guarded Ardennes region, which caught the Allies by complete surprise. In what became known as the Battle of the Bulge, hopes for an end to the war in 1944 were dashed. General Dwight D. Eisenhower, head of Allied forces in Europe, saw the assault for what it was: a desperate gamble.

The success of the German advance was partially predicated on bad weather, since Allied air forces clearly had air supremacy. But of course, the skies could not stay clouded over indefinitely. The sun would have to return to Europe. Eisenhower saw the Battle of the Bulge as an opportunity for the Allies to drain off significant manpower and war matériel from Germany, and he knew that this was truly the beginning of the end.

Jakob awoke when a fly landed on his face. The barn was hot and smelly, stiflingly hot in the August morning heat. He could hear other flies buzzing around him and a gentle scraping against the outside of the barn wall. He listened intently for a moment, concentrating on the sound, until he decided it was just one of the animals hitting its tail against the wall as it brushed away flies.

"Mmmm . . . What's wrong?" Galia asked as she awoke beside him.

"Nothing. Just the cows. I couldn't figure out what that noise was, but I think it's just one of the cows..."

"It's hot."

"Yeah. We should get up and go swimming."

"With the cast? No you don't!" she said playfully. "Just another few days."

"I can't wait to get it off."

A lot had happened since that afternoon when Galia had told Jakob that she loved him. Jakob hadn't fully realized how alone he had felt—alone and hunted—until Galia had opened her heart to him. The day after her declaration of love, she told Jakob that Aliz wasn't her name at all. She had only taken that name while she was being hidden by the Gazsis. Galia was her real name, Galia Bartalan, and she was from Budapest.

They quickly became close, and then there was a first kiss and hand-holding and . . . But finding themselves in bed together was a surprise for both of them. It had just . . . happened. Galia had been a virgin.

Galia's father was very strict, and she had never even dated when she was living at home. There had even been an arranged marriage, but her betrothed, whom she had never met, was living in Vienna, and so the war had changed everything. Perhaps that was how it happened. Maybe it was the freedom of being away from her family. Or maybe the uncertainty. For all she knew, she might never see her parents or younger brother again. Maybe Jakob was taking their place in a much different way. She had fantasies of Jakob as a brave partisan taking on the world of evil—the evil ones who had torn her family apart . . .

That must have been it. He was her savior, and it seemed so natural to give herself to him.

It wasn't that much different for Jakob. He had panicked and run away when he had come face to face with Rebecca and his young son, Thomas. A voice in his head told him that he should marry Rebecca and be a father to Thomas, but another voice told him he wasn't ready to have a family. He had run away to a life of danger and adventure in Prague, but the voice was never far away. He kept feeling guilty about leaving them there in Switzerland, but then he would rationalize that it was the war, and once the war was over he would return to them and do right by them. That rationalization was made a little more difficult as he lay in bed with Galia in his arms. He decided to put it all out of his mind and just live for the moment, a very common way of thinking among partisans and soldiers. We will live for today, for tomorrow we may die.

It was an idyllic time for both of them. The war was far enough away to keep them safe, but close enough to push them together. Once the cast was removed from Jakob's leg and he was pronounced fit by Joska, the tone of Galia and Jakob's love took on even more intensity. Their love-making became desperate and clinging, their kisses deep and lingering. They both knew what was coming.

Jakob began eating his meals with the family for the first time when his cast was removed. Before that Joska said it would be too dangerous. If soldiers were to drop by, it would be difficult to get Jakob to a hiding place with the cast hindering his movement. Up in the loft it was just a matter of closing up the panel that hid his little room.

Joska and Elga were aware that Jakob and Galia were falling in love, but the young lovers did their best to hide it. Joska had caught them kissing a couple of times, but neither he nor his wife knew Jakob and Galia were sleeping together. Galia would get up early to do her chores and slip into bed with Jakob for a couple of hours before reappearing in the kitchen with that day's collection of eggs.

Elga treated both of her guests as though they were her own children. She had doted on Galia since the day the young girl came to their farm. Galia was the daughter she had never had. But while she wanted Galia to be happy, she was worried about the affection she saw developing between Galia and Jakob.

"They're getting closer every day," Joska said as he paused while eating.

"The Germans?" Elga asked her husband.

"Germans? No, the Russians. In the East. They say they're closing in on Budapest."

"Russians . . . ," Jakob muttered under his breath as he shook his head.

"You don't like the Russians?" Galia asked.

"As a people?" Jakob asked in response. "The Russians are fine as a people. It's the Communists. The leadership. I've heard terrible things about Stalin."

"So you hate the Communists?" Joska asked.

"I don't trust the Russian Communists."

"I've had friends who are Communists," Galia said. "They were always—"

"You can't talk about them the same," Jakob interrupted. "I've had friends who call themselves Communists, too, but it's not the same as the Bolshevists in power in Russia. It's not the same as with Stalin . . . the purges before the war. He killed most of his good officers. They say if a Russian officer doesn't perform well, Stalin has him executed. He uses men like cattle. That's not the same Communism they talk about in coffee houses. I'm afraid there isn't all that much difference between Stalin and Hitler."

"Maybe you're just hearing war propaganda," Joska countered.

"All the same, I'd rather not be here when the Russians come."

Galia looked up at Jakob with a start. She knew he would be leaving someday, but this was the first time it had come up. "You're leaving?" she asked accusingly.

"Of course he has to go," Joska answered for Jakob. "We knew he was only here until he got well . . . got his strength back."

"When?" Galia pressed. "When are you going?"

Jakob looked at her blankly. He wasn't prepared for this confrontation. He had known all along that he would be leaving. She must have known it too. Why was she pretending to be surprised? Why did she look as though she had been betrayed?

"Am I going with you?" she continued.

"Child!" Elga exclaimed in an outburst that was very out of character. "What do you mean? You can't go off with him. Your father sent you here so that we could take care of you and keep you safe until after the war."

"After the war?" Galia asked, tears welling up as she looked Elga in the eyes. "There isn't any 'after the war.' I don't know if I'll ever see my family again. Don't you know what they're doing to the Jews? They're killing them. They're sending them to their concentration camps and killing them."

"That's just rumors," Joska interjected.

"It's true," Jakob said with a somber note of authority.

"Then I can go with you?" Galia asked.

"You'll be safer here," Jakob said as he reached for her hand, but Galia quickly pulled away, knocking over her chair as she got up and ran from the room.

Jakob was embarrassed by the scene and just sat back in his chair. It was Elga who got up and went after Galia. She found her out in the yard sitting beneath the huge oak tree, crying as she held her face in her hands.

Elga sat down beside her. Galia thought of Elga as old woman, but Elga was only in her midforties. She had had a hard life and looked older than her years. Born as the new century began, she was the second-youngest of eight surviving children. Infant mortality in the region was high, and her mother lost four children before they reached the age of ten. She had never known a home with electricity, indoor plumbing, or even running water. She and Joska were married as the First World War continued to rage around them, but they lived apart from that. For some reason, Joska was never called for military service, and they never questioned it. Elga's dowry was a lightly wooded ten acres of land next to the twenty acres that Joska's parents had given him. They worked side by side each day and into the night, clearing land and pulling rocks out of the fields with the help of one tired old horse and an ancient plow. They barely survived the first couple of years, their families giving whatever help they could offer. Then Elga became pregnant. They named their daughter Aliz, the name they had given Galia as an alias while she hid with them. Aliz was only three years old when she got an ear infection. Such a small thing—such a normal complaint for a child—but it wouldn't go away. And then it began to grow worse. When they lost their first child in the fall of that year, after the war had ended, the life went right out of them. It seemed Aliz had given them a reason to go on with all the endless back-breaking work, but now she was gone. They grew so tired. They forgot how to smile and laugh. To lose a child—even though it was so common in those days—it tears away a part of your soul, leaving a gaping wound that never completely heals no matter how much time passes.

It was almost two years to the day, the anniversary of Aliz's death, that Elga visited a doctor in the village some ten miles away and was told that, yes, just as she suspected, she was with child again. Her first response was fear. She was afraid that this child might die, too, and she didn't know how she could ever bear such a thing again. Joska was also apprehensive, but he didn't dare show it. He kept telling her over and over how everything would be fine and she should be happy that God had seen fit to send them another "little angel."

Little angel. Those were his exact words, and the most amazing thing happened when their little boy was born. Ferko was healthy and happy, and such a big baby. He seemed to bring with him the most incredible fortune for his family. The farm began to prosper, and they were able to buy a bit more land and a few more animals.

Aliz was never far from their hearts or thoughts, but Ferko filled their lives. Elga did everything she could to keep him safe. But of course, the time comes too soon when a young man wants nothing more than to be free of the "protection" of his parents. When the war came, it was soon clear that Ferko was growing restless. He was still a teenager, sixteen as Hitler's panzers rolled into Poland from one side and Stalin's troops from the other. The dramatic phrases of youth began slipping into his conversation as he would rail against the "evil tyranny" and "rotten fascists," mimicking speeches he had heard or read about. By the time the Germans occupied Hungary, he would constantly go on about how "our people" wouldn't stand for it. And then came the day when Lorencz stopped for a visit, a visit Ferko had requested in confidence. "He's not too young," Lorencz had said. "He's a smart boy. Would be a good fighter. We must fight . . ."

The conversation went on. Elga railed against them, the men who argued for it and her husband, who was beginning to accept the idea. "He mustn't go," she shouted. "Take someone else's son! Haven't we lost enough?"

But Ferko was hungry for the excitement, the thrill of adventure and the heroics of which he had so often dreamt. He would not die. How foolish his mother was to think it. *They* would die . . . all the evil Nazis. They would die, but certainly not he.

All of this, and now here she was sitting beside Galia, who was crying her eyes out because Jakob would not take her with him into the unknown battle lines to the west.

"We all knew he would be leaving," Elga said softly as she put a hand on Galia's shoulder.

"I thought . . . I . . ."

"What, child? What did you think?"

"I thought he would take me with him," she said as she started crying again.

"You don't know what you're saying! Don't you know how dangerous it would be?"

"Not with him."

"You think too much of him."

"No, no . . . He would protect me from anything. He would—"

"Didn't you hear what Lorencz said when he first brought him?"

Galia blinked back tears as she looked Elga in the eyes without answering.

"He said Tonda ran—"

"Jakob."

"Yes, Jakob. Jakob ran. Lorencz called him a coward."

"He didn't!"

"Yes, he did," Elga insisted. "Your heart hears what it wants to hear."

"But I . . ."

"I know. You love him . . . but you're so young. You can't—"

"Are you trying to tell me I don't love him?" Galia interrupted accusingly.

Elga put her hand on Galia's shoulder again. "I know what it feels like. I haven't forgotten. Aliz . . . I mean Galia . . . this is the first time you've been away from home. You're lonely, separated from your family, and then this handsome young man, wounded in battle, comes from nowhere and you take care of him. I would be more surprised if you hadn't fallen in love with him. But Galia, your parents brought you to us, and we promised to take care of you as if you were our own child. Jakob doesn't want to take you with him, and we can't let you leave."

"Am I a prisoner?" Galia asked defiantly, no longer crying.

"Don't be foolish! You know that's not true. You need to stay for your own safety."

"But I could go if I wanted?"

"Galia, please don't ask such a thing," Elga said, pulling the young girl to her as they sat beneath the sheltering oak tree. Just then a light rain began to fall and the air was filled with the wonderful smell of a hot summer day being quenched by a gentle shower. "I love you, little one," Elga said, meaning it with all her being, as though Galia had been sent as her chance to love her little Aliz once again.

Galia had decided at that moment, however, that she would go with Jakob. She would tell him tomorrow that he had to take her. She simply wouldn't let him go without her. She let Elga believe that she was convinced and said nothing more about it as she went to bed.

The next morning she got up early as always and

quietly made her way to the barn. She climbed up to Jakob's room and tiptoed softly to his bed. "I am going with you!" she declared as she pulled back the covers. "No matter what you say, I . . ."

Suddenly she realized the bed was empty, and her stomach dropped to her knees. Could it be? Had he really left? Had he crept out like a thief in the night?

She glanced around the little room to confirm that his things were gone and noticed a piece of paper folded on the wooden chair in the corner. She walked over to find her name printed on it. A letter! He truly was a coward! He couldn't even face her!

She grabbed the letter and crumpled it, tearing it to pieces and throwing it at the bed. She was filled with anger as she looked for something to break and found the porcelain water pitcher by the bed. She raised it over her head with both hands and threw it to the floor with all the strength she could muster, but even though it shattered into hundreds of pieces, it did nothing to release the pain, and she fell to her knees at the bed, sobbing into the sheets. "Bastard!" she cried as she let out a gut-wrenching wail, burying her face in the bed linens.

She cried for some time, and when she was finally cried out, she forced herself to pick up the pieces of the letter. Still kneeling, she laid them out on the bed to read. "My love," it began, and she became angry all over again. How could he have run off if he loved her? But she forced herself to read the rest. "It's all my fault. I do love you and I know you love me, but we can't be together now." The sentence ended there, and Galia realized she was missing a piece of the letter. She looked around and found the rest of it. Once she put it together, she realized there were parts crossed out. He must have been in a hurry. Just as interested in what he had scribbled out as she was in the rest of the letter, she held it to the light until she could make out the words: "I'm sorry we went as far as we did. I shouldn't have taken advantage of you." The letter went on: "Being older I should have known better, but I was weak. Your beauty and kindness were too much for me in a time when I have known too little beauty and even less kindness. I do love you. I will always love you, and, God willing, we will meet again someday when the world is a safer place. But I must go now, and I must go alone. You are better off here with Joska and Elga. They care very much about you. I didn't mean to hurt you. I was too blind to see this coming. You were sent by heaven to heal me. Not just my wounds, but my heart. I will never forget you for that. Please don't hate me." He signed it simply: "Jakob."

She read it again, and then again. She didn't know what to do. She couldn't go after him. She couldn't just let him go . . . but there was nothing she could do, and the tears came again, washing over her pain.

JAKOB HAD LEFT right after he returned to his room after dinner. He knew there was no other way, no better time. It had been such a happy time for him that it was just as sad and traumatic for him to leave as it would be for Galia when she found out he was gone. But he had to go.

He had no money and only a little food that he had squirreled away in case soldiers came and he had to leave quickly. Joska had told him that he could take one of the horses when the time came, since both of them were concerned that soldiers might ride into the farm someday looking for him. He knew he was in for a long, hard journey.

He had much time to think as he rode along. He thought about heading northwest to Austria. Or it would only be about five hundred kilometers to Munich as the crow flies . . . Munich? He could go back to Switzerland, but he wouldn't be able to stay there. Refugees were not allowed to stay in neutral Switzerland. His only goal was to reach the Allies rather than being caught up in the Russian advance, and he had no idea how long that would take. Maybe Italy was best . . . If he went through Austria, he could make his way to Italy through the Brenner Pass, but it was already autumn. It would not be good to start through the pass as winter began. It was far too unpredictable. He decided it would be best to return to Prague and see what happened. Then he could make his way down through Italy to Palestine. He was supposed to go to Palestine. His mother and Rebecca and Thomas . . . maybe even his grandfather would be there by then, if he was still alive. If any of them were still alive. For all he knew, none of them had made it through France. They could be sitting in a German concentration camp somewhere waiting to die.

He was thinking too much. It wasn't a good thing in days like these, endless wandering days when you lose track of time, when there is only day and night, sometime before now, now, and the days yet to come. He was beginning to regret that he didn't go with them when they left Switzerland. At least he would have shared their fate. Now he began to wonder if he would be all alone. Maybe they were all gone. Maybe he should have stayed with Galia and started all over. Maybe . . .

It was weeks before he got to Prague, arriving in that edgy, hot September as the future of Germany was being clearly and inexorably painted on a bloody canvas at a frenzied pace. It was that moment—that moment of hesitation before the executioner lets his ax fall—that moment when the spectator thinks it still might not happen. But the ax must fall.

He went to an old hiding place outside the city and settled in. It was hard to get back into the Prague state of mind—the state of mind that says you must never feel safe and secure and must trust no one. The time with Galia had been so . . . well, it had been the complete opposite. He never really thought for a moment that German troops would come looking for him at the farm. It was something he forced himself to think about as a possibility, an off chance, so he would be ready if the unthinkable happened, but he could never believe it in his heart. Back in Prague, though, everything was dangerous and unnerving. Anyone might turn him in.

After a few days he went to make contact with Ondra, who had sent him to Bratislava months before. They met in the early morning at a coffee stand in Prague's main train station. Jakob got there a little early and watched from across the great hall as people came and went. He was nervous, not knowing what to expect. He couldn't figure out why at first, but then it hit him as he lay awake the night before, thinking about the coming meeting. He had left Prague months ago with Jan and Sasha, and then suddenly here he was again, unannounced . . . and alone.

Ondra arrived early, too, along with a friend, and Jakob watched as they circled the area, checking things out just as Jakob had done. Jakob knew that this "friend" of Ondra's was probably not Ondra's only escort. He was just the one Jakob knew about. There were most likely others watching as well.

Ondra had an intense expression on his face, much too intense for the inconspicuous demeanor that he wished to display as he took in the train station with a series of sweeping glances. It was on one of these "sweeps" that he caught sight of Jakob. He had missed him at first. After all, Jakob looked rather rough after his trip, tired and scruffy with a half-grown beard, but Ondra recognized him nonetheless. Jakob was staring straight at him as he looked around the hall. When they made eye contact, Ondra made a face that could best be described as a grimace. He had been caught at the game, but Ondra was very astute, more than a step ahead of most, and he was sure that Jakob was alone. When they made eye contact, Ondra waved Jakob over with a big hand gesture, as one might call over an old friend.

They walked over to the coffee stand and ordered their coffee, then moved to one of the tables. They didn't say anything to each other for a couple of moments, a long uncomfortable silence, as they drank their coffee.

"Tell me a story, Tonda."

"A story?"

"I was very . . . surprised. Yes, I was surprised to hear that you were back. I thought it was understood that you and the others would stay in Bratislava."

"We never even made it to Bratislava."

"I know."

Jakob let the statement go. He just assumed that Ondra knew people in Bratislava who had been keeping an eye out for him and the others, waiting for their arrival. "Sasha is dead."

"Dead?"

"We were . . . I guess you could say we were kidnapped by a group of partisans just as we left the truck convoy. Jan was hurt when he jumped from the truck. His shoulder. The partisans sent him off somewhere. They said he would be safe until he was well enough to travel."

"Where?"

"Where did they send him? I don't know. I think the group he went with was crossing the border into Yugoslavia."

"And Sasha?"

"We were caught in a crossfire. It was a raid on a German column, and they got behind us. I saw him go down just before I was shot . . ."

"You were shot?"

"Shot in one leg, and the other was broken when my horse went down."

"Both legs?"

"Yeah."

"How did you get out?"

"I passed out. Somebody else pulled me out and

got me to a farmhouse. They hid me there."

"Who?"

"Who? You mean the farmers?"

"No, who got you out?"

"He was a great brute of a man. We called him Lorencz. I don't know if that was his real name."

"Where was the farm?"

"Southwest of Budapest about a hundred and fifty kilometers."

"What was the farmer's name?" Ondra asked quickly. It wasn't that he would know any of these people, or even thought that he might know them. He just wanted to see if Tonda—Jakob—could come up with the answers quickly. If he could give the answers off the top of his head, it meant that the story was probably true, or at least well rehearsed. But if he couldn't answer quickly . . .

"Gazsi."

"Was he married?"

"Joska and Elga Gazsi. They had a son named Ferko, one of the partisans. He was killed in the same battle as Sasha." Jakob stared at Ondra after rattling off the answers. "Why all the questions, Ondra?" he continued with an edge to his voice. "Are you planning to go to Hungary for a visit?

Ondra grimaced once again as he scratched the back of his neck, then let out a sigh and let his hand fall to the table. "I guess I didn't make it clear that you shouldn't come back here. You're useless to us now that they have your name, and you're in danger."

"I didn't know where else to go."

"Tonda . . . you've always been good at what you

do. You know what needs to be done, and even more than that, you've always seemed to understand the bigger picture . . ."

"Just say it, Ondra."

"It doesn't look good. You leave with Jan and Sasha. You disappear without a trace for a few months, and then you suddenly reappear out of nowhere without your friends . . . It just doesn't look good, Tonda, not good at all."

"And?"

"And no one will work with you. I don't blame them."

"So where does that leave me?"

"I believe you, Tonda. I think we owe you something. The least we can do is hide you. You can go underground."

"Underground? How long?"

"As long as it takes."

"Until the war's over?"

"It can't go on forever. The Americans think it will be over by Christmas."

"The Americans . . . ," Jakob said with a smile and shake of his head. "What do *you* think? I've just come a long way, and from what I've seen, I don't think the Germans are ready to collapse."

"It's possible."

"So I should hide out for God knows how many months?"

"You wouldn't be the only one. There are quite a few people who need to stay out of sight. We do what we can to help."

Jakob remembered the time almost two years before when he had returned from England and was hiding out from Abwehr agents when he had come into contact with Wilhelm Canaris. He thought he would go crazy back then, but maybe it was because of everything else that was going on at the time. Back then he had been waiting for word on his family when they were imprisoned in Theresienstadt. This time he would just be passing time. Maybe he could do it.

It only took a day for Ondra to make contact and set up a place for Jakob to stay. It was a small attic in the Nova Mesto district above a two-story warehouse. He could only stand up near the middle of the floor where the roof came to its peak. The two small windows were set up in the peak of the roof, just above his head, and on the first day he found a couple of boxes to use as steps so he could look out, even though he had been warned to stay away from the windows.

It wasn't long before the attic became a prison to him. He felt trapped. And he was bored. The nights were beginning to get colder as September came to a close, and Jakob started to question whether he could make it until the war ended.

He could see the first snow falling through the high window as he lay on his bedroll reading a book. It was already November, some seven weeks since he had gone into hiding, and the sight of that first snowfall actually made him cry. Was this what life came down to? Doing anything just to keep drawing another breath? And then he felt bad for thinking it. He knew what others were going through—the pain, torture, and starvation—and here he was feeling sorry for himself when he was being taken care of and was relatively safe. But he was so lonely. Even when they brought him food, it was anonymously; someone would leave something at the door at some time during the day and would pick up the remains after it was dark. Sometimes he could hear people moving things around in the warehouse and he would freeze. He was becoming like an animal, he thought to himself, like a little mouse peeking around a corner, only to scurry away in terror when people showed up. He wasn't sure how much longer he could take it.

Then one day everything was answered for him. The weather had warmed a bit, just enough to melt the snow, and he was glad for that, considering how cold it got in the attic. He was beginning to wonder if he might freeze to death as winter set in. Over the weeks he had spent in the old building, he had come to know its idiosyncrasies, all the strange little sounds that would come and go in the course of a day and when people might show up to work. No one had ever shown up at the building on a Sunday. Not that it would have been impossible. Who knows... The owner might have needed something, or it might even have been someone dealing in the black market, or a burglary. But when Jakob heard, from two floors below, the sound of someone making a rather dramatic entrance into the building, he sensed it was not a good thing. He quickly threw a few things into his small rucksack and left the attic, going down to the second floor. As he arrived at the stairs at the opposite side of the warehouse, he heard them coming up. He ducked back behind some crates and pulled out his pistol. He held his breath, still wanting to believe that it wasn't Gestapo or soldiers. But he knew it must be, and he wasn't going to let them arrest him. They would never let him live, and there was no question that it would be a slow and painful death. They stormed past him, leaving a man to guard the steps as they rushed up the stairs to the attic.

Someone had given him up. They weren't just checking a building; they knew exactly where to look. Jakob knew they would go through the warehouse floor by floor as soon as they realized he wasn't in the attic, and he knew had to make a desperate move. He couldn't shoot the man at the steps because he'd have all the others coming after him, not to mention that there was probably another soldier posted at the door downstairs.

Jakob slipped the pistol into his belt and pulled out a knife with a locking, spring-loaded blade. The man at the stairs was watching the other soldiers as they poured into the attic, and he gripped his rifle as he heard the sounds of things being thrown around up there. He was ready to shoot anyone who might get past the others and head for the stairs.

That was when Jakob came out from his hiding place and slipped in behind the guard. He had learned how to kill a man with a knife when he had been trained by the Abwehr for his "mission" in England, but this was the first time he'd had to do it. Jakob threw his left arm around the guard, covering the man's mouth and pulling him backward behind the crates. Even though the guard had his rifle at the ready, his first reaction was to try to throw Jakob off, just like the Abwehr trainers said it would happen. That was when Jakob flipped out the blade on his knife, sinking it into the notch in the man's collarbone and twisting it. As the guard's knees started to give out, Jakob pulled out the knife and made a hard, sweeping slice across his neck, opening the jugular, then let the man drop to the floor behind the crates.

It would be hard to describe how Jakob felt at that moment. He was shaking with fear and tension, and knew he had only moments before the others came down from the attic. He grabbed the soldier's rifle and made his way quickly down the stairs, trying to be as quiet as he could in case there was another guard at the front door.

Just as he thought, there was another guard, but he could see that the young man was smoking a cigarette. Rarely did anyone get past the first squad, but if they did, the second man would get them. Because of that, the soldiers who were posted at the front door knew that they weren't likely to see any action. Rounding up Jews had become routine for them, and they knew what to expect.

The sounds of Jakob's movements were still covered by the activities of the men in the attic, but Jakob knew that could end at any instant. Just as Jakob got to the bottom of the stairs, the soldier at the door turned toward him, but Jakob managed to duck behind a crate just in time. Making his way down an aisle, he managed to get within three meters of the door, still under cover. He was sweating as he closed in on the young guard at the door, and just as he was getting ready to rush him, everything went quiet. Jakob held still, frozen like a statue, as he waited for the noise to start up again when they began going through the second floor. It suddenly occurred to him that they might find the body of the soldier he'd already had to kill, and the thought made him even more nervous. Without realizing it, he shifted his weight from one foot to the other, causing the floorboards beneath his feet to creak loudly. The guard at the door jerked violently, dropping his cigarette as he grabbed for his rifle. At that instant, Jakob leapt from his hiding place, covering the distance between them in two long strides, bringing up the steel-clad rifle butt against the guard's face. The soldier crumpled to the floor, and Jakob ran out the door, still holding the rifle wrong way around.

There was a military lorry idling just outside the door with a driver standing nearby, obviously waiting for the squad to come out of the warehouse with their prisoner. The driver looked him up and down, and Jakob realized he couldn't just run away because this man would tell them which way he went. Still panting from the exertion of his escape, frenzied with animal-like fear as he faced yet another obstacle, Jakob knew he had to kill this man too. With a precision that surprised even him, he flipped the rifle end over end, like a soldier performing a drill, and shot the driver. The rifle shot exploded in the city street like a cannon, bringing the soldiers on the second floor of the warehouse to the windows. But by the time they looked out, Jakob was already behind the wheel of the truck, so it wasn't until it started moving that their eyes were drawn to the body of the driver lying in the middle of the street.

Two of the men from the squad broke out a couple of windows and started firing at the truck with sub-machine guns, but they never even came close to hitting it as they fired wildly into the street.

Jakob couldn't believe he had made it out of the warehouse, but he knew he had a ways to go before he could breathe easy. He felt he had no more than fifteen minutes before the men in the warehouse could contact their headquarters and alert others to look for him. It might be longer—in reality, it would almost certainly be longer—but that was about as much time as he could safely give himself. He couldn't trust anyone for help, since he didn't know who had betrayed him, so he felt it would be best to get to the outskirts of the city and hide the truck.

He was amazed at how easily he made it through the city. Taking side streets to avoid stoplights, he headed north toward the city limits, avoiding the area just beyond, where he knew from previous experience there would be a checkpoint. Instead he chose an extremely unorthodox route that included a bone-rattling jaunt across three pairs of railroad tracks and a patch of truck gardens.

When he cleared the field, he accelerated to the truck's top speed, a bit over eighty kilometers per hour, and ran it into a lake where there was a dropoff. Jakob swam out of the cab as the truck sank well below the surface. He could see the canvas top of the truck box under the water, but only if he was looking directly at it. Anyone driving by would never know the truck was there. Satisfied that it was hidden, Jakob got his bearings and set off on foot.

It was just gut instinct that told him to go north.

That would be the shortest distance to Germany, through the Sudetenland and then along the Elbe River valley through the Ore Mountains. All of his travel was on foot, being careful to avoid military or civil authorities, although just as a precaution, the last time he had seen Ondra he had gotten a good set of forged identity papers, including a medical report exempting him from military service due to a heart condition. Thus he felt he had a good chance of talking his way out of any confrontations.

If he could have traveled in a straight line, it was only roughly eighty-five kilometers to the German border, a short train trip or bus ride. But in that winter of 1944, having to avoid soldiers and police, he was lucky to go more than six kilometers a day. The snow, the cold, and the authorities weren't the only problems; it became increasingly harder to find food as he went along. For the first time in his life, he had to go through garbage cans looking for scraps, but wartime food shortages made for little waste. Jakob hadn't known that level of hunger anytime in his life. He couldn't remember the food shortages of the Great War, when he was just an infant, but he remembered his mother talking about how difficult that time had been. Talk, however, could never really convey what it was like.

When it's simply a matter of not having enough food, hunger is a continual gnawing presence, but in the first few days of going completely without food, there is a physical pain as your body rebels against the privation. Then the pain seems to lessen... or else a person just gets used to it, numbs to it, and that's when it becomes dangerous. The body turns to reserves of and fat and muscle to keep going. A person's mind starts to slow down. Everything focuses on food, on survival, and that's when illusions of what we are begin to fall apart. Our concepts of society and right and wrong and all those noble inspirations and aspirations begin to dim as it becomes clear that man is still, above all, an animal. Being born, living, and dying with a fundamental similarity to any other animal. More than once Jakob had come across a farm field where the snow had been clawed away by freezing hands as people before him had foraged for a frozen, rotting potato or beet, or an ear of corn. And even though others had already been there and almost certainly picked things clean, Jakob would still get down on his knees and rut through the snow and dirt, thinking he would find something that the others had missed.

At one time it would have surprised him to find himself in the company of others as he traveled, but his weakened condition didn't allow him the luxury of critical thought. The other people he joined on his journey, or who joined him, were refugees who also thought it best to get back to Germany. They traveled together, but they didn't exchange a single word. They all eyed each other suspiciously, viewing each other as competitors. They slept wherever they could find shelter. They might take refuge in a barn, getting an hour's rest before the farmer discovered them and told them to leave, or they might find a burned-out building or a house abandoned by others who were now refugees like themselves.

After several weeks of traveling, Jakob began to realize that he was getting sloppy. He was trudging along, eyes down on the road, working to keep one foot going after the other, when suddenly there was a hand on his shoulder.

"Papieren!" the young soldier stated forcefully.

Jakob had walked right into a military checkpoint without knowing it. He was lucky. Since he was still in a group of about twenty other refugees, the teenage soldiers only made a cursory check of identity papers and let the ragtag group through.

When they were a few hundred feet past the checkpoint, Jakob turned to one of the other refugees and asked where they were. The woman he asked was not surprised that he didn't know where he was. There was no emotion at all in her voice. "Germany," was all she said.

"Which direction are we . . . ?" Jakob started to ask.

"This is the road to Dresden. We're going to Berlin. We have family."

"Dresden . . . ," Jakob muttered to himself, trying to decide if he wanted to go there or turn west and work his way down to Munich. He decided that if he went to Dresden, he might be able to get transportation south. He could disappear in the crowds.

The road was no easier in Germany than it had been in Czechoslovakia. It was harder, in fact, since there were more roadblocks and checkpoints. It was February by the time he made it to Dresden.

The city was filled with refugees by then. By the end of January 1945, the Russians had swept through Prussia, making a vicious thrust at Berlin throughout the winter. They had also left a few small pockets of German resistance behind their lines, but none of these was a serious threat to their continued advance. When Jakob arrived in Dresden, the Russian front was only a hundred and sixty kilometers away—only about fifty kilometers from the outskirts of Berlin.

Jakob found it easy to blend in with the crowds in Dresden, just as he had anticipated, but the inflated population made it even more difficult to find food. If he were to believe the news and gossip that he picked up in the streets, it seemed the Russians were concentrating all their efforts to the north, at Berlin. He believed he had a good chance of getting to Munich just as he had planned. He decided to rest for a few days before heading south.

A man would have to be blind not to see the end coming for Germany as he walked the streets of Dresden during that terrible winter of attrition. The final assault of the German army in the west, a push through the Ardennes that would come to be known as the "Battle of the Bulge" by the British and Americans, had failed chiefly due to the air superiority of the Allies. Armies on both sides were quickly closing in on Germany, and even the inspirational propaganda of Herr Goebbels couldn't bring a glimmer of hope to the faces of a numbed and foreboding people. But no one could have guessed what the night would bring to the beautiful city of Dresden, the city known as "Florence on the Elbe."

Even though the days rarely had names for Jakob during this time, he did know it was a Tuesday evening when he drifted off to sleep in the company of a few other refugees from the eastern front. He knew because he had picked up a newspaper that day from an old man who had left it behind and, having nothing better to do, spent considerable time reading it from cover to cover. They were bundled in ragged blankets and layers of tattered clothes as they tried to keep warm in the shelter of a bridge. They had dug themselves in beneath the bridge, making a wall of packed snow to protect themselves against the bitter wind that swept up the river. They even managed a little fire, but for the most part the thing that would truly keep them from freezing to death was that they all huddled closely together, ignoring the normal rules of social conduct and the questionable smells resulting from a lack of proper hygiene.

It was a clear and crisp night with countless stars clearly defined against the black veil of space. There were few lights to be seen in the city, as a partial moon glowed radiantly over Dresden. It was a time when one might stop and notice the sky and a fearful phrase would creep into one's thoughts . . . "bomber's moon." It was part of the vernacular in that time and place. When the sky was clear, a pilot flying overhead could see his targets laid out neatly on the little model city below him. But it wasn't a model at all. It was a home with people and a school full of children and a church with people praying and a bakery with people standing in line for hours to get a loaf of bread . . . It was real.

But if you were walking through the streets of Dresden, the thought of a bomber's moon would probably quickly disappear, almost as soon as you thought it. Why would they bomb a city like Dresden? It wasn't the capital. There weren't any military installations or war factories. Why would they bomb Dresden? Why would they bomb London or Coventry?

Jakob awoke to the wail of the air-raid sirens some time in the middle of the night.

"What is it?" he asked sleepily as the others began to move toward the opening of their little cave beneath the bridge.

"Planes," one of his anonymous comrades answered as he looked up at the sky.

"Where are they going?"

"Here . . ."

"Here? Why would they . . ."

"We might want to get out of here. A bridge is always a pretty good target for bombers."

The four men looked at each other for an instant as they considered this bit of information and then agreed that the bridge might not be the best place to hide. Jakob didn't fully appreciate just how warm and cozy the snow cave had been until he was abruptly forced out into the frigid night air.

"Damn!" he said as he wrapped his arms around himself and started stamping his feet.

"Maybe they're just flying over," one of the other men suggested without much conviction.

"Then we could get back to sleep," another added.

"I think you're right," Jakob said as he stared up at the planes now clearly silhouetted against the moon. "They're just flying ov—"

Jakob went silent as his words were punctuated with the whistling of the first bombs as they cleared the open bay doors of the Allied planes. He had seen his fair share of artillery shells at other times, but he had never been in a major bombing raid. Each bomb shook the earth and sent a concussion wave through the air so that one could actually feel the vibration of the bombs falling one after another. But these bombs were different than the artillery shells he had seen before; these were incendiary bombs—filled with phosphorous or liquefied petroleum—so that they would start and spread fire. Great towers of flame would shoot up from the point of impact.

"Let's get out of here," one of the men shouted, shaking the others out of their trances as they stood transfixed by the scene playing out before them. They gathered up what few belongings they had and hurried across the bridge, making their way up a hill as the bombers continued their relentless assault on the city.

They could have kept going, but they all stopped to watch what was happening below. The fires in different areas had joined together and become a huge wall of flame moving across the city. The line of planes seemed endless as they kept dropping their bombs, even though it had been more than a half hour since the first bomb had fallen. And then a different sound was added to the cacophony of sirens and explosions and shouting. At first it sounded like the wind, but it wasn't. It was the sound of rushing air as all the fires started to heat up the atmosphere in the midst of the frigid winter night, and suddenly there was a vortex . . . a tornado made of fire. The updraft of the hot air swirled and danced, pulling up glowing embers and debris and sending it all up into the giant funnel, high up into the air where it would break free into a bright, sparkling cloud of orange and white sparks that would float down over the city. It was a holocaust . . . a consumption of humanity by flame. Just as a Jewish nation had been consigned to ashes that flew up Nazi-built chimneys a few hundred kilometers to the East, and Britons had perished in the blitz, yet more innocents were committed to the flame by these priests of war, sacrificed for their misguided beliefs of purity, honor, and revenge.

Jakob and the others stood and watched, at once both amazed and horrified by the hellish sight. They couldn't know what was going on down in the city. Some people were suffocated long before they were touched by flames as the fire sucked all the oxygen out of the area, while others were buried alive as buildings collapsed in on them in their hiding places. Thousands more were incinerated in the blink of an eye as they tried to outrun the fire in a mad dash to the river.

Jakob and the others did see people make it to the river. Many of them died as they leapt into the freezing water after having been burned in the fires. Many more were crowding the bridge as they tried to flee the city. Dozens were trampled to death as they tried to make this last push to safety.

The scene would stay with Jakob for the rest of his life. He kept thinking about what a horrible way it would be to die, trapped as fire swept in all around you. And worst of all, if everyone you loved was caught there too. He saw mothers with children among the people who were quickly filling the road out of the city, and he thought of the ones who hadn't made it out. What did they have to do with this war? But wasn't that the way it had always been? He told himself to stop thinking about it as he stopped to adjust the rags he wore so that he would be better protected from the cold, and then he forced himself to put one foot in front of the other and started off into the night.

The rest of his journey to Munich was a blur spent hiding from police and soldiers and hunting for food. Everywhere he went there were rumors and more rumors. "The Russians are five kilometers away!" "The Americans have crossed the Rhine." "Berlin has fallen!" "The British have surrendered because of the V2 rockets." "We can still win the war." Or from those who dared say it: "We never had a chance of winning this damned war."

But despite it all, spring came once again. People just didn't notice it.

It was about two months after he had left Dresden that Jakob arrived at the Isar River. The Isar was the river he had played in when his mother would take him to the English Garden as a boy. He knew he wasn't far from Munich now. He came close to a bridge and saw there was a sentry, and it suddenly occurred to him that the soldiers were American. He didn't know what to make of the Americans, so he just avoided them, as he had been avoiding the German authorities.

A few days later he came upon a boy of thirteen or fourteen who was crying as he sat beneath a tree in front of a modest little house that had sustained a bit of damage in some bombing raid or another. He only caught Jakob's eye because of his immaculate

Hitler Jugend uniform. Most people tried to hide the fact that they had had any association with the Nazi party, especially since the American soldiers were all around. The HJ uniform seemed so out of place with everything else Jakob had seen—the refugees, the looted stores, and the generally beaten down population. It made Jakob think of his own days in the Hitler Youth so many years before. The boy noticed Jakob staring at him, and even though Jakob said nothing—even though he was obviously just another dirty, ragged beggar—the boy wiped his eyes and said, "The Führer . . . the Führer is dead!" He said it with such pain and disbelief, it was as if he were telling Jakob that God himself was dead. And for the boy, who had known no other leader in his life, who had been told over and over again at school and on the radio, in newspapers and news-reels, that Adolf Hitler was like a god, it was just as though God had died.

Jakob didn't respond at all. He just walked away. Just another rumor, he thought to himself, but as he walked, as he thought about it some more, he began to believe it. A few days later the war was over in Europe, just as Jakob entered Munich for the first time since he left Rebecca there in 1938.

Munich had been beaten down by countless bombing raids in the months before the American Third Army Group under General George Patton rolled in to occupy the city.

All the memories of his youth were mounded up in great, mountainous piles of brick, mortar, and dust as he wandered through the Altstadt district. The churches, the city hall, and the Feldherrnhalle .

. . the museums and schools . . . the building where British Prime Minister Neville Chamberlain had asked Hitler to sign an agreement, a slip of paper that Chamberlain would later wave before newsreel cameras saying that it meant there would be "peace in our times" . . . that place too was beaten down. It was the time the Müncheners would call "the ruinen jahre," the years of ruins.

He walked from street to street, and each time he looked up expecting to see a familiar building, there was only a corner piece or a foundation or a pile of dust and stone to mark the spot. It was an overwhelming feeling of loss. He hadn't realized before how much it all meant to him, the feeling of belonging and identity that he had derived from these streets and buildings.

He kept going. North to the residential areas, to Schwabing. He passed the place where the apartment building had been, the apartment where his family had lived when they first came to Munich after the last war.

Nothing.

Every now and then he would see a person, a child or an old man or woman, come climbing out of a pile of brick and dirt. They were living there in the ruins. All the young men were still gone, in prisoner of war camps across the country; only the very old or the very young remained. But of course, you couldn't really tell age . . . Even a young woman looked old after months of bombing and starvation. The only thing these people were glad of was that it was the Americans and not the Russians who occupied their city. The American soldiers, however, were not so comfortable with the arrangements. After all, Dachau was only twenty kilometers away. What kind of animals were these people? And they kept hearing about the Hitler Youth, young boys who were told to keep fighting even after the surrender.

Before long, a strange thought came to him. He was almost at Gertrude Haas's apartment. Friedrich Haas's mother—Grandma Gertie—who had taken care of him when he was a boy. How old would she be now? Maybe Gertie had moved out. Maybe the building was gone. Maybe she was . . . After all, it had been seven years since he had seen her, just before the *Anschluss* in Austria.

When he got to the apartment building he saw that it had been damaged, but only in the back on the opposite side from Gertrude's apartment, or at least the apartment that had been hers. Should he go in? What were the chances that she could still be there?

He had the strangest feeling as he walked into the foyer. The familiar smell. It all looked the same. Maybe it was a portal to the past. Maybe he would walk into Gertrude's apartment and go back in time. He walked up the stairs and turned the corner to her door and knocked loudly. There was no answer, so he knocked again. There was still no answer, but he could hear someone moving around inside.

"Gertie?" he called out hesitantly as he knocked again. "Gertie, are you there?"

Nothing.

"Gertie, it's Jakob. Jakob Metzdorf. Gunther and Amalie's son . . ."

He heard movement again, and then he heard

someone at the door fumbling with the lock. The door opened just a crack and a single eye peered out, and then the door swung wide. Gertie had shrunk. It was a smaller version, but it was Grandma Gertie. Her snow-white hair was drawn back into a tight bun, her face speckled with age spots on pale white skin that looked as thin as paper, her eyes enormous as they gazed through heavy eyeglasses. But the eyes were bright as she took in the face of her little Jakob all grown up.

"Oh, my . . . Oh, my . . . Oh, my . . . ," was all she could say as she stiffly moved toward Jakob with her arms wide open. Jakob returned the embrace warmly as he bent over to take his delicate old nanny into his arms.

"How can it be?" she asked in genuine bewilderment. "How . . . ?"

"It's so hard to explain," Jakob began as he thought about how to tell her what had happened. "We left Austria so long—"

"Friedrich is dead," Gertrude interrupted somberly, saying it in the way that old people say those things they must constantly remind themselves of lest they forget.

Jakob didn't know it, but he wasn't surprised. "Oh no," was all he could say, trying to show sympathy that he didn't really feel. So many people had died, and Friedrich seemed lost so long before that he just assumed he was dead, if not physically, then at least dead to Jakob.

"And what about your mother and father?" Gertrude asked. "How are they? Are they all right?"

"Well, you know father died long ago, back in

thirty-four . . ."

"Oh, my, that's right," she answered. "I'm sorry, I'm sorry. My mind . . . I'm getting so old. Of course I knew that . . . But your mother?"

"She's well," Jakob said, "as far as I know. I haven't seen her for a year, but she was on her way to Palestine. I'm sure she's—"

"Palestine? What a terrible place!" Gertie blurted out with a surprising degree of animation. "Why would she go there?"

"Gertie, you know she's Jewish. She went to Palestine to get away from—"

"Shhh!" Gertie interrupted as she drew close to Jakob. "You mustn't say such things. They'll take you away."

"No, Gertie," Jakob said as he gently put a hand on her shoulder. "That's all over now. You don't need to be afraid of—"

"They took away those two children...," she continued, ignoring Jakob. "Hans and Sophie. Only four doors down the street. They took them away..." Gertrude had been looking around nervously as she spoke, but suddenly she looked into Jakob's eyes and the thick glasses magnified the tears that were filling her eyes as she began to whisper: "They killed her. Little Sophie Scholl. She was such a pretty little girl, and they arrested her and killed her in the prison. They said she was giving out letters that said bad things about Hitler, and they arrested her and..."

Jakob had never heard of Sophie Scholl or the resistance group in Munich called "The White Rose," and so he didn't know the significance of her story.

"It's okay," he finally said. "It's over now. You don't need to be afraid."

They finally sat down as they continued to talk, but they kept to the old days before the war. Gertrude talked a bit about the American soldiers who had marched in and occupied Munich, but only to the extent that she was glad it was the Americans, because she had heard horror stories about the Russian troops to the east.

There was little to eat, but she did her best to cook something for the two of them. It seemed so normal—so awkward and yet so normal—as they laughed and talked and finally hugged each other as they said good night. It was the first night Jakob had spent in a bed in months. He felt as though he could sleep forever. He thought he might as well stay for a couple of days while he decided what to do. He would certainly go to Palestine eventually, but how?

When he got up the next morning, he went out to look for food so he and Gertie could have a good meal and she could have something to keep her going for a while. It wasn't easy. There were thousands of people—desperate, hungry people—roaming through the streets. He heard rumors here and there of food. The American army was trying to get food in, but there were delays as things were getting settled, with surrendering German troops being set up in camps and transitional authorities being put in place. Jakob was good at it, though, because that was how he had survived for the past year. He was bold and ruthless. Me first. No mercy, no kindness. The others could have whatever he left behind.

He came through the door of Gertie's apartment

with a flourish. "I've found us enough to last for days! Come see!"

He looked over and saw Gertie sitting in the chair, but she didn't move. "Gertie!" he said loudly as he walked over to her. "Come see what I've got."

He knew. He didn't want to know, but he knew in that instant. She was dead . . . But how could it be? He had come all this way and found her, and she had been so . . . she had been fine. Why now? Why did she wait all that time and then when he came back . . . Maybe it was just a cosmic joke.

He cried. He knelt there in front of her, holding Gertie's hand, and cried. He had time to cry now, and there was no one around to see. He could cry for them all now.

It was as if Grandma Gertie had been waiting for Jakob, knowing that he would return and wanting to see him that one last time to say good-bye. It's strange the way things go, the way people live and the way they die.

It was several hours before Jakob composed himself enough to go out and report Gertie's death. He started walking, but then realized he didn't even know where to go. Just then he saw two American military policemen walking down the street. They were young men, husky farm-boy types who were eyeing any young girls who happened to walk by.

"Excuse me?" Jakob said in English with the British accent he had been taught in school.

"What's up, Fritz?" one of the MPs asked with a smirk as his attention was drawn away from the rather impressive derrière of a young fraulein who knew just how to use it.

Jakob knew it was an insult, but he let it go. "I need to report a death," he said.

"There's lots of dead people around these parts, Fritz. Ain't you heard? There's a war on."

"For Chrissake, Ed!" the other MP interrupted. "Let him talk." The second MP then turned to Jakob. "What is it, buddy?"

"My grandmother . . . my grandmother has died. In her apartment."

"That's a shame, pal. Ya gotta talk to the civilians, though. They're going through the rubble a few streets over. Supposed to be some bodies in there still. Go ask them what to do. They'll send ya to the right guys."

"Thank you," Jakob said with a nod.

"See, Ed? Treat 'em with a little respect and the Krauts aren't so bad."

"Too polite for me," Ed pronounced as they walked away. "Sneaky bastards."

That was the first time Jakob had come into contact with American soldiers. He wasn't very impressed. He followed the soldier's directions, though, and soon found a crew of men digging through a mountain of bricks that stood almost six meters high in front of the single remaining wall of what had once been an apartment building.

One man, whom Jakob judged to be about sixty years old, stood at the base of the mountain smoking a pipe and watching as the other, younger men dug through the debris. Jakob assumed he must be the man in charge, since he was doing the least amount of work.

"Excuse me?" Jakob said as he moved toward the

man.

The man looked up at him with an arched eye-brow. This wasn't the sort of work that brought many spectators these days. If it were a different place and time, a natural disaster perhaps, something out of the ordinary, then maybe a crowd would gather. But now there was so much destruction, with a mountain of wreckage on almost every street corner and so many dead bodies and missing people, that it was mundane and uninteresting work.

"I was told you might know . . . I'm not sure what to do. I . . ."

"Someone dead?" the man asked astutely. Obviously this wasn't the first time he had been approached.

"My grandmother."

"War casualty?"

"What?"

"How did she die?"

"I don't know exactly. Old age, I guess."

"I see . . . You could take her to the old army bar-racks by the hospital. They're using them as a morgue."

"The army barracks?"

"Ja, but she'll end up in a mass grave."

The man could tell by the look on Jakob's face that this wasn't what he had in mind.

"Of course," the man continued, "if she had a grave site already . . ."

"I don't know," Jakob said. "How could I find out?"

"Is her house still in one piece? Take a look around. A lot of older people buy grave sites. Look for her important papers. Maybe there's a contract."

"Maybe . . . ," Jakob said thoughtfully as he turned to leave, but then he stopped and shook the man's hand, thanking him before going back to the apartment.

It was strange coming back into the apartment and seeing Gertie there in her chair. He hadn't really looked at her before. Her mouth was open, as though she were about to let out a low, guttural wail, and she had taken on a distinctly greenish-gray color in just the short time since he had gone out to find help. He went into the closet in the bedroom and got a clean bedsheet, which he used to cover her up. He hesitated a moment before covering her face, as though the act would make her disappear from the world . . . or from his life . . . or from his heart. He wasn't sure. After a few moments, he turned his attention to the task at hand, looking to see if she had bought a grave site. He assumed she would keep her important papers in a box in a closet or a dresser drawer. He couldn't imagine Grandma Gertie having a safety deposit box in a bank, much less a lawyer or anyone like that to take care of things when she passed away.

He went into the closet of the second bedroom, and sure enough, he found a number of boxes carefully packed away on the shelves. He began opening them and found they were all sorted by type. One box was full of pictures. Another was full of paid bills, all carefully labeled as to when they had been paid and by whom. He even found bills labeled as having been paid by Manfred Haas, Gertie's husband, who had died more than twenty-five years before. Then he found a box with a few stocks in it, apparently from the company where Manfred Haas had worked. Judging by the date, before the Great War, the stocks were probably worthless, or Gertie would have sold them when hard times hit. And there it was . . . a deed to two grave sites in the North Cemetery, one for Manfred and one for her. She wouldn't have to end up as a nameless stranger in a mass grave. Jakob was pleased as he slapped the paper triumphantly on the bedside table and let out a sigh. He thought about how it probably didn't mean much of anything in the great scheme of things, but it meant something to him. What were the chances that he would end up there at that time to do this one last thing for Gertie? It seemed right.

By that time his curiosity started to get the better of him, and even though he had found what he had been looking for, he continued to go through the papers. That was when he found a letter from the SS expressing their sorrow over the death of Hauptsturmführer Friedrich Haas. Jakob was surprised to see that Friedrich had been killed in Prague early in 1942, especially since Jakob had been in Prague at that time. But of course, Prague was a big city.

And then another box caught Jakob's attention. He found it inside a larger box that was filled with letters from Friedrich, some that went back to when he was a boy. Jakob read through a few of the letters, as though it were required before he opened the smaller box. It was an unopened package about the size of a shoe box, with an envelope secured to it with a carefully tied string. It was heavy for its size.

Jakob shook it, but there was no rattling. Opening the attached letter, he read:

Dear Mother,

Please store this package with my things. I will take care of it when I make it home in August. It's just a few old war souvenirs that I've collected. I miss you and hope all is well. The man who has brought the package to you is a dear friend of mine named Kurt, but I am sure he has already told you that! I promised him that if he delivered this to you, you would make him a wonderful home-cooked meal! I will see you in a couple of months.

Love,
Friedrich

Now Jakob had to know what was in the box. He reasoned that if Friedrich had gone to all the trouble of having a friend deliver it in person, it must be some kind of contraband. Jakob opened it carefully, undoing the string and tape and then unfolding the substantial amount of brown paper which concealed a wooden jewelry box, polished and inlaid with different colors of wood in the pattern of a rose. He opened the little catch and found there were three drawers. It was hard to open the first drawer, but he kept pulling, letting up as the face of the drawer began to clear the box, afraid that it might come flying out unexpectedly. He then realized that the drawer was tightly packed with some kind of cloth, and that was why it was so hard to open. That was also why there had been no rattle when he shook it. He pulled firmly on the drawer and finally got it clear of the box. Then he lifted the cloth. He couldn't believe it! Diamonds! *Could they be real?* he asked himself. There must have been more than a hundred of them, and they were all of a respectable size. Maybe it was all glass . . . but why would Friedrich go to such trouble to send home glass?

Jakob then tried the second drawer, and when he pulled this one out he found it was full of gold rings. Mostly just simple bands, wedding rings, but a few with diamonds. That made no sense at all to Jakob. He couldn't imagine where Friedrich would have gotten that many diamonds, but the gold rings were an even bigger mystery. And then he opened the last drawer, resting it on his leg as he looked at what it contained. It seemed to be more gold. Strange little bright chunks with sharp edges here and rounded corners there . . . Suddenly the room filled with the sound of the box falling to the floor and the pieces scattering across the hardwood surface. Teeth! They were teeth. Gold fillings.

Jakob was overwhelmed as he suddenly realized what this box represented. The camps. This box was all that was left of countless Jews. Jakob had been made hard and cynical during the war. He had heard of the death camps in the East and had been in Theresienstadt, even if only for a couple of days. Even the camps that weren't "death camps" were filled with death. He had just passed by Dachau a few days before and heard people talking about what the Allies had found there. The Americans had made German civilians go through the camp—men and women and children—had made them go through as though they were all responsible for it and were now going to be held accountable. All of that . . . and yet. To hold a gold filling between your thumb and forefinger and realize that it had been pried out of someone's mouth and then sent home to Grandma Gertie as "a souvenir."

Suddenly Jakob was glad that Friedrich was dead. The dirty bastard, he said to himself as he sat on Friedrich's bed, and then he thought about how he had been so fond of Friedrich before the war. What had happened to him? How could he have changed so?

Once again Jakob gathered himself up. He would take the diamonds. And the gold. He would use it to get to Palestine. He couldn't think about it too much, about where it came from. He just told himself that he was alive and they were not, and he had to get by, and if this was how he had to do it, then so be it.

He found a few tools in the kitchen under the sink, and went out to get a brick from the street. He then spent an hour hammering on the gold fillings to flatten them out in a rather ridiculous attempt to make them look like anything other than dental fillings. He thought he might be able to make them look like battered coins, but when he was done he realized they wouldn't fool anyone.

His first thought was to find someone who dealt on the black market and get rid of the "coins." The diamonds and rings would be easier to deal with. Unlike the fillings, if he only used the diamonds and rings a couple at a time, he could say they belonged to him and his wife.

He packed it all into different areas of his small bag and then set out to find someone to take care of Gertie. He ended up walking to the cemetery, since few buses and trains were running. Those that were running were filled beyond capacity, with people hanging on the outside, many with just a toehold on a running board here or there.

Once he got to the cemetery, he found three scruffy-looking men leaning on shovels next to a grave that they had obviously just finished filling in. Two of the men appeared to be somewhere in their sixties, one slightly older than the other, and Jakob guessed the third man to be in his forties. The older men had beards, while the younger had a graying stubble.

"Excuse me?" Jakob interrupted politely. "Could one of you help me? My grandmother has died and I'm not sure . . ."

"They've got crews going through the rubble," the oldest man offered.

"But they just take people to the morgue, don't they? And then they go to a mass grave? But my grandmother already has a grave site here . . . all paid for."

"Yes, but we only have the three of us and we can't—"

"Are you in charge?" Jakob interrupted.

The younger man looked at the other two with a smirk. "Yes, I'm in charge," he said with a look that dared the other two to contradict him.

"Can I talk with you for just a minute over here?"

The man nodded and followed Jakob a few meters away from the others. "I have to leave the city," Jakob continued, "and I want to make sure Gertie is taken care of before I go."

"Do you have money?"

"I have a couple of diamond rings."

"Ja, I can help you out. Let me see the rings."

Jakob fished two rings out of his pocket for the man to inspect.

The man looked the rings over meticulously, so much so that Jakob wouldn't have been surprised if he had suddenly produced a jeweler's loupe.

"They're good rings. Nice stones," the man pronounced. "What do you want for them?"

"Just take care of Gertie . . . go pick her up in Schwabing. Whatever it takes to bury her next to her husband."

"Headstone?"

"No, not now. Her husband has a stone. I don't know if her name is engraved on it or not, but that can wait. I just want to make sure she doesn't get lost."

"The rings will take care of that. A cheap coffin and burial."

"Thank you. Could we go now?"

"Now? To get the body?" the man asked as he looked over at his coworkers, trying to judge how it would fit into their busy schedule. "I suppose we could. Give me directions."

"Could I just ride with you?"

"Ja, just show us the way," the man agreed reluctantly. "Do you have a priest?"

"No."

"No one to say anything at the grave?"

"No, but I'd like to be there. Uh . . . there is something else."

"What?"

"I have... If somebody had something to sell..."

Jakob stammered.

"To sell? Like what?"

"Some gold coins. Do you know anyone who might . . . ?"

"Just go to a coin dealer. You should still be able to find one around."

"But I'd rather find someone . . . more discreet."

"Discreet?"

"Someone who wouldn't ask questions."

"I don't know anyone like that. I take a few pieces of jewelry here and there to help someone out, but not the black market. I'll tell you this, though, you'd be a fool to go through the black market if you're leaving the city. If you can get into Switzerland you'd do better. Here you wouldn't get a tenth of what the coins are worth."

Jakob thanked him for the advice and asked again if they could leave to take care of Gertie.

The man turned out to be the hearse driver, and he drove them immediately to Schwabing, then did everything that he said he would. Two days later Jakob was the sole mourner as Gertrude Haas was lowered into the earth.

Jakob stayed at Gertrude's apartment for three more days, catching up on his sleep for as long as the food held out, and then left Munich.

There was tremendous confusion on the roads as Jakob made his way toward Italy. Throughout Austria, the roads were swollen with a great flood of refugees. There were civilians and soldiers and survivors of the German concentration camps, those who were either returning home or passing through on their way to other countries, or those who were just trying to get away from the Russian occupiers to the east.

When Jakob got to Salzburg a few weeks later, he stopped by the house his grandfather had owned. He couldn't go in, of course. He didn't even consider knocking on the door to see who lived there now. *Is Ethan still alive in England?* he wondered. He decided it would be better not to think about it anymore. He had to stop thinking about these memories that kept drawing him in. The past was past.

Acting on the advice of the hearse driver in Munich, he decided it would be a good idea to detour through Switzerland if possible. He would sell off Friedrich's loot from the camps and open an account in a nice, safe Swiss bank. He would keep out just enough to get to Palestine and send for the rest later when things had quieted down.

On his way out of Salzburg he saw signs pointing to a camp of some kind. He asked the store clerk about it when he stopped to buy food and was told that the Allied occupiers were setting up a new kind of concentration camps in the area. They called them "Displaced Persons" or "DP" camps, and they were being set up because the Allies didn't know what to do with all the refugees pouring into the area.

The store clerk warned Jakob not to remain in Salzburg if he didn't have a place to stay. People living on the street were constantly being picked up by American patrols and taken to the DP camps. The clerk whispered to Jakob that the Americans had put Nazis in charge of the camps. For all he knew, Jakob could have been a Nazi trying to keep a step ahead of the authorities. There were certainly enough of them on the roads. Countless Nazi war criminals, concentration camp guards, and the like were trying to get out of Germany and Austria—out of Europe entirely—as quickly as they could. They knew there would be trials coming up.

That was why Klaus Grunewald was making his way through Linz, Austria, at the same moment that Jakob was hearing about the DP camps outside of Salzburg. Klaus had barely survived the commando assault that Jakob had led against his small squad on the Swiss border roughly a year before, but neither of them had known, or knew to this day, that the other had been there. And neither knew at this moment that the other was so near. Nor could they know how close their lives would run or how intertwined their futures would be.

CHAPTER 3

The Second World War ended in Europe on the eighth of May 1945. Victory in Europe, or "VE-Day," left many Germans wondering how they had ever come to such an end.

The end of the war left many people in a state of oblivion. The Americans coined the phrase "displaced persons," which was a blanket label applied by military authorities to anyone who had no place to go. If a Polish soldier had been taken prisoner and sent to Hamburg to work in a factory, and then in 1945 found that he had no way to get home, he would be labeled a displaced person and sent to a DP camp. If a Jew survived the final death march of the prisoners of Auschwitz as the Russian army closed in, he would be labeled a displaced person and sent to a DP camp.

The Displaced Persons camps weren't intended to be prison camps. They were designed to keep a large transient population under control at a time when the Allies had their hands full trying to put nations and economies back together, while at the same time trying to sort out Nazi war criminals still on the loose. The irony of the camps was that sometimes, particularly under the administration of General George Patton in Bavaria, Nazis or Nazi sympathizers would be put in positions of authority within the camps. Many believe this was not just a coincidence, considering General Patton's anti-Semitic leanings.

Another startling development for Jews who had survived the Holocaust was that those who returned to Poland not only found Polish families occupying their homes and businesses, but many Jews were killed when they dared return to reclaim their property. In the little town of Kielce in Poland, the good Polish citizens rose against the returning Jewish population in 1946 and went on a rampage, killing dozens of Jews in what would become known as "the last Pogrom." Is it any wonder that the thought of a Jewish homeland in Palestine became an idea that these people would pursue at any cost?

"THEY'RE HELPING THEM get out," Kolya announced.

"The priests?" Nicolai asked.

"Not just the priests . . . even higher."

"Higher? You mean inside the Vatican?"

"A name keeps coming up. A cardinal named Hudal."

"Have you told Petrovich?"

"Yes."

"Yes what?" Nicolai asked impatiently. "What did he say?"

"Infiltration."

"Infiltration? What about the Nazis? Aren't we supposed to track the bastards down anymore?"

"Feliks says we are to infiltrate. We need to know who is involved and just how far it goes."

"But the Nazis are . . ."

"Don't worry about the Nazis now. That war is over."

Kolya Doboszemski and Nicolai Ostrechnokov wasted no time making contact with the people they had been observing. The Russians had taken Vienna and obtained a great deal of information from

German and Austrian prisoners with their time-proven methods of extracting information.

Russian agents had very little trouble getting into areas controlled by American and British forces during the period immediately after the war ended because of lax security. After all, the Americans and British had gone to great lengths to stress to their regular soldiers that the Russians were their Allies and friends . . . at least while that was policy. But that changed within a few months of the end of the war.

Once security tightened, if a Russian officer took the chance of asking for asylum with American or British troops, they would send him back to the Russian lines as part of the new Allied policy, most likely to face imprisonment or even execution as a deserter. It was a very confusing time, and one could hardly blame an American GI for turning a blind eye to a Russian who wanted to escape Communism . . . But then what if that Russian were a spy trying to get through the American or British lines?

Kolya and Nicolai, whose cover names were Konrad and Helmut, knew what to say to the priests and their helpers in northern Italy—that the godless Communists had to be stopped, and that between the Fascists and the Communists, at least the Fascists believed in God and church. To the Germans they were helping, they said they wanted to do all that they could to help "German patriots" escape the misguided judgment of the Allies.

They posed as Germans rather than Italians because their first assignment was in the area at the end of the Brenner Pass, where there was a significant German population that had first come to the region during the Papal wars of the sixteenth century. It was a place where certain Germans eager to get out of Germany could find refuge.

There were countless military roadblocks in the days right after the war, but their effectiveness in turning up war criminals was compromised by the overwhelming number of refugees.

WHILE KOLYA AND NICOLAI were setting up shop in northern Italy, Jakob Stein-Metzdorf had managed, as he passed through the Salzburg area, to get a new set of forged papers using the name Stein, his mother's maiden name. He thought he might as well be Jewish since he was going to Palestine. It just so happened that the man who sold Jakob the papers, in exchange for Jakob's wedding ring, was Jewish. The man mentioned the *Brich-ha* in passing.

"The what?" Jakob asked, thinking he had just misunderstood a German word.

"*Brich-ha* . . . escape. I thought you said you were a Jew?" the man asked with a sidelong glass.

"I *am* Jewish," Jakob insisted.

"But you don't know Hebrew?"

"No . . . ," Jakob hesitated, embarrassed at this shortcoming.

"Have you ever even been inside a synagogue?"

Jakob just looked at the man sheepishly.

"But you're Jewish?" the man asked doubtfully.

"Yes. My mother is Jewish."

"Not your father?"

"No."

"Were you raised Jewish?"

"No. They never talked about it much.

"Then why say you're a Jew? Why would you want the aggravation?" the man asked, with a crooked smile that revealed little brown teeth as he said the word *aggravation*.

"The Nazis told me I was a Jew," Jakob answered. "They destroyed everything I had. Now I've got nowhere else to go."

"Palestine . . ."

"Ja, that's where my family's gone. I hope they made it. I'm going to look for them there."

"So . . . Hitler made you a Jew," the man said with a shake of his head as he smiled his crooked smile once again.

Armed with his new documents—and they were a good forgery at that—Jakob made his way west to Innsbruck and then on to Switzerland. He had gone roundabout from Munich to Salzburg and then to Switzerland, but he felt more comfortable getting papers in Salzburg, since he thought he might still have some contacts there. It proved to be a simple matter for one such as himself who had fought as a partisan and survived the war by his wits.

While Austria hadn't experienced anywhere near the level of destruction that Germany had, it was still the same war-torn landscape. Jakob couldn't help but wonder about some of the people traveling on the road with him. Some seemed like ordinary men and women, some traveling with children and babies, but others . . . It became a sort of game as Jakob tried to pick out the former concentration camp guards and German SS officers who had left their uniforms behind as they tried to get out of the country.

He didn't talk to anyone as he made his way to Zurich. He didn't want to draw any attention to himself because of the gold and diamonds he was carrying, the treasure Friedrich Haas had looted from the concentration camps and sent to his mother in Munich. Switzerland was a detour on his journey south so that he could exchange the diamonds, the rings, and the gold teeth that he had tried to hammer down to male them look like anything other than dental fillings. After depositing most of the money in a Zurich bank account, he would use the rest to make his way to Palestine.

When he got to Zurich, he wasn't exactly sure how to proceed. He knew a bank wouldn't take the gold and diamonds directly, but a jeweler might. As he left the main train station, he noticed a sign for a rare coin dealer and decided that would be a good place to start.

Charles Garrick looked up as Jakob entered his shop. He had always been able to size up people as soon as he saw them walk in. He could tell if a woman was looking to buy a gift, or had just come in to sell a family heirloom because she had fallen on bad times. And he had seen quite a few men like Jakob since the war ended. They came in nervously and began looking at the coins laid out in glass cases, pretending to have an appreciation for ancient coins and commemorative medals. They would wander around the shop expecting Charles to jump up and ask them what they wanted to buy, and then they would let him in on their little secret— that they weren't there to buy, but had something to sell. Some were embarrassed as they opened a little sack and let nuggets of gold spill out onto the counter; some were proud, as though they thought themselves so much smarter than the rest because they had come out of the war with something to show for it.

"Excuse me?" Jakob said as he cleared his throat. "Are you buying now? Do you buy diamonds?"

"I'm always buying. It just depends on the quality and price."

"I have a few . . . and some gold."

"Gold?"

"Rings and . . . coins."

Charles knew better than to ask too many questions. He wasn't about to ask what kind of coins or where they came from. "Do you have them with you?"

Jakob let the pack he had been carrying slide slowly off his shoulder and come to rest on the counter. His eyes watched Charles all the while as he started to bring out the cloth bags that he had traded for the wooden chest. There were three canvas bags, each weighing several kilos, each about the size of a melon.

Charles maintained a poker face, but he was eager to see what Jakob had brought him. "I'd better lock the door," he said, as he made his way around the counter and secured the lock before returning to his seat in front of Jakob.

The first bag Jakob opened was the gold teeth that he had hammered out so they wouldn't look so obvious, but Charles knew exactly what they were. Jakob untied the bag and let a few pieces of gold cascade onto the countertop. Charles picked up a coin and looked at it, then quickly glanced at Jakob's eyes. It was nothing more than a blink, but that was all it took. Jakob knew the shopkeeper knew what he held in his hand and where it came from.

Charles said nothing as Jakob opened the bag containing the wedding rings and then finally the bag with the diamonds, hundreds of diamonds. The diamonds impressed Charles and he couldn't hide it.

"My, my . . . ," Charles said as he pulled up a jeweler's loupe and picked up a dozen or so of the diamonds, adjusting a nearby lamp to give himself more light. "You have quite an assortment here. Some good, some bad. Mostly small . . . but so many of them."

Jakob waited silently as Charles inspected a number of diamonds before letting the loupe drop from his eye. Charles rubbed his eyes for a moment and then carefully put the diamonds back with the others.

"Some nice ones . . . some nothing more than chips," Charles repeated. "How many are there all together?"

"Three hundred forty-eight."

"How much are you expecting?"

"I'm not sure. I thought I would talk to three or four buyers . . ."

"I'm interested in buying. I assume you'll only sell it all or nothing?"

"I'd like to take care of it all at once."

"The gold is also of varying quality . . . 250,000 Swiss francs. I would buy everything for 250,000 Swiss francs, no questions asked."

Jakob hesitated for a moment. "I thought it might

be worth more . . ."

"There are other considerations here, sir. Remember, I said there would be no questions asked. There could be some embarrassing questions if someone were more curious about the origins of these diamonds than I am. I think that part about not asking questions is worth a considerable amount in itself."

"If I were to agree, how long would it take for you to get the money?"

"One day."

Jakob considered for a moment. The thought of cashing in loot from the camps was terribly unnerving. He didn't take it lightly, and he just wanted to be done with it all. He was sure everything was worth five or six times what he was being offered, but he just wanted to be done with it.

"Cash?"

"A bank draft."

"I'll be back tomorrow."

"The day after tomorrow," Charles corrected.

"The day after," Jakob repeated in agreement.

Jakob didn't breathe easily until he had the bank draft deposited in a new account and some cash in his pocket. Now it was done. Untraceable. No police or military personnel rushing into the shop as Charles handed him the bank draft. Nothing had happened, and no one would ever know. He had no plans for spending the money unless absolutely necessary. It was just a bit of security in the face of an insecure future. He wouldn't starve to death.

Now he was in no hurry. He took his time making his way to Italy. Almost a week later he arrived in Moreno, the first town of any significance when entering Italy via the Brenner Pass. This was the place he had been told about when he got his papers in Salzburg. This is where he was told the *Brich-ha* sent Jews down through Italy. It lay in a valley at the base of the Alps, guarded by a few medieval castles perched on mountain slopes. Moreno was in a grape-producing region, which in better times hosted an Octoberfest renowned throughout Italy.

Jakob entered the valley looking for a place to sleep.

It began to rain as he walked along the streets of Moreno after coming down from the mountains. It was early evening, and he ducked into a small café near the church in the center of town. The restaurant was filled with people, including quite a few soldiers. Jakob had lost track of the days and didn't realize it was a Saturday.

It wasn't as though everything stopped when he walked into the café, but many of the patrons raised their heads here and there to look at him as he stood at the door, just to see if he was friend or enemy. He dropped his small pack and sat alone at a small table against the wall. It felt so good just to sit down after walking all day. He put his head down, running his fingers through his hair and rubbing the back of his neck.

There were a half dozen soldiers sitting at the large table next to him, and he was surprised to see one of them smiling at him. "Looks like you've had a hard day," the soldier commented. It wasn't the sort of thing Martin would normally do, but he could identify with how worn out and tired Jakob looked.

"A lot of walking," Jakob said with a forced smile that quickly faded.

"We're infantry. Know all about it."

"British?" Jakob asked, even though it was obvious from the uniform.

"Attached. H.M.J.B."

"What's that?"

"His Majesty's Jewish Brigade."

"Jewish Brigade? Are you serious?"

"Yes, I'm serious. Most of us are from Palestine. What's wrong? Don't you like Jews?"

"I'm Jewish."

"That's what I thought. I have a good sense of people. You're not Italian . . . obviously a refugee. There are only two kinds of people coming through this area, and the other kind doesn't care to be seen in public."

Jakob nodded in agreement, and Martin invited the newcomer to join him and the other soldiers for a couple of drinks at their table. They talked about the war, Martin and the other soldiers about their fight up through Italy and Jakob about his time in Prague. Jakob tried not to get carried away as he talked about fighting with the partisans, being careful not to drink too much so that he wouldn't say too much. Hours later, after the storytelling and laughter had died down, he left them with a promise to return the next night.

The next day Jakob awoke in a comfortable bed in a private room of a rustic little mountain inn. Outside it was a quiet, dew-covered morning, and the blankets were warm and comfortable. For the first time a particular thought crept into his mind, a thought that should have been there long before. "The war is over."

It just didn't seem true before, but on this particular morning in this quiet valley, the war seemed done with . . . even though there was much more to go through, and he certainly knew it. It wasn't going to be easy putting a life together, but at least the war was over.

He got up and took a shower, then went downstairs for breakfast. It was just a roll and some cheese and a cup of coffee—a simple breakfast—but it just seemed so . . . civilized!

"Tomorrow is Sunday, sir. Will you be leaving?" the hotel owner asked.

"No, I think I might stay another week if you have the room."

"Certainly," the proprietor answered, happy to have a polite guest who didn't ask for credit.

Jakob then took off to see the town of Moreno and possibly a bit of the countryside. It seemed as though he was just on vacation, a feeling he rather enjoyed. He walked the streets and wished he had a camera to record the sights; not that it was a big town, just picturesque. As he stood on the bridge overlooking a small river that ran through the town of Moreno, he noticed a marble cross in the water below. An old man was walking by, and Jakob couldn't help but ask him what the cross meant. Why was it there? Surprisingly, the old man spoke excellent German. His answer was that the cross had no meaning; it had been thrown in there as an act of vandalism. And yet Jakob still stood on the bridge looking at the cross. It seemed to mean something to him . .

. something lost in a terrible flood, and Noah had been told to gather the world once more and everything had been washed away . . . and nothing would be the same again.

Jakob ended up back at the same restaurant that night and the next, meeting Martin there each night. He and the British infantryman were becoming fast friends.

"How's it going?" Martin called out as Jakob entered. "You're still here?"

"I like it here," Jakob answered as he joined Martin at a table. "I thought I might stay and rest up a bit."

"So . . . you came from Prague?"

"Munich, originally. I didn't go to Prague until after the *Anschluss*."

"The *Anschluss*? You were in Austria?"

"Oh, right . . . Yes, we left Munich and went to Salzburg where my grandfather lived. Then we moved on to Prague just before the *Anschluss*."

"You said you fought with the partisans?"

"Yes, but not 'til after Heydrich was killed in forty-two.

"Forty-two?"

"That was around the time they closed down the universities. I had tried to stay in school and get a degree, but after Heydrich was killed they . . . well, they murdered thousands. I just couldn't pretend anymore. I couldn't get through without being a part of it."

"But you're Jewish! How could you stay in school that long? Didn't they throw all the Jews out of every school?"

"My mother is Jewish. Since my father wasn't a Jew, the Germans said I was a Mischling . . . half a Jew. Fewer restrictions. So, what's with all the questions?"

"Curiosity . . . ah . . . well, I was thinking of asking if you . . ."

"If I what?"

"There are some of us who go out sometimes . . ."

"Out where? For a party?"

"I guess you could call it a party. Sometimes we get word that there's someone special in the area."

"Special?" Jakob asked, wondering where this strange conversation was going.

"You know Jews aren't the only ones coming down through the pass, don't you?"

"Of course!" Jakob scoffed. "Nazis are slipping through here like rats deserting a ship."

"Right enough. Well, we have some of our boys out checking about, and sometimes they find out that a particularly nasty sort is coming through the area."

"And you . . . pay him a visit?"

"Exactly."

"You're asking me to come along?"

"I guess so."

"Why?"

"There are times when it might be useful to have a civilian working with us. Being from Munich and familiar with that area, I get the feeling you could help us out. That is, if you're interested."

"I suppose so. What do I do?"

"First off, it depends on the others. You should come with us tonight as a sort of test run. We'll see if we can work together."

They talked a while longer, having another beer before parting company, agreeing to meet by the church later that evening.

It was a strange feeling for Jakob as he prepared to go out that evening. Just that morning he had felt so good about the war being over, and now he was getting ready for another mission. But there was also a sense of excitement as he picked out his darkest clothes and then slipped the Walther pistol that he had been carrying for months into his belt. Tonight was different, though. Instead of carrying the gun to protect himself, he now had a sense that he was about to become the hunter.

Martin and three other soldiers in British uniform appeared out of the pitch black night in an American jeep promptly at 11:00 P.M., as planned, the headlights washing over Jakob as he sat on a bench in front of the church.

"Ready?" Martin asked as the jeep ground to a halt a few feet away.

Jakob had barely squeezed into the tightly packed back seat of the jeep before it jerked forward and quickly accelerated, throwing him back. Martin was obviously anxious to get going. The rapid acceleration seemed a bit contrived, though, since the jeep topped out at only sixty kilometers per hour, but the dim headlights and the fact that Martin never let the accelerator pedal up from the floorboard made for a hectic ride in the top-heavy vehicle.

"I'm Edward," one of the men beside Jakob said as the jeep bounced along the dirt road.

"David," said the other, "and that's Deron in

front."

Jakob tried to shake hands, but he was barely able to move his arms because he was wedged in so tightly. Just then Martin took a rather sharp curve at full speed, and Jakob could have sworn the jeep was about to roll over, but he seemed to be the only one who thought so, since David and Edward sat quietly without saying a word.

"What if we tip?" Jakob asked Edward, trying to appear calm.

"Not to worry," Edward answered with a smile. "Jeeps are light. The survivors can right it up and be on their way in no time."

They drove for about fifteen minutes before reaching a winding mountain road, an ascent that slowed the jeep considerably. After another twenty minutes they pulled into the long, circling driveway of an old castle of relatively small size that had been converted into an expensive hotel. The soldiers jumped out with their Sterling submachine guns at the ready as soon as the jeep stopped at the front door.

Martin handed Jakob a British Sten. "Do you know how to use this?"

Jakob looked over the submachine gun. It was the basic British-issue mass-produced gun, little more than a gun barrel with a metal rod for a shoulder stock and a stamped metal tube for a receiver, with a thirty round magazine jutting out of the side. "Pull back the bolt here . . . safety here. Right?"

"That's about it," Martin answered. "Just a sardine tin with a barrel welded on. Let's get on with it, then."

Jakob looked up at the castle and saw a curtain open and close quickly on the second floor. He looked over at Martin to see that he was seeing it at the same thing. Martin quickly motioned for Deron to go around back in case anyone tried to leave by a back door. Martin then took out his Webley revolver and used the butt of the pistol to hammer on the thick, heavy oak door. The banging echoed loudly throughout the castle and into the night. After a brief pause he called out, "British Military Authority! Open up!" and pounded again on the door. When no one answered in the next few moments, Martin tried the door and it opened. Obviously they hadn't been expecting a visit.

Jakob, Martin, and the other two filed quickly into the entryway, where they were met by a tall, thin man in a robe who asked in German who they were and what they were doing breaking into his hotel.

"We understand you have a special guest tonight," Martin began as he signaled David and Jakob to go upstairs, "and I'm sure you realize it's a crime to harbor . . ." Jakob could hear Martin's loud voice continuing in the hallway below as he and David came to the first room at the top of the stairs. David cautiously tried the doorknob. "Cover me," he whispered to Jakob as he crouched down with his gun at the ready. Jakob was amazed at how quietly David moved, searching the room quickly and efficiently before returning to Jakob. "This one's empty."

"I think that's the one where I saw someone at the curtain," Jakob said as he motioned to a door down the hall.

"Right . . . This one's yours, then," David replied

with a wry smile. "We always take turns. Are you up to it?"

"I'll give it a go."

David stood beside the doorjamb and motioned for Jakob to go in. Jakob did just as David had done at the previous room, trying the knob, but this door was locked.

"I'll kick it open and you move in," David whispered.

Jakob nodded and got ready. The door exploded inward as the soldier's heavy boot made contact, and Jakob rolled into the room, coming up with his machine gun pointed at a very surprised middle-aged man who had obviously been sleeping. The hotel guest began to fumble with a lamp on a bedside table, and Jakob shouted at him to put his hands up and stay perfectly still. David entered the room just as the light came on.

"That's not him," David said curtly, withdrawing from the room, but Jakob stood transfixed, staring at the man in the bed, who was staring back at him. Thinning gray hair, sunken tired eyes, a middle-aged man putting on weight. But even caught by surprise in bed he had a military bearing, as if to ask, "How dare you disturb me?"

It was Klaus Grunewald. And Klaus recognized Jakob in that same instant because of Jakob's uncanny resemblance to his father. In fact, Jakob was ten years younger than Gunther Metzdorf had been when Klaus had put a gun to his head and killed him in front of the Neues Rathaus in Munich in the years before the war.

Jakob had never expected such a thing—would

never have expected it in a million years!

And the same was true for Klaus, as he debated whether he might survive if he grabbed for the Luger pistol beside his right leg under the bedcovers. Neither knew the full extent of the other's crimes against them, but each knew they were now enemies. They also both knew that they had something on one another. But at that moment, in that place, it was a stalemate.

Jakob backed out of the room without saying a word.

Klaus let out a deep sigh as he heard shouting in the hallway and the sounds of a struggle. They had found their man, and at least for tonight, it wasn't him. He knew he would leave in the morning.

Jakob couldn't get Klaus's face out of his mind, even as he struggled to hold onto the man that he and David had caught while David fought to manacle their captive.

Martin smiled briefly as he saw them bringing Hans Kleidenveld, a malevolent-looking man in his early thirties who shouted and spat viciously at his tormenters, down the long stairway.

"We are sorry to have disturbed you," Martin said loudly, so he could be heard above Kleidenveld's curses as David and Jakob dragged him out the door. "Good night."

As they ushered Kleidenveld out, Deron was in the driver's seat of the jeep waiting for them. He drove at a considerably slower speed than Martin had, since Edward had to ride on the back with a rather tenuous toehold on the *Jerry-can* shelf, a little step on the back of the jeep where a twenty-liter gas can would normally be strapped. Martin sat in the passenger seat in front, twisted around so that he could talk to Hans, who was tightly sandwiched between David and Jakob in the back seat.

"Are you Hans Kleidenveld?" Martin asked.

Their prisoner said nothing.

"Are you Hans Kleidenveld?" Martin repeated, much louder this time.

The prisoner still didn't answer, and Martin sat back in his seat. After a moment he motioned for the driver to pull over. As Jakob looked over at their prisoner, he could tell he was now getting nervous as his eyes darted from man to man.

Martin was the first out of the jeep as Deron shut off the engine, leaving the headlights on. Martin motioned for Jakob and David to bring the man along. "You have his papers?" he asked David.

"Right here."

"Let's see, then," Martin said thoughtfully as he paged through the documents, moving in front of the headlights and motioning for David and Jakob to bring the man closer. "Guiseppi Martinelli . . ."

David and the other soldiers smirked.

"That's funny," Martin said as he raised the back of his hand slowly to the prisoner's chin, as though carefully taking in the man's countenance. "You don't look like what I would think of as an Italian."

"Ah," he continued as he looked back down at the man's papers, as though making a key discovery. "It says here you are a watchmaker. An Italian watchmaker."

Martin then turned away and took a couple of steps before pulling something out of the breast pocket of his tunic. "Now here," he continued slowly, "is a picture. A picture of a man . . . or what passes for a man. Here is a picture of an assistant to the commandant in charge of the Jewish Ghetto at Lodz. A place where people were robbed of . . . of *everything*. They starved, they died of disease . . . If they broke even the slightest rule of the German guards, they were shot right there on the streets, even little boys, just because they would try to sneak food into the Ghetto to their families. They would be shot right there and their bodies left to rot. And even *that* wasn't enough. Soon all the Jews of Lodz who somehow stayed alive were sent to the death camps, where they were gassed and their bodies burned and the ashes plowed into the earth." Martin paused as though trying to catch his breath.

"Here is the picture of a man," he continued once again, "who revelled in that death and killing. And the most amazing thing . . . he looks just like an Italian watchmaker!"

The prisoner let his head hang down. Jakob, still holding onto the man's arms, could feel something shift, as though his knees were about to buckle.

"Are you Hans Kleidenveld?" Martin growled as he held the picture up to Kleidenveld's face.

"And who are you?!" Kleidenveld cried out as he suddenly lifted his face, color quickly filling the cheeks that had been a pasty white just an instant before. "Who do you think you are to drag *me* out into the night?" he shouted with all the rage in his body. "Are you some dirty Jew? Half a dozen dirty Jews to arrest one German officer?"

Martin was normally a very composed man, but

he had had enough and took a step forward, back-handing Kleidenveld so hard that the former German officer almost fell to his knees.

"You dirty, rotten cowards!" Kleidenveld shouted. "Beating a man with his hands tied behind his back. You *Jews* . . . you dirty sons of Jew whore bitches! Untie my hands and I'll take you all on! Let me loose and see how brave you are!"

"Do it," Martin said hoarsely as his stare bore into Kleidenveld's eyes.

David quickly fumbled for the keys and undid the manacles.

"Now!" Kleidenveld ordered as he rubbed his wrists, which had been marked by the tight-fitting handcuffs. "You will take me to your superiors and I will—"

"Are you Hans Kleidenveld?" Martin interrupted in a conversational tone, a sharp contrast to the shouting of an instant before.

"Yes," he answered perfunctorily, feeling that he was now in control of the situation by virtue of the fact that they had taken off the handcuffs and that Martin was now calm. "Under the terms of the Geneva Convention of 1929, I am surrendering to you as—"

"Shut the fuck up!" Martin shouted, using the crudest American colloquialism he could think of.

Kleidenveld was shocked but quickly composed himself. "Come now . . . There is no reason to—"

Suddenly Martin brought his boot up sharply between Kleidenveld's legs. Kleidenveld fell to his hands and knees in a spasm of retching and cough-ing. Martin then took a step forward and put a hand on Kleidenveld's head, holding it as though it were a football being set for a shot into the goal, and brought his knee up savagely, sending the man sprawling into the dew-covered grass.

Martin then pulled out his Webley pistol and surprised Jakob by offering it to him. "I'm afraid this is your baptism . . . Can you do it?"

Jakob had never liked violence in the specific. He had been in battles and done what was necessary on missions, but this was different. It was cynical and vengeful, but he also understood it. He knew why Martin had lost control, and he also knew that there was nothing certain if Kleidenveld were turned over to military authorities. He had probably already been in a POW camp before escaping and making his way to Moreno. What if he just walked away again? Perhaps some people did deserve to die. Perhaps even by Jakob's hand . . .

"Can you do it?" Martin asked again.

Jakob looked at him and then looked down at Kleidenveld. "Yes." He then walked over to where Kleidenveld lay. The German officer looked up at him and saw the trepidation in his eyes.

"You don't have to do this," Kleidenveld said, struggling to get out the words. "You can just turn me over to the military police and... You won't have to get blood on your hands. You don't have to do this... You *shouldn't* do this... You *can't* do this..."

The hand in which Jakob had been holding the Webley dangled at his side, but when Kleidenveld said the word *can't*, Jakob suddenly saw the faces of the dead, people he had known, people he had seen die, the people he had seen in Theresienstadt . . .

And at that moment he could. His hand had been like a pendulum at his side, a sword of Damacles over Kleidenveld's head, and suddenly it moved and there was an explosion that filled the night as the weapon jerked in his hand.

"The river is right over there," Martin said as the smoke from the gaping wound in Kleidenveld's head, which showed so clearly in the jeep headlights, slowly dissipated.

David and Edward took the body and threw it into the river. No one said a word as they drove back to town. The next day when Jakob met Martin for a beer at the restaurant, they didn't mention the previous evening at all.

A few days later Jakob was walking along the road when Martin pulled his jeep up beside him. "We've got another visitor . . ."

WHILE JAKOB AND MARTIN were planning their next excursion from Moreno, Klaus Grunewald was wending his way southward through Italy, having left Moreno scant hours after his midnight encounter with Jakob.

The owner of the castle where Klaus had stayed that night was only a distant contact for the people who were actually helping him get out of Europe. It wasn't a highly organized spy ring. Klaus only had a piece of paper with some directions and a name on it to find his next destination, in the same way that he had gotten a piece of paper with a name and directions that had sent him to Moreno. It was, in fact, merely the beginnings of an effort by certain members of the Catholic Church, of the Vatican itself, to take sides in what they saw as the world's next great political battle.

The pope himself, Pius XII—Eugenio Pacelli—had expressed the opinion to his subordinates that between the Fascists and the Communists, at least the Fascists had allowed the church to exist, whereas atheism was a basic tenet of Communism. He viewed Communism as the greatest evil and said that the Germans, however distasteful some of their actions during the war may have been, were warriors against Bolshevism. "My enemy's enemy is my friend . . ."

Pope Pius XII's position was fraught with irony, considering that during the war a great many Catholics had risked and even lost their lives protecting people from the Nazis all across Europe. This was especially true in the Italian city of Assisi, some hundred and sixty kilometers to the northwest of Rome.

In Assisi, on the slopes of Mount Subasio, stands the Basilica di San Francesco. It marks the place where Giovanni di Bernardone was born in the eleventh century. Giovanni's father, Pietro, didn't like the name his wife had chosen for their son while he was away on business, and so on his return he changed his son's name to Francesco. Francesco di Bernardone would eventually break away from his family after receiving a vision in his dreams, telling him he had a destiny to fulfill, wherein God himself told Francesco, "Go and repair my house which has fallen into ruin." This was the beginning of Francesco di Bernardone's life of religious devotion that would eventually lead to his canonization as St. Francis of Assisi, founder of the order of Franciscan monks.

During the war, when the Germans occupied the country after the capitulation of the Italian government in 1943, Catholic priests and Franciscan monks in Assisi worked with Jewish refugees, making the city a center for supplying Italian Jews with forged identity documents to protect them as they went into hiding. Within two years the tables were turned as agents of the Catholic Church began granting sanctuary to Nazi war criminals trying to escape from Europe before Allied military authorities could catch them and bring them before the Nuremburg tribunal.

Klaus was already tired by the time he approached the town of Assisi and began making his way up the foothills below the basilica, among the contoured rows of grape vines and groves of bent, scraggly olive trees. Eventually he reached the steps leading up to the basilica, continuing to climb the steep and narrow streets of Assisi to the small shop near a group of church administration buildings, where he was to make contact with the man who would take him to his next hiding place.

"Signore Brindisi?" Klaus asked in a nicely turned Italian accent that only hinted at his German origin.

"Yes. May I help you?" the shopkeeper answered in a pleasant tone.

"Si, Signore. I have been told . . . ," Klaus began haltingly. "Scusi, sprechen Sie Deutsch?"

"Ja, ein bischen," the shopkeeper replied warily.

"I was told to find you. I was told by a friend."

"A friend? What friend?"

"Eugenio. From Rome."

"Eugenio . . . ," the shopkeeper said thoughtfully, waiting for the rest of the message.

"Eugenio said we must watch the heavens . . . and beware of Ursa Major."

The shopkeeper grimaced at the reference to the big bear. "I told them this was ridiculous," he commented, "but they insisted this was how it must be done. You can call me Luciano, but not around other people. Around other people you don't know me."

Klaus nodded his head and then followed as Luciano led him into the back of the shop, where a boy about twelve years of age was sweeping the floor. "You must follow this boy. He knows the way. There will be food and a safe place to sleep. Good luck."

"Grazie," Klaus said as he followed the boy out the back door. Once outside, the boy pointed at a small motorcycle and then got on it, gesturing for Klaus to get on behind him.

"No, no," Klaus laughed. "I've seen how Italians drive. I'll drive, and you just tell me where to turn."

The boy was clearly put out, but he did as he was told, and they headed out town, about four kilometers up Mount Subasio to the hermitage, "Eremo Delle Carceri."

Klaus would never know that the shopkeeper, Luciano Brindisi, was actually the Russian spy, Nicolai Ostrechnokov.

That was the way the "ratline" worked. The Germans just wanted to get out of Europe before they got caught up in the Allied search for war criminals and weren't particular with whom they dealt. The Vatican, however, was operating on what they considered to be a higher theological plane. They believed that since the church was eternal, it operated on a level above the politics of the moment. They had to see past the suffering the Nazis had inflicted, the premise being that the time of the Nazis was now over and that from this point on, the Russian Communists would inflict even more damage on the world, most notably on the church itself. The French intelligence community believed that there was some merit to that idea, at least the part about the Soviets being the next threat to *their* political aims, and so they were instrumental in helping Vatican operatives set up the ratline.

Russian intelligence had made it a priority to insinuate intelligence operatives, not only into the Eastern European countries that Russia now occupied, but wherever they could in Western Europe under the cloud of confusion that accompanied the surrender of Germany. Russian agents came across the "Vatican ratline" shortly after its inception and infiltrated it quickly, not to stop escaping Nazi war criminals, but to put themselves in a position to see what other anti-Soviet plans the Vatican might develop. It proved to be an invaluable move for Russian intelligence, because soon thereafter British and American intelligence agents discovered the ratline and also tried to infiltrate it so that they could use German intelligence to combat the Soviets. The net result of all the subterfuge was that the Soviets were in a position to compromise American and British intelligence for years to come, because the American and British intelligence agencies soon tried to co-opt Vatican agents who were actually

Soviet agents!

But none of that meant anything to Klaus Grunewald as he moved down the pipeline to the shipping port of Bari, where passage was arranged for him on a ship bound for Syria. Why the Middle East? Because the Arabs could see the handwriting on the wall, and Jewish lobbying for a homeland in Palestine meant there would soon be a battle to keep that from happening. Thus they would gladly enlist the aid of any German battle-trained officers to train their own troops. "My enemy's enemy is my friend . . ."

WHILE KLAUS GRUNEWALD was making good his escape from Italy, Jakob Metzdorf was still in Moreno, where he and Martin had another mission lined up. As it turned out, it would be their last mission.

Word had come down that Bruno Kress was now in the area. Kress had been a lower echelon commander in the Einsatzgruppen, the units that followed the Wehrmacht into Poland in 1939 as Germany and Russia divided the conquered nation. The Einsatzgruppen were the Waffen SS detachments charged with rounding up and executing Jews as they came under German military authority. Those early days were the "experimental" phase of the Jewish genocide. Systems were developed whereby the Einsatzgruppen would go into a village, round up the Jewish population "for deportation," and then murder them using specially designed vans. The vans were modified at the factory to vent the engine's exhaust directly into the back by means of a lever, which would cause any living thing held in the van to die from carbon monoxide inhalation. It was a slow and agonizing death. The victims would scream and retch before dying in a pool of their own vomit, feces, and urine. The drivers of these vans often complained about the inconvenience of this form of murder. It was very disturbing to hear the screams of dying men, women, and children, even if they were just Jews. Similar complaints were coming from other troops. When there were larger Jewish populations, the trucks were deemed too slow and inefficient. Shooting Jews was faster and cheaper. A system was designed wherein a pit, much like a standard "tank trap," would be dug. The Jews would be marched in a line of some ten or twenty people and made to stand at the edge of the pit, and then they would be shot with machine guns. An officer or some other designated person would administer final shots to kill off anyone who had only been wounded, and then another group would be brought in to be shot, and they would fall in on top of those murdered before them.

Commanders of these operations soon began to complain that it was putting a great emotional strain on their troops to kill unarmed civilians. That was why the Totenkopf division of the SS eventually turned to camps set up specifically for the mass murder of Jews and to Xyklon-B as its favored method of execution. It was still a messy operation, as those in charge of cleaning out the gas chambers had to deal with the problem of untangling corpses because the victims would climb over each other in a last desperate attempt to climb up to "good air." It did, however, have the advantage of dispatching larger numbers at one time, and the camp setting meant that the SS guards could force Jewish inmates to do the disagreeable work of dealing with the corpses.

Bruno Kress was not a major catch. He was unique in that he not only survived the Russian front, but even the defense of Berlin, and managed to make it all the way to Austria, where he was eventually caught by the Americans. He was just one more in a long line of Nazis responsible for multiple cold-blooded murders of an unarmed civilian population. He was a man who deserved to die for his crimes. He was just one more of the nameless army of evil-doers that allowed this monstrous crime against humanity to be perpetrated. Another man who gave over his morality and conscience, like so many had done before, until he was the end of the line and it was his finger on the trigger, his hand on the lever, and he would say he was only following orders.

It makes one wonder, *Did it begin with the first body?* Was that all it took to give permission to all the rest? When that first Brownshirt took to the streets of Munich and started a riot in which a Jewish man or woman was killed, was that first—that very first—fatality all it took to give permission to all the others? That taste of blood on their lips? That proof that it could be done, that they could take that first Jewish life with impunity, without consequence? Was that enough to validate all the hatred and anti-Semitism of generations of Germans? Was the fact that the first innocent victim *could* be killed with impunity enough to bolster their demented dreams of

Eugenics, the nightmare of perverted science that was social Darwinism?

Rhetoric. The past is past. The dead are buried. Ashes are spread to the winds. Justice is a human concept to endorse morality. Morality is an imposition of society. If the entire society of a nation endorses an immoral act as a moral act, then so it is. But a nation called immoral in a group of nations is just like one person being accused of immorality in a group of people. The larger society will judge and call it justice, not always for the best, but that's the nature of humanity. If you believe in God as some higher meaning, a God that molds us in different ways—perhaps the gentle loving hands of the potter or the blacksmith working iron through fire and strength— then we are like children and "his" reason is beyond our comprehension. Perhaps the Jews were chosen to teach humanity this lesson of fire, beyond our comprehension, a lesson of what terrible things men can do and how we must beware of . . . of us. It has been said in circles of lesser understanding that the Jews call themselves "the chosen people" as a point of pride, but most Jews came to understand long ago that they had been chosen for many things, many of them sad and almost unbearable. They were the first to speak of one God, and they suffered greatly for it through generations. For believing in God, for not believing in "the right God" . . . for reasons beyond reason. And then there are those who said their fate was a lie, or others who said that their suffering was nothing by comparison to the suffering of another people. Even the dead are challenged when they're Jewish.

Bruno felt safe. He was staying with Dieter and Magda Stuben. He had made a daring escape from an Austrian prison camp, walking out with a couple of the civilian workers after bribing them to bring in some civilian clothes. Well, it wasn't daring. The camp was in the American sector and the Americans just weren't as motivated as their Russian counterparts in eastern Austria. If a prisoner walked out here or there, it wasn't the end of the world. But then they often didn't know who they were guarding. They thought for the most part that the Germans in their charge were just the German equivalent of themselves—some poor slobs called up to serve their country—and now they had lost the war and had to sit around in a POW camp until the bureaucrats straightened everything out and let them go home.

Bruno had been an SS captain. He believed in the killing. He knew the Jews had to be eliminated, and the duty fell to him. He had to be hard. He had to do it, and then he could get on with his life. He actually came to appreciate the role. He came to like walking along with a pistol at the ready, the power of life and death in his holster with no hesitation to use it. He had no regrets. He knew the Americans were too naïve to understand, and the other European countries . . . well, they just didn't have the stomach to do the job. The Russians . . . well, of course, Russia was run by the Jews. They were barely human. The "Untermenschen." And now he was forced into hiding, but it would all pass soon enough. This was the price for their failure in not killing all the Jews. They had been too soft. Bruno knew why things were the way they were.

It was a Tuesday evening, about eight o'clock, as Bruno and the Stubens relaxed in the sitting room after dinner, listening to a radio performance of classical music. The French doors leading to the veranda were open to the beautiful view of the valley. Bruno rested his elbow on the arm of the overstuffed chair as he reclined and lazily moved his hand back and forth in a poor attempt at emulating the conductor's movements.

A loud knock on the front door brought Bruno immediately to his feet. "Are you expecting anyone?" he asked Dieter anxiously.

"No," Dieter answered just as anxiously, since his head was also on the line if he was caught harboring Bruno. "No one ever comes without calling . . ."

"I'd better go," Bruno said as he grabbed his jacket from the chair and started out.

"I'll keep them busy," said Dieter as he started for the door. "Come back later. If it's safe, I'll put the light on in your bedroom. You can get some supplies before you go."

Dieter opened the front door to find a man in uniform standing there. "Yes?" he asked.

"We're looking for someone," the young American captain in the doorway began. "We were told he might be staying with you."

"Staying with me? No . . . we haven't had any houseguests for—"

Dieter was interrupted by the sounds of a scuffle behind him, and an instant later someone shouted, "Got 'im, Cap'n!" from the other room.

"Excuse me, Herr Stuben," William Hanlon said

with a self-satisfied smile as he pulled out his government-issue .45 automatic and pushed past the surprised host.

"Bruno Kress?" Hanlon demanded accusingly as he entered the sitting room where a huge American MP, who dwarfed Bruno, now held the fugitive with a firm grip on his shoulder.

Bruno said nothing, neither confirming nor denying his identity, which was good enough for Hanlon. "My name is Hanlon. American OSS. You are under arrest. You'll be treated as a prisoner of war with all the—"

But then it was Hanlon's turn to be interrupted as the room suddenly exploded in motion and confusion once again when Jakob burst through the front door, pistol in hand, and Martin and the others came in through the veranda doors. "Nobody moves!" Jakob shouted from behind Hanlon. Martin, David, and Edward disarmed the two MPs who had accompanied Hanlon. Jakob and Martin hadn't counted on the Americans being there, but once they saw the jeep outside, they decided that they were still going to take Kress. They had heard rumors about the Americans protecting Germans who agreed to work with them. They decided that wasn't going to happen with Kress.

When Hanlon spun around to face Jakob, Bruno Kress decided this was his one chance to escape, and he pulled away from the MP and went for Hanlon's pistol. Bruno was familiar with the .45 pistol and knew that if he could put his finger between the hammer and firing pin, he could grab the gun and pull it from the captain's hand without fear of it going off. But when Bruno grabbed the pistol, Hanlon wouldn't give it up, so Bruno pulled him off balance, throwing him to the floor. When Bruno pulled back, he shoved the MP who had been restraining him a moment before, and the large GI fell on top of Hanlon, who was scrambling to get up. Martin and the others moved to try to stop Bruno, but they weren't going to shoot for fear of hitting someone other than Bruno. Bruno was counting on that reaction.

Jakob never moved during the mêlée. He had his gun trained on Bruno the whole time, and when Bruno pulled the slide back on the .45 and brought the gun up to fire at him, Jakob fired four shots point blank at Bruno as soon as he was clear of Hanlon and the MP. When Jakob's first shot hit him in the lower torso, Bruno cringed in pain and fired a shot into the floor, but he was dead by the time Jakob fired his last shot, and he fell to the floor like a bag of sand.

"Damn it!" Hanlon yelled, assuming that he wouldn't be the next target. "We needed him! Who the hell are you people?"

"Shut up!" Jakob shouted back angrily. "Get their guns," he continued to Martin, but their guns had already been taken when they first entered the house. Martin knew Jakob was about to panic.

"Down on the floor! Get your heads down," Jakob ordered Hanlon and the MPs, "and count. Count to a hundred. We don't want to hurt you, but we will if you come after us."

Martin casually moved toward Jakob and put a hand on his shoulder, guiding him as they backed out the door after David and Edward.

"Should we go after them, sir?" one of the MPs asked as he looked up at Hanlon after a moment.

"No," Hanlon said as he sat up on the floor.

"This bastard isn't worth it," he continued, waving toward Bruno. "See if he's dead."

"Who the hell were they?" the large MP asked.

"They're just some of those damned vigilantes. I'd guess they didn't expect us to be here. Never heard of them trying to take a prisoner before. We must have surprised them."

"Well, they sure as hell surprised me!"

Hanlon shot the MP a disapproving glance in response to his unsolicited comment.

Jakob decided that was a bit too close as he and the others sped off down the road. He hoped beyond hope that the Americans would do as he said when they ducked out of the veranda doors. Fighting off the Americans wasn't part of the deal. He couldn't understand why they were there in the first place. Somebody must have gotten their wires crossed, because Jakob had been told it was the Americans who had initially given them the information about Kress's whereabouts.

A week later Martin told Jakob that the Jewish Brigade was being transferred.

"Transferring you? Where?"

"Belgium."

"Belgium? What's in Belgium?"

"Nothing. I think that's the point."

"What do you mean?"

"You can't believe the British don't know what we've been doing. They must be afraid of the repercussions if word got out."

"The avenging Jews . . ."

"Yes. All well and good if it's discrete, but to say the British army supported the summary executions of people who are now civilians . . ."

"But they're war criminals."

"That's for the court at Nuremburg to decide, I guess. Most British understand why we've done what we've done, but they can't support it as policy."

"How do *you* feel about it?"

"Me?" Martin asked with a menacing grin. "I just wish I could've killed more of the bloody bastards. I don't regret it at all."

"So that's it. Done. We just let them get away with it."

"We're not the only ones, you know."

"What do you mean?"

"I heard about a group out of Hungary. They're a partisan group that didn't disband when the war ended . . ."

"A partisan group *after* the war?"

"Right, they're the ones who set up the *Brich-ha*. Kovner. They came through this area asking for volunteers and supplies from the Jewish Brigade."

"And they're going after war criminals?"

"Not exactly. Their first goal was to set up the *Brich-ha*, but they also had a plan to . . . ," Martin began, considering what he was about to say.

"A plan for what?"

"I shouldn't tell you. This is the kind of thing they would kill you for if they found out you told anyone."

"I took the same oath you did to the Haganah. I

may not agree with everything we do, but I'm no traitor! Don't even insinuate that I would . . ."

Martin looked Jakob square in the eye and took a deep breath. "Poison . . . They're going to poison the water supply in a German city."

"No!" Jakob said in disbelief, continuing adamantly, "That's just an old anti-Semite jibe . . . the Jewish well poisoners."

"No, it's true. They say a big city. They're supposed to get into the water works and poison the water after it passes the filtration."

"You can't be serious! There would be thousands of innocent people who—"

"Innocent people?" Martin shot back. "Thousands of innocent people? There were *millions* of innocent people in Poland and Hungary and Czechoslovakia and . . . all over Europe! Millions!"

"But this kind of vengeance . . . We would be just as bad as the Nazis."

"This is not open for discussion. I guess I shouldn't have told you. Do I have your word that you'll never repeat any of this to anyone?"

"My word?" Jakob repeated with astonishment. "You can't seriously think I would go telling anyone . . ."

"No," Martin agreed as he held out his hand to Jakob. "Of course not. Forget it. I'm sorry I said it."

There was an awkward pause as they both calmed down.

"So . . . what will you do now?" Martin finally asked, breaking the silence.

"What will I do?" Jakob repeated thoughtfully with a sigh. "I guess it's time for me to leave too."

"The *Brich-ha?*"

"Why not? I don't have any reason not to believe my family hasn't made it to Palestine."

"They could use you," Martin said with a smile. "You're a good man, Jakob. We'll need a lot more like you when the time comes."

"When do you think you'll get back?"

"Here?"

"No, Palestine. How will I find you?"

"I'll find you. I've got news for you, friend. I'll see Haifa before you do."

"What?"

"You're going in as a Haganah soldier, not a refugee. You'll help the crew keep order on the trip, but a small boat will get you and a couple others off the ship before you get close enough to be challenged by the British ships. They'll take you in for a night drop."

It was a week or so later that Jakob started on his way south. The *Brich-ha* was a long, hard road down the mountainous length of Italy. There wasn't much sympathy for the pilgrimage of Jews. Many Italians felt they had been the victims in some great political drama beyond their control and that somehow these Jews were a part of it. Not as the cause, but as haunting reminders of the terror and destruction. They had walked with death.

Jakob was struck by the different kinds of people traveling alongside him. Some were so drawn and gaunt, he was surprised they could walk. There were families with mothers carrying newborn babies, and single men and women, old and young, along with orphaned children. They all traveled on foot for hundreds of miles. Most of them had crossed the snow-covered Alps in little more than rags.

Just as Martin had warned, it was several weeks before Jakob arrived in Bari. Bari had been a busy seaport on the east coast of Italy since the time of the Roman empire—even before the Roman empire. It was paradoxically a dirty, industrial city of the twentieth century that somehow seemed to be stuck in the nineteenth century. Jakob liked it because it was one of those urban centers in which he always felt he could find a hiding place if necessary. That had become very important to him as a result of his experiences in the war. He was always aware of his surroundings as he traveled. The people he passed all seemed to be watching him, but they weren't staring at him in particular; they always noticed strangers. Nonetheless, it was disconcerting to walk down the street and pass a couple of men who were talking and laughing, only to look up and see their eyes veiled in suspicion.

"We heard you were coming."

"Heard I was coming?"

"Martin," the young man said with a smile.

"You know Martin?"

"I've met him . . . he's my brother-in-law."

"He's a good man."

"I know. My sister keeps telling me."

"So . . . what next?

"Everything is set. You leave next week."

"Will there be a lot of people on the boat?"

"A full load."

"A good ship?"

The Haganah man just gave a shrug of the shoulders as he arched his eyebrows, as if to say, "What do you expect from this kind of thing?"

The danger was not only implied, it was inherent in their activities. After all, their goal was to get the British out of Palestine and claim it as their homeland while simultaneously keeping the surrounding Arab nations at bay.

The Haganah refugee ships had taken on a completely different role as the war ended. Originally, they had simply been a means to increase the Jewish population in Palestine by attempting to smuggle illegal immigrants past the British authorities. Once the war ended, however, British naval resources freed up from other areas were sent to the Middle East, making it almost impossible to get sizable groups of immigrants through. That, coupled with the dramatic increase in the number of refugees trying to get to Palestine as Holocaust survivors tried to emigrate, caused a change in the strategy of Jewish leaders. The point was no longer to get immigrants into Palestine; it was to make sure that the world knew that Jews couldn't get into Palestine.

The British were in the unenviable position of playing out the anachronistic role conferred upon them by the League of Nations known as the "British mandate" in Palestine. As outdated as Kipling's racist notion of "the white man's burden," the mandate assigned the British the paternal duty of keeping the peace between Jews and Arabs in that country.

The ruling powers in Britain could hardly believe it as they watched their empire slip through their fingers after the Second World War. Financially, the war had cost them so much that war austerity programs would continue for years after the cessation of hostilities. In human terms, it seemed incomprehensible that so many British lives had been lost in defense of colonies that would simply be released when the war ended. It was so difficult for them to imagine Britain as a secondary, or even less than secondary, influence on world events that they felt they had to maintain their position wherever they could. The Middle East became a test site. Could the British Empire maintain order based on its reputation? Could the British leaders stand up and find a resolution to the situation, dictating the terms through their own force of will? And could such terms be enforced?

CHAPTER 4

*There is a strip of land that runs along the
Mediterranean Sea, west of the River Jordan and
the Wadi Al Arabah, from the Negev Desert in the
south to the Sea of Galilee and the Golan Heights
in the north. This land of Canaan is a crossroads
between North Africa and southwest Asia that has
been conquered and reconquered many times over
the centuries. Assyrians, Babylonians, Persians,
Alexander the Great, Muslim Arab armies, the
Seljuks, Mamelukes, the Ottoman Empire—they all
invaded or occupied the land that would become
known as Palestine at one time or another. The
Hebrews came to the land of Canaan almost 2,000
years before the birth of Jesus Christ, but they were
conquered and expelled by different rulers at different times until finally being driven out by the
Romans in the second century C.E. in what
became known as the Diaspora.*

*During the First World War, British Foreign
Secretary Arthur Balfour issued the statement that
became known as the Balfour Declaration. The
Balfour Declaration stated that the British government supported the founding of a Jewish homeland
in Palestine, because at the time the British wished
to gain support of the Jewish community throughout the world. When the war was won and the
Ottoman Empire was defeated by Allied forces,
administration of the Middle East fell to the
British. Talk of establishing a Jewish homeland
was tabled until "the appropriate time" might present itself.*

When it really counted, however, when Nazi

Germany was marching toward the zenith of its murderous power and policy of genocide, British government officials not only failed to follow up on the Balfour Declaration, they completely contradicted it with the issuance of the White Paper of 1939. The White Paper closed off the last point of escape for European Jews by severely limiting immigration to Palestine for the foreseeable future.

It's not hard to understand the reasoning behind the White Paper of 1939. The British simply chose Arab oil over Jewish lives. That's the way of the real world. Other nations would make the same sort of choices throughout history. It takes oil to run tanks and ships, and besides, in the aftermath of the war, the British "Pilate" could always claim he had no idea what the consequences of this action would be. That was where the situation stood as the Second World War ended.

The movement known as Zionism began in the late eighteenth century in France in the aftermath of the Dreyfus affair, a military trial in which a Jewish officer was dishonorably discharged from military service and imprisoned for a crime he didn't commit. It was later shown that Dreyfus was chosen as a scapegoat and convicted because he was a Jew. Theodor Herzl, an Austrian journalist, proposed that the Dreyfus affair was evidence that Jews would never truly be accepted or allowed to live in peace in non-Jewish societies. Thus Herzl began the Zionist movement with the stated goal of returning European Jews to the land of their ancestors in Palestine, where they would build a Jewish homeland as a modern Jewish nation.

Subsequent state-sponsored acts of terror known as Pogroms, notably in Russia and Poland before the First World War, soon motivated many Jews to move to Palestine in anticipation of the day when a Jewish nation would be declared. The movement started off slowly with formation of a Jewish community in Palestine known as the "Yishuv." Those in the Jewish settlements faced many hardships as they tried to farm land of questionable agricultural value while fighting off Arab raiders, who viewed them as Europeans stealing their land, violating the centuries-old territorial claims of a tribal culture regardless of the fact that the Jews had purchased the land.

As the Second World War ended, the Holocaust added a new impetus to the Zionist movement. It was no longer just a matter of Jews escaping social injustice in their adopted homelands; now it was viewed as a matter of life and death for the entire Jewish community. No one had believed millions of Jews could be systematically murdered before the war, and now the Jewish community couldn't believe that it would not happen again!

An additional ingredient to the explosive situation in the Middle East was the anti-colonial sentiment sweeping across the world. Many colonies felt that since they had fought alongside the Allies, they had earned the right of self-determination. So at the same time the Jews were looking to create an independent homeland, the Arabs were looking to end colonial occupation, whether it be the British in Egypt and the Middle East or the French in North Africa.

Many British soldiers in Palestine couldn't understand why they were there. It was obvious that they were hated by both Jews and Arabs. Many a British Tommy would ask out loud over a pint:

> *"Why don't we just leave the desert and let the
> damned Jews and Arabs fight it out amongst them-
> selves?"*

A hot wind blew Rebecca's long black hair away
from her face into a fluttering mane as she
stood amid the gravestones with Thomas at her side,
looking down over the city of Jerusalem.

She had decided on the spur of the moment one
day that she and Thomas should take the bus to
Jerusalem. They had been in Israel for almost two
years and had not yet made it to Jerusalem, a bus
trip of little more than an hour from where they
were living in Tel Aviv. She just wanted to make a day
of it. They spent hours making their way through
the narrow, winding cobblestone streets of the
walled city. They went about their journey casually,
stopping now and again to inspect the wares of the
street vendors or to explore a religious shrine, finally
exiting the walled city and climbing the Mount of
Olives just to see what they could see. She never
could have imagined as she looked out across the
skyline that she was about to witness one of the more
dramatic incidents of the conflict between Jewish
guerrillas and the British authority of the mandate.

Before Rebecca and Thomas had even started
their climb, a group of men had entered the kitchen
of the King David Hotel, which was the headquarters
of the Criminal Investigation Division of the British
military in Palestine, along with other British government offices. The men were members of the Etzel,
also known as the Irgun Z'vai Le'umi, which had

been formed as an offshoot of the Haganah some sixteen years earlier when some of its members felt that the leadership wasn't aggressive enough to reach their goals of creating a Jewish homeland. The leader of the Etzel, a Polish émigré named Menachem Begin, had ordered the assault in retaliation for a British crackdown on Jewish insurgents a few weeks before. Begin wanted to send a message to the British authorities that they couldn't strike at the Jewish underground with impunity.

"Achmed!" Emile called out as he searched the kitchen. "Damn it, Achmed! Where the hell are you? If you don't finish those damn dishes, I swear I'll—"

Emile never finished the sentence as he turned a corner and found Achmed standing against a wall with his hands up, his eyes ablaze with fear, as a man with a bandanna covering his face held a gun to his head.

"What . . . what the . . . ," Emile stuttered.

"Shut up!" someone said as a hand grabbed Emile's throat and he felt the muzzle of a pistol press coldly against the back of his neck.

"What do you want? We don't have no money here. You want food? Take it! Take what you want!"

"Shut up!" the voice commanded again. "How many more?"

"What?" Emile asked, having no idea what the man with the scarf over his face wanted.

"Who else is in the kitchen?"

"Just three. Three cooks."

The man let go of Emile's throat and pushed him toward Achmed. Two other masked men appeared from out of nowhere, and the leader motioned for them to go get the cooks. Everything moved so quickly that the cooks were instantly standing alongside Emile and Achmed, looking just as scared.

"What're you going to do with us?" asked one of the cooks, an Englishman.

"You're just going for a little ride. If you shut up and do as you're told, you might get out of this alive."

One of the intruders then blindfolded the kitchen staff, and he and another man ushered them out to a delivery truck that had been backed up tightly against the delivery entrance. The kitchen staff could hear that something was being unloaded at the same time that they were being shoved into the back of the van, but they obviously couldn't see the heavy milk cans. The delivery van drove off as soon as the transfer of prisoners and milk cans was complete, and the Irgun members who were left behind struggled with the cans as they moved them down into the basement, interspersing them with other, empty milk cans. Once the milk cans were in their hiding place, the leader of the small band pulled off the lids, exposing the gelignite inside. He then carefully placed a blasting cap in each of the four cans and set the timers for thirty minutes.

When the men then calmly left by the kitchen entrance, that was the cue for another Irgun member who stood at a nearby telephone.

"CID, Inspector Hanley," Frank Hanley answered absent-mindedly, bent on finishing up some paperwork as he was getting ready to leave.

"You have twenty-five minutes," the voice on the other end said with a thick accent.

"What? What's that?" he asked, focusing on the call.

"In twenty-five minutes. There is a bomb."

"A bomb? Is this some kind of joke?"

"You have twenty-five minutes before the bomb explodes," the voice said crisply as the line suddenly went dead.

"Hello? Hello?" Hanley shouted, but the caller had obviously hung up.

Frank Hanley got up from his desk and rushed to the captain's office. He rapped on the door and stuck his head in. "Sir!" he said urgently, interrupting the captain, who was talking to a tall and very thin man in a dusty suit.

"Hanley, I'm in the middle of something."

"Yes, sir, but I've just gotten a call—"

"I'm sure it can wait. This is—"

"A bomb sir. Someone says there's a bomb."

"Where? Was anyone killed?"

"No, sir, it hasn't gone off yet. They say there's a bomb here."

"Here? In the hotel? Don't be ridiculous, Hanley! We've got security at all desks and all the doors. No one could get in to—"

"They sounded serious. Said there was only twenty-five . . ." Hanley stopped and anxiously looked at his watch. "Well, it's twenty now. Twenty minutes."

"Calm down, Hanley. It's obviously a hoax. Maybe it's a diversion. Trying to keep us busy."

"Are you sure, sir? Shouldn't we evacuate the building?"

"That's just what they want us to do, Hanley. We'd be playing right into their hands. Just think of all the confusion . . . It would be the perfect time for them to pull something. No, I think it's just a ruse."

"But sir, can we take that chance?"

"It's a ruse, Hanley. Get hold of yourself. We've had these calls before and they've all come to nothing."

"But—"

"I've got things to attend to, Hanley."

"Sir, could I at least take a couple of men and do a quick inspection?"

"If you do it *quietly*. I don't want a panic."

"Yes, sir. Thank you, sir."

"Right . . . now be on your way."

Hanley rushed down the hall to the CID front desk. "Have we had any deliveries today?" he asked the sergeant on duty.

"Yes, sir. Delivery of paper and office supplies to the storage room down the hall."

"Anything else?"

"Couriers. Lots of letters and such."

"But the paper delivery was the only big delivery?"

"That's right, sir."

"Come with me. Was there anything unusual about it?"

"Unusual, sir?" the sergeant asked as they hurried down the hallway.

"A new delivery man? Anything like that?"

"Yes, sir. Now that you mention it, it was a different man. Never seen him before. It's right in here."

Hanley pulled open the door and made a quick inspection, but found nothing unusual. "Is this everything?"

"Uh . . ."

"Think, man!"

"No, sir. I'm sure he took part of the delivery upstairs. Let me check the log."

The sergeant scurried back to the desk with Hanley hot on his heels. "Here it is, sir. He went up to the third floor. I believe he had three or four boxes on a dolly."

"I need a couple of men to go with me upstairs," Hanley said as he looked at his watch. "Christ! Only twelve minutes."

Just then a couple of soldiers entered the lobby and the sergeant called out, "Tim! Hugh! You're with Hanley. Quick time!"

"What's it all about, Inspector?" Tim, the younger of the two, asked as they rushed up the stairs.

"We've got a bomb call. Captain says it's a hoax, but we're going to take a quick look about. We don't want to start a panic."

"How long do we have?"

"About ten minutes!"

They cleared the stairs in a heartbeat, and Hanley, out of breath, asked the receptionist about deliveries. She said they had had the same supply delivery as the CID downstairs and pointed to a storage closet down the hallway. Hanley and the others rushed to the storeroom and quickly pulled out the boxes, carefully setting them out and opening each one cautiously, finding nothing but reams of typing paper. Hanley looked at his watch. It was past twenty-five minutes. *Captain must have been right,* he thought. *It was just a hoax . . .*

Hanley hadn't even finished the thought when the world fell apart all around him.

Rebecca and Thomas turned suddenly when they

heard the earth-shaking thunder, in time to see a billowing black cloud rise above the Jerusalem skyline.
Although Rebecca couldn't see it from her vantage
point, the explosion had blown away a huge piece of
the building, as though some monster had taken a
bite out of the side of the hotel. Dozens of people
were killed in the explosion, including Hanley and
the two men with him, the captain and the tall, thin
man he had been meeting with, Dickerson from the
British Foreign Office, who had come to discuss the
effectiveness of the crackdown on the Haganah.

"This is not good," Rebecca said under her breath
as she watched the cloud rise higher and higher.

"What is it?" Thomas asked.

"It's something bad. We'd better get back to the
bus station. It's time to go home."

"But Mommy, we haven't seen the—"

"I'm sorry, Thomas, but we've got to go now."

Rebecca surprised her son by hailing a taxi, something he had never seen her do before. It was the
first time Thomas had ever ridden in a cab.

It was hardly more than twenty minutes from the
time they had seen the smoke of the explosion to
when they were boarding their bus, just as it quickly
pulled out of the station. Rebecca was glad that she
had round-trip tickets, since the panic was under
way and the ticket windows at the station were
already overwhelmed with people.

"We heard some kind of explosion," she said to
the bus driver as they boarded. "Do you know what
it—"

"Are you kidding me? Everyone knows. They blew
up the King David."

"Blew it up?"

"Big explosion. Lotta people killed and hurt."

"Who?"

"Who?!" the driver repeated in disbelief, astounded that a complete stranger would ask such a question. "It doesn't pay to know too much around here," he finally replied when he had regained his composure. "And believe me, it doesn't pay to ask too many questions."

Within hours there was a curfew in Jerusalem and Tel Aviv, with British troops ordered to shoot to kill anyone defying the order.

That was the way things went in Palestine after the war. The end of the war in Europe signaled an increase in the fighting between the British, the Haganah, and the Arabs with the sudden influx of combat-proven Jewish partisans from Europe. There would be a period of calm, and then suddenly a terrorist act would outrage one group or another, and then an act of vengeance would follow. And all the while Jewish guerrilla forces were trying to steal weapons from British garrisons or bring them in from other sources for the all-out war they knew would be coming. The Haganah, however, had another priority in mind. Their goal was to bring as many refugees as possible into Palestine. The Yishuv wanted to increase the number of Jews in Palestine as quickly as possible because reaction to the talk of an independent state of Israel made it clear that, however independence came about, it was sure to be a bloody affair.

Actually, the Haganah pursued two methods of bringing Jewish refugees to Palestine. One was to smuggle people across the borders and have them live "underground" with false papers, and so on. The second method, however, was a propaganda campaign designed to sway world opinion. These people rarely set foot on Palestinian soil, although at the very least they were that much closer to the land of Canaan. The Haganah would load ships with thousands of ragged refugees and then make sure the world press took note as the British put these survivors of the Holocaust into new, British concentration camps.

And the British never swayed. British agents watched ports all over Europe for potential Haganah ships, doing whatever they could to stop the ships somewhere else before they could force a confrontation with the British in Palestinian waters. Palestine became an important newspaper story, with reporters always ready to witness modern British warships once again demanding the surrender of some overloaded, antique ship filled with Holocaust survivors.

It was almost a year after the King David Hotel exploded into world newspaper headlines when two British soldiers patrolling a stretch of shoreline outside of Haifa noticed something.

"There!" Teddy shouted as he pointed out to the water.

Reg Witherspoon strained to see what Teddy was pointing at through the darkness as their jeep bumped along at full tilt down the highway that paralleled the coastline south of Haifa. He could hear the whine of another engine over the sound of the jeep's motor and could tell it was being pushed to the limit, but he couldn't make out the boat.

"I see it!" Reg finally shouted back. "Someone's going over the side! Pull off now!"

The jeep slid into the soft sand, the rear end skidding sideways as Teddy floored it. In an instant they were on the beach and heading for the spot where the person who had jumped out of the boat would most likely come ashore. "There's our little friend," Reg continued as he spotted a figure rising out of the water at the beach. Reg pulled his pistol as he abandoned the jeep and raced off with Teddy close behind.

"Halt!" Teddy shouted, firing a round from his pistol as the man started to run.

The man stopped in his tracks and waited for the two British soldiers to catch up.

"That's a good lad," Teddy continued in a condescending, out-of-breath tone as he came to a stop and motioned with his pistol for the man to put his hands up. "That's good. Keep your hands in sight, and now we'll go for a ride—"

"I don't think so," came a shout from behind them.

Teddy and Reg both spun around at the same moment to see three men with submachine guns leveled at them. "Now don't make us shoot you . . . ," the voice continued ominously.

"Christ, Reg! You were supposed to be watching our backs."

"Shut up, Teddy. Three of 'em with bloody machine guns . . ."

"Gentlemen, please don't argue. Just drop the pistols and step back, and we'll be on our way."

The soldiers did as they were told, and the man who had just come out of the water walked over and picked up the pistols, slipping them into his belt as he walked over to the others.

"You're late," Martin whispered to Jakob when he got close enough.

"Couldn't be helped. We had to dodge a couple of patrol boats."

"Gentlemen," Martin called out to the soldiers, "I'm afraid we're going to requisition your jeep."

"Damn it!" Teddy said under his breath.

"Now, now . . . If you start walking now, you should make it to Haifa by midday."

"Go to hell, you rotten kike."

"Well, now, that's not very polite. After all, the Arabs would have just killed you."

"Don't do us any favor, Jew boy. You kill us and the whole British army will hunt you down and—"

Martin had had enough and fired a burst from his machine gun over their heads. Teddy and Reg immediately hit the sand, each coming up with a mouthful as the Haganah men ran for their cars and sped off.

"Russian?" Jakob asked as he looked at the machine gun that rested on Martin's lap.

"They never jam. We get all kinds of guns. Not many machine guns, though. Russian Mosin Nagent, Czech pistols, American Krag Jorgensen, and of course, British SMLE."

"How do you keep the ammunition straight?"

"Every man for himself. It's their responsibility to keep enough ammunition for their rifle or get a rifle to match whatever ammunition they can get.

There's one hell of a black market. Lots of guns available from the war. We get quite a few guns shipped in from America . . . the Jews there . . . but we only get about one in ten. The rest get seized at one port or another en route."

"So they all help the British?"

"You've got to remember the mandate is from the League of Nations. They play on that in the United Nations, as if the United Nations was a direct successor to the League.

"But the League of Nations failed miserably. Why would they want any association . . . ?"

"You know the Brits. Everything from the monarchy to horse theft is based on common law. They can only think in terms of succession."

"Their time is over . . ."

"They don't know it."

There was a brief pause as they rode along until Jakob changed the subject. "So, what are we up to now?"

"First, we need to get you settled in. Then we'll talk, you'll meet some people, and we'll go from there."

"Good enough. Any idea how I can find out if my mother and the others made it?"

"They have a Red Cross office set up here. They get messages from people. Even if they were stopped and sent to Cyprus, there could be a message. How long ago would they have arrived?"

"Good question. I suppose it could be anywhere from two years to . . ."

"I've seen some pretty old messages on their boards. . . But you're sure they made it?"

"Not at all. I don't know for sure what happened to them."

"Well, the best place to check would be here in Haifa and then in Tel Aviv. After that, I don't know. I think there's an International Red Cross office in Europe that only deals with DPs, but I don't know how successful they are at locating people. There are millions of refugees."

"I'll start in Haifa and see what they say," Jakob answered with a note of finality.

It wasn't long before they saw the lights of Haifa. It was about three o'clock in the morning, long after the 9:00 P.M. military curfew, so they had to hide the jeep and continue on foot. Haifa rambles down from mountain to sea, with an ancient mosque cut into the mountain at the south end of the city and the seaport at the northern end of the city. The police station and city hall are also at the northern end of the city. That, of course, was where the greatest concentration of British military forces was to be found. It was a hard climb to the top of the hills behind the mosque, where the Haganah had set up a safe house. Martin assigned one of his fellow soldiers, a man named Izzy who was about the same age as Jakob, to stay with the new arrival.

"Close the shades before you light the lamp," Martin cautioned. "We're leaving now. I suggest you and Izzy keep a watch, but you probably don't have anything to worry about. I'll be back tomorrow with your papers and show you around the city."

"Papers? They gave us papers before we left Bari."

"They just changed them again . . . new signatures. Don't worry about it, just a minor hitch."

"First or second?" Jakob asked Izzy, referring to whether he wanted to take the first watch or sleep.

"I'll take first," Izzy said in a thick Romanian accent. "You sleep."

"Good. Wake me in a couple of hours," Jakob replied as he handed Izzy one of the pistols he had taken from the soldiers on the beach. He then fell into one of the cots, fast asleep almost as soon as his head hit the sack of hay that posed as a pillow.

Morning came early, a bit too early for Jakob. He had gotten used to getting along without sleep during the war, a common complaint of soldiers that surprisingly doesn't get mentioned much when men talk of their combat experiences. But Jakob had quickly gotten over the habit of going without sleep when he was in Moreno. He slept like a playboy there, going to bed long after midnight and sleeping well into the morning. He and Martin had done all of their "work" in the middle of the night. That was how they operated. Not unlike the "Nacht and Nebel" ("night and fog") method of the German Gestapo. Catch them with their pants down. Surprise them in their sleep and make them disappear so quickly that it seems almost like a dream to those who are left behind.

Martin had a lot to do that day, so he showed up at the house at 5:30 in the morning to get Jakob and Izzy on their way. He brought clothes with him. It certainly wouldn't do to have them looking like newly arrived refugees. Jakob had to look like he had lived in Palestine for years—like he had been born there.

"The first order of business is to get you familiar

with the city. Your papers say you are from Tel Chai, a small village to the north. You are from a nearby kibbutz and are here to recruit immigrants and buy livestock. There are Arabs living all over Haifa, but we are now in the predominantly Arab neighborhoods. Down there is the German cemetery—"

"German cemetery?"

"German missionaries came here around the turn of the century. I guess they wanted to convert *everybody*. Muslims, Jews, Arabs, Turks . . ."

"The piers . . . ," Izzy said as he pointed down the coastline.

"There are piers all the way down the coast here, but there, to the north, that's where they bring in the immigrants. The city offices are up the hill from there.

The three of them caught a trolley and were soon standing at the north piers. "Have you heard of the *Patria?*"

"*Patria?* No," Jakob answered for both himself and Izzy.

"It was a French ship. Back in forty. That's probably why you didn't hear about it . . . with the war going on. There were a couple of broken-down old ships ships loaded with Jewish refugees from Europe who had spent weeks trying to get here. When they finally made it, the British took them off the other ships and put them on the *Patria* so they could be taken to Cyprus and put in the detention camps there. We couldn't let that happen . . ."

"We?"

"The Haganah. We were doing everything we could to get people out, and then when they got here they ended up in a prison camp in Cyprus. We had to stop them, so it was decided that the *Patria* had to be sabotaged. They smuggled some explosives onboard in loaves of bread and then tried to blow a hole in the hull of the ship."

"What happened?"

"The man on the ship didn't know his explosives. He used too much. He was only supposed to cripple the ship so the refugees would be taken off, but instead he blew a hole so big that the ship tipped and sank. People started jumping over the sides. Those that tried to slide down the hull as the ship leaned to one side got cut so badly by the barnacles that they died. Many of those who jumped from the other side, a thirty-foot drop into the water, made it. Hundreds died."

Jakob just shook his head. "Let's go take a look at the city hall," Martin continued. They climbed the roads lined with two- and three-story buildings, all built of the defining cream-, tan-, and orange-colored sandstone.

The city hall was cloaked in a barbed wire fence that drove home the tenuous nature of the Britons' hold on the city and the country at large.

"Looks pretty secure," Jakob commented.

"It is," Martin concurred. "I'll have to show you the prison in Jerusalem."

"Jerusalem . . . ," Izzy said thoughtfully.

"A lot to take in, isn't it?" Martin said with a smile

"I never thought I'd make it to Palestine."

"So, where's the Red Cross office?" Jakob asked.

"Not far. We might as well go now."

The Red Cross office was located in an old storefront building where the dust of centuries had been ground into the worn floorboards. The woman sitting behind the desk at the front door had a pleasant voice and face. She politely asked how she could help Jakob and his friends.

"I'm looking for my family. We were separated and. . ."

"How long?"

"What?"

"How long have you been separated and where did you last see them?"

"I last saw them in the summer of 1944 on the Swiss border."

"And you think they're in Haifa?"

"They said they were going to try to get to Palestine."

"They didn't say where in Palestine?"

"No . . . They weren't on holiday. They couldn't make plans like that. They were determined to get here however they could. It would be up to the captain where they ended up."

"I'm here to help. You don't need to be rude," the woman said curtly. "You can't imagine how may people we get through here."

"I'm sorry, I'm just a little . . . I don't know where they are. This is the first place I've started to look. The name is Stein, and I—"

"Dorothy Iverson," the lady interrupted, introducing herself. "We should start by looking through the files. I'll need names, married and maiden names . . . Is there *anybody* they might know here that they might have tried to find?"

"It looks like you have some work to do here,"

Martin said as he pulled out a chair for Jakob to sit in. "We'll go do some other things and meet you back at the house."

Jakob spent hours looking through individual files and then finally the old messages that had been left at the Red Cross office over the past years.

They all looked the same. "Shemuel, we have gone to Jerusalem. You will find us on the Jaffa Road outside the old city walls. We will wait for you however long it takes. Love, Mother."

It didn't take Jakob long to understand the immensity of his task. There were thousands and thousands of files, and that was just in the Haifa area. There were also offices in Jerusalem and Tel Aviv, with Tel Aviv being the largest office.

He spent some time wandering through the city before returning to the safe house. He made a sandwich and decided to catch up on his sleep. He was awakened by Martin just as the sun was setting.

"We're going to Tel Aviv."

"When?"

"Tonight. Something's up. A ship is going to run the blockade."

"In the dark?"

"No. We're not sure exactly. They've got over four thousand people on board, a lot of them camp survivors, and they're being followed by a British cruiser."

"They won't let them dock, will they?"

"No. The only chance is to get close enough to shore so that they can swim for it."

"Jump over the side?"

"It's either that or they go to the camps on Cyprus."

"I suppose there are women and children . . ."

"Of course."

Jakob and Martin were just two of a number of Haganah men called to Tel Aviv as quickly as they could get there. The ship, an American ship called the *President Warfield,* manned by a crew of mostly American Jews, had picked up thousands of Jewish refugees in a French port. They had only barely managed to leave the French port before an order was issued by the harbormaster, under pressure from the British, that would have pulled the sailing papers, stranding the ship there indefinitely.

The ship was then trailed by a British cruiser across the Mediterranean to the coast of Egypt. That was where it was sailing that night as Martin got his marching orders. The British thought the ship might try to disembark her passengers there, in Egypt, and then smuggle them into Palestine later. It was a very Biblical premise, the Jews being led across the desert into the land of milk and honey. But the cruise along the Egyptian coast was just a ruse. The men of the *President Warfield* had no intention of landing anywhere but in Palestine. Their plan for the following day was to sail up the coast of Palestine, staying outside the two-mile limit of territorial waters until they were near Tel Aviv, and then make a dash for the shore with everything the ship's engines could muster.

"What if they make it to shore?" Jakob asked as he and Martin sped along a dusty road toward Tel Aviv with two other Haganah soldiers in the back. "Won't the British just arrest them?"

Martin glanced over at Jakob with a smile. "Let

me tell you a story . . ."

Jakob smiled too. Martin hardly ever answered a complicated question with a direct answer. He always started out the same way: "Let me tell you a story . . ." Not that the answer was so complicated, but Martin's stories always included a little propaganda. In his stories he would always try to educate Jakob. He would talk about what life in Palestine, as he knew it, was like—who the people were and therefore why they would undoubtedly, ultimately, win.

"There is a mountain in northern Palestine," Martin began. "Actually there are a lot of mountains in northern Palestine, but there is one mountain in particular on the border of Syria that has a kibbutz . . . You know what a kibbutz is, don't you?"

"A farm . . . ?"

"That's a good start, but it's more than just a farm. It's a farming community. A commune. Nobody owns anything and everybody owns it all together. You get a place to live, food to eat, and clothes on your back, but that's it. Don't say it too loud, because Communism is a dirty word now, but a kibbutz is what Communism was supposed to be like. You come in with nothing and you leave with nothing. Just like life. So there was this mountain with the kibbutz at the foot of it, and on the mountain were British soldiers watching the border. They were supposed to keep Jews from sneaking into the country. So one day a man comes into the kibbutz in the night, under cover of darkness as they say. He sneaks in and finds the head of the kibbutz and says he's got over a hundred refugees on the other side of the mountain, trying to get into the country. 'Can you help us?' And so the members of the kibbutz meet to discuss it, and the next day they have a plan. They all. . . everyone, every man, woman, and child . . . start up the mountain and just walk past the British soldiers. The kibbutzim are unarmed and calm and peaceful. There's no shouting or anything. It's like they're out for a nice little stroll on Shabbat. They cross the mountain to where the refugees are hiding, tell the refugees to come with them, and they all cross back over the mountain together, returning to the kibbutz on the other side. The British soldiers are so surprised they don't know what to do. They didn't fire a shot. And why should they? They weren't being attacked. They should shoot unarmed women and children just for going on a walk? So the refugees just blended into the crowd, and by the time the British got around to investigating the kibbutz, the refugees all either had papers or were sent on their way to other communities."

"That really happened?"

"Of course it really happened!" Martin replied with all the indignation he could muster.

There was a military curfew in Tel Aviv, just like in Haifa and Jerusalem, and so, just like in Haifa, Martin, Jakob, and the others had to leave their car at a safe house outside the city limits and walk into the city, taking care to avoid patrols and sentries.

It was an ominous feeling as they cautiously worked their way through the city, finally making their way to a darkened house on Allenby Street. There were lights on in many of the houses and apartments along the way. Did they all know what was coming tomorrow?

"What do I do?" Jakob asked the next morning as he and Martin made their way across the city to the beach, having split up with the other two Haganah men when they left the house.

"We're going to spread out in the crowd. We have to play it by ear. We may even need to start a riot if it comes down to it. Keep an eye on me. Do what I do. If these people start swimming to shore, we'll need to get them through the crowd and keep them away from the Brits."

"The crowd? Do you think there will be a lot of people there?"

"Of course there will be. It's all been arranged."

"So *everyone* knows what's happening today?"

"No, they only know as much as they need to know. Some people have been told there will be a protest, and so they'll be there, and that will draw other people . . . Nothing draws a crowd like a crowd . . . And then when the ship comes into sight, we'll make sure everyone sees it."

"Do we know when?"

"Our best guess is early afternoon. We'll be waiting for a couple of hours. Let's get something to eat. We'll just blend into the crowd."

Tel Aviv was quite a surprise for Jakob. He hadn't expected it to be so normal. He thought the Holy Land would be populated with Biblical people—shepherds and Arabs in long flowing robes and headdresses wrapped in gold braid, devout Jews with full beards dressed in black bobbing up and down as they offered prayers, and priests and nuns on holy pilgrimage to the birthplace of Christ and the Via Della Rosa. Not that these people weren't there, but in Tel Aviv they were few and far between. Most of the people in Tel Aviv looked like . . . like him. Average people, some looking more "Semitic" than others, many looking very European, most just non-descript people.

They stopped at a small food booth on Dizengoff Street, and Martin ordered sandwiches of sliced meat served on pita bread with chopped, pickled cabbage.

"What *is* this?" Jakob asked as he cautiously approached the sandwich.

"Just eat it," Martin said with paternal impatience, as though Jakob should know Martin would never give him anything that wasn't good.

"There's the beach," Martin said with his mouth full. They had walked for a while, and he had just gotten his first glimpse of the water.

"So now we just wait?"

"Just a day at the beach . . . ," Martin said, looking up and down the area as they got closer.

"What does he look like?"

"Who?"

"I don't know. Whoever it is you're looking for."

"Too obvious?"

"It's different than in the army. A little subtlety goes a long way."

"Whoa! That's not very subtle," Martin said with a pointed nod as a woman in a very impressive bathing suit paraded past them.

"Don't we have some business to attend to?" Jakob asked.

"That's the worst thing about the army. You walk by a beautiful woman . . . and believe me, some of those Italian women . . . But then you see the mother and you know where they're headed."

"I didn't realize you were such a Renaissance man."

"Don't joke. You ever look at those women? I love a big ass. Those women in Italian paintings all got big, beautiful asses."

"You think about this a lot, don't you?"

"You don't think about women?"

"Of course I think about women, but I don't get obsessed with them."

"What kind of women do you like?"

"I don't know . . . I've never thought about it like that. I just . . ."

"You had many women?"

"Had?"

"You know . . . made love. Have you been with many women?"

"Not many. You?"

"Nah. I'm cursed. I fell in love too young. Got married at seventeen."

"Seventeen? Why so young?"

"Her father thought it would be a good idea . . ."

"Oh, you got into a little trouble?"

"Well . . . I love her. It's not like it was a bad thing. It's just . . . seventeen is too young for a man to have a wife and baby. And with the war . . ."

"Too many temptations?"

"No. I wouldn't say that . . . Just the *right* number of temptations." There was a smile and a brief pause before Martin continued. "How long you been married?"

"I'm not."

"But you said you were looking for some girl and your son."

"Yeah, but I didn't even know I had a son until a couple of years ago. We were kids and . . . Well, I found out I had a son."

"Are you going to marry her?"

"I don't know. I don't know if it would do anybody any good if we got married because we thought we had to."

"Do you love her?"

"Love?"

"Oh, I see!" Martin said with a laugh as he grabbed Jakob's shoulder and gave him a shake. "You've become a cynic! I guess you're just about the right age. How old are you?"

"Thirty."

"Thirty . . . Yeah, that's it. You've finally figured out that all the schoolboy shit is just a joke, and now you think there's no such thing as love."

Jakob smiled and shook his head as he looked down at his feet and shifted the white sand around with his tattered boot.

"Well, don't give up yet," Martin said as he slapped him on the shoulder. "There's something to it all. It's just that it's hard work. Love was never easy, and everybody's got to figure it out for himself."

They had been waiting for just over an hour by then, waiting for something to happen. There was a noticeable increase in the number of people on the beach. It could have been the group Martin said would be coming, or maybe it was just because the clouds were starting to clear and the beach looked inviting.

Jakob was surprised when a man just walked over to them and began talking. "That's them," he said as he nodded toward a ship now clearly silhouetted on the horizon. "We've just gotten word that they're starting in. Whatever happens . . . it should all be over in the next half hour."

The ship didn't look any different than any of the other ships working their way along the coastline, but then it made a sharp turn and headed toward the beach. Another ship was closing in on it as it turned, a British cruiser that had been following it all the way down the coast. The people on shore couldn't see, but the crew of the *President Warfield* had rolled out a banner that hung down the sides of the ship proclaiming a new name for the vessel: *Exodus 1947.*

The people on shore started taking notice, especially when the Haganah agents interspersed in the crowd began making loud comments.

"Damn," Martin said as he and Jakob watched intently, waiting for their moment.

"What?" Jakob asked.

"There . . . another cruiser is coming in alongside."

Jakob could see the other cruiser closing in quickly on the starboard side of the *Exodus* as the first cruiser moved into position on the port side. The engines of the refugee ship were no match for the British cruisers.

Aboard the ship, Mendel Lubinsky, a twelve-year-old orphaned refugee from Poland, could feel the tension rise as it became apparent they were going to be boarded. Men on the *Exodus* started coming up from the hold with canned food and potatoes. Those were the weapons they would use against the pistols, rifles, and cannons of the British military. But it wasn't as crazy as it sounded. Their goal wasn't to defeat the British navy in an open battle. All they wanted to do was delay them until the *Exodus* could run aground and as many refugees as possible could jump ship and make it to shore, where they would be taken in by the Haganah.

"Attention crew and passengers of the *President Warfield*," a tinny voice blared across the open water from the rapidly approaching battle cruiser. "You have passed into restricted waters in violation of the British mandate of 1919. Turn back now or you will be boarded . . ."

In the wheelhouse, an American volunteer stood steady at the helm, aiming directly for the beach. "Look!" yelled one of the other men in the cabin, pointing at the second British cruiser, which was now pulling up along the port side of the *Exodus*. "They're going to hit us!"

"They're going to catch us in between. Go tell the others. Get ready to fight them off."

But the others didn't need to be told. They knew what was happening, and they were as ready as they could be.

"Attention crew of the *President Warfield*," the nasal voice repeated in its perfunctory and unmistakably English rhythm. "You are in restricted waters in violation of the British mandate of 1919. Cut your engines and prepare to be boarded."

In moments the *Exodus* was being knocked from side to side as one cruiser squeezed the former luxu-

ry liner up against the other and British sailors
began to leap onto the decks of the refugee ship.

There was a sudden hailstorm of raw potatoes and
food tins as the refugees and crew started their bar-
rage against the sailors. Although it may seem slightly comical, it's no small thing to be hit square in the
face with a tin of hash or stewed tomatoes. Mendel
aimed carefully with a potato at a sailor he saw bringing his billy club down hard on the shoulder of a
young woman who was clawing at his face. He gave it
everything he had, and the potato exploded into a
dozen pieces as it hit the sailor in the ear. The sailor
yelled out in surprise and the woman scrambled
away. Mendel was pleased to see that there were
actually a few drops of blood trickling down as the
sailor's hand went instinctively to his ear, but the
boy's smugness soon gave way to terror as the sailor
looked over and started after him. He ran for the
bow, but stopped for an instant as he came to a
group of sailors pushing their way into the wheelhouse. They were just about to break through the
line of refugees guarding the wheelhouse when Bill,
the American volunteer, came to the door, holding a
fire extinguisher menacingly over his head. He was
about to throw it at the sailors when a shot rang out.
Bill crumpled to the floor and the sailors rushed
past, taking control of the helm.

It was over.

The sailors started rounding everyone up and
consolidating the group. When it was all over, there
were a few wounded sailors and dozens and dozens
of wounded refugees, three of whom, including Bill,
would die from their wounds.

A few hundred yards away, on the Tel Aviv beach, the crowd was quieting down. There had been all kinds of shouting and yelling as the sailors clashed with the crew and passengers of the *Exodus,* but when things quieted down on the ship, the people on the beach began to quiet down too. It was as though they were all on the ship together, a bond that surpassed the physical distance, an emotional response that could only be explained by understanding the overwhelming desire of the refugees, survivors of the Holocaust, to get to Palestine in the first place.

Martin's was the sole voice that roared out "Bloody bastards!" at the top of his lungs.

"Get the British out!" Jakob yelled in response, and other people began to shout, too, until a tidal wave of voices swept the beach, all demanding with one phrase or another for the British to let the refugees be, to let them come home.

Jakob kept shouting, caught up in the spirit of rebellion, when suddenly he felt someone tugging at his arm. He pushed Martin aside, both to give himself some room and to let Martin know that they were probably about to be arrested, and spun around to face his attacker. He was ready to punch his assailant in the face when he realized it was a woman who had grabbed his arm and she wasn't trying to arrest him. It was his mother!

Amalie had been at the market with Thomas when she saw that something was going on at the beach. Drawn toward the commotion, they walked to the beach and stood on the sidewalk, waiting to see what would happen, just like so many others that day.

The instant Jakob shouted, she knew it was his voice. It had been years since she had seen him, but she knew his voice so well that the moment she heard it, her head snapped in the direction it was coming from. She had thought she had heard his voice on other occasions, expecting him to show up at any time, and had been embarrassed when she accosted a stranger thinking it was Jakob, but that didn't stop her. She walked toward the voice like a sleepwalker, with Thomas in tow, as the crowd began to erupt. Making her way through the sea of humanity, she finally found herself standing behind the man who had shouted. She drew back as he spun around, ready to attack her.

"My God!" Jakob gasped as Amalie embraced him. "How did you . . . ?"

"You made it!" she sobbed as she crushed him in a bear hug. "Thank God you made it!"

Jakob was speechless, as was Martin, staring at the two of them. "My mother," Jakob explained in amazement. "It's my mother!"

Just then Amalie realized that she had let go of Thomas's hand in the crowd, and she broke free of Jakob and started calling for the little boy. Thomas was only a few feet away in the crowd, and Amalie found him and pulled him to Jakob.

"It's Thomas," she shouted to be heard above the crowd as she virtually threw the little boy into his father's arms.

"Thomas," Jakob shouted. "Thomas . . . do you know me?"

Thomas was quiet, surprised that his grandmother had thrown him into this strange man's arms in the midst of everyone shouting around him. He just shook his head no.

"I'm your father," Jakob continued. "Your father..."

"Handsome boy!" Martin piped in.

Jakob was stunned.

He had heard the stories of people who had lost their families, and he had been prepared for months of searching. On the one hand, he thought he might have a better chance of finding her just because she had traveled with the others out of France. More people would touch more lives and increase the chances that he would run into someone who knew something about her. But on the other hand, he didn't even know if they had made it out of France at all, or if they were even alive.

He certainly didn't expect to run into her by accident on the beach. It was, in fact, the furthest thing from his mind as they awaited the fate of the *Exodus 1947*.

"The others said I should be prepared for the worst," Amalie said as she maneuvered her way down the sidewalk. "But I knew . . . I knew . . . ," she continued with a deep sigh, one of the many deep breaths she took as she almost ran down the sidewalk, carried on by her excitement.

"Grandma," Thomas whined. "I can't keep up."

"Oh! I'm sorry, Liebchen. I'm just so happy and I want to get home," she said with a smile as she slowed for an instant, but suddenly Martin stepped in and swept Thomas up in his arms.

"Of course you are!" Martin said with a grin.

Thomas laughed as Martin tickled him and threw him over his shoulder, carrying the boy feet first as Martin picked up the pace again, walking beside Amalie with Jakob bringing up the rear.

"How long have you known my son?" Amalie asked Martin as they turned up Gordon Street.

Jakob was walking close behind them, and Thomas's head bobbed in front of him with every step Martin took. Thomas was staring at Jakob intently. Jakob looked away, pretending to watch the traffic on the street, but in reality he was embarrassed by Thomas's stare. But it was just a reflex, and he soon found himself returning his son's stare. Thomas was indeed a fine-looking boy, just as Martin had said. He seemed a little small for his age, but Jakob was taken back by how much they looked alike, how much Thomas resembled pictures of him as a boy. It wasn't the sort of thing a boy would notice. Jakob would never have known when he was nine years old that this boy could have been his twin. It's the sort of thing that people find out as they grow older and start seeing all the connections in the world.

Martin had been talking with Amalie as they walked along, and it suddenly occurred to him that something was going on as Thomas had stopped squirming. He glanced over his shoulder and then suddenly stopped dead in his tracks.

"Here," he said as he turned to Jakob. "He's your son. You carry him. He's wearing me out." He tossed the boy playfully into Jakob's unprepared arms.

"My God!" Jakob exclaimed with a groan. "You *are* a big boy!"

Thomas laughed and tried to get down, but Jakob held on and flipped him over until he was holding Thomas upside down by his legs.

"Put me down! Put me down!" Thomas protested through laughs and giggles, and Jakob swung his arm under Thomas's back, kneeling down as he stood Thomas on his feet.

Thomas was still giggling, but then he suddenly stopped and his face became serious. He looked deep into Jakob's eyes.

"Are you really my father?"

Amalie and Martin just stood by and watched the exchange.

Jakob just nodded his head yes. He had a strange, apologetic look on his face, as if to say, "Sorry, kid, sometimes we just don't get the best parents . . . We don't always get the father we deserve."

"Where have you been?" Thomas continued with childish innocence.

"I . . . I . . . ," Jakob stuttered, not sure how to say it, not even sure himself about why everything had happened the way it had, why he had been away so long. "The war," he finally offered lamely. "It was the war."

"Are you going to stay with us now?" Thomas pressed on.

"Well, I might have to . . . I don't know if . . . ," he stammered again, and then he looked up at Amalie and Martin, as if they might get him out of this. But Amalie wanted to know the answers to those same questions, and Martin clearly felt that this was something Jakob had to face on his own.

"Yes," Jakob answered simply as he turned back to

Thomas.

"You're going to stay?!"

"Of course I am. Where else would I go?"

Thomas could hold back no longer as he leapt for Jakob and wrapped his arms tightly around his father, almost knocking him over.

Jakob returned the embrace as his son melted into him. He felt as though he had just lied to Thomas, but what else could he say at a moment like this? He told him what he wanted to hear, but he was afraid that he might not be able to keep his word.

Thomas released his grip and Jakob stood up, taking Thomas's hand in his as they all continued on their way.

"We've been here in Tel Aviv for almost a year now. The British are getting more and more aggressive, but then so are the Haganah."

"Of course they are, now that the war is over. It's like David Ben Gurion said when the war started . . . We—"

"Yes, I know. 'We'll fight the White Paper like there was no war and the war like there was no White Paper.' We've all heard it."

"You don't agree?" Martin asked in such a way that said he couldn't believe every Jew in Palestine wasn't squarely behind the Haganah in everything it did.

"I'm not so sure. The British have used their troops to save many Jewish lives in Palestine over the years."

"They also made it illegal for Jews to have guns when the Arabs were rioting in the thirties. They closed immigration while millions of Jews were being killed in Europe."

"You're Sabra, aren't you?"

"Yes, I was born here. I spent my childhood on a kibbutz in the north called Kfar Giladi on the border with Syria. My parents were some of the first kibbutzim there. Why do you ask?"

"I could tell."

"Oh, I see," Martin said.

"What?" Jakob asked.

"Some say that the Sabra are . . ."

"What is a Sabra?"

"In the Jewish community," Amalie explained, "Jews born here are called Sabra. It comes from the name for cactus fruit. It's tough and prickly outside but sweet and tender inside. They have some harsh words for camp survivors. They can't understand how it happened. They call survivors 'pieces of soap.'"

"We're not all like that."

"This is it," Amalie announced as she headed for a doorway. "This is the apartment."

"So," Jakob began as they climbed the two flights of stairs, "how have you been getting by?"

"I work as an accounting clerk in a factory. Before the war they were a small company that only made brass kerosene lamps, but during the war they were refitted for making bullet casings. They grew so much that when the war ended they expanded their product line. Now they also make kitchen utensils and stoves."

"How did you find that job?"

"It's not a very nice story," Amalie answered with a note of embarrassment.

Martin's eyebrows arched as he waited for the details while Amalie unlocked the apartment door. Thomas rushed in ahead of them and disappeared into one of the bedrooms.

"When we came to Tel Aviv we had nothing. All four of us living in this apartment. We spent almost all of our money to rent this apartment for three months..."

"Four of you?" Martin asked.

"Thomas, his mother and grandmother, and myself."

"Rebecca is living with you?" Jakob asked with obvious alarm.

"Of course she is! We have to stick together. But as I was saying, we were in a desperate situation. The neighbors were all very kind and even gave us some chairs and sometimes food. One lady was very nice. She was so fond of Thomas. She had lost her daughter and grandson in the war. He had been about the same age as Thomas. She became very attached. Would you like some tea or coffee?"

"Coffee, if it isn't too much trouble."

"No trouble. I always make some for myself. So, as I was saying, she was very fond of Jakob." Amalie stopped and smiled as she realized her mistake. "I mean Thomas, of course. Well . . . one day she was in a car accident. She was just walking along, crossed the road, and a car didn't even slow down. She looked terrible. I went to visit her in the hospital and she asked me to tell her employer what had happened. I went down to talk to them and . . ."

"You took her job?" Jakob asked as he tried to move the story to its conclusion.

"They said they had to get somebody immediately. I told them I could fill in until Laila was better. But she had internal bleeding. She died a day later."

"You don't need to feel guilty about it," Jakob said.

"I know . . . I don't think I feel guilty, it's just that..."

"Not the best circumstances," Martin offered.

"Yes, I guess that's it. I was so sad about Laila, and yet I . . . I profited when she died."

"Maybe she would have wanted it that way. Maybe that's why she asked you to go talk to them," Martin continued

Amalie gave a half smile and nod of her head.

The small apartment was filled with the wonderful smell of food simmering away on a little kerosene stove, and when the conversation paused, Martin looked toward it.

The stove Amalie used was the sort one might use on a camping expedition. It was made of brass and sat on a table in the little kitchen, but the way Amalie kept it brilliantly polished, it looked like an art object or an antique samovar showpiece.

"See!" Amalie said proudly. "That's the stove we make. We're so old-fashioned here. No oven. We have an old icebox instead of a refrigerator. It's not so bad, though. You get used to it."

Amalie's daily routine was dramatically different from what she had known before the war. She had to go to the market every day, carefully shopping for bargains, trying to buy a special something now and then—a chicken here or a piece of beef there—but overall it was a very austere diet.

That's not to say it was all bad. She had made friends at the marketplace down by the seashore that became a big part of her social life. It was no embarrassment to have nothing since there were so many others, Ashkenazim refugees like herself, who were also struggling to get by. It might sound like a joke, but it's easier to be poor when you have a lot of friends to be poor with. Every now and then her thoughts would wander back to those days in Munich before Gunther was killed, those days out in Fürstenried, where they had a nice house and a car and Gertie Haas would do all the cooking and housekeeping in exchange for her room and board. It was almost like having a maid, but so much more, since she had grown to love Gertie. It was as though Amalie had chosen a new mother to replace the one who had left her when she was only twelve, and had chosen well to find a friend like Gertie.

She was making potato soup, her old recipe from Munich, improvising with whatever she could afford at the market. Tonight the soup would have chopped cabbage and sausages.

Amalie busied herself making coffee as Thomas slowly came back into the room carrying a chess-board with both hands.

"Oh, my . . . ," Amalie said as she saw Thomas coming. "Thomas has found a new playmate."

"You play chess?" Jakob asked.

Thomas smiled as he nodded and set the chess-board down on a little table next to the chair where Jakob was sitting.

"Does he play chess?" Amalie repeated with a laugh. "If he had his way, he would play chess all day long. It doesn't matter if he wins or loses. He goes from one game to another, and on and on. Eight years old!"

Amalie was interrupted by the sound of someone unlocking the apartment door. A quick look at the clock and she knew it must be Rebecca. She tried to get to the door, but as she moved, Thomas ran ahead of her.

"Momma!" Thomas called out with joy as he wrapped himself around her legs, hugging her as soon as she appeared in the doorway.

"Oh, my!" Rebecca said with a laugh, but as soon as she looked up from the little boy at her legs, she noticed Amalie was looking at her in a strange way. "What is it?" she said as she ran her fingers through her windblown hair. "What's wrong?"

Amalie didn't say anything. She just glanced over at Martin.

"Oh . . . we have guests," Rebecca continued, but then she realized it was Jakob sitting in the corner chair next to Martin, and she froze.

Jakob didn't know what to do. He just sat there too.

"My God . . . ," she finally said.

"He said he's my father," Thomas said as he looked up at his mother. "Is he?"

Rebecca didn't answer.

"Is he?" Thomas persisted.

Jakob finally got up and walked over to her, standing within inches.

"Is he?" Thomas asked again.

Rebecca looked down at Thomas as though snapping out of a trance. "What?"

"Is he my father?"

"Yes, of course he is," she answered without looking down at her son.

Jakob slowly, cautiously reached out and touched Rebecca's hair and then gently embraced her, as though she were made of glass. She returned the embrace just as gingerly.

"So . . . ," Amalie began, trying to end the uncomfortable silence. "What are you going to do now?"

"I don't know," Jakob said as he released Rebecca from their awkward embrace and looked over at Martin.

"You'll need a place to stay," Martin answered, expressing the obvious.

"Well, of course you'll stay here," Amalie declared. "You'll have to sleep on the floor for a while. But you'll have a roof over your head." She paused for a minute and looked over at Martin. "You'll stay for dinner, of course."

"Dinner? Do you have enough?" Martin asked. "We've dropped in by surprise . . . Should I get something more?"

"That's a good idea," Jakob said as he stood up. "Let's make a quick trip to the store. It won't take a minute."

"I can go by myself," Martin announced, cutting Jakob off as he started for the door.

"No, I'll come too," Jakob insisted.

"Are you coming back?" Thomas asked innocently.

"Of course we are!" Jakob laughed. "Won't be long," he added reassuringly, giving Martin a congenial pat on the back as they exited.

"What the hell are you doing?" Martin asked once

they were out on the sidewalk.

"I just wanted to get out for a minute."

"Can't face them?"

"No. No, that's not it. It's just a lot to . . . It's all such a surprise . . . God damn it! It's a lot to take in."

"You're not going to run out on them, are you?"

"No, damn it!" Jakob spat out with frustration. "We're just going out for some bloody groceries!"

Martin couldn't help but smile and shake his head. They didn't say anything for a few minutes as they walked.

"She's quite a looker," Martin finally said.

"Rebecca? Yes. She's even prettier than before."

"There's a butcher. We'll get some cold meats and bread."

Jakob felt better as they walked back to the apartment. That was it . . . he just needed some air.

When they got back, they found that Abigail, Rebecca's mother, was also there. Martin stayed for dinner but took his leave soon thereafter. Jakob had enough stories to get through the evening as the returning hero while carefully avoiding his seamier adventures, including his affair with Galia.

"Oh, my God, you saw Gertie?" Rebecca asked.

"Yes . . . she was living in the same apartment. But she passed away while I was there."

The room became silent.

"It's like she was holding on until I got there," Jakob continued quietly.

"She was really something," Amalie said. "Like a mother to me."

"Friedrich is dead. He died in forty-two."

"Forty-two?" Amalie asked, thinking of her meeting with him in Prague in May of that year and wondering what had happened, but she said nothing more.

Jakob answered by saying that he was tired and it was time to get some sleep. It was almost midnight, and everyone agreed except for Thomas, who was already asleep on Rebecca's lap as they shared the one old easy chair in the apartment.

Amalie brought a couple of blankets and a pillow for Jakob to use in the living room. As he reached to take the blankets, she put her arms around him tightly. "I'm so glad you're here. I missed you so much," she said as she gave him a peck on the cheek and a few tears started down her cheeks. "I didn't even know if you were alive."

"I know. I know . . . I was afraid I wouldn't find you. I was in Haifa and they couldn't tell me anything. If you hadn't found me on the beach . . ."

They stood for a moment until Amalie wiped her eyes. "Well, let's get some sleep. I'm off to work at seven, but we'll talk tomorrow afternoon."

They didn't even have a couch, so Jakob laid one blanket down as a mattress and covered himself with the other and turned out the light. He lay awake thinking for quite a long time. Just as he was starting to drift off to sleep, he heard something and strained to see in the darkness. After an instant he could see a form moving toward him. It was Thomas, carrying his pillow and dragging his blanket behind him. He started to spread the blanket on the floor when Jakob said something.

"What's wrong?" he whispered.

"I thought you might be afraid sleeping alone,"

Thomas whispered back as he lay down beside his father.

"I see. It's a good thing you're here."

Thomas didn't say anything else. He just rolled in close to Jakob and put his arm across his father's chest. Jakob looked down and smiled, putting his arm around Thomas and petting him on the back as he drifted off to sleep.

Abigail was the first one awake and up the next morning. As she shuffled toward the kitchen to make coffee at about five o'clock, she stopped as she noticed Jakob and Thomas asleep together. Amalie came out an instant later and stood beside Abigail. "Will he stay?" Abigail asked in a whisper. Amalie just shrugged. Deep down she was sure Jakob would stay, but she had been wrong about him before.

"Another mouth to feed . . . ," Abigail said with a sigh. As soon as she said it, she realized how terrible it sounded, but they were all working so hard just to get by—three woman lucky to find work but barely earning enough to pay rent and buy food. Normally, Amalie would have felt a mother's irritation at hearing such a comment about her son, but she had been thinking the same thing. The two women looked at each other, and when their eyes met, each instantly recognized that the other felt the same contrasting emotions—joy at having Jakob there and worry over the problems it would create—and they both laughed.

Amalie and Abigail were always the first to leave in the morning. They went about their usual routine, sharing a breakfast of coffee and a hard roll, and left for work. Neither Jakob nor Thomas awoke.

It was an hour later that Rebecca got up and started for the bathroom, and she, too, stopped in her tracks. She had assumed Thomas was up until she saw him in the living room lying next to Jakob. She went to get herself ready for work, then returned and sat in a chair, just watching them sleep.

She didn't know what to do about Jakob. He had just walked out of her life in Switzerland, and now he came sauntering back in. Would he really stay? Did he have it in him? She was sure he had been killed in the war, although she never said it out loud, not wanting to upset Amalie. So here he was, as big as life, and all the old questions came back to life along with him.

She sat there mulling things over for ten or fifteen minutes and then decided it was time to get Thomas up for school. She knelt down and shook him gently to wake him, and he rolled onto his back, rubbing the sleep from his eyes with the backs of his hands.

"Come, Sweetheart . . ."

Thomas made some incomprehensible sound of protest, but she insisted, and soon he was getting up.

Jakob watched them scurry about for several minutes and then got up also. "I should take a bath," he said as he quickly pulled on his pants.

"Do you have any clean clothes?"

"I've got a knapsack around here somewhere . . ."

"Here it is!" Thomas called out as he brought the bag in from kitchen. Jakob smiled at the boy and tousled his hair as he took the bag.

"So . . . what are your plans for today?" Rebecca asked tenuously.

"I would guess Martin will come back for me."

"Are you leaving?"

"Leaving? No . . . I'm here to stay. I thought I made that clear last night. Martin and I just have some things to do. I'll be back this afternoon"

"I just wanted to make sure. Are you going to—"

"I think we need to talk," Jakob said, cutting her off.

"I have to go to work! I can't—"

"No, I mean tonight. I have some money. We could go out. Is there a restaurant we could go to so we can be alone and talk?"

"Uh, I suppose we could . . . Yes, in one of the hotels down at the beach."

"Let's do that," he agreed as he embraced her— the way he should have the night before, without hesitation, without holding back.

"We've got to go," Rebecca said, pulling away after a moment. "I have to get Thomas to school and I have to go to work."

"Where do you work?"

"A bakery."

"A bakery? That sounds like fun."

"Fun?" she said with a wry smile and shake of the head. "No, it's not like the bakeries in Munich, with sweets and cakes. We just make bread. It's like a factory," she continued wearily as she helped Thomas put on his worn jacket. "I stand at a table with four other women, and we cut loaves from the dough and slide them in and out of the hot ovens all day long."

"Well, then," Jakob began, trying to make her feel better, "you'll be ready for a nice dinner tonight."

She forced a quick smile and then disappeared out the door.

Jakob had been right about Martin. He showed up at the apartment in a beat-up old truck at around ten o'clock that morning. "Are you ready?" he asked as soon as Jakob opened the door.

"What are we up to today?"

"We've got some people to meet."

It was time for Jakob to be introduced to the Haganah organization in Tel Aviv. He would be at the first level, just a soldier in the field as it were, but Martin's recommendation would serve him well. He would have to tell his story of how he survived the war to a tribunal of sorts, whose members would judge whether he should be allowed to enlist in their secret army. He passed the test while keeping his secrets. He had enough to tell about Prague and Hungary and his affair with Galia to give them a well-rounded picture of his successes and failures. His story, along with the background of his family's arrival in Palestine before him, seemed to convince everyone that he wasn't a British plant and should be given a chance.

Martin and Jakob then spent the next few hours talking about how Jakob would fit into Haganah operations in the area. Martin finally delivered Jakob to the apartment in the late afternoon.

"I'll be leaving town tonight. If they have something for you, they know where to find you."

"Do I need to keep in touch with anyone?"

"No. I'll be back before sundown on Friday. You just settle in."

Martin paused as Jakob got out of the truck. "How

are things with you and . . . ?" he continued cautiously.

"Rebecca? I don't know," Jakob said though the window of the truck, leaning on the door after slamming it shut. "We're going out tonight . . . an evening alone to talk. I think she's angry with me for all the time she's waited. Maybe we can work it out . . . I just don't know."

"Well, good luck," Martin said with a wry smile and a wave good-bye. Jakob shut the door and watched as Martin ground the old truck into gear and lurched off down the street.

When Jakob knocked on the apartment door, it was Abigail who answered. "Oh, that's right. You don't have a key yet," she said as he followed her in. "What were you up to today?"

"Looking for work. My friend Martin was showing me around."

"Rebecca says you're going out for dinner tonight."

"Ja . . ."

"It's been a long time. The three of us work hard just to keep food on the table. For a while there, the only food we had was the day-old bread that she brought home from the bakery."

"Abby, just say it," Jakob said with a sigh as he stood in the kitchen watching while she started to make dinner.

"Say what?" she asked with a lilt as she studied the potatoes she was scrubbing in the sink.

"Whatever it is you're leading up to."

"It's just that we're having a hard time here. We can't support you too."

Jakob laughed. "Support me? Where did you get that idea?"

"We've seen all these refugees coming in. We know all about the Haganah men. The women work like dogs and the Haganah end up in jail. You're not going to come in here and . . . and . . ." She stopped scrubbing her potatoes and leaned on the sink, not sure herself whether she was going to cry or start throwing things. But then she looked Jakob in the eye. "You're not going to come in here and break her heart again."

"Break her heart?"

"What do you *think* happened when you left her there in Switzerland?" she asked in a nasty tone. "Don't tell me you think everything was just fine! She was counting on you, Jakob. And you just walked away."

"She didn't ask me to stay. She said she understood why I was . . ."

"You don't know anything about women, do you?" Abby said in a louder voice. "You never should have put her in that position at all. Why should she *have to* ask you to stay?"

Jakob didn't have an answer and was grateful to be interrupted as the door opened and a teenaged boy came in with Thomas in tow. The boy stayed close to the door as Thomas ran over to Jakob, wrapping his arms around his father's waist as he called out "Tateh!"

It surprised Jakob, but Thomas was just reenacting the scene he had witnessed when his friends greeted their fathers. It wasn't that he was so sure of Jakob; he just wanted so badly to have a father.

Whatever his reason, it hit the mark. Jakob scooped the little boy up and hugged him warmly. "How's my boy?" he asked as he held Thomas in midair and looked him in the eye.

"We're going to a movie tonight!"

"That sounds like fun," Jakob said as he let Thomas down and turned to the teenaged boy. "And who   are . . . oh, you must be Aubin. You came with them from France."

"Oui, Monsieur. I've heard a lot about you."

"Yes, and they told me all about you last night. They said they couldn't have made it without you."

"That was a long time ago," Aubin replied shyly, dismissing his role in the escape.

"Don't let him fool you!" Rebecca said as she came into the apartment, catching the exchange. "He saved our lives in those last days."

"Where do you live now?" Jakob asked.

"David and I live together."

"David? David Frieder?"

"Yes. He's been like a father to me."

"David's a good man," Jakob agreed

"David had such a hard time when his father died," Rebecca added. "He told me he didn't know how he would have gotten through it if Aubin hadn't been there." She put an arm around Aubin's shoulder and gave him a quick squeeze. It was obvious they were close.

"Well, how was your day?" Jakob asked Rebecca. "Are we ready to go?"

"Ready? Don't be silly! I've got to wash up and change," she answered as she headed for the bedroom. "It will take me about a half hour."

Jakob settled in to wait, watching from a chair in the living room as everyone went about their business. Thomas and Aubin helped Abby make dinner and then went on to play a game on the floor at his feet. Before long, Amalie came home and began telling everyone who would listen how her day had gone and what was planned for the next day and the weekend coming up. It was all very domestic, this extended family and the home they made, and Jakob felt like an audience rather than a participant, a stranger on the outside looking in. He understood why Abby had warned him about disrupting it. It was comfortable. Certainly not elegant or affluent, but comfortable—the way they all fit into the picture.

Finally Rebecca reappeared. She was dressed very simply in a nice white blouse and gray skirt. Very modest and presentable. She had on the slightest touches of make-up, something she rarely used, but enough to show that this was a special occasion. She was very pretty. At that moment Jakob would have said beautiful, because it was such a transformation from how tired and rushed she had looked less than an hour before.

"Oh, Rebecca!" Amalie exclaimed as Aubin gave a flirtatious whistle.

"Down, boy," Jakob said with a big smile as he got up from the chair. "That's my date you're whistling at!"

"Thomas, you be good at the movies," Rebecca instructed as she gave him a quick peck on the forehead. "We won't be too late," she added as Jakob escorted her to the door.

"Don't wait up," Jakob countermanded with a wink as he closed the door behind him.

There was the strangest little silence as Rebecca and Jakob left, something between Abby, Amalie, and Aubin. In Austria, they have an expression for when people are having a conversation and there is a sudden, unexpected silence in the midst of it. They say "an angel flew in the window." This pause was like that. In that instant, they all knew what the result of the evening would be—that everything they had built since arriving on their own in this strange land was about to change. They weren't sure how; they only knew things would be different. Thomas looked up at Aubin and then at his two grandmothers. "When do we eat?" he asked, and they all went back about their business and the small talk resumed.

It was only about seven o'clock as Jakob and Rebecca wandered down the sidewalks toward the ocean. It had been a beautiful day, and as the sun started to fall toward the horizon, everything was warm and calm.

"So . . . what do you think of Tel Aviv?" Rebecca asked as they strolled.

"The city?" he asked with surprise. He didn't think that would be the first question on Rebecca's mind. "It's ah . . . it takes some getting used to. Not like Europe."

"No, it's definitely not like Europe. I'll have to take you to Jerusalem. If you think Tel Aviv is different, Jerusalem will really surprise you."

"Well, I didn't mean different in that way . . . not exotic. Tel Aviv is put together in a strange way. It has no history. All these different people thrown together. Jerusalem would probably seem more familiar to me. Places I've heard of all my life."

"I see what you mean. When we first came here we were just happy to get out of Europe. We felt safe at last, like we could breathe. We just took it for what it was."

"I didn't say I didn't like it," Jakob added, now on the defensive. "I just said it was different."

It was an awkward start to their evening, and things didn't get much better as they made their way to the seashore. At one point, Jakob commented on a building with some unusual architectural feature, and Rebecca made an amusing remark about a group of children playing in the street, but other than that it was a long, quiet walk.

"There's a nice restaurant in that hotel," Rebecca said as they came to the beach, "but it's sort of expensive."

"That's fine," Jakob replied. "I can afford a special night."

"What's special about it?"

"You and me . . . that's all."

"I just thought of something funny."

"What?"

"You and me. We've known each other for all these years. What is it? Fifteen years now?"

"That sounds about—"

"All these years . . . we have a son together . . . and this is our first date!"

Jakob finally smiled. Rebecca smiled too. They had been out together many times back in Munich when they were teenagers, but back then they had only thought of themselves as friends.

Rebecca kept walking, but as she did, she turned away from the hotel she had pointed out to Jakob and headed for the shore. Jakob followed, not knowing what to make of it. She stopped a few feet short of the farthest reach of the gentle waves as they rushed toward her and then retreated just as quickly. Without a word, she sat down, taking in the giant canvas being painted before them as the sun came closer to the horizon and colorful ribbons spilled out across the sky. She brushed a few strands of hair away from her face that had been blown there by the gentle breeze coming in off the ocean. Jakob sat cross-legged next to her.

"What are we doing?" she finally asked.

"What do you mean?" Jakob countered.

"Why are you here?" she asked accusingly, as though she knew his dark ulterior motive and there was nothing for him to do but admit it.

"Why am I here?" he countered incredulously. "Where else would I be? There's nowhere else for me to go."

"Is that it? Just because you had nothing else? Or..."

"Or what?" Jakob prodded. "Say it. Ask it."

"For me? Me and Thomas?"

"Of course for you and Thomas."

"Of course?" she repeated with a damning pause, her hands outstretched in bewilderment, and then brushed back her hair, holding her head for an instant. "How can you say it like that?" she continued, starting with a whisper. "Is it really all that clear to you? After everything that's happened, you come back . . . I haven't seen you for almost three years. I didn't even know if you were alive. And you come back, and the most passionate thing you have to say to me is 'of course'!"

He reached for her face, thinking he could gently take her cheek in his hand, but she pulled away. "Don't!" she barked fiercely.

He tried to move closer and put his arm around her, but she pulled away again, rolling on her side. He rolled right along with her and it turned into a wrestling match as he took her in his arms. He thought he could hold her and force her to listen, but Rebecca slipped an arm out of his hold and slapped him sharply on the face. He turned away from the stinging slap and she pulled her other arm free and started hitting him, and then the tears came.

"You bastard! You damned bloody bastard!" she shouted as she pounded on him, taking him completely by surprise. He tried to deflect the blows as she continued. "How could you leave us there? How could you leave us like that!"

Jakob recovered and rose up on his knees, overpowering her and falling on her once he held her arms down. Rebecca was sobbing uncontrollably. She didn't want to cry. She had thought she could just tell him to leave her and Thomas alone if it came down to it. She could live without him. They could get by, just like they had done since they arrived in Palestine. She didn't need him. But all the bravado was gone now.

"You disappear . . . Last year we found out that Max was killed."

"What? How?"

"They took him to Dachau and he ended up in Auschwitz."

"Oh, Rebecca . . . I'm so sorry."

Jakob's cheek touched hers. They were both flushed and hot. Rebecca was shaking from the exertion of trying to fight him off.

"I'm sorry . . . ," he whispered in her ear. "I never should have left you."

It was more than she could take. She was prepared for the excuses. She was prepared for him to say he was leaving. She was prepared to tell him to go. All of that. She was prepared for everything . . . except that he would say he was sorry.

"I . . . I told myself I had to go. A voice in my head said it was the right thing to do, that I should sacrifice to . . ." He stopped and took a deep breath. "But it was all a lie."

He had to stop then. His throat tightened and he couldn't say anything more. It hurt him to see Rebecca like this. He let go of her and rolled onto his back in the sand. They both lay there side by side, looking up at the last bit of fading daylight. He had never meant to hurt her . . . or Thomas . . . Now it was all clear.

"I was afraid. And later, when I was in Dresden..."

"Dresden? You mean when it burned?"

"I had to leave Prague, and I was trying to go south. I was there, just outside the city, when it was bombed. It was so horrible. I saw a mother and her children . . . her clothes where smoldering. She had actually been on fire, and she just held her two children so tightly. She would have died for them."

He stopped again as he relived the moment. "That was when I knew I had to come here," he continued. "I don't know how to explain it very well. Before that, in Switzerland, I suppose it felt like everything was being forced on me. And then suddenly, watching that firestorm as though I was standing at the edge of hell, a witness as that woman fought her way out . . . I realized everything was being *given* to me."

He looked over at Rebecca, who was watching him intently as he told the story.

"I suppose it all sounds stupid to you. A mother never has questions like this. Only a father, an absent father . . . I guess you never had any questions, so you can't understand. I wish I could take it all back. I would give anything if I could change the past . . . but I can't."

He stopped talking and rolled onto his back again, staring up at the sky. After a moment he felt Rebecca's hand taking his.

"All those times when you said 'it's the war,' I got so angry with you . . . ," Rebecca said quietly. "I think that's it. The war just stole that piece of our lives. Like a children's picture puzzle. When that piece was taken, the rest just didn't fit like it should have. Doesn't that sound stupid? Selfish. Love and happiness doesn't mean much when everything is disappearing. Just survival. And now we don't know each other."

"You know what I think?" Jakob asked after considering everything Rebecca had said.

"Hmmn?" she murmured.

"I think you're thinking too much. I think we

have to take things the way they are at this moment and start from here. We can't change the past. And we can't let it swallow us up. We have to decide what we want to do now and let the rest of it go."

"That's ridiculous."

"Well . . . that's what I was thinking," Jakob countered half-heartedly in the face of Rebecca's dismissal.

"You know what I think?" Rebecca then asked.

"Hmmn?" Jakob grunted.

"I think I'm hungry."

"Hungry?" Jakob repeated as he looked at her. "I know a nice restaurant in a hotel nearby. A friend pointed it out."

"You don't say?" Rebecca said as she stood up and brushed the sand from her blouse and skirt. "That sounds good."

They hadn't walked more than a few steps when Rebecca casually asked, "Should we get married?"

Jakob laughed.

"You're right," she agreed. "It is funny."

"It's not that. It's the timing. Ten minutes ago you were beating the hell out of me."

"I know why people marry young," she continued as though she hadn't heard him. "They're too stupid to know any better. They have all these illusions about love and happiness. I don't think I have any illusions left."

"When I think about love, it's always your face that comes to mind," Jakob said, stopping to answer her profound assertion. "When I think about getting married . . . it's to you. It's always you. I don't know what you expect of love, but that's as close as I've ever come. Maybe I shouldn't say this, but the truth is that there have been other women. But you're a part of me, Rebecca. You always have been. I kept trying to find you again."

She wasn't sure if she believed him. She was embarrassed when he said it and turned away.

"There are more of us than you think," he continued as he started walking again. "People whose lives were interrupted, those years just stolen out of the middle somewhere. We can't pretend all those things never happened, but now we have a chance to put it back together. It's not a fairy tale, but . . ."

His thought just trailed off and they continued on to the restaurant. When they were seated at their table, the conversation turned to memories of Munich. They conjured up the names of friends neither had thought of for years and stories from the good times before the war. They drank some wine and had a very respectable meal, and afterward they ended up back on the beach under a star-filled sky. They talked for hours, and suddenly Rebecca said she had to get home to bed so she could get to work the next morning.

CHAPTER 5

Even as the Second World War was raging in Europe, plans were being made to find some way to ensure world peace when the fighting ended. Once again, as with the League of Nations after the First World War, the proposed answer was an international forum wherein disputes could be resolved before they evolved into larger conflicts.

The refusal of certain key nations such as the United States to become members of the League of Nations proved to be a fatal flaw of that assembly. Without the backing of the major powers, there was no force behind League resolutions. Nations censured by the League for violating its code of conduct would simply withdraw from the League and that would be the end of it.

But the United Nations was carefully constructed, with the Security Council made up of the so-called "Super Powers" and other major nations. It was seen as a way to ensure the presence of influential countries, but at the same time, with the veto power afforded members of the Security Council, it also ensured constant, frustrating deadlocks.

One of the early challenges for the United Nations was the proposal to end the British mandate in the Middle East and partition Palestine into an Arab zone and a Jewish zone. The problem was studied again and again, with various proposals offered for a peaceful solution, as Jewish agencies shamelessly played on the guilt of the world, holding up the Holocaust as the definitive reason for such a partition. It was a game of politics that the Yishuv was determined to win at any cost, because they viewed it as a matter of life and death. If it meant "exploiting" Jewish children by lining them up as the newsreel cameras clattered away, extending their little arms so that the world could see how the Nazis had tattooed them with numbers as they readied them for slaughter, then so be it. They knew they had to put a human face on the question of partition. Those who might be able to reject the abstract political idea of creating a new country based on a centuries-old claim of citizenship might not be so ready to deny a "safe home" to children who had only barely managed to escape a Nazi gas chamber. But for the survivors of European Jewry, never had it been so clear that the end justified the means.

Some naïve diplomats believed Palestine to be somewhat like an orange: peel off the skin of the British mandate and then you could separate the Jewish segments from the Arab segments, and that was all there was to it. In truth, of course, neither the Jews nor the Arabs were willing to compromise on the partitioning of Palestine. And the British, barely managing to keep some semblance of order, wanted to wash their hands of the whole matter as the international press increasingly characterized them, not as peacemakers, but as the villains who would send pathetic concentration camp survivors to detention camps when they attempted to enter Palestine.

Consequently the birth of Israel was not to be a peaceful transfer of authority, as prescribed by the UN, but rather a bloody, butchered operation, as open warfare between Arabs and Jews broke out on November 29, 1947, with the announcement of the UN agreement to partition the country.

Things developed quickly between Jakob and Rebecca in the months following that night on the beach. To understand what happened, you have to take into account the times in which they were living. They decided to move in together. Even though it was 1947, it isn't as strange as it sounds. What with Thomas and all, people just assumed they were married. And yet they were still cautious about each other. With their history, jumping into marriage just didn't seem right. It wouldn't have been fair to either of them. So when Jakob said that he had found a big apartment, and that Thomas could have his own room if Rebecca moved in with him, she agreed. It was a matter of convenience. Amalie and Abby were at the point where they could afford the rent for their apartment by themselves, so it wasn't a hardship to have Rebecca and Thomas move out, except on an emotional level.

On an emotional level, it was a major change for everyone. Thomas, for example, had been like a little prince in that home with his mother and two grandmothers. Now he was suddenly in a new apartment with a real father to replace the one he had imagined for so long.

Jakob, Rebecca, and Thomas all had to come to grips with the reality of their new lives in the face of what they had each imagined in one way or another since that moment of promise in Switzerland. They had each nurtured some fantasy of what it would be like when the war was over and they could live a normal life. But just as it should have, the façade broke down after the first month. The first argument was about how Jakob had found the apartment on his own. It was a great surprise, and Rebecca was glad to move at that point, but the seed festered for weeks until she finally spoke up. There was shouting and some tears, but most important of all, they found that the world didn't end. Rebecca found that Jakob didn't expect her to be a silent, empty-headed maid, and Jakob found that even though his intentions were good, it was more important to talk to her. And to listen.

And Jakob had to learn that Thomas wasn't just a little copy of himself. He also began to realize that being with him now didn't make up for all the time before. Thomas could be sad and quiet at times, and Jakob was surprised to find that he couldn't break through to him then. Jakob had no idea in the beginning what kind of work lay ahead. And then at other times, Thomas would run up to Jakob and leap into his arms, wrapping his legs around him with wonderful, adoring abandon.

But there was more positive than negative. It was also a wonderful time of discovering each other. If it wasn't happening the way they had imagined in their fantasies, at least they were coming together as a family.

"Bubbaaaahhh!" Thomas called as he rushed in and wrapped his arms around Amalie.

"Ohhh!" Amalie said as she returned the hug. "How is my little darling today?"

"I'm good."

"And school?"

"School is almost done."

"And that makes you happy?" Amalie asked as she touched her nose to his while still holding him in her arms.

"Yes it does. I get to spend more time with Tateh. He says we'll go to Jerusalem next month."

"Jerusalem? What for?" she asked as she let him go.

"He has to work there, and he said I could come with."

Jakob walked in just then and tousled Thomas's hair as he gave his mother a peck on the cheek.

"I'm going to see if Avram is home," Thomas said as he went out the door.

Jakob went to the stove and peeked into the soup kettle while Amalie finished up in the kitchen. "That looks like a lot for just you and Abby," Jakob commented as he stirred the soup and took a taste from the wooden spoon.

"Myra and Leonard are coming over. I cook the dinner, they bring some wine and cards, and we make a night of it."

"Myra and Leonard?"

"They live down the block. They're from Berlin. They've lived here for years."

"Before the war?"

"Goodness, yes. They were here before the Great War."

"Oh, real pioneers, eh?"

"Yes, they lived on a kibbutz for a while. Then Leonard finally bought a little shop here in Tel Aviv. He's a butcher."

"A shochet?"

"No, just a butcher, but let me tell you a secret, my son . . . it's a good thing to have a butcher as a friend. When we were living off little more than the day-old bread Rebecca brought home from work, it was really something for Myra and Leonard to bring along a package of stew meat or a nice chicken."

"Important friends . . ."

"It's not a bad thing to be friends with a butcher," she repeated, "and they were always so good about it. It never felt like charity. Remember how we used to take a cake or flowers whenever we visited friends in Munich? It was just like that."

Jakob burst out laughing.

"What's so funny?"

"I was just thinking of Mrs. Heggenburger back in Munich. That stuck-up lady who hired father to do the plans for her house and then invited us to dinner. Imagine if we had showed up for dinner at her house and dropped a dressed chicken on her mahogany dining table! She would have had a heart attack!"

"Mrs. Heggenburger? I haven't thought of her in years. Now you're just making fun of me."

"No, no . . . I know what you're saying. It just struck me as funny."

There was an awkward silence as Jakob looked over the apartment and Amalie gave the soup a good stirring.

"So . . . what is it?" she finally asked. "Are you going to tell me, or do I have to guess?"

"What?"

"You never stop in for nothing. What is it? Do you need money?"

"Money? When have I ever asked you for money?"

"There's always a first time," she said dryly, trying to be funny.

Jakob just smiled and shook his head. "You think you know me so well . . ."

"Well, I know when you have something to tell me."

"You really take the fun out of things."

"Take the fun out of things? Are you saying I'm not a fun person? Ask my friends, they'll tell you. 'That Amalie Stein, she's a riot!' they say. 'She makes me laugh so hard I wet myself!'"

"Fine, fine . . . you're a fun person."

"So out with it. What's the news?"

"We're pregnant . . . well, Rebecca's pregnant . . . We're going to have a baby. *Another* baby."

"Pregnant? My God!" she exclaimed as she held a hand to her mouth, but then in the next breath, as though at the end of her rope, she blurted out, "Why won't you get—"

"Married?" Jakob interjected, cutting her off. "Yes, Mother, we're getting married. We've been talking about it, and this is . . . well, it's the deciding factor."

"The deciding factor? You make it sound like a business deal."

"No, no. I mean we had already decided to get married. We've been in the new apartment for months now, and things . . . things are good. We just weren't sure when to get married. Now we're just going to do it a bit sooner."

"This is a good thing, Jakob. You and Rebecca are good for each other, and you need a wife. And that son of yours . . . he worships the ground you walk on. You need to take on some responsibilities and settle down."

"He calls me Tateh," Jakob said with a smile and a

chuckle, as though Thomas had made up the name on his own.

"I've heard."

"He's got a friend in Hebrew class from the Ukraine, and that's what he calls his father . . ." Jakob paused for a moment as he looked out the window. "I didn't know it would be like this," he continued as his voice filled with emotion.

"A boy loves his father," Amalie said with a smile as she put an arm around her son's shoulder.

"Sometimes it scares me. I'm afraid I'll let him down. And sometimes it's so right."

"I'm very fond of Rebecca. You learn a lot about somebody when you go through hard times together. She's a good person."

"And you like Thomas a little, too, don't you?" Jakob asked with a smile.

"What? He's just my reason for living, that's all."

"How is work going?"

"Not too bad, but there are rumors going around that the British are going to close us down."

"What?"

"They say that we were needed during the war when we were making bullets, but now we're just upsetting the economy in the area because there are too many Jewish businesses."

"That's ridiculous. Where did you hear that?"

"I work in the office. Kiva said she heard that's what they told Mr. Mengershausen, the owner. He's employed a lot of illegal Jews at the plant, and the British want to punish him as an example to others."

"I don't understand why they can't see what we..."

"Don't be naïve, Jakob. It's oil. England must have

oil, and the Arabs control it. They have to be hard on the Jews or the Arabs will cut off the oil."

"I know. I'm not naïve. I'm just foolish enough to think that human lives should count for something. Why keep being so damn harsh when at the same time they're putting the mandate before the UN so they can wash their hands of it?"

"They don't want to wash their hands of us," Amalie stated plainly. "Politics is an interesting world. You can't just look at what they say. You have to look down the road. It's a game of chess. The British Empire is disintegrating. They're almost certainly going to lose India. The world is shrinking for them. They're like a sad old man who's about to lose everything and desperately grabs for everything he can get. I think they're putting it before the United Nations because they don't believe the UN can come up with a better answer, and so the mandate will be reaffirmed. If that happens, they'll feel free to do whatever they like."

"I can't believe the United Nations can't come up with something better than the British mandate."

"Don't be too surprised. The Jews have been left out in the cold too many times over the past four thousand years to be surprised by another disappointment. Don't ever tell anyone I said it, but I'm beginning to think the Irgun and the other extremists may have the right idea."

"You don't mean that!"

"I'm afraid it might come down to that. We can't be nice little Jews waiting for the world to hand us something. We have to fight for it."

"My God, Mother. I never thought I'd hear *you* say

something like that."

"Well, I'm not saying I'm for it. I'm just saying I'm afraid that's what it will take. But it scares me too. If we have a state born of terrorism, what will we bring down on ourselves?

"You know . . . I don't think these are the sort of talks my friends have with their mothers."

Amalie broke into a smile and laughed. "Not exactly your image of a sweet old grandmother?"

"You sound like you're getting ready to take over the Yishuv."

"I don't think politics are for me. Sam Frieder once told me, 'Politics is the art of compromise.' I don't think I'd do too well."

"Napoleon didn't compromise either, and look how far he got."

"Oh, so now you think I'm another Napoleon!"

"Well, if the funny hat fits . . ."

"Enough of that. So why are you going to Jerusalem?"

"There's a lawyer there. He has an office here in Tel Aviv, and I'm going to see if he'll hire me."

"But you don't have your degree."

"A friend told me I might be able to work in the office while finishing my degree."

"That would be wonderful. So . . . why are you *really* going to Jerusalem?"

"You know I can't tell you. You don't seem to understand that the Haganah is supposed to be a *secret* army."

"Zei nit kain Golem!"

"Dear God!" Jakob exclaimed, rolling his eyes and laughing. "Now you're speaking Yiddish?"

"Don't make fun. I like it. It's a very colorful language. Don't change the subject. What's in Jerusalem?"

"A law office that might . . ."

Oh, so David Ben Gurion won't let you tell your own mother?"

"Ben Gurion isn't in charge of . . . Wait a minute. How do I know you're not a British spy?"

"If I were, would I tell you?" Amalie replied coyly.

"That's it. Not another word. I've delivered my news, and now I'll gather up my son and leave."

"Right. Just go, you rotten son," she said as Jakob gave her another peck on the cheek, but she reached up and took his face in her hands as she suddenly got serious. "Whatever it is," she continued, "be careful."

"I'm always careful. I wouldn't take Thomas with me if I thought there was any danger. You know that."

"Of course!" she exclaimed with a comical slap to her head. "Oh!" she continued. "I forgot to tell you. I got a letter from Eleonore today."

"A letter from Aunt Eleonore? Do you know how long it's been since I've gotten a letter?"

"Well, dear, we have been living in the same place for three years now. I sent a letter to Eleonore as soon as we landed."

"But how did you . . . ?" Jakob started, but then cut himself off. "Oh, Louis's university!"

"Of course. Everyone is fine. She was saying they would come here one of these days. But of course, she never will. They lived in Vienna for years without ever visiting us in Munich. It's a lot farther from

England to Palestine than from Vienna to Munich! But then again, she said it was Father who really wanted to . . ."

"Grandfather Ethan is still alive . . . ," Jakob said with relief in his voice. It was the question he hadn't wanted to ask.

"Oh, Jakob . . . it never occurred to me that you didn't know. How stupid of me. Yes, Father is fine. Eleonore and Louis found him soon after they arrived in England, still living in that cottage in Ipswich."

"I just had an idea," Jakob said brightly. "If they do close down the factory, you should take some time and go to England to see Grandfather."

Amalie laughed out loud. "You do come up with the most ridiculous . . . If I lose my job, how could I afford a trip like that?"

"I've got a little extra money. I could pay for it."

"Don't be silly. You've got a family now. You can't throw your money away like . . . And what about Abby?"

"Abby will be fine. How old is Grandfather now?"

"What?"

"How old? What is he? Seventy something?"

"Let me see," she said with a sigh as she calmed down. "Seventy . . . seventy-six! My God, he's going to be seventy-six this year."

"I think you should go. You'll just have to believe me that I can afford it. Don't ask questions . . . just go."

"Alone?"

"No. You'll take someone with you."

"Aubin," she said as a thought suddenly struck

her.

"Aubin?"

"We were just talking the other day. He wants to find out if somehow his brother survived the war."

"How did they get separated?"

"He told us his brother was taken away with others from an orphanage while Aubin hid in some nearby woods."

"A younger brother, or older?"

"Younger. His name is Etienne. He was about five years old, I think."

"That doesn't sound good. Too young to work . . . If he went east . . ."

"I told him that."

"You did?" Jakob asked with surprise, not expecting her to be so straightforward in such a difficult matter.

"Of course I did. I thought it would be kinder in the long run. We've taken care of Aubin . . . loved him for years now. I felt like his mother telling him. Should I lie to him and have him go off searching?"

"Well . . . what are you suggesting now? How long would it take to try to find him? He could be anywhere."

"Aubin has an aunt . . . She was the one who put them in the orphanage to keep them safe. We could try to find her. She might know what happened to his brother."

"So you'll go?"

"If they close the factory . . ."

"I think you should go regardless."

"Just take off?"

"Call it business. Call it a holiday if you want.

Don't let the chance slip by. I hate to bring it up, but what if Grandfather were to die and you never got to see—"

"Jakob!"

"I'm not saying it to upset you! I just think it would mean so much to you to see him, them, again. You could see Aunt Eleonore and Louis and the girls.

"When?"

"Right after I get back from Jerusalem. About two weeks. That will give you time to make arrangements."

Amalie stared at him for a moment, perhaps in disbelief, as she considered that it could actually happen, and then she smiled. "I'll write Eleonore a letter now."

JUST AS AMALIE had suspected, the appointment with the lawyer was just a cover story for Jakob while he did some Haganah business. He was supposed to get information about a police station on the Jaffa Road near the old walled city. He had been keeping a low profile since arriving in Palestine, so Martin and the others felt he was a safe choice for a mission like this.

The British had armed Jewish militias in Palestine during the war when it appeared the Germans might continue their advance through Egypt and invade the Middle East, but when the German threat ended in 1943, Jewish defense groups were ordered to stand down. The Yishuv had lobbied the British government to form a Jewish brigade from the outset of the war, but there was strong resistance from the British Foreign Office. Many British officials felt that the threat posed by the presence of a trained Jewish military force in Palestine after the war far outweighed any benefit a Jewish brigade might provide during the war. Nonetheless, His Majesty's Jewish Brigade was formed in 1944. When the Jewish Brigade was sent home soon after the war, all Jewish troops and militia units were ordered to turn over their guns just as Arab violence was rising in response to renewed talks of partitioning Palestine to form a Jewish homeland. And just as British officials had feared, members of the Jewish Brigade joined the Haganah on their return to Palestine and used their talents against the British mandate.

One of the most pressing concerns of the Haganah units was the acquisition of guns, not only for their current fight against the British, but more important, to prepare for what might be an all-out war waged by the Arabs when a Jewish state was declared.

The Haganah could buy guns through the lucrative black market dealing in weapons "salvaged" from battlegrounds across North Africa, but funds were very limited. Money was being donated to the Yishuv from around the world, most notably from American Jews, but it wasn't enough, and the British did what they could to stop it. When the Irgun kidnapped and hanged two British soldiers in response to the British executions of Jewish prisoners found guilty of terrorism, the British Foreign Office issued a statement to the effect that the rope used by the Irgun had been bought with money donated by American Jews. Not in those exact words, though. It was worded in such a way as to say that the money naïvely donated by kind-hearted Americans to help feed Jewish refugees was actually being used to buy weapons for terrorist organizations in Palestine.

Another way for the Haganah to get guns was to stage raids on British storehouses and take back the weapons that had been in the hands of Jewish soldiers just a few months before.

Jakob brought Thomas along with him on his trip so that he would look like a tourist. Jakob had never had what one would call "Semitic features," and so he wouldn't raise much suspicion as he and Thomas slowly wandered down the Jaffa Road from the Ron Hotel to the Jaffa Gate, casually passing the British police station twice a day.

And that was all there was to it for Jakob—he and his son strolling back and forth, having lunch nearby on two occasions. Jakob was only supposed to see how many soldiers and police officers were there at any given time, when the back entrance was used, and how secure the building was. It might seem a waste of Jakob's talents, but he knew it was part of his training.

On the last day before they returned home, Jakob and Thomas were standing outside the walled city.

"That's where we saw the smoke," Thomas said.

"Smoke? What smoke?"

"Mama and I were here before. We were standing over there," he said, pointing to a spot a few meters down the hill. "There was a big boom and then black smoke over there."

Jakob didn't know that his son was talking about the King David Hotel, but he suddenly realized that

Thomas had never known a life without guns and
bombs going off around him. He was born in the
second month of the war, and now at eight years old
in Palestine, it didn't look like peace would be coming any time soon.

Their return trip to Tel Aviv was uneventful. The
raid on the police station by a half dozen Haganah
men that resulted from Jakob's "research" was little
more than a footnote in the newspapers, since no
one got hurt and they only managed to get a dozen
rifles and some ammunition.

Jakob stopped by Amalie's apartment a few days
later to see how she was doing, and after greeting
him with a hug and kiss, she told him she was out of
work.

"They did it," she said with a sigh. "The British
closed the factory."

"The British? How did the British close the factory?"

"I don't know. I just know that's what I heard. I
worked in the office, and I know they were making
money. It's only closing because it's Jewish-owned."

"Now you're starting to sound paranoid."

"That's the talk going around. I didn't make it
up."

"Well, have you thought about the trip we talked
about before I went to Jerusalem?"

"I don't know . . ."

"Don't think about it. Just do it. If you keep thinking about it, you'll keep coming up with reasons not
to go."

"I suppose you're right. I mentioned it to Aubin.
He seemed apprehensive, but he said if I wanted to

go, he would go too."

"Apprehensive? Why?"

"I'm not sure. Maybe just memories of the war."

"Doesn't he want to see that aunt you talked about?"

"He doesn't know if she's alive. Maybe he doesn't want to go and find out she's dead."

"He'd rather go on not knowing whether she's dead or alive?"

"I know it doesn't make sense, but . . ."

"Well, you know how I feel about it. I think you should go. I think it would be good for you. And probably for Aubin too."

It took a bit more convincing, but Amalie finally agreed to make the trip, and Aubin kept his word. A few weeks later, in the first week of October, they were waving good-bye from the railing of a ship bound for Greece. From Greece, they would land at Bari in southern Italy and take a train to Rome, then from Rome to Paris. From Paris, they planned on going to Nancy, where Aubin would see if his Aunt Claire still lived in the same house. They would only spend one night in Nancy before going on to Calais, where they would take a ferry to Dover, and then on to Nottingham University, about three hours north of London, where Louis taught botany. It was Aubin who insisted they would only spend one night in Nancy before going on to England. He said they could stop back on their way home if he had anything else to do there. It sounded confusing to Amalie, and she suggested they just divide the time, spending three days in England and three days in Nancy, but Aubin insisted and she finally agreed.

She felt that whatever his reasons, it was something he would have to work out himself.

Aubin was not a good traveling companion. Not for Amalie, at least. He was very quiet as they traveled, while she, on the other hand, was excited and wanted to talk. He would sleep endlessly. Whenever she tried to talk to him as they sat across from each other in a train compartment, he would stare out the window and reply in monosyllables. They reserved beds in a sleeper car on a night train from Rome to Paris.

The second-class sleeper coach had four bunks, and Amalie and Aubin found themselves sharing the coach with two young men. One was an American serviceman on leave, the other an Italian who appeared to be a student, although a bit old for a university, perhaps twenty-six. He was probably one of countless young men whose education had been interrupted by the war and were now trying to put their lives back together. The American was a clean-cut young man from some large city in Texas who had been drafted a month after his high school graduation.

Aubin was already lying in one of the lower bunks with his face to the wall and Amalie was sitting on the other lower when their two roommates came in, the Italian first, the American following a moment later. As the American threw his bag up onto a shelf, the Italian introduced himself in French, saying his name was Matteo Guscetti. It was the most god-awful butchering of the French language Amalie had ever heard. She knew she had a German accent when she spoke French, but it was subtle. There was nothing subtle about Matteo's rendering. And then the American introduced himself as Dan Lofgren, also in French, but with a heavy Texas accent that made Matteo sound like a native Parisian. Amalie was polite, but she didn't say much as a discussion began to develop in which Matteo proudly stated that he had taught himself French and Dan said that was quite a coincidence as he, too, had learned French on his own. It was a fascinating exchange as Amalie strained to catch any semblance of what she knew as French from their conversation, which was quickly becoming animated as it developed into other areas and Dan and Matteo tried desperately to make themselves understood.

Out of the corner of her eye, Amalie noticed that something seemed to be wrong with Aubin. He was shaking, and it appeared that he was crying. She started to get up to see what was wrong when he suddenly got up and, hiding his face, ran from the compartment. She followed him out, calling his name. He kept going until he got to the end of the hallway and stopped in the passageway between the cars. When Amalie caught up with him, he was leaning against the wall, his faced buried in his arms. She put her hand on his shoulder.

She had to speak loudly in the passageway to be heard over the sound of rushing wind and the staccato click-clack of the wheels against the rails.

"Aubin . . . what is it? What's wrong?"

When he turned to face her, she realized he wasn't crying at all, but laughing!

"Did you hear them them talk? It was so funny, I couldn't stay there anymore. I would have embarrassed them!"

Amalie began to laugh too. It was the first time Aubin had smiled since they started the trip, much less laughed out loud.

"I couldn't understand a word they were saying at the end," he continued, wiping away the tears that had come from laughing so hard.

"I thought something was wrong," Amalie said as she laughed along. "I thought you were crying."

Their laughter subsided and Amalie looked up into Aubin's eyes. "*Is* there something wrong? You haven't been yourself."

"I know . . . I guess it's coming back to France. Seeing Aunt Claire. The time before we left was so bad. I never told you everything."

"You don't have to if you don't want to."

"I've got to tell someone," he said quietly, but he was obviously becoming agitated. "I turned Jews in to the Gestapo!"

Amalie was startled by the unsolicited confession, but before she could respond, the door from the next car burst open and a man in uniform appeared. It startled them both, giving them the eerie sensation that the authorities had been listening, and now that Aubin had told his dark secret, they were there to arrest him. In truth, however, it was just the conductor checking tickets.

Once the other door had slammed shut after the conductor stamped their tickets and moved on, Aubin nearly collapsed. "My God, I thought he heard me."

"So did I . . ."

She was waiting for Aubin to continue when the

train went into a curve and they were jostled about a bit, and Aubin reached out to steady her.

"Do you remember when we left Lyon . . . the man who attacked us?"

"Yes, I'll never forget Sam Frieder swinging that shovel!"

"Well, that was René," Aubin said as he started to tear up. "I was supposed to bring people to him."

"People?"

"Jews. I would be out on the street, and if I saw someone who looked . . ."

"How did you ever get started doing that?" Amalie asked incredulously, knowing that Aubin was only twelve or thirteen years old at the time.

"I got caught without any papers. They took me to the police, and this Gestapo man slapped me around. He said either I helped them or they'd send me to Drancy."

"Aubin, you were just a boy. They used you!"

"I can still see . . . ," he began, and then the tears really started to come. "There was this family. They had a little girl, and I can still see her face. They told me I was helping them."

"Don't do this to yourself," Amalie said firmly as she started crying too, seeing how much pain Aubin was in. "Would you rather it were you who had died?"

"I think about that."

Amalie couldn't help but throw her arms around him. He was so skinny for his seventeen years that her arms easily went completely around him. "We all had to fight to stay alive," she said into his ear. "And   it wasn't always . . . It wasn't always fair, but you can't look back on it now and say it was wrong. We did what we had to do."

Once again, they didn't say anything, but just held each other.

"You'll come with me when I see Aunt Claire?"

"Of course I will."

"There's something else I didn't tell you."

"What?" Amalie asked, not sure she wanted to hear it. It was as though Aubin was suddenly testing her after all this time. What other terrible secret could he have?

"I killed my brother," he choked out.

Amalie didn't let go, but she did pull back enough to look Aubin in the face.

"Etienne . . . My mother died in childbirth . . ."

"I know. You told me."

"I always blamed him for my mother's death."

"But you said the Nazis took him with the other children."

"They did. But just before that I wished he was dead. That morning . . . when the trucks came . . . I knew what it was. I don't know how, but I knew I had to run away. I could have gotten Etienne. I could have gone upstairs and gotten him . . . taken him with me to the woods. But I didn't. I just ran for the door to save myself!"

"Oh, my little one! You don't know that! You think back on it now after all these years, and you think you know. But everything happens in a moment. If you had gone for him, you probably would both have been caught. You don't even know for sure that he's dead. Aubin . . . you have to find some way to forgive yourself. If your brother is dead, it's because an army of German soldiers came here with orders to kill him, that innocent little boy. *They* killed him, not you. You were just a boy yourself, and you couldn't stop the whole German army."

That was enough. Aubin was sobbing in Amalie's arms. The train conductor came back through and passed by them without a look, and they paid him no notice.

"Let's just take it as it comes," Amalie finally said as she fished a handkerchief out of her coat pocket and wiped her eyes, then wiped Aubin's cheeks in true motherly fashion. "We'll go to Nancy and see if we can find your aunt and then start from there."

When they had composed themselves, Amalie and Aubin returned to their compartment, where Matteo and Dan were still deep in conversation. As he and Amalie prepared to climb into their bunks, Aubin managed to smile at her as the cacophony of accents filled the compartment. Before long, Matteo and Dan bid each other good night and they all drifted off to sleep.

Amalie and Aubin were traveling light, with only one small suitcase apiece, so it was a simple matter to catch the next train to Nancy the following morning. Aubin was calm after the cathartic encounter with Amalie in the passageway the night before. The first thing they did after arriving in Nancy was to find a cheap hotel where they could leave their bags.

Nancy is part of France's most notable iron mining and industrial area. After taking a bus to a rather run-down part of the city, Amalie let Aubin take the lead as they walked a short way, stopping in front of a pretty little house in the middle of the block.

"This is where she lived the last time I saw my aunt."

"Well? Are you going to the door?"

Aubin looked at her with a forced smile, then started up the narrow sidewalk with Amalie close behind. His knock on the door was rather timid. After they waited a moment without getting a response, he gave Amalie a sheepish look that suggested, "Nobody's home. Let's go!" But Amalie stepped in and gave a much firmer knock, followed by a grunt and nod of her head, as if to say, "Now *that's* the way you knock on a door."

Finally, they heard the sounds of someone moving about inside and then undoing the lock.

"Yes?" asked the pleasant-faced woman of about forty who answered the door. Giving Aubin only a quick glance, she looked at Amalie and continued, "I'm sorry, but if you're collecting for charity . . ." Just then a strange look crossed her face as she stopped in mid-sentence and looked at Aubin again.

"Aunt Claire . . ."

"Dear God! Is it you? Is it . . ." She moved toward him and reached out to touch his face. "Aubin?" She whispered his name as if she were afraid to say it, as though he might disappear if she said it out loud.

"It's me, Aunt Claire," he finally said as he embraced her.

"How? Where have you been? They said all the children were taken. They said you were dead."

"I hid in the woods. I made my way to Lyon."

"Lyon? Why didn't you come here?"

"I thought you didn't want us. I thought that was

why you sent us away."

"Didn't want you! I sent you there to save your lives! To keep you safe!"

"I know that now. I know. But I was just a child. I..."

"Madame," Amalie interrupted. "May we go inside?"

"Oh! Yes, of course," Claire agreed as she opened the door to them. "Uh," she continued hesitantly, "we haven't . . ."

"Oh, this is Amalie, Aunt Claire. Amalie Stein."

"We found Aubin in Lyon," Amalie explained. "He came with us to Palestine."

"Palestine? You've been to Palestine?"

"Yes, we took him with us," Amalie answered for Aubin.

"Took him with?"

"Virgil . . . ," Aubin said to Amalie in bittersweet recollection, and then continued as he addressed Claire. "He was their guide. He insisted I go with Amalie and her family."

"Just like that? Out of the blue?"

"Virgil had lived on the streets as a boy. I guess that's why he wanted to help me."

"What about Etienne?"

Aubin stopped for a moment, and Amalie was worried what he might say after their conversation the previous night.

"He didn't . . . I couldn't get to him," Aubin explained with a tremendous sadness in his voice. "He was taken with the others. I don't know if he's dead or alive."

"They told me that all the children were taken from the orphanage and sent to Drancy. The authorities told me they went to Auschwitz from there, that there was no hope. I didn't know what else to do."

"You couldn't have known," Amalie offered, trying to comfort her.

At that moment none of them knew what to say to each other—Amalie because she felt like an outsider, Aubin because he had never considered what it would mean if he did in fact find Claire alive and well, and Claire because she was still in shock from the surprise.

"What are your plans?" Claire finally asked.

"We are on our way to England," Amalie replied. "Aubin came along as an escort. He didn't know if he would be able to find you. He just assumed something terrible had happened."

"Terrible? No. We made it through the same as most others. There wasn't a lot of fighting here."

"We?" Aubin asked.

"Oh, I got married... it was right after the war... to Michel. I knew him before the war. He was always so kind. He helped me when I sent you and Etienne to ...," Clair began, but then she started to cry as she tried desperately to explain. "We thought we were saving your lives, Aubin. Please tell me you forgive me. We thought you were out of harm's way in the mountains at the children's colony."

"I do, Aunt Claire," he said as he moved to her side and knelt by the chair where she sat, putting a comforting hand on her shoulder. "I know now. It's very clear to me. Like Amalie was telling me just last night, we can't blame ourselves for what the Germans did."

They stayed like that for a moment in silence. "I

didn't come here to accuse you of anything," he continued. "I came because you're the only family I know. I came to see if you knew anything about Etienne.

"I don't know anything for certain. I've been told that I should assume he's dead. There just wasn't much hope for a child on his own at Auschwitz." Just then Claire's demeanor changed completely. "Oh! The money!"

"Money?"

"It wasn't that much . . . a few thousand francs. Your grandparents gave it to your mother for your education. She put it in a Swiss bank. Before your mother died she told me to give it to you when you turned sixteen. When I thought you were both gone . . . well, I went to Switzerland, to the bank, and tried to get it. The accounts are in your names, so they said I had to have a death certificate! I told them that the Germans weren't in the habit of giving out death certificates from the camps, and they said they were sorry, but there was nothing they could do to help me!"

"Death certificates?" Amalie asked incredulously.

"Yes. That's what they said."

"So the bank ends up keeping the money if the family can't get a death certificate?"

"I suppose . . ."

Amalie just shook her head in disbelief.

After they talked for a while longer, Claire invited them to dinner. They met Michel when he came home from work about an hour later. Most of the conversation that evening was between Aubin and Claire as she told him about his family. He had probably heard some of it before, but he was younger than twelve at the time, and children rarely pay attention to such details at that age. It seems Claire was not his only living relative. She was the sister of Aubin's father, and they had a brother who had moved to Italy years before. Aubin also had family on his mother's side who had managed to emigrate to America before the war. Aubin's mother would have gone, too, but his father was already in the army and she wouldn't leave him.

After dinner Aubin and Amalie returned to their hotel, since Claire's house was far too small to accommodate guests. Aubin assured Claire that he would stop and see her on their way back from England. He also asked if she knew what kind of papers he would need to get the money from the Swiss bank.

When Amalie and Aubin continued their journey to England the next day, Aubin's mood had changed dramatically. He and Amalie talked constantly on the train, the ferry, and then the English trains. They talked about his family, trying to recall what Claire had said, and then they talked about Amalie's family. She told Aubin about her sister Eleonore and how she had hated her at times as a child, and about their mother's death. Aubin was profoundly affected by it all. His past—the guilt he felt—had been so terrible that he had closed off those memories and never talked about them because he thought he was uniquely evil. He thought if he told anyone, they would know what a terrible human being he was. And now he began to wonder about all those things. He was beginning to think it was the time, the situation, that had made it all terrible. He was beginning to think that he wasn't so unusual.

Soon it was Amalie's turn to be nervous as she faced her door to the past. Although she certainly didn't have anything as ominous to face as Aubin had, still it had been such a long time. The door opened, and there was Louis's round face filled with a smile so big it hardly fit. Eleonore was soon right beside him, talking nonstop as she escorted Amalie and Aubin into the house. Their daughters, Sophie and Rachel, were also there awaiting Amalie's arrival. Sophie, the eldest at twenty, had already married an American soldier and had a three-month-old baby. And then Ethan came downstairs. There were tears in his eyes as he embraced the daughter he hadn't seen for so long. Amalie was surprised to see that he was wearing a yarmulke, but Eleonore had warned her that he was much more religious than he had ever been when they were children.

The conversation for the rest of the day and that evening was loud and unceasing. Like waves rolling one after another on the shore, one topic would fade into the next and the next, and so on. The baby, Louis's work, Ethan's work, Sophie's husband, Aubin and his aunt, Jakob and Rebecca getting married, and on and on.

Amalie was surprised by how well it all went. She and Eleonore not only didn't argue, they were actually friendly. Time had changed them both for the better. The three days went by so quickly Amalie could hardly believe it. But on the last day, Aubin surprised her.

"We should stay a few more days."

"What? But what about your aunt? I thought you wanted to see what you could find about Etienne."

"I know. I think it's going to take longer than a couple of days."

"Well, I don't think we can afford much more than. . ."

"I don't think I'm going back."

"What?"

"I don't think I'm going back to Palestine."

"What?" she repeated in disbelief.

"I . . . If I get that money my mother left, I can go to Poland. I have to look for Etienne. I have to know one way or the other."

Amalie's heart sank. She knew in her heart that Etienne was dead. She knew it, but she couldn't say that to Aubin. She thought he had come to terms with that in the past few days, but now she saw it clearly. He had been afraid to even think about it, and now that he was past that, he had to cling to the hope, however small, that Etienne had survived.

She knew she couldn't change Aubin's mind, so she just agreed that they should stay in Nottingham a few more days. And then something even more shocking came up the next day. When Amalie told everyone that Aubin was going to stay in France, Ethan announced that he wanted to go back to Palestine with Amalie. Amalie, Louis, and Eleonore laughed at the idea, saying they knew he wanted to visit, but this was hardly the time.

"I don't want to visit. I want to live there."

"Live there?" Eleonore asked. "Don't you like it here? Don't we treat you well?"

"It's not about that, Eleonore. I'm seventy-five

years old. Let's face it, I'm not going to live much longer. I'm an old Jew who wants to live in the Holy Land. Why is that so hard to understand?"

"Father, on the day we left, a half dozen people were killed on a kibbutz in the north. I don't know what's going to happen, but some say there will be a war if they make a Jewish state."

"Then why are you going back?" Ethan asked accusingly.

Two days later, Louis drove Aubin, Amalie, and Ethan to the train station. A day after that Amalie said good-bye to Aubin. It was like she was leaving her own son. She tried not to cry, but she couldn't stop herself. She held onto him so tightly. And worst of all, she knew the kind of pain and disappointment that awaited him.

Several days later Jakob couldn't believe his eyes when his Grandfather Ethan got off the boat with his mother instead of Aubin.

CHAPTER 6

On the last Thursday of November in 1947, hundreds of thousands of radios in countries around the world were tuned in to a landmark broadcast. People were listening to the vote of the United Nations on whether or not Palestine should be partitioned into two roughly equal states: one an Arab Palestine and the other a Jewish homeland. Taken against a confusing backdrop of countless studies and commissions surrounded by propaganda, unceasing politicking, and attempts to find some middle ground that would have majority support in the region, the partition vote was a bastardized compromise, a potential starting point that diplomats hoped could eventually be molded into a lasting solution. The final tally was thirty-three countries in favor of partition and thirteen against, with the thirteen "nays" being cast by Moslem and Asian countries.

The Arab nations decried the vote as the worst kind of Western imperialism, calling it the theft of ancestral Arab lands by Westerners with the consent and support of other Western nations. They used the term "Westerners" in reference to the Ashkenazim leadership of the Yishuv, ignoring their Middle Eastern ancestry.

In true Middle Eastern fashion, not only did the Palestinian Arabs begin fighting in the streets, but so did extremist Jews who were also unhappy with the compromise.

Members of the British government and British military personnel were also displeased with the vote, as it signaled the ignominious end of the

British mandate in Palestine. They had endured Jewish terrorism, Arab terrorism, and severe international criticism brought about by media coverage of their handling of Holocaust refugees, and in the end they had nothing to show for it. In what many consider one of the most singularly acrimonious acts ever perpetrated by the British government, policies prohibiting the existence of Jewish militias and ownership of arms were enforced right up to the end of the mandate. And then, when the mandate ended on the fourteenth of May in 1948, they immediately withdrew all of their troops, leaving the Jewish community unprotected as Arab armies massed on all sides of Palestine.

The day after the British withdrawal, there was fevered discussion among Jewish leaders as to whether or not they should declare a state at that time or call for UN intercession and postpone statehood until the situation was under control. But in the end, on the fifteenth of May, David Ben Gurion read the Israeli declaration of independence and the nation of Israel officially became a state.

Thus began what Israelis would call "The War of Independence" and Arabs would refer to as "The Palestinian War." Overnight the Haganah changed from an underground guerrilla force to the mainline military defense of Israel. Many of the splinter groups, including the Irgun, agreed to cooperate with the Haganah, even though there would be significant disagreements for some time to come. A notable example of such conflicts occurred when David Ben Gurion ordered Haganah forces to sink a supply ship that was smuggling in weapons for Irgun forces, weapons that, while des-

perately needed in the war, would have shifted the balance of power toward the Irgun.

In retrospect, it would seem that a major factor in saving Israel from being destroyed in almost the same instant it was being born was the confusion of leadership in the Arab armies. The Arab leaders had all assumed that their overwhelming superiority in manpower and weapons would make short work of the Israelis, and it was this overconfidence that left them without a unified command for their attacks.

The lack of unified command, however, was certainly not the only reason Israel survived. The Israeli soldiers fought with incredible courage and heroism. If the Israelis fought better than the Egyptians, Syrians, Saudis, Iraqis, and Lebanese, it was because they knew what was at stake. If they lost the war, they couldn't simply withdraw to fight another day. If the Israelis lost, it would mean more than just the imprisonment and death of Israeli soldiers, more than the deaths of their families and the massacre of hundreds of thousands of Jews. It would mean the end of Israel.

Five years before David Ben Gurion announced the independence of Israel, the German Afrika Korps was being forced into Tunisia as American troops advanced from the west and the English closed in from the east.

Even though the Germans were in an untenable position in 1943 as they faced complete withdrawal from North Africa, certain German officials took the time to issue an ultimatum to the Jewish population of Tunisia. Jewish representatives were told that if their people did not present German authorities with a huge ransom, they would face immediate deportation to German concentration camps in Eastern Europe.

The Tunisian Jews collected and turned over the equivalent of almost ten million deutsche marks worth of gold, jewelry, and other valuables, hoping to appease the Germans and buy their freedom. The Germans, however, never intended to honor the agreement. The treasure, consisting of everything from wedding bands to gold Kiddush cups, had hardly been melted down into gold ingots by the time the Germans began rounding up the Jews of Tunisia.

The deportations began soon after, only to be interrupted by a final attack by American and British forces who captured thousands of German soldiers and relieved the German Afrika Korps of their last foothold on that continent. Before the noose was drawn tight, however, the treasure stolen from the Jews of Tunisia was loaded on a patrol boat bound for the island of Sardinia, a fuel stop on its way to the Italian mainland. From there it was to eventually make its way to Germany and a storehouse assigned to none other than Heinrich Himmler, leader of the Waffen SS.

As fate would have it, the gold would never make it past that first port of call. There was a small harbor in the south, some ways away from the Italian naval base—a secluded inlet with steep, windswept slopes used only during the peak fishing season by a few local fishermen. The Germans used it as an auxiliary military refueling station for smaller boats. This was where German patrol boat number 99708 stopped to refuel after leaving Tunisia. Normally such a trip wouldn't require refueling, but supplies in Tunisia were stretched to the limit as the Germans evacuated key personnel, so the fuel tanks hadn't been filled completely when they left. The patrol boat was also using extra fuel, since its cargo exceeded the normal load.

There were only four men stationed at the refueling dock. They were playing cards, trying to kill time on a boring Tuesday afternoon, when number 99708 came into the harbor. The men all jumped up, spilling their cards out onto the table as they left. They were at the petrol pumps and ready to go, standing at attention, as the boat maneuvered into place.

Few words were exchanged as the diesel fuel started gurgling into the nearly empty tanks. Franz, the man at the hose, looked over the ship and was surprised by how low it sat in the water. "Heavy load . . . ," he said to one of the ship's crew, but the young sailor just grunted.

"Wie geht's?" called out Gregor, one of Franz's comrades on the dock.

"Good flow. The pump's working faster since you rebuilt it. We're about half way . . ."

"How's the oil pressure?" Gregor called out to the captain, who was clearly impatient as he watched Franz at the pump.

"She's running a little hot . . . ," the captain, Micah Eerdmann, answered. Eerdmann was not normally at the helm of a patrol boat. He was an SS captain who had commandeered the boat under the direct orders of Himmler's office for the sole purpose of transporting the valuable cargo.

"That could just be the extra load. You're pretty low in the water."

"No choice," Eerdmann replied. "We do as we're told. They're evacuating."

"Well, maybe we could . . . ," Gregor began, about to suggest a minor adjustment, but just then he heard the distant drone of airplane engines.

"Ours?" the captain asked.

"Not sure . . . ," Gregor answered as he held his hand up to block the sun as he scanned the sky.

The four crewmen on number 99708 looked at each other. The light patrol boat might stand a chance at full speed, but not with such a heavy load.

When one of the planes cleared a nearby hill, Eerdmann saw the familiar markings on its side. "Break off!" he shouted to Franz as he pulled the throttle a third and started moving away from the dock.

Franz tried to pull the nozzle out, but it was difficult with the boat already moving. He climbed on the ship's rail as the fuel hose kept feeding out and just barely got the nozzle out before the hose reached the end of its tether. He then realized he was ten yards from the dock. He looked at one of the crewmen and the crewman looked back at him, and he decided he would stand a better chance in the water, so he jumped.

"Throw them over!" Eerdmann shouted. "Throw the crates overboard. They can come back for them later!"

And so the crew began hoisting the heavy crates up to the rail and letting them fall into the water, each box sending a splashing fountain into the air as it plunged beneath the waves. They were about two hundred meters from the dock by the time the crew got into the swing of tossing crate after crate overboard in a sort of bucket brigade.

The pilots of the two British Hawker Typhoons had been talking to each other as they flew over. One pilot was suggesting that they had gone far enough and should turn back, but just then he saw the patrol boat heading for open sea. Eerdmann was sure they had missed him, and he tried to stay as close to shore as he could while leaving the bay, but then the right wing of one of the planes dipped gracefully and the engine strained ever so slightly. It then straightened out and went into a dive, bearing down on the slow-moving boat. The pilots assumed it was a disabled ship, judging by how slowly it was moving, and therefore an easy target for one plane, so the other pilot just watched as his wingman went in for the kill.

Eerdmann looked up anxiously as the plane's engine began to whine when it started its rapid descent toward its prey. He was counting on this kind of approach and purposely kept the throttle down so that the pilot would judge his bomb release based on their current speed. Eerdmann looked back at the crew as they picked up their pace. Crate after crate crashed into the ocean while the plane got closer and closer. Suddenly the whine of the Typhoon's engine changed dramatically into a fierce wail as the pilot released his torpedo and pulled up from the dive, straining the engines as he climbed. The pilot was surprised that there was no machine-gun fire from the patrol boat, but Eerdmann had yelled at the crew to forget the guns and keep dumping cargo as he waited for the precise instant when the plane's torpedo slipped below the surface of the water. He then yelled for them to hang on as he pushed the throttle all the way open and the bow of the ship lifted up from the sudden force of the thrusting engines.

Two of the crewmen fell to the deck as they lost their balance, having just let go of a crate they were throwing over the side. They rolled across the deck all the way to the back of the boat. They were all waiting to see if the captain had gambled well . . . and he had. The torpedo slipped past the ship and continued in to the shore, where it exploded.

The Typhoon pilot, realizing he had missed, circled around. Now it was time for the other pilot to give it a try, like boys in a marksmanship competition with their slingshots, each knowing that they had to go in turns.

The crewmen on the patrol boat kept working feverishly to get the last half dozen crates over the side, their desperate situation producing a rush of adrenaline that gave them added strength, so that those last crates weren't dropped into the sea from the ship's railing, but tossed quickly over the side in graceful arcs. The second Typhoon began its run at the boat, but by now the heavy cargo was all gone and the patrol boat's deck-mounted machine guns began to chatter angrily at the approaching plane. Without the extra load, Eerdmann had the maneuverability to dodge the torpedo and escape the Typhoon's parting strafing run virtually unscathed. The dock, however, wasn't as lucky. Just as the second plane broke off from the patrol boat, it joined the first plane in strafing the dock before they were forced to return to their home base because of dwindling fuel supplies.

The first pilot hit an above-ground fuel tank, which set the dock on fire, and the second plane went after Franz and Gregor as they ran from the dock. Franz had just climbed out of the water a few minutes before, but now both he and Gregor dove in on a dead run, barely escaping the machine-gun fire. But the strafing continued up to the small barracks, and the incendiary rounds set them on fire. The planes then pulled up and were soon out of sight as they made their way home.

Franz and Gregor crawled onto the shore at about the same time. Walter and Emil were trying to put out the barracks fire with the fire hose from the dock and doing a good job of it, but then there was another explosion as the gas drums in the storage area began to explode from the heat of the dock fire.

"Silly bastards should have put out the petrol fire first. They're worried about their beds, and now the petrol's all gone," Gregor said to Franz as he took off his shirt and gave it a good wringing. "There's going to be hell to pay."

"They don't have to know. We just tell them the petrol was the first to go."

"Why?"

"Why not?" Franz answered back. "Why do you

have to make things so hard?"

"Why should I lie for those lazy little boys? No skin off my nose if they get court-martialed."

"Court-martialed? More likely prison . . . or even death. Doesn't seem worth it for a few barrels of petrol."

"Ja, right. Well, it looks like we're out of business. What do we do now?"

"I'm going out to see what they threw over," Franz answered.

"Are you crazy? It's probably just some general's winter clothes being shipped home for the season."

"No, I've got a feeling it could be something important . . . or valuable," Franz said with a wink.

"What if they come back? The boat, I mean."

"No. They're halfway to Rome by now," Franz insisted. "I just want to go out and take a look. I'll be back in twenty minutes."

Gregor went up to help sort out the barracks while Franz grabbed a crowbar out of a toolbox and hopped into a small boat, taking off for where he thought he saw them start to throw the crates over.

The water in the harbor was very clear and only about twenty feet deep where Franz stopped, but you had to know what you were looking for, or the shape of the small crates would have just blended in with the rocks and seaweed. Franz, forty-six years old at the time, had always been a good swimmer, and the little rowboat he was using always had an underwater swimming mask and a snorkel, since it was the boat they used around the dock to inspect ships that came in for fueling.

Franz went down with the crowbar and started to

open one of the crates. The crates were well built and too heavy for him to bring up by himself, and it took two more dives before he was able to open the crate as it lay at the bottom of the harbor.

The crate was filled with papers, files in folders completely filling the box. He grabbed a handful and went up to the boat, where he peeled the wet pages apart and read them. They were personnel files. Nothing special. Franz wondered to himself why these files had been given a priority shipment out of Tunisia. Maybe it was just bureaucracy. Someone ordered an office cleared and they took everything, regardless of importance. That was probably it. Just a stupid mistake by panicked SS men. *They're not really supermen,* Franz thought to himself. *They must make mistakes too.* He looked the papers over one more time, going through the various folders. He decided to try one more crate. That would tell the story. If it contained the same kind of papers, then it was just some ridiculous mistake.

He dove in and opened another case and came up with more of the same. But he couldn't stop. *Just one more,* he thought to himself like a child pilfering candy or, more to the point, a gambler trying one more throw of the dice. The third box also contained papers, but this time they were laid flat in the box instead of standing up, like the others had been. Franz was so upset that he just pushed the box over and started for the surface, but as he looked back, he noticed there was something else tumbling out of the box besides papers. He continued up to get his breath and after a moment dove back down. He grabbed at the smaller boxes that had fallen out of the crate, pulled one of the heavy packages wrapped in newspaper to his chest, and swam back to the surface.

Once back in the boat, he unwrapped it to find that it was a crudely made ingot of what appeared to be gold. His heart started racing. He made another dive and found that half the crate was filled with ingots and then covered with files.

Once he was back on the boat, he took a moment to examine his find more closely. It was a small ingot, not what you would expect a gold bar to look like. It was much cruder, as though poured into a handmade clay mold. He could even see a couple of fingerprints cast into the precious metal. But it was certainly gold. Franz just held it for a moment as he tried to decide what to do next.

Meanwhile Micah Eerdmann came up with an idea as his boat raced across the water. He knew what was in those crates, but only because he had looked for himself. The bombing and strafing would be his alibi. There had been witnesses back at the dock that the boat had been attacked. Who was to say that the planes hadn't caught up with them after they left the bay?

Eerdmann looked at the coastline and saw that the cliffs were still deserted. They were about two miles out when he started turning the boat back in toward the island. The four crewmen were sitting on deck watching the sky for planes and catching their breath after the sudden exertion of ejecting their cargo.

"Are we going back?" one of the men shouted to make himself heard above the engines. Eerdmann

turned to them and pulled his pistol, calmly shooting all four men before they even knew what was
happening. He knew that even if someone was in
the area, they never would have heard the shots over
the boat's engines. He came in close enough to the
shore where he felt he could swim, but where the
water was deep enough to ensure that the boat
would disappear completely. He looked at the
deserted shoreline, and when he was certain there
were no possible witnesses, he throttled the engine
down. He then went onto the bow and worked at
dismounting the machine gun from its yoke. The
gun was very heavy, so once he had the yoke pin
removed, he tried to let the gun just slide out of the
yoke to the deck rather than trying to carry it. He
then dragged it down to the cabin, where he aimed
it down the stairs at the floor of the lower deck. He
went back for the ammunition belt and then loaded
the machine gun. The gun was hard to fire now that
it was out of its support, and it jumped around as he
tried to concentrate his fire into one spot to break
through the hull. But he kept firing until he was positive the ship was going down. The last thing he
wanted was for the boat to stay afloat long enough to
run aground somewhere. The water was coming in
fast when he began thinking about what to do with
the bodies. If he left them on deck they might float
free. Now he had to work fast as he grabbed each
corpse by the shirt and dragged it to the galley.
When he grabbed the third man there was a groan.
Eerdmann was so surprised that he completely lost
his footing and fell to the deck, desperately scrambling for his pistol. He emptied his gun firing blind-

ly at the man and hit him once in the head. The
man had been so badly wounded by the first gunshot that he was clearly no threat, but Eerdmann
had lost his nerve.

Once Eerdmann recovered, he realized the water
was only a foot and a half from the railing. He left
the other two men on deck and jumped into the
water. He had heard that as a ship went down, a
whirlpool formed that would suck in anyone who
was too close, so he swam as fast as he could to clear
the ship. When he thought he had gone far enough,
he turned to look. There was nothing. No boat, no
debris, no floating bodies. He then continued swimming to shore.

He knew he would have to eliminate the men at
the dock. Maybe they were already dead, since he
had heard some sort of explosion, but if they
weren't, he had some friends who could help. Now
he just had to convince Himmler's office that the
boat carrying those important files had been
destroyed by Allied planes.

Within two weeks the refueling station was closed
down as Franz, Gregor, Emil, and Walter were reassigned. Gregor never made it out of Italy. He was
killed during the fighting on Sicily. Emil and Walter
suffered a different fate, however. They were identified as having served at that refueling station when
they were transferred to the mainland, and one day
they were arrested by a couple of SS men. They
never arrived at headquarters for questioning on
charges of dereliction of duty based on what happened at the refueling station. They were both murdered and their bodies dumped into a drainage

ditch alongside an isolated Italian road.

Franz was the only one to make it out of Italy. He ended up on the Russian front just ahead of the SS men who were looking for him, and they lost track of him as the Russians began their relentless advance across Eastern Europe a few months later.

Micah Eerdmann managed to convince the necessary people that the patrol boat had been shot out from under him, and so he survived the questioning. But he was to be punished for his failure. He was immediately sent to the Russian front.

Eerdmann survived his assignment through his ruthless abuse of others. He spared nothing and no one as he organized various lines of defense. He used concentration camp inmates to dig tank traps and would kill them indiscriminately as a warning to others of what would happen if they didn't work hard enough. He oversaw the execution of thousands of Russian prisoners of war and became a symbol of Aryan resolve and determination in the face of the oncoming "Untermenschen" who would destroy the fatherland. He was even featured in German newsreels as an ideal of the German officer who would never consider surrender or accept defeat. That was how Bill Hanlon of the American OSS first heard of him, through captured German newsreels.

Eerdmann managed to escape the final Russian assault on Berlin, conveniently being "cut off" just before the final closing of the ring around the German capital. At the instant that Adolf Hitler was raising a 7.65-mm Walther semiautomatic pistol to his temple and simultaneously biting down on a cyanide capsule, Micah Eerdmann was moving toward the advancing American Third Army, under the command of General George Patton, as it moved into Bavaria. He ended up in an American POW camp in Austria, never knowing that it was the same camp where a battle-scarred and shell-shocked German veteran of the Russian front named Franz Beckman was also being held prisoner. It was also the then current residence of a balding, middle-aged SS man who had been one of the staff officers in charge of the Theresienstadt concentration camp and, when that camp closed down, the Auschwitz-Birkenau complex in Poland—a man named Klaus Grunewald.

There were more than four thousand men in that prisoner of war camp, and the American intelligence officers were overwhelmed trying to find out exactly who was who. They were looking for war criminals as the world geared up for the Nuremburg trials, a proceeding that, at the insistence of the Russian delegation, included in its charter a pronouncement of collective guilt against the German people. That is to say that every man, woman, and child, *every German citizen,* was to some degree responsible for the Second World War and the atrocities committed during that conflict.

In light of that atmosphere, Nazis were few and far between. Virtually every prisoner in the POW camp was just "a soldier who did his duty and followed the orders that he was given . . . no more and no less."

Klaus wasn't comfortable in surroundings that lacked order and position, but of course, that was a complete contradiction to the necessity of hiding his past. For some reason, Klaus was the one that Franz Beckman took to. Franz was living in a fantasy world and had decided that Klaus was his dead friend Gregor. At that point Klaus was not opposed to living in his own dream world, and so he began to humor Franz just because it was something to do, someone to talk to who wouldn't ask the wrong questions.

"Don't worry, Gregor," Franz would say, "we're almost there. It will all be over soon, and then we can go back and get those crates."

Everyone else would push Franz away or threaten him. His lunacy scared them. But Klaus would just smile and agree, having a soft spot in his heart for the crazy old man who had given everything, including his mind, to the fatherland.

"Don't worry, Gregor . . . ," Franz started in again one afternoon, but Klaus had had a bad day and didn't want to put up with it again.

"Shut up, Franz," Klaus growled. " Keep that shit to yourself . . ."

"Shit?" Franz repeated, recoiling with surprise. "That's not a very nice thing to say. That much money is hardly . . ."

"Money?" Klaus asked, allowing himself the possibility that Franz, even though crazy, might be on to something.

"Ten million marks will take care of all of us for the rest of our lives."

"Ten million marks?" Klaus repeated with a chuckle as he stroked his chin. It was obviously ridiculous, but what a nice little daydream.

"Of course . . . You remember. They had to throw

it over the side. Himmler doesn't need it. We can go back for it, Gregor. We can get the others together and all go back for it after we win the war. You, me . . . Walter and Emil . . . we could get it all."

Klaus thought Franz must just be rambling again, but it was a boring day and so he could invest a little time in a crazy old man's story of lost treasure. "So we could go back to . . ."

"Sardinia, Gregor . . . Sardinia. We could get a boat and . . ."

"Ja, Sardinia. right outside of . . ."

"Those damn planes. But I guess it's our fortune after all. If they hadn't bombed us, they never would have thrown the crates over and we wouldn't have the chance to go back for them."

"But the water was so deep . . . ," Klaus prompted, trying to get more information.

"No it wasn't," Franz protested. "It wasn't more than thirty feet deep out by those rocks."

"But what if somebody else has found them?"

"Found them? Not likely. No one ever goes out there . . . And remember, we *moved it* so if they came looking, they'd have a hard time," Franz went on, and then he suddenly stopped and looked Klaus dead in the eye. "You remember the secret?" he challenged.

"The secret . . . the secret . . . ," Klaus repeated.

"You'll never find it without that. Just like a safe-cracker! Right, left, right."

"Ja, that's it!" Klaus repeated with a smile. "Like a safecracker. Right, left, right."

Franz went on about that day on the docks and how he hadn't told anyone but Gregor about what he'd found when he went out that day, how they had managed to move all the crates to an underwater cave. He kept repeating the same things over and over again.

Franz's madness had been a result of all of the strains of the war, the loss of his family, the defeat of Germany, the constant artillery barrages and infantry charges of the Russians . . . It had all run him down until he finally ended up wasting away in that American POW camp. Maybe he would have ended up the same way regardless of the war, wasting away in his warm little house with his wife at his side, but Franz never made it out of that prisoner of war camp. One day Klaus went over to wake him up and that was all there was to it. Franz had died in his sleep.

Klaus wasn't terribly sad. Not that he wasn't go to miss Franz, but he didn't feel there was anything to look forward to, and so the thought of Franz dying in his sleep didn't seem like such a bad thing. Franz had nothing more to worry about. He had probably died happy in a dream world somewhere before the war where he and his wife and family were on holiday in the Mediterranean, recovering his sunken treasure.

Klaus didn't think much about Franz after that. He had much more important things to worry about. It was just a few weeks later that he and a couple of fellow prisoners, after a bit of planning and bribery, had managed to walk away from a work detail outside the camp fence. He took a chance and went to see his wife and son in Munich.

Klaus's first three sons had died in the war, the

last one being one of the thousands who froze to death at Stalingrad. But Klaus had a fourth son, too young for the war.

Klaus had been with the Einsatzgruppen when the Germans and Russians carved up Poland in 1939. He spent the next two years murdering Jews. He told himself it was right and it needed to be done, as he saw unarmed men, women, and children stripped and led to common graves and then shot. Babi Yar was the last that he could take. He watched naked children being shot and falling into that garbage pit on top of their mothers and fathers, and he couldn't do it anymore. He walked into his commanding officer and started crying, telling him how he should be court-martialed and how he was letting the men down and letting Germany down, finally insisting that the officer shoot him. Klaus considered it an incredible failing of character that he must never talk about. The officer had him taken to the hospital, where Klaus completely fell apart.

Eventually he was sent home for an extended leave after his time in the hospital. In his vulnerable state, with the arrogance and braggadocio gone, he and Katrina clung to each other and found comfort with each other. Soon after, Katrina shocked her husband by telling him that at age forty-six he was going to be a father again. Katrina was nine years younger than her husband, and the pregnancy went well for her. She delivered a beautiful son in July of 1942 when Klaus had been reassigned as a staff officer at Theresienstadt.

After escaping from the POW camp and getting some money from Katrina, he headed south to Italy.

He made some connections through the other prisoners and tapped into the escape route being laid out by members of the Vatican staff. That was how he came to be in Moreno on that strange night when none other than Jakob Metzdorf had burst into his hotel room looking for some other German officer.

When he left Europe, he went to Transjordan, thinking it might be a place where they could live, since many of the Arab nations had been friendly with Nazi Germany during the war. He tried to start a business importing dry goods, but his heart wasn't really in it. The company made a profit and was a good front for his new identity as Edward Bortner, but he couldn't see living the rest of his life as a glorified store clerk. He then decided on a bold course of action. He went to the court of the Jordanian king and offered his services as a military advisor.

That was how Klaus Grunewald happened to be at a forward observation post one scorching hot July day in the desert outside of Jerusalem.

He was constantly amazed at how the Israelis could prevail in these skirmishes where they were incredibly outnumbered and outgunned, but he soon understood why. The Arabs knew they outnumbered the Jews. They knew they had artillery, tanks, and airplanes. They knew there was no way the Jews could win. The problem was that *the Jews didn't seem to know they couldn't win.* The average Arab soldier expected the Jews to just lay down their arms and surrender when faced with such impossible odds, and when the Jews—these "Israelis," as they called themselves—launched attacks instead of surrendering, they often caught the Arab soldiers by surprise and ended up taking prisoners.

Klaus also soon began to understand that while all of Israel's neighbors were at war with Israel, these neighbors had different reasons for fighting and different goals in mind. Their alliance was only a vaguely coordinated affair in which different armies were assigned to different regions, but their objectives were not clearly defined, nor were they updated as the war progressed.

Klaus had just focused his field glasses on an antique American tank with a six-pointed Mogen David painted on its turret, the *only* tank the Israelis had on the field in that area, when he saw the puff of smoke from the cannon that preceded a thunderous salvo. He dropped to the floor just as the shell found its mark, completely destroying the south wall of the observation post. The Jordanian soldiers, disoriented by the explosion, the debris, and the cloud of thick smoke and dust, staggered out of the former school building and right into the waiting arms of an Israeli squad.

The Israelis quickly disarmed their captives and led them away. The squad leader then noticed Klaus, who had crouched down in the wreckage, hoping that the dirt would camouflage him and the Israelis either wouldn't see him or would assume he was dead. The first thing the squad leader noticed was that he wasn't wearing a uniform like the others, although he was wearing something similar to a British khaki uniform, and then he looked at the face and realized this wasn't an Arab. The Israelis knew that the Arabs were employing mercenaries, although the British commanders preferred to call themselves "professional soldiers," and so Schlomo Meicelzinsky, the squad leader, tried to decide if this man was a British commander or . . .

Schlomo signaled one of his men over to him.

"What is it?"

"That one . . . ," Schlomo said under his breath. "I think he's alive. Go check."

The soldier cautiously made his way over, and when he nudged Klaus's shoulder with the bayonet fixed to his rifle, Klaus slowly looked up. The Israeli smiled. Klaus wiped his eyes and stood up. The soldier signaled for one of the other men to take Klaus and went to confer with Schlomo.

"He's German," the soldier said as he looked Schlomo intently in the eyes.

"German?" Schlomo said with surprise. "Why do you say that?"

"He said 'Scheis' as he tried to get the dirt out of his eyes."

"Keep him separate from the others."

While Klaus was very good with dialects and did his best to sound British, the interrogation officers at the Israeli camp believed Schlomo. The Israelis knew that their Arab neighbors welcomed Nazi war criminals who felt that the annihilation of the Jews might still be carried out on this new battlefield.

Klaus was the last to be interrogated after all the Jordanians had been questioned.

The interrogation officers planned their attack carefully. It was just like a Hollywood spy movie. They had drawn the tent flaps and turned on the light hanging from the center pole, pulling it down low so that it shone right in Klaus's face. One officer sat across from Klaus at an old weather-beaten table while the other officer stayed behind him, pacing back and forth as the interrogation got under way.

"Guten Tag Herrn. Ich heisse Oscar. Wir haben fur Sie weniger fragen, bitte, und wenn Sie uns mochten mitgesprecht, wir konnen . . ."

"Terribly sorry. I don't speak the language," Klaus said. "Do you speak any English? I speak a little French . . . Parlez vous—"

"Come now," Oscar interrupted. "We know you're German."

"German? Don't be ridiculous," Klaus protested. "My family . . . well, we came from Germany originally . . . but my family has been in Britain for over a hundred years."

"I see . . . and your name is . . . ?"

"Bortner. Edward Bortner."

"Edward Bortner . . . And you just happened to be on the battlefield?"

"I . . . I was just . . ."

"You realize we consider mercenaries just like any other Arab soldier. We'll hold you for the duration."

"A mercenary? Don't be ridiculous. I'm just a grocer. A businessman."

"A businessman?" the pacing interrogation officer asked dubiously from behind Klaus.

"Yes . . . Yes! I know it sounds silly. I was just curious, and I knew one of the officers and asked if I could just come up and take a look. It just seemed fascinating."

"So you didn't get enough of the last war?"

"I never saw any of it. I'm just—"

"A grocer?"

"Well, not quite. I import dry goods. I'm just a businessman. A businessman with a bit too much curiosity. The wrong place at the wrong time."

"Not a German?"

"Heavens no!"

"Not a Nazi?"

"A Nazi?!" Klaus erupted almost hysterically. "Good lord, no!"

"Well, I guess we just got some bad information then," the officer seated at the table said casually as he got up and started to put together a few file folders. "I guess you can handle it then, what?" Oscar continued, speaking to the faceless officer who had been pacing behind Klaus, putting a comical, heavy English accent on the word *what*.

Now Klaus was really worried. He knew something was up, but he had no idea what. It was not out of the realm of possibility that he might be executed right then and there.

"English . . . ," the faceless officer said slowly, doubtfully.

"That's right," Klaus answered nervously, determined to stick to his story to the end.

"Where in England?"

"Uh . . . the south."

"Sussex?"

"West. West of Sussex . . . ," he stammered. "A little village. You would never have heard of it."

"You must be familiar with that old English saying then."

"Saying?" Klaus asked as he brought his hand up to wipe the sweat away from his eyes.

"You keep turning up like a bad penny."

Klaus was completely confused and couldn't help turning to look at the officer. He didn't know what to think when he finally realized that it was Jakob Metzdorf. This could be Jakob's chance to get rid of him. When they were in Moreno, it had been a surprise. They were both out of their element. But Jakob was obviously in control here. Klaus still didn't know after all these years if Jakob knew that he was the one who had killed his father. He decided to gamble. He would play the old uncle in trouble.

"Jakob . . . Little Jakob," Klaus said with a mix of desperation and relief in his voice as he played the role to the hilt. "You've got to get me out of this!"

"Got to?" Jakob recoiled. "Why should I? Besides, it would look a little suspicious if I let you go."

"I . . . I can make a bargain," Klaus, suddenly remembering Franz's story from the Austrian prison camp.

"Bargain? What kind of bargain?" Jakob asked.

"Money."

"Money? Are you crazy? You'd have to have a lot of money to buy your way out of this."

"Ten million marks . . ."

Klaus had never believed Franz's story for a moment, but now he thanked God he had run into the crazy old man. If they bought his story—if they actually took him out of the country—he knew he could get away somewhere along the way.

"You've got ten million marks?!" Jakob asked incredulously. "Where did you . . . ?"

"I don't have it. I know where it is."

"Where?"

Klaus just smiled wryly.

"And . . . ," Jakob continued, "you'll show us where it is in return for letting you go?"

"And one million of those deutsche marks."

He knew he had Jakob's interest and that by asking for a million marks he gave his story a bit more credibility. If he had said he would give them all the money just for his freedom, they wouldn't have believed it.

"A million deutsche marks? And where did all this money come from?"

"North Africa. It was shipped out when Tunisia fell, but it never made it back to Germany."

"What a marvelous sense of humor. I hope you still have it after we check into your background . . . But I'd dare to guess right from the start that you weren't in North Africa, were you, Uncle Klaus? I seem to recall you were in the region of Prague in 1944."

"Yes . . . I heard you were in that area too."

"Careful, Uncle Klaus," Jakob said as he put his hand on the pistol holstered on his belt. "I lost more than one friend to the Germans, who said they were shot trying to escape. I'm not above using that excuse if you push me."

"Calm down, Jakob. I know where I'm sitting. That's why I brought up the money. I know you're a reasonable man."

"Absolutely. Now . . . back to North Africa?"

"No, I never said I was in North Africa."

"But you know about this money . . ."

"I have a source of information . . ."

"Someone sold you a treasure map in a bar?"

Jakob countered with a grin.

"Firsthand. Firsthand information," Klaus pronounced emphatically.

They continued talking for almost an hour in a sort of verbal fencing match in which neither of them wanted to say anything that would be of advantage to the other, playing a game of cat and mouse. Jakob was interested in the money, since his adopted homeland was in a desperate situation that could be made a little better with a few million deutsche marks. Although money wasn't a panacea, it would help.

Jakob decided he had gotten all he could out of the game and called the guards as he stood up and prepared to leave.

"It's not a bad offer, Jakob. I only want ten percent. You could buy a lot of ammunition with nine million marks. Perhaps even another American tank. Then you'd have two . . ."

"I'll talk it over with my superiors," Jakob said curtly as he started to leave the room. "Oh, by the way . . . your little jokes might not go over too well with the others. I suggest you watch yourself. This isn't a good place for a Nazi officer to start insulting Jews."

The comment made Klaus's blood run cold, but he knew he had a role to play if they were going to believe him, so he had to act as though he had the upper hand, even in defeat.

Jakob then left as the guards took Klaus to a holding pen to await his fate.

A couple of hours later Jakob was sitting in another tent with a friend of his from Tel Aviv, Baruch

Mummenstein, an Israeli intelligence officer originally from Brooklyn who had come to Palestine right after being released from the American army in West Germany after the war.

"Are you crazy?" Baruch asked as he shook his head. "You want to take off on some wild-goose chase while we're in the middle of a war? I don't think you know how bad things are . . ."

"I thought nine million marks could buy a lot of rifles."

"Assuming this money exists. What next? Pirate's treasure in Bermuda?"

"This is a little different. We *know* the Nazis looted most of Europe during the war. Why would Rommel be any different? Why *wouldn't* there be Nazi loot out there?"

"And you want me to commit men and money to finding it while we're in the middle of a war, surrounded by the enemy? If it wasn't for the Mediterranean, we wouldn't even have a place to have our backs up against!"

"I know, I know. But I know this man. I believe him."

"You trust him? "

"No, I don't trust him. I just know he couldn't make up a story like this. He doesn't have it in him. I'm ninety-five percent sure that he's being truthful."

"And the other five percent? What about that?"

"He knows I'll shoot him if he's lying. Nothing's for certain, but if you just give me a couple of weeks—"

"What? And a boat?" Baruch interrupted, raising his voice as he started to gesture wildly at Jakob's presumption for even asking such a thing. "We don't have *anything* to spare."

"And no money for the trip?" Jakob added.

"No! There's absolutely no money for this."

"All right. Then how about this . . . I go with just a couple of men. We take a look. If we find it, then you send help."

Baruch just looked at Jakob, huffing and puffing with exasperation as he considered it. "Your dime?"

"My dime," Jakob repeated, nodding his head in agreement. "Two weeks. Just two weeks, no more. We just go take a look."

"This will have to go through channels. I can't say yes. We'll have to talk to the general.

"He's a good man. He knows how to gamble."

General Guri Ben Tzuriel met with Jakob and Baruch a couple of days later. Jakob had gotten a few more details from Klaus, and after Ben Tzuriel heard them out, he sat thinking for a moment before responding. "It's a fact that the Germans forced the Jews of Tunisia to pay a ransom . . . and there has been talk . . ." He leaned back in his chair and sighed. "But there's always talk. I don't know. It sounds crazy, but these are desperate times. If word ever got out that I gave the go-ahead for a treasure hunt, I'd be laughed out of the army. I'd be laughed out of the country."

Guri then leaned forward on his desk and smiled as he continued. "But of course, they couldn't get me out because there's no one to replace me!"

"We go?" Jakob asked.

"Strictly on your own, you understand," Guri said, once again serious. "You're not going in as part of the Israeli army invading Italy."

Jakob just nodded.

"Then you go. We'll give you some funds. You draw a couple of good men, but you all go as civilians. Tourists."

"What if we have to terminate our prisoner?"

"You do it as civilians."

"That's not good . . . ," Baruch muttered.

"Don't be sloppy. You could be arrested and put on trial," Guri said as he looked Jakob in the eye. "They could put you to death if you're in another country."

"If they catch us . . ."

"If they catch you."

That night, instead of returning to the front lines outside of Jerusalem, Jakob returned home to see Rebecca and Thomas before he left, saying only that he would be gone for a couple of weeks and couldn't tell them any more than that. In the morning he traveled to Haifa where, with the last bit of help the military could give him, he arranged passage on a supply ship.

He had chosen one of his traveling companions, Josef Fedorovich, from his unit outside of Jerusalem. Josef was about the same age as Jakob. He had been a language professor in Kiev before the war and had joined a group of partisans soon after the Germans invaded. Jakob figured Josef would be the interpreter for the group, but he also needed some muscle, so he took Baruch's recommendation and also asked a twenty-two-year-old combat-trained Sabra named Ben Nagan to come along. Within forty-eight hours of Klaus's capture, the four were on their way to the island of Sardinia.

So far, the only concrete information Klaus had given Jakob was that they would need to get to the southern part of Sardinia. Jakob was willing to play the game for a little while, but he let Klaus know that if they didn't come up with something, it would go very badly for him.

Klaus knew that Jakob meant it when he looked at Ben. Ben was not the sort of Jew that came to mind when Klaus thought back to his days at the concentration camps. But then Klaus, even in the middle of it all, had never understood the nature of those camps. He only knew the propaganda.

It was only a four-day journey to Sardinia, much different from the experience of those, including Jakob, who had come to Israel aboard tired old, overloaded Haganah ships. Klaus worked very hard as they traveled to try to remember everything Franz had told him. If he didn't have some new information for Jakob by the time they reached Sardinia, he was fairly certain that he wouldn't make it off the ship. When they disembarked at the port of Cagliari, Klaus said they should get rested up that night and get under way in the morning. They would have to go from inlet to inlet to find the right place.

"You don't know where it is?"

"Not precisely. We have to investigate. There is a layout . . ."

"What do you mean?"

"The lay of the land. There is a group of hills that look like a dog's head."

"You've got to be joking!"

"No, no . . . The inlet we're looking for . . . the

ridge on the west of the harbor, the hills. They look like a dog's head. I swear it. I'm not making this up."

"A dog's head . . . ," Jakob said with a heavy sigh and a shake of his head. "We've got a lot riding on this . . . *You've* got a lot riding on it too. You'd better be right."

"You'll have to trust me on this."

Josef couldn't help but laugh. Klaus just glared at him.

They were bound to draw attention, since there weren't a lot of tourists coming to Sardinia in 1948. One might have thought Ben looked like an Italian with his black hair and deeply tanned face, but Jakob and Klaus were clearly northern European, and Josef, with his high cheekbones and Slavic features, perhaps stood out most of all as a foreigner, although he spoke flawless Italian. Klaus also spoke Italian, but he decided to keep this to himself as it might come in handy at some point.

Because of his fluency in Italian, it was Josef who made the arrangements for the night when they found a hotel. They all shared the same room, which wasn't unusual for European travelers, considering the economy so soon after the war, but they hadn't done it to save money. They all stayed in one room so that they could keep an eye on Klaus.

The next morning they rented a car, no small task on the island. The owner of the hotel had a brother-in-law who had an old car, a little prewar Italian sedan that was terribly beaten up and rusted, and he wanted a substantial amount of money for it, but Josef was a consummate negotiator and talked the price down.

"What do you want the car for?" the brother-in-law asked.

"We're just on holiday. We wanted to do some sightseeing and possibly some diving."

"Diving? Why don't you stay here? The best diving is right here."

"Too crowded. We want to get out on our own. Explore the coastline a bit."

"You have to be very careful out there. There's no one to help you. They say that some of the bays still have unexploded mines from the war."

It was hard going as they traveled narrow dirt roads that were little more than cow paths connecting one inlet to the next. Klaus was starting to get worried as they kept driving. Nothing looked right. And as if that wasn't bad enough, everyone was getting edgy as they bounced along in the hot, crowded little car.

"How long are we going to keep this up?" Ben asked impatiently.

"As long as it takes," Jakob replied.

"When the time comes," Ben said maliciously as he looked over the barren coastline, "when we find out he's been lying all along, this will be a fine place to take care of our friend here."

"Shut up, Ben," Jakob growled.

Klaus pretended not to hear the exchange as he kept an eye on the hills ahead of them.

They spent hours rumbling and bumping along the cliffs, stopping constantly to have Klaus look over the shoreline. Time after time Klaus would shake his head and walk back to the car, saying that it must be "a little" farther down the coast. But he wasn't looking for the landmarks he had described. He was looking for a way to escape.

After several hours, Josef drove out onto a small peninsula that jutted straight out from the cliffs. The wind was picking up as they all fought their way out of the car and looked out over the ocean. It was a beautiful scene with a bright blue sky and the waves crashing loudly at the base of the cliffs below, where they formed torrential tide pools that rose and fell like a beating heart in the ocean's body. Jakob stood at the point of the cliff like the master of a ship standing on the bridge while Josef sprawled out in the grass.

Klaus was kneeling down at the cliff's edge, taking in the view while Ben kept watch, trying to appear casual but still looking like a guard.

"Do we have any field glasses?" Klaus finally asked.

Ben just shrugged his shoulders and so Klaus turned to Jakob. Jakob went to the car and pulled a pair of binoculars from his pack in the tiny trunk.

"What is it?"

"Over there," Klaus said as he pointed in toward the cove below them. "Is that a burned-out shack?"

Jakob took the glasses Klaus offered and looked hard at the rocky shore. He saw the debris that Klaus had pointed out. It was very close to a road that led up the cliff into brush and trees. "I don't know. It could be just about anything. Fisherman's shack . . . It could be a broken-up fishing boat."

By then Josef had gotten up and was looking too. "We could go down and take a look," he said. "We haven't found anything else."

"Yeah, why not," Jakob agreed as he headed for

the car with the others close behind.

Jakob was at the wheel this time as they back-tracked to where they thought the road should be, but they couldn't find it. There was such heavy scrub brush overgrowing the ocean side of the road that they couldn't see anything, including the cliffs from which they had seen the road in the first place.

"It's got to be here!" Jakob said after they made three trips back and forth in the area where they thought the road would come out.

"Let's go back to the point and take a better look from there," Josef suggested, and so Jakob floored it, spitting dirt and gravel as evidence of his frustration.

Once back on the peninsula overlooking the cove, they visually followed the road as far as they could to where it disappeared into the thick overgrowth.

"We obviously went past it," Josef commented to no one in particular.

"Let's try it again," Jakob said as he started back to the car.

"If we can't find it this time, I'll take the rope and go down the hill, find the road from there and work my way back up.

This time Jakob drove more slowly as they all stared into the brush looking for any hint of the gravel road that cut off down to the beach, but they still couldn't find it. They pulled off the road and Ben got the long climbing rope and gear out of the trunk. They looked through the dense overgrowth for any kind of passage and eventually found a tiny winding path that went into the thick brush. "A goat path," Josef said with a laugh, and Ben worked his way through, finding a sturdy tree where he tied off the rope and began a descent into the overgrowth.

Jakob jumped when he heard Ben yell out "Damn it!"

"Are you all right?" Jakob shouted.

"I'm okay. It's just the damn thorn bushes," Ben called back. "They're thick. My shirt and pants are torn."

"Can you keep going?"

"I'll go as far as I can."

They waited anxiously for a few more minutes until Ben finally called up again. "I made it. I can see the road."

"Where?"

"About twenty-five meters to my right. I'll climb over. I'll have to get rid of the rope."

"Are you sure? Is it safe?"

"I think I can keep a good hold on the brush as I climb. It's not as steep over here. Not like the cliffs."

"Be careful . . ."

The three of them started walking up the road to where Ben said they should find the cutoff, but they still couldn't see any evidence of a road.

"I'm there."

"Where are you?"

"At the road. It's washed out. It must have washed out a long time ago. That's why we couldn't see it. There's an overgrown ravine here about twenty feet wide. We'll never get the car down here.

"Should we just forget it?"

"I don't think so."

"Why not?"

"Because I can see the cliff from here, the cliff where we started . . ."

"And?"

"And it looks kind of like a dog's head."

Jakob turned to Josef and Klaus with a look of disbelief. "Don't joke with me, Ben," he shouted.

"No joke. You'd better come down here."

"Can we come down from here?"

"No, not where you are. Come down the way I came down, but watch out for those damn thorn bushes!"

"I think we've got a real problem here," Klaus said as they walked back.

"What's that?" Jakob asked.

"If that cliff was the right cliff . . ."

"Yeah?"

"I didn't understand what it meant before, but the crates are supposed to be in a cave at the dog's paws."

"The dog's paws? What the hell does that mean?"

"Let's take a look and I'll let you know."

They each climbed down to join Ben, Klaus going first so they could keep an eye on him, and then they made their way down to the wreckage they had seen from the cliff. Klaus was in the lead. First he went to what he had thought was a shack, and sure enough, it had been a small building. It could have been the barracks that Franz had told him about. He then looked out toward the cove and started walking toward the shore.

"What is it? Is this the place?" Jakob asked.

"It could be . . . ," Klaus answered hesitantly. It had all just sounded like a fairy tale or some sort of setup for a swindle—or just a crazy old man's foolish dreams. Klaus had planned to make a break for it that night when they returned to the hotel. He was sure he could lose them in the harbor town. He had even picked out an escape route. But now he realized Franz's story . . . might be real?

"What are you looking for?"

"These," Klaus said as he stepped a few feet into the water. "Dock posts. This is where the dock was..."

He looked over at the cliffs to the west and then said under his breath, "It's true. It's really true."

"And those are the dog's paws," he continued out loud as he pointed to the base of the cliffs.

Jakob finally realized what Klaus meant. The cliffs to the west looked somewhat like the outline of a dog's head, and down at the water, the jumble of treacherous boulders and the bubbling tide pools looked like the dog's paws. It was a bit of a stretch of the imagination, but he saw it.

"Is that where it's supposed to be?"

"Caves. There are caves over there. I saw the water going in and out. I don't know how we can make it in and get back out again."

"We can do it," Ben said without hesitation.

"We should watch for a day . . . see what the tide does," Josef offered.

"We don't have the time. We'll get a boat and come back tomorrow morning. We'll see how things look then. Ben, do you think you can find this place from the sea?"

"Easier by sea than it was by land."

"Then let's go back. We'll get an early start tomorrow.

No one said a word as they began their trip back to the hotel. They were all lost in thought about what tomorrow might bring. The danger, the challenge . . . and the treasure? Or the disappointment. The gold might not be there at all. That was Klaus's conclusion. He just didn't think the gold could still be there after all this time. Five years . . . It didn't seem possible that no one would have come around for a look. What about those sailors who had thrown the treasure overboard in the first place? They must have tried to come back for it. If not for Germany, then for themselves, at least in the three years since the war had ended. Where were they?

It was a good question. Only Micah Eerdmann knew the answer.

WHILE JAKOB AND CREW were exploring the Sardinian coastline, Eerdmann was about to be summoned to a meeting with an American OSS man in Rudesheim. Eerdmann had been given money and a new identity in return for working with the OSS.

"Micah Eerdmann is an evil, black-hearted S-O-B," Bill Hanlon pronounced as he slapped the file down on the desk in front of his friend, Jack Walsh. "He would fuck your grandmother and then make her pay for it."

"Well, he's never met my grandmother. She's—"

"Doesn't matter."

"You should let me finish! She's a real—"

"I'm telling you, Jack, it doesn't matter. If not your grandmother, then your dog. The man has no soul. He is the personification of evil, and we've taken him on as a customer."

"They can't all be winners, Bill. You knew the business. We're going for quantity here, not quality. If these guys can get us the information we need against the Reds, it doesn't matter if he does screw my grandmother. They're all snakes. The trick is just not to get bit."

"Well, he's coming in today. It's time to get him out of town. Somebody recognized him the other day. 'The defender of Berlin. Hero of the Reich.' What bullshit! He must have killed a couple of hundred prisoners of war and concentration camp prisoners with his own hand when they were building tank traps outside the city. Then he ran like hell when the Russians started to encircle Berlin."

"Sounds like a real piece of work."

"Well, now we're stuck with him. If we don't get him out of the country, he'll scream like a stuck pig when they catch him. He'll spill his guts."

"Why not just kill him?"

"Too risky. Our other clients are watching. They want to see how we treat Eerdmann. If we screw this up, we may never get another piece of good intelligence from them."

"We're gonna get bit in the ass . . ."

"Not if I can help it," Hanlon said forcefully as he grabbed the file folder and stormed out.

An hour later he was trying to work things out with Eerdmann.

"So . . . we get you out of Europe and down to South America."

"South America?" Eerdmann asked in a very clinical way, not distressed, but just curious why.

"There's been a strong German community in

Argentina for years. We have contacts. They'll take care of you, and everybody gets what he wants."

"So you really think it's that bad? You think I can't stay here?"

"Absolutely not! If people recognize you it would ruin everything. And I'm sure I don't have to remind you that if we're out of business, we can't help you at all."

"What if I just moved to Italy?"

"Doesn't work that way. If we take you out, we take you all the way out."

"It will take my family time to . . ."

"No, not the whole family. You go now. Tomorrow. Your wife can take care of things here and follow later, but we have to get you out now. Word about something like this travels fast. You wouldn't believe how fast. I wouldn't be surprised if the Russkies already have someone on the way to see if you're living around here. And if they don't find you here, they alert their whole operation. That means Italy, France . . ."

"You think it's that bad?"

"I *know* it's that bad."

"All right. I'll go, but I have to stop in Sardinia for a week before I leave."

"Sardinia? What the hell for?"

"I was in Sardinia when we withdrew from North Africa. I left something there that I want to get. Sentimental value . . ."

"We're not travel agents here. We're trying to keep a low profile with this. We can't let you go wandering all over the . . ."

"I doubt the United States government would like

to be put in a position where they have to explain our dealings."

"Are you trying to blackmail me, you son of a bitch? You better watch your step, Mister. We might end up a little red in the face if this all came out, but you'd probably end up at the end of a rope! Now, excuse me for talking plain, but that doesn't sound like a very good trade on your part."

"I need to go to Sardinia."

"Why?"

"I can't tell you."

"How long?"

"Just a week . . . maybe two. But no more than two weeks."

"Two weeks?" Hanlon asked as he looked Eerdmann in the face. "I'll check. Maybe we can give you one week, but I'm not making any promises."

"I . . . ," Eerdmann began, about to say that he would go no matter what Hanlon's superiors in American military intelligence said, but then he reconsidered. "I can't ask any more than that. Will you call tonight?"

"I'll call now. As soon as you leave, I'll be on the phone."

"Let me know," Eerdmann said as he got up and went to the door, pausing as he added emphatically, "It's very important."

True to his word, Hanlon called the colonel and told him about Eerdmann's request, leaving out the part about him threatening to expose the whole operation. The colonel thought about it for a moment, knowing that Eerdmann could make things ugly, and said that it didn't seem too unreasonable. "One week. You go with him, Hanlon. Keep a low profile. We have a few details that you can wrap up in Rome, and then you meet him in Sardinia and make sure he gets on the right boat."

The trip to Rome was very uneventful, just a long train trip in the company of an American OSS officer who fortunately had enough paperwork to keep him busy so that they wouldn't be forced to exchange false pleasantries or slip into any unpleasant confrontations.

Hanlon and Eerdmann parted ways at the Roma Termini train station, the main train station in Rome. Hanlon was headed for the Vatican offices just off St. Peter's Square while Eerdmann was headed for . . . Jakob and Klaus.

Eerdmann had been waiting for the opportunity to return for the gold, but as he himself would have said, timing is everything. He couldn't very well have taken off for a weekend while his wife and daughters were still in Rudesheim and then just not show up again. Now was the perfect chance. When Bill Hanlon suggested Argentina, it was just too perfect. Eerdmann not only knew that there was a large German community in Argentina, he had even been in contact with them. He had been corresponding with one former German officer in particular that he had known for years, going back before the war.

There was a group in South America which believed that one day Nazism could be revived, and they were biding their time and resources until that time might come. They called their dream "the Fourth Reich." They lived off money that had been confiscated and otherwise stolen during the war and hidden away in secret international bank accounts, most notably in Switzerland. Switzerland had made all the financial transactions that Germany couldn't make during the war. Switzerland's "neutrality" allowed them to deal with both sides during the war, and they made considerable money "legitimizing" funds that Germany had confiscated from all over Europe.

Eerdmann now confided in his friend that he needed help to recover a very valuable shipment. He knew he couldn't do it all by himself, but he was also convinced that there really could be a Fourth Reich. He believed that if he turned over a significant portion of the money to this group, he could make a deal where he and his family would be protected and live "in a manner befitting people of substance."

After parting company with Hanlon, Eerdmann made a beeline for a small hotel near the Spanish Steps. He settled in and took out a book, reading as he waited for the arrival of his associates. A couple of hours later there was a knock at the door.

"Signor Macelli?" the young man asked when Eerdmann cautiously opened the door.

Eerdmann looked him over for an instant. One couldn't be too careful. The young man was thin and good looking . . . too good looking.

"Yes?"

"I'm your guide."

"Come in," Eerdmann said.

This was somebody hired by his friend in Argentina through Die Spinne. Die Spinne was an underground network not unlike the Vatican ratline, but far more secretive, which had been set up by Otto Skorzeny. Skorzeny was the daring German commando who had led the squad that rescued Mussolini from a mountain prison when the dictator had been arrested after the Italian capitulation. Skorzeny had also led a group of commandos that posed as Americans during the Battle of the Bulge in Belgium in December of 1944, making their way behind American lines to spread confusion and commit acts of sabotage. Skorzeny had gone before an Allied war tribunal and been released on the grounds that he never committed any act that went beyond the accepted rules of warfare.

"So . . . ," Eerdmann said with a sardonic smile as he landed heavily on the bed, gesturing toward the chair for the young man to sit. "What did you do in the big war?"

"I turned seventeen on the day our tank moved into the Ardennes."

"The Ardennes? That was quite a campaign."

"We laid siege to Bastogne. We could have taken it, but the Luftwaffe . . ."

"Ja, ja . . . that's a long time ago. And what do you do now?"

"I'm a mechanic. An automobile mechanic."

"Where?"

"In Köln."

"And why are you here?"

"Because I was told you needed help. I have six men ready to help us."

"And you know all of these men?"

"Ja wohl! I know them all. They were in my unit. They are loyal to a man. They would die for you if you ask."

"Let's hope it doesn't come to that," Eerdmann muttered in response to the young man's exuberance, and then he remembered to ask for the second password. "Oh . . . and one more thing. Where is the center of the universe?"

"In the tempered steel heart of every SS soldier."

"What do I call you?"

"Kurt."

"Good . . . You're a handsome young man, Kurt. Too handsome. You'll stand out in a crowd."

Kurt didn't know what to say to this.

"Dirty yourself up a bit," Eerdmann continued. "Let your beard grow. Don't shower for the next few days and get yourself a dirty old hat. We're not out to impress the girls on this trip."

"Yes, sir. When do you want to leave?"

"Tomorrow morning. Early. Meet me here at 5:30."

The next morning Kurt knocked on the door just as Eerdmann's watch showed 5:30 A.M. Eerdmann knew the boy must have been waiting outside for just the perfect time to knock.

"Let's go," was all Eerdmann said, and they were soon on their way to the train station and then out of Rome to Civitavecchia, where their crew was waiting and where Kurt had chartered a large boat.

Once they were out to sea, Kurt handed out pistols to Eerdmann and the rest of the crew, and then started inspecting the surplus scuba gear that they had purchased. They would be ready for anything.

AT THE SAME TIME in Sardinia, Josef was looking over *their* collection of gear in the bottom of the fishing boat they had rented. They had dropped anchor close to the caves at about nine o'clock in the morning under a cloudy sky. "Scuba?" Josef asked, not knowing that word in English.

"Self-contained underwater breathing apparatus," Ben answered as he looked over the equipment.

"Oh. First letters."

"Acronym," Klaus said with a note of superiority.

"Have you ever used it before?" Jakob asked Ben.

"The man who rented it to me showed me what to do. We don't have time for an instructor, and we certainly don't want to have anyone with us on the boat. There would be too many questions. Don't worry. It's not like we're going to do any deep diving."

"We may not even need to dive," Klaus said as he looked over the hoses and regulator.

"I'm just worried about getting caught in those caves," Jakob replied. "I feel better having it in case something goes wrong and we get caught in there."

"Why did you only get one?"

"It was all he had. You don't know how lucky I was to get this one."

"Who's going to use it?"

"I thought I would go down first," Jakob announced. "I'll go in and take a look around the caves while Josef keeps an eye on the boat and you two let me down on a rope."

"Are you expecting trouble?"

"To tell you the truth, Ben, I don't know *what* to expect."

"It looks pretty calm," Ben said as he looked out at what appeared to be a gentle river of water flowing among the boulders that littered the shore, moving in and out of the mouths of the four caves as the waves rolled onto the shore and receded.

"Which one is it?" Jakob asked Klaus.

"I'm not sure. I only know it's in a cave at the dog's paws."

"You don't have any idea which cave or how far in it is?" Jakob asked with an angry edge to his voice. "These caves could go on for a long ways."

"Wait . . . ," Klaus said, holding up his hand as though about to receive a vision. "That's right. He said it was like a safe. Right, left, right. We turn at the first right, then go to the left and then to the right. Like a safe combination."

"That's good, but we still don't know which cave or how far. We could be going a long ways if it's the wrong cave."

"Maybe the first right means the cave to the right, not a turn inside the cave . . . ," Josef offered.

"That's possible," Jakob said. "Well, let's go in."

Jakob had to keep reminding himself about the nature of his relationship with Klaus as he got wrapped up in the thrill of the treasure hunt. He knew that Klaus was trying to ingratiate himself, and that he would try to get away at the first opportunity.

Klaus, on the other hand, had known exactly what he was doing as he tried to lull Jakob into a false sense of security until the moment when he would try to escape. But suddenly he was beginning to believe his own story. The gold might be there. And if it was, he wanted his piece of it.

Ben and Jakob gathered up some equipment and tossed it into the little dinghy at the back of the boat. Without saying a word, Jakob pressed a coil of rope into Klaus's hands when he hadn't made a move to help. Klaus threw the rope into the dinghy and helped them lower it into the water.

Once they had rowed to the shore, Josef watched them as they stood there looking at the caves. Jakob would walk over to the cave and then back to Klaus. He walked back to the cave and threw a few stones in, probably out of some futile desire to judge the depth and nature of the cave.

"I'll go in," Ben said.

"Do you know anything about land mines?" Jakob asked.

"I know enough not to get blown up."

"Good. Take a look at this."

They walked over to the first cave, and Jakob pointed inside to where someone had painted a warning in German and Italian.

"Caution. Mines. Do not enter," Ben read. "Why would they mine the caves?"

"I don't know," Jakob answered. "It could have been written by the men who put the gold in there . . . if it really is in there."

"It could have been booby-trapped for the Allied invasion," Klaus said.

"The Allies didn't invade here. They invaded Sicily."

"But they could just as well have landed here. The caves could have been mined in anticipation of them being used as cover during an invasion," Klaus explained.

"So you think there really are mines in there?" Jakob asked.

"It's possible . . ."

"Possible? Damn it, it's possible someone just painted that to keep anyone from going in and finding a few million marks worth of gold! Anything's possible. Maybe there were mines in there, but they were removed years ago. I need to know if we should chance it."

"I say we do it," Ben answered curtly, getting on Jakob's nerves as though he were suggesting Jakob was afraid to go into the cave.

"So do I," Klaus agreed.

"I'm not against it as long as we all understand the danger. I've disarmed a few land mines in my day, but a booby trap in a wet slippery cave . . . ," said Jakob, shaking his head. "Watching this water go in and out . . . it could be just like getting flushed down a toilet."

"Can you work your way in along that ledge?" Ben asked as he looked over the cave wall.

"I was looking at that. It's a narrow ledge. One slip and we'll go for a slide. If there are mines, we'd slide right into them."

"We could make a dummy and let it slide in on the water," Klaus said.

"A dummy?" Ben retorted. "We don't have anything like that!"

"It doesn't have to be perfect. Just something about the same size, weight, and buoyancy as a man," Jakob added. "We let it slide in on a rope and pull it back out. That should trigger whatever's down there.

"A couple of life preservers, some brush . . . ," Klaus suggested. "Tie it all together."

"Let's do it," Jakob agreed, and with that Ben took

the dinghy out to the boat for tools and the life preservers.

It took a considerable amount of time to get everything together, about two hours, what with having to chop down the brush, tie it all together, and size it. They dubbed their mannequin "Walter," as Klaus said all good dummies should have a name. The next step was to find good cover—not a problem considering the large boulders on the beach— and then to let the ocean waves wash the dummy into the cave. They waited for an explosion, or maybe even multiple explosions, as Walter entered the cave, but there was nothing.

"Let's pull it out," Jakob said after they had payed out about thirty meters. It came back up easily as he pulled. "Almost there . . . We should see Walter right about—"

Before Jakob could finish the sentence, there was a flash and a loud explosion. Smoke started pouring out of the cave entrance.

"Damn!" Klaus said as he watched the smoke billowing upward.

But Jakob could still feel the dummy on the rope, so he kept pulling.

"What gives?" Ben said as the dummy came out of the cave completely intact.

"It was just a smoke grenade," Jakob said as he pulled the dummy the rest of the way out to where they were hiding behind the rocks. "He's just singed a little around the edges. That wasn't any mine. It had to be a trip wire and a smoke grenade."

"Too loud for a smoke grenade," Klaus said as he looked over the dummy.

"It was the cave. It echoed. The cave just made it sound bigger. It's just a booby trap to keep people out. It wasn't even meant to kill anybody . . ."

"Ja, you must be right," Klaus said as he looked back at the cave and then continued to himself under his breath, "That would be just like Franz."

"I say we go," Jakob then announced. "Get the torches."

Ben swam out to the boat one more time, gathering flares and flashlights as he told Josef about the explosion, that no one was hurt and they were going in.

"Are we ready?" Ben asked as he came running up the beach.

"I'm going to tie the rope around my waist, and you're going to keep a hold on me," Jakob said. "If everything goes well, then we'll go from there."

Klaus knew that his moment was at hand. Ben would be busy with Jakob, and Josef was alone on the boat. Klaus was sure Josef wouldn't shoot him. Klaus was much bigger than Josef, and knew he could easily wrestle him over the side.

He would wait until Jakob was in the cave, and while he and Ben were holding the rope, he would let go. Ben would have to stay with the rope, and that would give Klaus the chance to row out to the boat, throw Josef overboard, and be gone before Jakob and Ben could go after him.

Jakob was wearing cut-off khaki military pants as a swimsuit with a British commando knife on his belt, tied down to his leg. He tied the rope around his waist and put his flashlight, which was on a string loop, around his neck. Then he started into the cave. He hadn't made it more than three steps when the water rushing into the cave changed direction and washed back out, catching him by surprise and causing him to lose his footing on the smooth, slippery rock. He caught himself as he fell and the rope suddenly drew taut, keeping him from sliding into the cave.

"Are you hurt?" Ben called out, his voice echoing in the cave.

"I'm fine," Jakob shouted back. "I just slipped. But I've broken the light. Pull me back."

Ben gave a good hard pull and Jakob slid out of the cave with the next backwash of seawater.

"That looks like fun," Klaus said with a wry smile.

"If I don't get killed," Jakob countered acerbically. "The floor of the cave is too slippery on that incline. I can't just walk in. This time I'm going to start off laying on my stomach. I'll just slide in with the waves, so you two have to be ready with that rope."

"Wait a minute," Ben said as he looked around the beach. "There . . ."

"What?"

"Let's get those planks there, that piece of the wall from the shack."

"For what?"

"You can lay down on it as you go in. That way you won't get cut up if you run into some sharp rocks..." Ben trailed off as he started on his way to get the boards.

Klaus sat down on the rocky beach to wait since it would take Ben at least twenty minutes to walk over to the old army barracks and back. Klaus shaded his eyes as he looked up at Jakob standing over him.

"Let me guess . . . You're going to ask me again if it's really down there."

"I could get killed going in there . . . drown . . . break my neck," Jakob said as he looked over the beach and hills. "I'm willing to take that chance. But if you know it's a wild-goose chase, now would be a good time to tell me."

"We came all this way. We found the harbor. We found the caves . . . For all I know, there are a couple of dozen crates down in that cave," he answered, pausing for an instant before concluding with "Right, left, right."

"And you're sure this is the right cave?"

"Jakob," he said as he ran his fingers through what hair he had left, "I've seen that look in your young friend's eyes. I know he would just as soon kill me as not, and I'm not in the habit of risking my life for nothing."

Jakob just grunted. He sat on the rocky beach a few feet away from Klaus as they waited. He wanted reassurance, but what could he have expected from Klaus?

The boards that Ben brought back weren't very sturdy, but nonetheless, it was a good idea, and they would provide some protection as he rode the sea wash into the cave.

"We'll tie a piece of rope on the raft for you to hold," Ben instructed, "and you'll have the rope around your waist too."

"Good enough. If I tug on the rope once, that means to stop letting out rope. When I pull it once after that, then start letting the rope out again. If I tug twice or more, pull me up. Let's go."

Jakob dragged the raft over to the stream and paddled backward, feet first, into the cave. The waves rolled in again and he was flushed into the cave's entrance, immediately disappearing into the darkness.

Jakob's eyes adjusted to the dim light coming from the mouth of the cave, and he could still see as he slowly descended on the slight incline into the cave. He was surprised by the first backwash as the waves hit the back of the first cavern and rolled back, sweeping over him.

Ben thought the push of the wave was Jakob tugging on the rope, but he wasn't sure. His voice came echoing into the cave again. "How are you doing?"

"Fine," Jakob shouted back. "Everything is good. Keep going."

"Were you pulling on the rope?"

"No. That was just the waves. Keep going."

Ben and Klaus started feeding out the rope again, and Jakob reached around for the flashlight as the light from the mouth of the cave grew dimmer. He started to wonder if he shouldn't have gone in head first, but no, that wouldn't have worked. Still . . . it was awfully hard to twist around to see what was coming up in the cave. The floor of the cave appeared to be leveling out for a ways, so he gave a tug on the rope and they stopped letting it out

Jakob stood up in the cave. The ceiling was still high at that point. He figured he had gone about twenty-five meters by that time, and he scanned the walls with the flashlight, looking for any sign of an opening to his left. He couldn't see any opening, but the cave began to curve at that point so that he could only see about five meters ahead. He gave a tug on the rope and started to walk into the blackness. He could feel that the floor of the cave was just as slippery as it had been at the opening of the cave, and when he realized he was starting on a new incline, he got the raft and started down again. The water was deeper at that point as he descended, and he thought there must be a portion of the cave completely under water. They might have to use the scuba gear after all. As he started around the corner, he heard a strange sound that he couldn't identify; he only knew that whatever it was, it probably wasn't good. He twisted around and tried to get the flashlight on the source of the sound, but he couldn't quite reach, so he took the string holding the flashlight from around his neck and tried that way. That was when he glimpsed a shadow on the wall. His flashlight had passed over it quickly, and he couldn't quite make out what it was. He kept getting closer as the rope kept feeding out, and then he caught sight of it again. It was another opening, another cave leading off from the main one, but it was also the source of the strange sound. Before he knew what was happening, a surge of water pushed him toward the dark opening. He knew he didn't want to go in blindly, but the force of the water moved him just enough so that his feet went in first. He started to panic when he couldn't feel anything with his feet. He grabbed desperately for the raft, but the more he struggled to steer it, the more he lost control, and one of the boards suddenly separated from the raft and floated down the other passageway into the cave. There was nothing to hold onto, just the smooth, slippery floor and walls of the cave. Suddenly the lower half of his body was enveloped in the darkness of the other opening as the flashlight danced wildly over the walls while he struggled to pull on the rope so that Klaus and Ben would stop feeding it out.

Back at the mouth of the cave, Ben knew something was going wrong as the tension on the rope changed. There was a marked difference from when they had been gradually feeding out the rope, and now as it was suddenly like pulling . . . dead weight. Then he felt the desperate tugs as Jakob struggled to signal them and tried to climb the rope, but the rope was so wet that he couldn't get a hold of that either.

"Pull him out, damn it!" Ben yelled to Klaus, but Klaus didn't seem very concerned at all. In fact, Klaus picked that moment to let go. The rope slipped about four feet before Ben caught it, friction burns cutting into his hands as he held tight and tried to pull Jakob back out.

Ben couldn't waste his energy yelling at Klaus as he tried to pull Jakob up, and Klaus knew this was his chance. All he had to do was get to the boat, throw Josef overboard, and take off. Klaus took off at a dead run for the dinghy, quickly making his way out to the boat. Josef had heard Ben shout, but he was too far away to make out what had been said. Now he watched as Klaus approached, assuming that Klaus was coming for some tool or other supplies.

"What? What is it? What's happened?" Josef asked with concern as Klaus climbed into the boat.

"Hurry! They need you on shore," Klaus said as

he took a wide stance and grabbed Josef's hand, suddenly twisting Josef's arm behind his back and pushing him toward the edge. Klaus thought that was all there was to it, but he had misjudged Josef. As a little Jewish boy in Warsaw, Josef had learned how to fight dirty since the first bullies had picked on him in school. When the time came that he decided to become a partisan fighter in the Ukraine, where he had been a university language professor, he learned every dirty move he could in hand-to-hand combat. Instead of falling over the edge, Josef grabbed the rail with his free hand, fell to his knees when Klaus released him, thinking he was going overboard, and twisted around so that he slid underneath Klaus, between Klaus's legs. Josef then brought up a powerful short jab to Klaus's . . . very sensitive organs. Klaus fell to the bottom of the boat like a sack of potatoes, and within a couple of minutes Josef had him hog-tied so tightly that Klaus's fingers were starting to turn blue as Josef dropped him into the dinghy and headed for shore to help Ben and Jakob.

Back in the cave, Jakob had let out a scream when Klaus let go of the rope and he slipped four feet into the darkness. The rope had slipped up from his waist, giving him an even greater sense of falling until it finally tightened up under his arms, putting a sudden strain on his shoulders. He was now hanging by the rope while Ben was doing everything he could to pull him out, but the rope kept slipping little by little. Jakob was sure he was going to die as he tried to get his bearings. He ran his hands over the wall and scraped at it with his feet, trying to find some nook or cranny where he could get a handhold or foothold. He looked up and realized that he could see the beam of the flashlight at the opening where he had dropped it. Then he realized that the string he had tied around the flashlight was hanging down into the opening. He was within an inch as he reached for it above his head, but he couldn't quite make it. He tried again to climb the rope, but couldn't do it.

He tried one more time, determined at the very least to get the flashlight, and managed to pull himself up enough to catch the string, and then suddenly the flashlight came tumbling into the cave, hitting him on the head as it fell. "Damn it! God damn it to hell!" he shouted. The rope was still slipping bit by bit as Ben lost his hold, and Jakob could feel the ever so slight pulses that meant he would soon be falling into the abyss below. After he recovered from the knock on the head, he noticed that the light was still visible. "It couldn't have fallen very far," he thought to himself, and he twisted around on the rope so that he was now facing away from the wall.

"I don't believe it . . . ," he said out loud as he looked down. There was the flashlight, not six inches from his feet at the bottom of a shallow pool of water. The entire drop from the opening of the cave was barely six feet.

Just then he started rising up toward the mouth of the cave as Ben, now assisted by Josef, pulled him up. Once he got clear of the opening, he pulled on the rope once.

"What was that?" Josef asked.

"He . . . he pulled on the rope. Once!" Ben answered with amazement, having been sure that they were pulling up a dead body. "He's all right! He wants us to stop pulling."

"Are you sure?"

"We'll wait a minute . . ."

Back in the cave, Jakob gathered up about ten feet of rope and then gave another tug so they would let out some more.

"That's it! He wants some more rope," Ben said, obviously relieved as he started feeding out rope again.

Jakob carefully worked his way back to the opening he had just come out of and gave another tug. Ben and Josef held firmly as Jakob put his weight on the rope and lowered himself into the next passageway. He then picked up the flashlight at the bottom of the shallow pool and started into the new passage. The strange noise he had heard before was another small passageway, barely big enough for a man to crawl into, which led off to the left. The water from the shallow pool filled this smaller cave, and there was also the sound of air, not only going into the passage, but coming back out again. It sounded like the cave was breathing. Jakob figured there must be another opening, maybe just a crack in the cave wall that went all the way to the face of the cliffs. He kept on moving slowly, careful not to lose his balance. He was looking for that last turn, that last cave that should be off to his right . . .

"We've got to get him out of there," Josef said as he and Ben stood ready at the rope outside the cave.

"He'll let us know when he's ready . . ."

"No. The tide will be coming in soon. It comes in fast around here. That's what they said back in

Cagliari."

"We'll get him out before the tide comes in," Ben said tersely, as though Josef was being foolish.

"He's a long way in there. Maybe forty meters. We don't have much more rope anyway."

"We'll give him ten minutes," Ben said decisively.

Back in the cave, Jakob noticed that he was actually walking uphill. The passage narrowed a bit and made some relatively sharp turns and twists, to the point that he had the distinct feeling he had made a full circle. He had only gone another twenty feet, but it seemed farther. He was just about to turn around and go back when he saw another passage to the right. But that couldn't be it. It was only three feet high and maybe as wide. He thought it must be a little nook cut out of the stone. He turned the light on it, expecting to see the back of the nook, but there was no back. He knelt down and still couldn't see the end of it. Another black recess . . . He got on his hands and knees and crawled in, and as he turned up the flashlight, he couldn't believe the size of it. It was like a cathedral with crystalline stalactites pointing down from a ruptured dome of a ceiling. It was the biggest cavern he had seen in the cave. Some of the calcium deposits sparkled as the beam of the flashlight passed over them. It was hypnotic as he turned around the cavern, taking in all the strange and beautiful shapes. He didn't even notice at first when his flashlight danced over the weathered boards. Then it came to him the second time. There they were, behind those rocks, laid out in proper military fashion. Twenty-four neatly stacked cases. He didn't believe it. He did believe it.

He walked over and stood in front of the crates, reading aloud the words stenciled on the sides. "Achtung! Priority 1 shipment. Interference with the shipment of vital materials is a criminal act. Office of Reichsführer Heinrich Himmler, Berlin."

He pulled out his knife and went at the top crate, struggling to pry the lid off. It didn't come easy, even after being dumped in the ocean and weathered for years in the cave. The screeching protest of the heavy nails resounded in the cavern as the cover finally gave way. And there it was. Bar after bar, crudely shaped ingots of gold.

He held that first ingot in his hand and played with it, feeling its smoothness, its weight. A bar of gold. The letters RSHA were also crudely stamped into the bar, and in the same instant that he read the stamp, he thought of where it had come from. He remembered the box he had found in Gertrude Haas's apartment. Gold rings . . . *gold teeth* . . . He felt an involuntary shudder go down his back. His thoughts went back to the crates, trying to figure out how they would get them out. It wouldn't be easy with that last narrow passageway.

Suddenly there was a tug on the rope. He couldn't figure out what was happening, since they had never discussed what it meant if Ben tugged on the rope, but he didn't have time to think about it, as suddenly he was being pulled out of the cave at an alarming rate. "What the hell?" he thought to himself as he moved down the narrow passageway, and then he noticed that he was walking in water where the passage had been dry just a few moments before. By the time he got to the area with the six-foot drop and the shallow pool, he was faced with a rushing torrent coming into the passage, and the water was up to his waist and climbing. But the tension on the rope never stopped, and he was pulled right into the pool and up through the passage, barely having an instant to take a breath before being immersed in the saltwater onslaught. He was starting to think he would drown as he flew up the cave, underwater all the way, and then he felt the first blast from the waves rolling into the cave, and suddenly he was going back down the way he had just come. An instant later the rope was pulling him out again, and just as he was about to let out his final breath, he broke clear of the mouth of the cave.

He came up gasping, just enough to catch one quick breath before being washed back in, and then Ben and Josef gave it everything they had and pulled him tumbling out onto the stony beach, as though he had just been born from the cliff.

Jakob was stunned as he lay on the bed of rocks, and Josef and Ben came running over to him.

"Jakob! Jakob, are you hurt?" Josef asked as Jakob convulsed, coughing and spitting out seawater.

"My God!" Ben said as he looked down and saw the single gold ingot that Jakob had managed to hold onto through his traumatic ride. "You found it! It's really there!"

"It's all there . . . ," Jakob rasped out. "Just like you said. It's all there . . ."

Jakob looked up, expecting to see Klaus. "Where's Klaus?"

"He tried to run," Ben said, and then, changing the subject, "What happened down there? I thought we lost you."

"Where is Klaus?" Jakob repeated.

"He tried to steal the boat," Ben answered.

"He ran when you got into trouble," Josef added. "Came out to the boat, tried to throw me off."

"And?" Jakob asked impatiently, almost shouting.

"And he thought it would be easy to get rid of me," Josef said with a grin. "He found out better. He's tied up in the dinghy. We had to pull you out because the tide started coming in so fast."

"Good thing you did. I wasn't paying attention. Could've drowned in there."

"You still didn't say what happened," Ben persisted.

"That first time it was just a dropoff. I couldn't see, and I didn't know how deep it was, but it turned out to be only a couple meters."

"I was sure you'd been killed."

"Well, it sure scared me!" Jakob said as he stood up, feeling better now that he was back on firm ground. "Not much else we can do today. Let's pack up and we'll get started early tomorrow."

Jakob smiled as he climbed into the boat and saw Klaus trussed up in the corner with his hands and feet all tied into a neat little knot, as though he were about to be put on a spit. "My, my, Uncle Klaus, aren't you full of surprises?"

"I'd appreciate it if you'd loosen these ropes. I can't feel my hands or feet anymore."

"You should have thought about that before you tried to throw me over," Josef chimed in as he climbed into the boat behind Jakob.

"You're lucky it wasn't me," Ben said as he followed, throwing the bale of rope in before him, barely missing Klaus's head and splattering him with water. "I wouldn't have kicked you in the balls . . . I would've cut 'em off and fed 'em to ya."

"Come now, Jakob, you can't blame me for trying to get away. It's every prisoner's duty to try to escape."

"For all you know, you might have killed me by letting go of that rope, Uncle Klaus. *That's* not every prisoner's duty. That sounds personal to me."

"If I give you my word that I won't try to escape, will you please get these ropes off?"

"Your word? That's an interesting thought. I will have to admit, though, we'd look rather strange carrying you up to our room like that."

"God only knows what they'd think we were doing up there," Ben said luridly.

"We'll cut you loose," Jakob finally conceded as he knelt down and cut the ropes. "But next time . . . ," he continued soberly as he laid the cold knife blade against Klaus's throat, playing with it, "we'll kill you. No more chances . . . no hesitation."

Klaus knew he meant it. When they got out to the boat, Jakob and Ben straightened up the gear as Josef started the engines and pulled anchor, and Klaus began packing things away, too, as if he were just part of the crew and everything was normal.

Once they were on their way, Klaus sat next to Jakob. "So . . . what happened down there? Did you find anything?"

"Nothing," Jakob said. "The rope just got caught. We'll try one of the other caves tomorrow."

That night Jakob talked with Ben and Josef separately so that one or the other would be with Klaus

at all times. He told Ben to find some more rope—
some kind of harness—so they could start to bring
up the crates, and also some fishing and camping
equipment. He decided that they would set up a
camp on the beach, pretending to be fishermen, so
that as they brought up whatever crates they could,
they would be ready for transport when a ship came.

He assigned Josef the task of getting a message
through to General Ben Tzuriel, no small job considering the state of communications in Israel at the
time. The phone and power lines were limited and
subject to sabotage by the Arabs. The big question
for the general was how soon he could get a ship to
them.

Jakob knew they would be exposed on the beach.
If the Sardinian authorities discovered the gold, they
would confiscate it. He was counting on the fact that
no one else in the world would suspect that there was
hidden treasure in that small, secluded harbor on
Sardinia.

When Jakob had picked up that first bar of gold
deep inside the cave, it was virtually the same
moment that Bill Hanlon was telling Micah
Eerdmann he would be leaving Europe.

That night as Josef was trying to arrange for some
ship to be sent for the gold, Bill Hanlon and Micah
Eerdmann were on their way to Rome.

Two days later, while Jakob, Ben, and Josef were
harvesting the gold from that sparkling cavern,
Micah Eerdmann and his friends arrived in Cagliari.

It was very hard getting the crates out of the cave.
On the first day, Jakob had gone down and accompanied each crate back up. The whole day's work

only netted five cases. On the second day, however, he decided that he wouldn't try to come up with each case. He would go in on a raft like that first attempt, and then he would stay in the cave, carrying half-full boxes from the crystal cavern to the dropoff and sending them up on the raft. It wasn't that they couldn't have figured out that system in the first place; it just took Jakob time to get comfortable with the cave and also to trust Josef and Ben. When they started using the new system, it went very smoothly. They had a dozen more crates out by the time the tide came in.

Klaus realized early on that Jakob had lied to him and had to give him credit. It must have taken a lot to keep such a secret, and if he hadn't, Klaus certainly would have tried to tell someone, anyone, so that there might be an ensuing rush of treasure hunters, which he could use as cover for another escape. But that wasn't going to happen now. They all knew what was going on. Klaus was tied up most of the time, sitting within clear sight of Ben and Josef as they worked. Today they were all carrying pistols. Now it was all certain, and they were all business.

Jakob wasn't going to take a chance on going back to Cagliari. For the rest of their time in Sardinia, they were going to camp on the beach, placing their tents as close to the cave as possible so that virtually every move in and out of the cave was hidden from view.

That night Jakob talked with Klaus, saying that he felt their original agreement was still in force, and that if Klaus gave his word not to escape, he would still get ten percent of the gold. He wondered if either of them believed it.

"You have my word," Klaus said.

"But we still have to tie you up."

Jakob wondered when a ship would arrive. Josef said he had been promised it wouldn't take more than three days, but Jakob was worried. Every day they spent on that beach made it more likely someone would see them. Just as he was falling asleep with Klaus tied up on a cot beside him, he wondered if tomorrow would be the day they would be discovered.

"Is this really necessary?" Klaus groaned. "It's really hard to sleep like this."

"Go to sleep."

BACK IN CAGLIARI, Micah Eerdmann had no idea that *his* gold was being taken right out from under his very nose as he ate his dinner and conspired with his hired friends. Similarly, Bill Hanlon had absolutely no idea what his evil little friend Eerdmann was up to. At least not until his meeting in the Vatican offices right after he and Eerdmann had parted company.

Bill Hanlon sat down to a very civilized yet very secret lunch with Father Bruncatti, his liaison with the clandestine Vatican operations. Hanlon had known for quite a few months that the Vatican was an amateur affair, but he had tried to help them to the extent that he could co-opt people from within their operation. He would hear of a particularly interesting candidate for the OSS operation and convince him that he could stay in Europe under their protection in exchange for services rendered. That was how he had come across Micah Eerdmann, much to his later regret.

"I'm afraid we have made a rather unpleasant discovery," the priest said casually as he sipped from his glass of wine.

"What's that, Father?"

"One of our contacts, one of the members of our organization . . ."

"Yes?"

"Well . . . it seems he wasn't who we thought he was."

"Wasn't who you . . . ? C'mon, Father. What are you saying?"

"It seems our Signor Brindisi was . . . well, he was a Russian."

"Russian?" Hanlon said, stopping his fork in midair as he was about to take a bite of his salmon.

"We heard from some of your OSS men. We don't know if he actually is Russian, but it seems he was working for, or with, the Russians."

"You're telling me there was a Russian spy in the network?"

"That seems to be the case."

"Well, what happened to him? Where is he now?"

"Ah . . . well . . . he's gone."

"Gone? What do you mean 'gone'? Dead?"

"No! Heavens no. Our people would never kill. He's just disappeared, and after doing some looking, it seems your people have come up with some information indicating that he had been working with the Russians. And now he's just disappeared."

"So what you're trying to tell me is that a Russian

intelligence agent . . . maybe more than one Russian intelligence agent . . . infiltrated your escape route."

"Yes. I'm afraid so."

"And so he . . . they . . . may have the same information we have. They may even have gotten information about . . ." Hanlon stopped and took in a deep breath as he considered the consequences. After in instant of silence, his temper erupted. "Christ!" he yelled as he banged his fist on the table and threw down his fork. "God damn it!"

"Please, Mr. Hanlon. Is that necessary?"

"Do you have any idea what kind of damage this could do?"

"I'm afraid I really don't. I know it's a bad situation, but this just makes me realize how naïve we were. We're not exactly in the spy business here. We don't appear to be . . . good at it."

"Now there's an understatement. Who the hell was he? Where was he assigned?"

"It was our Mr. Brindisi . . . At least that was the name he used. He helped our friends along as they went through Assisi."

Hanlon froze for an instant. Assisi. That's where he found Eerdmann. What if Eerdmann had been a plant? What if all the information he had gotten from Eerdmann had been fed to him through the Russians? Hanlon realized he was about to get bitten by his snake. Did he really go to Sardinia? For all Hanlon knew, Eerdmann was on his way to Moscow at that very moment. Hanlon realized he'd better go to Sardinia and see if he could catch that lying bastard before he got away.

And so the game of tag began. Bill Hanlon was on

his way to Sardinia the next morning, knowing that it was a long shot that Eerdmann was there, much less that he would find him. And all the while Hanlon kept asking himself how he ever could have trusted Eerdmann in the first place.

Taking the chance that Eerdmann started in Cagliari, since it was the main port of Sardinia, Hanlon fell back on his old ways as a former police officer from Philadelphia. He decided that if Eerdmann had stopped in Cagliari, he would have rented a car or boat. Hanlon spent a few hours looking around, checking out any place that would rent to tourists. Things were still slow since the war, so there weren't that many places to check.

"There were four men. One of them could be the one you're looking for. They rented a scuba tank. They were asking about any diving spots to the south. Old harbors . . ."

"And one of them was German?"

"More than one. At least two, maybe three. But one looked like . . ."

"Like what?"

"Signor, we had a bad time under the Germans as they were leaving. I saw a lot of things. One of these men seemed like a German officer. I don't know. Maybe it's just my old age, but that's what I thought when I looked at him."

"That's good enough for me. Do you know where they went?"

"They asked about this area," the old man said as he pointed at the map on the wall of his office. "They rented a car from my brother-in-law. Then they rented a boat. I'm sure they were talking about this area, even though they were very quiet about it."

Hanlon was sure that was it. He was sure he was hot on Eerdmann's trail, and by sheer coincidence he was.

When Jakob awoke the next morning, it was to the sound of Josef shouting something in Italian. He peeked out of the tent and saw a boat near theirs with a half dozen men on board. They didn't look like fishermen. He reached for his pistol and pulled on his shirt, but as he was about to leave the tent, the boat engines opened up and the boat sped away in a wide arc, heading east.

"What was that?"

"I'm not sure. They asked if the diving was good, and I told them I didn't know, that we were fishing."

"Tourists?"

"I suppose it's possible. But I don't know why they would be out so early or why they left. Even if we were fishing, it wouldn't stop them from diving." Josef stopped, thinking it all out, and then continued. "I don't know why they would . . ."

"Why they would be diving here," Jakob said, finishing Josef's thought.

"You don't think . . . ?"

"The gold?" Jakob said thoughtfully. "After all these years and suddenly we all show up at the same time? I don't know . . ."

"What do we do?"

"We keep going. It's probably nothing. We can't let our imaginations get the best of us. It's just a coincidence."

On the boat, Micah Eerdmann was wondering almost the same things as they sped away to the east.

They were so close. Could it just be a coincidence? He didn't know anything about the island. For all he knew these fishermen camped out there every year. He had the boat pull up near the shore as they rounded the point so that they wouldn't be seen from the camp, instructing one of his men to climb the hills so he could spy on the camp and see if they actually were fishing. If they made a move to the other side of the harbor and started diving, his man was to fire three shots and Eerdmann and the others would move in and take care of them. But if it was just a coincidence, he didn't want to chance drawing attention to himself. He would wait a little while.

Jakob and the others got to work laying out the ropes and harnesses, hoping it would go faster now that they knew what they were doing and hoping that help would arrive soon.

Eerdmann's man up on the cliffs couldn't see what they were doing, just that they weren't going out fishing. But they also weren't moving to the other side of the harbor. He signaled to Eerdmann with a mirror and the boat moved in to pick him up.

"What's wrong?" Jakob asked Ben as Ben stood on the beach looking up at the cliffs.

"I saw something."

"What?"

"I don't know. A flash of light . . . something."

"Did you see any movement? People?"

"No. I wasn't really looking. I just caught it out of the corner of my eye."

"Maybe we should get ready to move. It wouldn't be good to get caught here."

"Leave the gold?"

"Look how much trouble we're having getting it out. If someone else comes, we'd do better to let them try and then harass them while they're working. This isn't a very defensible position."

"What if it's the authorities?"

"If we're being watched, it's probably that boat from this morning. We haven't seen anybody else out here. It's best to be prepared. What have we got on the boat?"

"The five crates from the first day."

"What about ammunition?"

"A few boxes."

"We'll go out and bring it in," Jakob said, referring to Klaus and himself. "You straighten things up . . . get the ropes and harness out of sight."

Jakob saw a boat coming around the point as he and Klaus rowed the dinghy out. It looked like the same boat he had seen that morning, but he wasn't sure.

"What do they want?" Klaus asked in a lyrical way, happy to invite trouble.

"I'm sure it's got nothing to do with us."

Eerdmann had his pilot bring the boat in to where he thought the majority of the crates would have gone overboard, and they dropped anchor. Two of the men with him were experienced divers, and they were over the side within a few moments of arrival. They scoured the dive sight and came up with nothing. After a half hour of trying different places and theorizing about drift, silt cover, and so on, they came to the conclusion that there was nothing there. Not even pieces of the crates had shown up.

Eerdmann found himself staring at Jakob's boat as they sat there discussing the possibilities. *It's just a coincidence,* he said to himself, but then he stood up and said resolutely, "Let's check out that boat."

Jakob had taken all the ammunition back to the camp along with two crates and was making another trip when Klaus announced that the other boat was heading toward them.

"Don't say a word," he cautioned Klaus. "I'll do all the talking." He thought about taking off, trying to outrun them, but where would he go? And he couldn't just leave Ben and Josef on the beach like that. He started the engines but kept the throttle down.

"Of course . . . ," Klaus murmured mockingly.

Josef and Ben also noticed the boat moving in and went for the bolt-action Carcano rifles they had bought in Cagliari. "Take cover and get ready," Ben said.

"But Jakob . . ."

"Wait and see," Ben said. "If they kill him, they come after us next.

On the boat, Jakob nervously adjusted the Walther pistol in his pocket as Eerdmann's boat came closer.

"How's the fishing?" one of the men asked in Italian.

Jakob only spoke a little Italian from his days in Moreno. "Not so good," he said with a heavy German accent.

"Sprechen Sie Deutsch?"

"Ein bischen . . . ," Jakob answered, as though he were walking into a trap.

"Are you fishing?"

"A little . . . Not much luck . . ."

Eerdmann stepped forward and took over the conversation. "You have a nice boat. Do you mind if I come aboard?"

"Actually, we were just about to leave. We're breaking camp and . . ."

"I'd really like to see your boat," Eerdmann insisted as two of his men drew pistols.

Jakob drew his pistol at the same instant. They stood there for a moment, just staring at each other.

"Jakob, you don't stand a chance," Klaus said.

"A very wise decision, sir. It would be a good idea if your son listened to you. Just drop the pistol. I just happened—"

"He's not my father," Jakob interrupted as he dropped the pistol in the boat.

Eerdmann glared at Jakob. "I would have preferred you throw that over the side, but as I was saying, I just happened to be looking for something. I lost it a few years ago, left it behind, and now it doesn't seem to be where I left it."

"You're Micah Eerdmann," Klaus said. "I remember seeing you in the newsreels. Defender of Berlin."

"And you are?"

"Obersturmbannführer Klaus Grunewald of the SS."

"Really . . . ?" Eerdmann said dubiously.

"Here is my SS tattoo."

"And what are you doing here?"

"That's a long story."

"I don't really have time for long stories."

"How about this . . . I know where your crates are."

"You bastard!" Jakob said. "You think they won't kill you too?"

"Jürgen," Eerdmann said to the man beside him, "get the pistol."

Jürgen climbed up on the rail, about to leap from boat to boat, but suddenly a shot rang out and he crumpled into a heap in the boat. Ben had shot him from shore.

Jakob jumped for the throttle and the engines roared to life, but one of the others on Eerdmann's boat threw a line at the same instant and tethered the boats together, so that all Jakob accomplished was to start the boats going around in a circle.

"Damn it," Ben shouted back on the shore.

On the boat, it was Klaus who reached Jakob first and wrestled him to the floor. He was immediately joined by another of Eerdmann's men, and together they subdued Jakob. As things were thrown about in the mêleé, the last two cases of gold were uncovered, and Eerdmann immediately recognized the boxes.

"What do we do?" Josef asked Ben back on the beach.

"Don't shoot at the boat. We don't know if Jakob's dead or not. Shoot over their heads. Maybe he can break free in the confusion."

When rifle fire started coming from the beach, the men on the boat started shooting back blindly with their pistols, since they couldn't tell where the shots were coming from.

Eerdmann looked at the crates in the boat and shouted, "Take both boats. Rolf, you take that boat! Let's go!" And so as Josef and Ben kept firing, both boats pulled out and took off to the west.

"Is that it?" Josef asked as he stood up from his position behind one of the boulders and watched the boats disappear from sight.

"No. They're coming back," Ben answered, and Josef knelt back down.

"Not now," Ben reprimanded, annoyed that Josef took him so literally. "They're going to come back when they find out the rest of the gold is here."

"But Jakob wouldn't . . . ," Josef began, but he stopped in mid-sentence as it dawned on him... "Klaus."

"Of course it was Klaus," Ben growled. "He probably had this planned all along."

"You mean from the start? That doesn't make sense. Why would he have tried to escape?"

"Maybe it was all a setup. Right from the start."

"From the start?" Josef repeated. "I can't believe that. I don't think he was sure the gold was here until he saw those first crates."

"Then who was that on the other boat?"

"Think about it!" Josef countered. "They stop by in the morning to see who we are, and then they come back in the afternoon and dive on the other side of the bay. It took them *hours* before they tried to board our boat."

"And . . . ?"

"Klaus said the crates had been moved. Who would be looking for them in the harbor?"

"The men who dropped them there in the first place!"

"Exactly," Josef exclaimed.

"If that's true, then Jakob is in big trouble," Ben said as he looked out at the point where the boats had disappeared. "They won't hesitate to kill him. But I don't know how Klaus fits into all this."

"And all we can do is . . ."

"Wait," Ben said, finishing Josef's sentence. "And get ready for them."

Eerdmann had only gone about a kilometer up the coast when he had the boats come to a stop. He got into Jakob's boat, found some tools on the floor, and opened one of the crates, pulling out an ingot. He then pulled back the canvas tarp that had been covering the boxes. "Eins . . . zwei . . . ," he said loudly as he looked at Jakob and Klaus. "But that's not right. I was sure there were more than that."

Jakob was still being held on the floor with his arms behind his back. "That's not all of them," Eerdmann continued as he knelt down with his face close to Jakob's. "No, that's not nearly all of them, is it?"

Jakob didn't say anything.

"What about you, Obersturmbannführer Klaus Grunewald?" Eerdmann continued as he walked over to Klaus, who was leaning casually against the railing. "Do you think that's all of them?"

"No," Klaus answered simply.

"Good. At least we agree on that. So now we need to understand each other. I believe that you are trying to steal my gold. Is that right?"

"I didn't know it was your gold."

"You didn't . . . What exactly are you doing here?"

"I was in a bad situation. I was in trouble and I tried to bargain . . ."

"You seem to be getting ahead of yourself," Eerdmann said as he started to pace a couple of steps. "*My* gold," he said emphatically. "There was no one else who knew about this place."

"Franz."

"Franz?" he said, throwing a hand into the air. "I don't know any Franz who—"

"He was on the dock."

"The dock? What are you talking about?"

"I met Franz in a prisoner of war camp . . ."

"Get to the point."

"He was there on the dock when the crates were thrown over. He moved—"

"Damned incompetents!" Eerdmann roared as he kicked the cover of the crate across the boat in a frenzy, only barely missing Jakob. "I was told they had been taken care of."

Klaus recoiled imperceptibly, still maintaining his calm demeanor, as he realized Eerdmann might not be a man he could reason with.

Eerdmann's face was now beet-red as he approached Klaus. "Now where have you hidden my gold?" he demanded.

"*I* didn't hide the . . ."

Eerdmann began to grind his teeth and his hands started to shake. "I don't give a damn who did what," he growled through clenched teeth, "I just want to know where the boxes are now."

Klaus straightened up, standing at full height, a full six inches taller than Eerdmann. "We are fellow officers in—"

"We *were*," Eerdmann interrupted.

"We gave an oath that said for as long as we live," Klaus countered before going on. "I need your assurance. I will tell you where it is if you can grant me safe conduct out of the area."

"If you don't tell me I will have you shot."

"Then I have nothing to lose if I am dead either way."

Eerdmann looked at him for a moment, staring him down and thinking how he didn't have time for this game.

"Who is this?" Eerdmann asked as he pointed at Jakob, appearing to change the subject.

"He is a Jew."

"A Jew? Do you often travel in the company of Jews?"

"I was helping the Arabs in Palestine to fight the Jews. I was captured."

"Oh, I see. Captured by the Jews. So they made you come here?"

"Yes."

"You told them about this place. And . . ."

"It was not a good situation."

"So you offered them my gold to—"

"I didn't know it was your gold. I didn't even know it was really here. I was just trying to get my head out of the noose."

"I . . . I just find this all very hard to believe. I think you should give me something to believe in here. If this is some Jew who forced you to come, why don't you shoot him for me right here and now?"

Jakob looked at Klaus, but Klaus just looked down at the pistol Eerdmann was handing him. The other men on the boat put their hands on their pistols, just in case Klaus made the wrong move. Klaus raised the gun, pointed it at Jakob, and pulled the trigger.

"Excellent!" Eerdmann said as he took the gun back.

Even though the gun wasn't loaded, Jakob was not amused at the way Klaus had so easily pointed it at him and pulled the trigger. He didn't even want to guess whether Klaus thought the gun was loaded or not.

"Now let's try it with a clip."

"I have a better idea," Klaus said.

"A better idea? I don't know . . . this sounds like a very good idea to me."

"Those men on the beach who were shooting at us . . . I think we could get them to leave if we offer them this one."

"We?" Eerdmann said as his eyebrows arched. "Is there a *we*?"

"If we get rid of *them, I* will show you where the crates are . . . and *we* all get what we want. You get the gold and I get a ride out of here."

"You just want a ride out of here?"

"Wherever you're going. That's good enough for me. I can get by."

Eerdmann just looked at Klaus again as he thought about the offer. He knew it was time to do something. He could kill them both and then go after the others on the beach . . . Maybe this Grunewald could save him the trouble. But could he trust him?

"I could give you this pistol . . . ," Eerdmann started. "First, you and 'your son' help get those crates onto my boat. Then you and he will take that boat and convince them to leave, leaving all their guns on the beach, in exchange for his life. We'll be watching you, and if you make one wrong move we'll kill you all. If everything goes right, you can jump over and swim out to us while they leave."

Klaus knew it was a setup. It was too easy. But there wasn't any way out of it. He would have to play it by ear.

Jakob knew it was a setup, too, but he was willing to go along. He figured he stood a better chance with Klaus. If he could get into the water . . . If Ben and Josef were ready . . .

"Can you trust them?" Kurt asked under his breath.

"Of course we can't trust them. If there's a chance to get the others into the open, we'll get rid of them all at the same time. If not, we'll just have to do it the hard way."

Back at the beach, only about fifteen minutes had passed when Ben and Josef saw a different boat approaching from the east as they were preparing for Eerdmann's return.

"Now what?" Ben exclaimed. "They said no one ever comes out here. It's turning into a damn regatta."

"Hello! Hello on the beach!" Hanlon called out as he came in close to the tents on shore.

Ben leaned his gun against the boulder he had been using as cover and stepped into sight, waving.

"I'm looking for some friends of mine," Hanlon continued. "They were going to do some diving."

"There were some out here this morning, but they're gone."

"Do you remember which way they went?"

"You're American?"

"Yes . . ."

"These are friends of yours?"

"Yes, friends of mine," Hanlon repeated. He didn't understand what Ben was asking. He thought Ben just didn't understand English very well.

"I think you'd better come in here," Ben said.

"Come in? What the hell are you talking about?"

"If you don't want to be shot," Ben said as he motioned for Josef to step forward so Hanlon could see him and the gun he had aimed at him. "You must throw your anchor and swim in here."

"What are you? Pirates?"

"Pirates?" Ben said, unable to hold back a laugh. "*You're* the pirates, you and your friends. They kidnapped our friend and—"

"Hold on there!" Hanlon protested. "We're all mixed up here. I'm with the OSS."

"OSS?" Ben asked.

"Office of Strategic Services. American military intelligence. When I said they were my friends . . . Well, first let's make sure we're talking about the same bird. I'm looking for a man named Eerdmann. Micah Eerdmann."

"He didn't give his name."

"All right . . . I'll lay it out on the table here. He's a former Nazi officer. I've been sent to arrest him."

"That could be him," Josef interrupted, still pointing his rifle at Hanlon. "They had guns. They were looking for something, but we ran them off. But they took our friend. I think they might come back any time now."

"Do you have any papers to prove your story?"

Ben asked.

"I'm not going to get through this without getting wet, am I?" Hanlon asked.

"I'll come out," Ben said as he dove in and swam to the boat.

Hanlon had the right papers and even a picture of Eerdmann that Ben identified, although he wasn't absolutely sure, since Eerdmann had been a substantial distance away when he saw him.

"And you say they're coming back?"

"I'm certain."

"What were you going to do?"

"Wait and see what he has to say. I don't think he killed our friend. I think he's going to rob us."

"Just to steal the tents and equipment?" Hanlon asked doubtfully.

"That's all we have."

Hanlon remembered that Eerdmann had talked about finding something he had left behind. He assumed Eerdmann had just wanted these fishermen out of here. He decided this might be his best chance to catch him.

"Maybe we can help each other," Hanlon said. "I've got a little something here . . ." He pulled out an M3A1 submachine gun. "Is there any sort of cover close by?"

"Cover?"

"A place to hide. Somewhere I can hide with the boat."

"There's some brush close to the water over there," Ben said as he pointed.

"Let's cover the boat and wait for a while. If they come back, we'll have quite a surprise for them."

Ben grabbed a saw and ax they had brought along for setting up the camp and took off in the boat with Hanlon. It didn't take long to get sufficient coverage for good camouflage from the thick brush.

"Well, I guess there's nothing else to do but wait," Hanlon said, and Ben just raised his eyebrows and shrugged, heading over the side to swim back to the camp.

"Are you sure they're coming?" Josef asked when Ben walked out of the waves. "It's been over an hour."

"That's what worries me. I don't know what's taking them so long. Unless . . ."

"Unless what?"

"Unless they're coming overland."

"Overland? That doesn't make sense. The road's out."

"They don't know that, unless Klaus told them. Maybe they're splitting up. Sending a couple of men over the hill. They can see right into the camp from there."

"This is not making me feel better."

Ben was right on the money. Eerdmann had ordered two men to climb the hill, but it was hard going up the cliffs and Eerdmann was growing impatient. He was just about to go whether they had made it or not when somebody caught sight of them waving at the top of the cliff.

Eerdmann had the boat start off slowly for the cove, with Jakob's boat still in tow. He still had to give his men on the cliffs time to climb down, since they only had pistols. If they had had rifles, the top of the cliff would have been a perfect sniper's post, but with pistols they had to get a lot closer. Now Eerdmann was down to four men on the boat besides himself, armed with pistols and one submachine gun.

Bill Hanlon had been waiting under camouflage for almost a half hour by then, and he was getting impatient too. He sat in the captain's chair with the "grease-gun," as the M3A1 was known, resting on his leg and four extra clips of ammunition on the throttle lever shelf. He decided he would hold back until the last minute. If the fishermen on the beach were right, this would be a hostage situation and the timing would be critical. Try to separate the hostage before the shooting breaks out, decide who to shoot first, and then give it everything you've got.

On the beach, Ben jumped up when he heard the first rumbling of the slow-moving boats. "Here we go," he said as he grabbed the binoculars and watched them clear the point.

"I think I saw them!" Josef said as he ran over to Ben. "I think I saw somebody moving on the hill there. You were right."

"I only count five on the boat."

"How many were there before?"

"I think it was seven . . . But I don't see Jakob and Klaus."

"Are you sure?"

"No, there they are. They're still in our boat."

"What do you think they're up to?"

"Depends on what Klaus said. If they know the gold is here . . ."

"Trade us Jakob for the gold?"

"I think they just want to get us out into the open.

If we let them give the orders, we'll never get off this beach alive. We have to surprise them . . . do something they aren't expecting."

"Like what?"

"Well, you have to take out those men on the cliff. Can you do that?"

"If I can spot them. I think I know where they are."

"You take the binoculars and sit back there and concentrate on that, no matter what happens out here. You watch my back and I'll take care of the rest."

"What about the American?"

"I'm counting on him to surprise them enough so that we get the upper hand. I think we can get Jakob out of this and hold our position here on the beach until our ship comes."

"Hold out for the ship? That could be days!"

"What should we do, leave the gold?"

"If it means our lives, yes."

Ben was so single-minded that he had never considered surrendering the gold. "Let's just work on getting Jakob back now. We can talk about the rest later."

"I'll take care of the men on the cliff," Josef said resolutely as he headed back to his post.

Just as Josef was running back to cover with a better view of the hillside, Bill Hanlon was looking through his binoculars and growling, "I got you now, you dirty rotten bastard." He had a perfect view of Micah Eerdmann. "Think you're gonna leave me on the hook . . . ," he continued as he planted a sweaty hand on the throttle, just waiting for the moment.

"Grunewald," Eerdmann said as he leaned over the edge of the boat, "here is a pistol. I will give you the rules one last time. If you make any funny moves, you will be the first to die. If you cannot convince them to leave, you will be the first to die."

"I'm starting to see a pattern here," Klaus said as the man guarding him left the boat for Eerdmann's and set Klaus and Jakob adrift.

"Yes, a very simple pattern. Even you should be able to understand it. Everything is up to you. If everybody is smart, I will let you all live. A reward for making my life that much easier."

Neither Klaus nor Jakob said anything until they came up closer to the shore and Klaus throttled down the engines. "Well, get up. Let them see you."

Jakob had been sitting in the boat waiting for this moment of truth. He had hardly said a word through their period of captivity, knowing what those kind of men were like. He knew he couldn't talk his way out of it, so he just had to wait until he was out in the boat alone with Klaus. "What are you up to, Klaus?" he asked in a dry, gravelly voice.

"Just what they said," Klaus answered as he stood tall at the wheel, putting the engines into reverse so that the boat would come to a stop in the water.

"And you believe they'll let us go if we all get into this boat?"

"He gave his word."

"His word?! You would risk your life on that man's word?"

"We have to do something. What do you suggest?"

"I suggest we break for the shore. We can fight them off there."

"And I end up on a ship heading back to Palestine?"

"Israel," Jakob corrected tersely. "And no. We have a deal. We found the gold. You get your ten—"

"Now who's supposed to be the fool? Why don't you get up and call Ben and Josef."

"They won't come."

"You have to convince them. That's what a leader does, Jakob. It's your job to do whatever it takes to save their lives."

"I don't believe this will save their lives."

"You're a coward, Jakob! You've always danced on the fence. You never make the hard choices!" Klaus began to shout as he started waving the pistol at Jakob.

"Klaus, get hold—"

"Ever since you were a boy! You are a Jew, you aren't a Jew . . . Which is it today? You don't even know who you are. Just like your father. When the hard choices had to be made, he just couldn't do it. He had to die. I had no choice!

Klaus's words hit Jakob like a slap in the face. "You?" he asked with stunned disbelief. "Of course!" he continued. "Why didn't I know it all along?"

"And I'd do it again. I loved your father. He was my truest friend . . . But sometimes a man has to do things. He has to be strong and do what must be done." Klaus paused for an instant, honestly affected by that bloody crime of years before, but then he lashed out at Jakob again. "Look at you! I know about that little boy of yours," he spat out. "He had to wear your star. He had to wear your star while you were pretending to be some great soldier or spy.

Your son sat rotting in that camp with a dirty little star on his coat that should have been yours. I should kill you. I should kill you now, but I won't. This is the life I owe you for your father. Do us both a favor now and let it go. We're even."

"We're not even. We won't be even until I kill you!"

"Well, if that's the way you feel about it . . . ," Klaus said as he pulled the trigger.

Because he was so agitated, Klaus had not really been aiming as he waived the pistol around. The bullet caught Jakob in the arm and pushed him backward into the water, where a crimson cloud quickly engulfed his body as he sank to the bottom.

Eerdmann couldn't understand what was going on. It looked like they were having some kind of argument instead of calling for the others to come out. Was it for his benefit? Some kind of show to distract them from some elaborate escape plan? He didn't get a chance to figure it out because at the same instant Klaus shot Jakob, Bill Hanlon opened up the throttle and moved out from his hiding place.

When Klaus heard a boat start up, he turned to see what was happening just as a bullet fired from the shore sang past his ear. Klaus threw open the throttle on his boat, and suddenly the water was alive with activity as all three boats were moving around, trying to outrun or cut each other off.

Eerdmann's men on the hill opened fire on Ben when he fired at Klaus, allowing Josef to locate them on the hill. Josef killed one man right off and then kept firing at the other.

Eerdmann didn't know who to go after first. Bill Hanlon had completely surprised them and was on them almost before they could get their engines going, firing his machine gun all the while. Eerdmann couldn't believe his eyes when he saw that it was Bill Hanlon on the other boat, and when he realized he already had two men down on the boat, he assumed it must be an ambush by OSS agents and decided he'd better make a run for it.

Back on shore, when Ben saw that Josef had the man on the hill pinned down and Hanlon was taking care of the other boat, he grabbed the scuba gear and dove into the water, heading for the spot where he had seen Jakob fall in. He would never have guessed that Klaus would shoot Jakob like that. He couldn't understand what was going on between them out there, but the gunshot completely surprised him.

Ben put on the tank and mask while under water and was soon on his way to Jakob. He found him motionless about twelve feet below the surface and grabbed him around the shoulder, pulling as hard as he could in a desperate race to get him to shore. He tried to give Jakob the mouthpiece, but he wasn't breathing, so Ben just concentrated on getting him to shore. The only thing that saved Jakob was that he had passed out when he was shot and hadn't taken in much water. Ben somehow got him to cover as pistol, rifle, and machine-gun fire kept going off around them. By that time, he had no idea what was happening or who was winning the battle. He just concentrated on resuscitating Jakob.

Josef had been firing steadily at the area on the

hill where he thought the second man was, and finally he saw him roll out from behind a rock, either dead or dying. Josef then concentrated his rifle fire on Eerdmann's boat as it sped out of the bay with Hanlon in hot pursuit, but then Hanlon abruptly broke off and headed back for shore. An instant later, black smoke began pouring out of his engine compartment. Josef kept a close eye just in case Eerdmann came back to take advantage of the situation. Hanlon's boat floated in toward shore on the inertia, and suddenly he ran for the back and jumped in the water. The black smoke turned to flames, shooting ten or fifteen feet into the air, and then there was an explosion. Hanlon was clear of the boat when it exploded and soon made it to shore.

Only then did Josef run over to Ben and Jakob. "Is he alive? Is he alive?"

"Yes . . . ," Jakob gasped. "I'm . . . still . . . alive . . ."

Ben was inspecting the wound. "Don't talk. That must hurt like hell with the salt water."

By then Hanlon had trudged over. When he saw Jakob, he knelt down and looked the wound over too. "Well, it's not too bad, but he's gotta have that looked at. Looks like a lotta blood. Put some pressure on it." Hanlon stopped a moment and looked at Jakob's face. "Y'know, you look kinda familiar to me."

Jakob just looked up at him. For some reason, Jakob would never forget Bill Hanlon's face from that day in Moreno when Jakob had killed Bruno Kress.

"God . . . damned . . . bastard . . . shot me," was all

Jakob could gasp out.

"Yeah, wasn't that a bitch?" Hanlon commiserated. "They killed my boat. I'm going to have a hell of a time explaining that one. And then the sonofabitch gets away to boot."

"To hell with your boat," Ben said angrily. "If we don't get him some help fast, this is going to be bad."

"Well, I don't know, but I think that's what they're here for," Hanlon said as he pointed to a small freighter coming into the bay.

There are moments in life . . . Well, let's just say that for Josef, a man who had been forced to live in the woods for five years scrounging for food, dirty and cold, while fighting the Nazis who had killed so many of those that he had loved—for that man to look up in a desperate moment and see an Israeli flag flying from the ship that had come to help them—that was the defining moment in his world. It didn't matter that it was just an old freighter in need of paint. Josef couldn't stop watching as the little figures lowered a boat and headed for shore.

It was a little embarrassing for Ben, once Jakob was taken care of, to tell Bill Hanlon that he was a prisoner of the Israeli army. Hanlon couldn't believe what he was hearing, but then someone drew a gun on him, blindfolded him, and took him out to the ship too.

Then out came the equipment. They had a portable winch, ropes, and skids, and Ben and Josef oversaw the recovery of the remaining crates of gold.

Hanlon was getting a little worried when the ship started out of the bay, but after a while Josef came down to tell him they were going to drop him off in Cagliari.

"Well, that's a relief," Hanlon said as Josef took off his blindfold.

"I don't know why they didn't take this thing off earlier."

"Course ya do," Hanlon said good-naturedly as he made himself comfortable on the bunk. "There was something I wasn't supposed to see. You must have been loading something. Don't suppose you'd tell me what it was?"

Josef smiled at the American. He liked his straightforward attitude and mistook it for naïveté. "It's probably better if you don't know."

"Good enough," Hanlon replied. "How's your boy doing? Is he going to make it?"

"Yes. The doctor says he'll just need some rest."

"So what happened to the guy who shot your friend?"

"He got away in all the confusion."

"Was he with Micah Eerdmann?"

"I don't think so," Josef said thoughtfully, disregarding Ben's view that Klaus had somehow planned the attack from the beginning.

"We must be pretty near Cagliari by now. Could I talk to your friend for a moment before I go?"

"I don't think that would be a problem."

They made their way down the narrow gangway to the sick bay, and Hanlon smiled as he saw Jakob lying awake, staring out the porthole. "They say you're going to make it," he said. "I'm glad to hear it."

Jakob just smiled politely.

"You probably saved his life, coming out when you did," Josef said from the gangway.

"That's okay. He saved my life once too."

"What?" Josef asked as a look of surprise crossed Jakob's face.

"Yeah. I never forget a face. Up in northern Italy . . . a little town called Moreno. Big old Nazi named Bruno-something-or-other got the drop on me with my own pistol. Damndest thing. But your boy here shot him dead."

Jakob tried to protest, but he wasn't very convincing in his weakened state.

"No, don't try to deny it," Hanlon continued. "I know it was you. But don't worry, someday we'll get together again when you're feeling better and talk over old times."

"We'd better go now, Mr. Hanlon," Josef said. "We're coming into the bay. They'll take you in on the launch."

"What's your name again, friend?" Hanlon asked Jakob.

"Jakob," Josef answered for him. "Jakob Stein."

Jakob groaned, but Josef didn't know why.

"Well, I'll be sure to remember that, Jakob Stein. I'll sure be certain to remember that."

After they returned to Israel, Jakob spent a couple of months at home recuperating from his wound. While he was laid up, the United Nations established a cease-fire in Israel. A month later Count Folke-Bernadotte, a Swedish member of the UN commission trying to come up with a peace plan, was being driven to his headquarters in Jerusalem when a jeep pulled out and blocked the way. Suddenly members of an Irgun splinter faction called the Stern Gang rushed up to Bernadotte's jeep and raked it with submachine-gun fire.

The day after Count Folke-Bernadotte was assassinated, Rebecca Stein gave birth to a boy they named Yigal Shemuel Stein. Rebecca had chosen the name Shemuel to honor David Freider's father, and Yigal . . . well, they just liked the name Yigal. Jakob was a very proud father, and it soon became obvious that Thomas was going to be a very protective older brother. Perhaps he wanted to make sure there was someone there for Yigal, whereas he had felt so alone.

And the war continued.

The Tunisian gold made its way back to Israel without incident and was kept secret by the government because of its origin. It's not that survivors of the holocaust wouldn't have wanted it donated to the nation, but the concept of Nazi loot from the death camps and Jewish communities was so emotionally charged that the chance for a political disaster was very high. It was a desperate time that called for desperate measures, and the decision was made to "reprocess" the gold and market it outside of the country, using the proceeds for the war effort.

CHAPTER 7

In 1954, the chief area of interest for the Israeli intelligence-gathering agency known as the Mossad, or "the Institute," was the state of Egyptian affairs. The Egyptian monarchy had recently been overthrown by a group of army officers led by Major General Muhammad Naguib. The officers, including Colonel Gamal Abdel Nasser and Anwar as-Sadat, declared a republic in Egypt. A few months after the coup d'état, Major General Naguib was replaced by Nasser. Israeli intelligence knew from the beginning that Nasser was a man to be watched. There were suspicions from the start that Naguib was just a front man, a general who would lend credibility to their government.

Nasser became a popular leader, not just in Egypt, but throughout the Arab world, as he let it be known that one of his primary goals was to put an end to the last vestiges of British colonialism in his country. He was riding the wave of nationalism that was sweeping the former colonies of Western European countries as the concept of colonialism crumbled like a wall of sand in a desert windstorm.

The Germans, of course, had been divested of the vast majority of their overseas colonial interests by virtue of their losses in both world wars. Now it was the turn of the French and English. When Britain gave up its governing interest in India in 1948, it was the death blow to the once-great British Empire, and it gave strength to all other anti-colonial movements throughout the world, including those in the French colonies of Tunisia and Algeria. Colonialism, which had once been touted as a symbiotic relationship between a strong industrial nation and underdeveloped nations whereby the strong nation gained access to natural resources and the underdeveloped nation was infused with capital that stimulated its economy, was now seen as a purely exploitive, racist, and degrading abuse of the underdeveloped nations. Colonialism had become a dirty word as one colony after another demanded self-determination as nothing less than a basic human right.

Nasser of Egypt made it clear both in private and in the rhetoric of his public speeches that, short of a British embassy, he wanted no other British presence in his country.

The biggest point of contention regarding British and French withdrawal was the Suez Canal. The building of the canal in the previous century had been a joint British–French project. They had supplied the concept and capital while the Egyptians provided the backs on which tons and tons of sand were carried. Nasser capitalized on the misuse of his people, as any good demagogue would, and began making noises that the French and English contribution to the project was nothing compared to the loss of Egyptian lives during the building of the canal. The validity of that point being one for philosophers in an industrial age, Nasser seized upon it as a political expedient. His ultimate goal was to nationalize the canal, but that was a long way off. Now was the time for speeches and posturing, making the soil ready and planting the seeds of his future.

Despite the Israelis' history with the British,

specifically the acrimonious end to the British mandate only six years earlier, they were not happy about the prospect of a British withdrawal from Egypt. Nasser's hatred of Israel at that time was basically rooted in the antagonistic rhetoric of all Arab nations toward Israel. It may not have been anti-Semitism as Westerners would define the term, but rather the fact that many Arabs viewed the Israelis as Western Europeans who had stolen Arab lands in just one more example of Western colonialism. Whatever the genesis of the conflict, the religious and political aspects were soon irrevocably intertwined, and there seemed to be no hope for real peace in the foreseeable future.

When Ethan Stein came to Palestine with his daughter just before the UN vote on partition, he was enraptured with the Holy Land. In England after the war, when restrictions against foreign nationals were lifted and he was allowed to travel freely, Ethan began to attend services at a nearby synagogue. He had seen all the newsreel footage of the concentration camps as the Allied armies moved into Germany, and while some saw this as proof that there was no God and turned away from religion, Ethan was drawn back to the Judaism of his childhood. When his daughter Eleonore asked him how he could still believe, he would quote God's response to Job in the Torah: "Where were you when I laid the foundations of the Earth?"

Once in Palestine, he insisted on visiting Jerusalem that first week. The next spring, while Arabs and Jews fought in the streets after the partition, in the weeks before the announcement of independence, Ethan insisted that everyone celebrate Pesach. Jakob was out fighting with a Palmach group, but Amalie, Abby, a noticeably pregnant Rebecca, and Thomas sat around a table on the first night of Pesach as Ethan read from a Passover Haggadah. It was the first time for Thomas, and he was uncomfortable when Ethan called upon him to read the four questions, but at least he had heard about it before in Hebrew school. Rebecca wanted Thomas to know about his Jewish background and had enrolled him in Hebrew school, but only for a couple of years. Thomas didn't fully understand why Ethan started to cry when he came to the final line of the Haggadah.

Of that group, other than Ethan, their Jewishness seemed to simply fade as time went on. It was that casual attitude that soon came between Ethan and his family. It wasn't long after Jakob, Rebecca, and Thomas moved in together—a move that greatly dismayed him—that Ethan decided to move to a kibbutz in retirement. He wanted Amalie and the others to join him in his faith, but he understood when they didn't. After all, he himself had slipped away. It had taken time for him to see. He had faith that someday they would join him.

In the years after independence, after the excitement of Ethan's arrival had waned, visits to the kibbutz became less frequent until finally a routine developed of family members visiting him one Sunday a month and bringing him to Tel Aviv for Yom Kippur and Passover. It was during those years that Thomas developed his lasting memories of his great-grandfather, memories that got mixed together with stories of the history of the Jews in Palestine, until somehow he decided that his great-grandfather had been one of the pioneers . . .

"Pioneers," Mrs. Yedidah said as she partially closed the book she was holding, carefully inserting the thumb of her right hand to keep her place. "That was what they were. Half a century ago they came to a place called Palestine, virtually a wilderness, and now after all these years of struggle, we have a homeland called Israel."

"You, too, are pioneers," she continued as she walked down the three rows of tables that served as desks in the musty little room of the former office building, now converted to a school. "Pioneers in this new state. Not like the first pioneers, but you are the ones who will build our Israel and make it a modern state. You are the ones who will make the desert bloom."

Thomas Stein rolled his eyes as he looked at his friend Pista. They had heard the word *pioneer* so many times before. It was always said in reverent tones, telling them that they were on a holy mission to build this Jewish homeland. Thomas and Pista had talked about it before. They decided that being told they were pioneers was just a nice way of saying they were poor and had to work hard.

Thomas was quickly brought to attention as Mrs. Yedidah's book slammed down on the table in front of him. It hurt her thumb as she slammed it down, but she wouldn't dream of letting it show. She was steeled by the fact that she clearly struck terror into the little boy's heart.

"Thomas," she said slowly and deliberately, "how many people came to live in Israel last year?"

Everyone in the class was looking at Thomas, not so much because they wanted to know the answer or because they wanted to know if *he* knew the answer . . . they just wanted to see Thomas suffer. Not Thomas in particular, of course. It could have been anyone. It was like watching a horrible accident, so terrible that it could make you physically sick, yet so fascinating . . . Thomas looked at Pista, but Pista had no idea what the answer was either and gave a subtle shrug of his shoulders. He couldn't have communicated the answer to Thomas even if he wanted to, what with Mrs. Yedidah towering over his friend's right shoulder.

Mrs. Yedidah saw Thomas looking at Pista and the answering shrug. "Thomas . . . ," she prompted in an ominous tone, pausing for dramatic effect, "we talked about this last week."

"Lots?" Thomas replied meekly, and the other children, including Pista, started to laugh. But Mrs. Yedidah held up her hand, a hand seemingly as powerful as the one with which Moses had parted the Red Sea, and the room instantly fell silent. Was she going to slap him?

"Lots . . . ?" she repeated in such a sad, disheartened voice. Thomas was obviously so disappointing that she could hardly hold her head up. Unable to look at him, she just shook her head and turned away. "By next year, children, if people keep coming to Israel in the same numbers, our population, the number of people living in Israel, will be double what it was when we became a state. *Double!* I don't know if you can understand what a fantastic thing that is now, but someday you will. Someday you will be proud to tell people that you were here from the beginning."

School seemed to go on forever that day, as it so often did for Thomas. He was a good student, but there were just so many other places he would rather be. The clock over the cracked blackboard loudly clicked off each five-minute increment, but Thomas had noticed on the first day of school months before that each time it clicked, the minute hand would first move backward before marking off the passage of time. It got to the point where Thomas would watch the clock just waiting for that instant so that he could verify that while he was in school, time was indeed going backward and that was why the day seemed so long. He had once heard a Yiddish saying that roughly translated as "for every step forward I take two steps backward." That was how the school day went.

The day finally ended with a frantic closing of books and shuffling of feet as the children desperately made their way to freedom.

Thomas and Pista met up with other friends and started on their daily rounds. They would go to each boy's house to deposit schoolbooks and then check to see if there was any chance of a snack. There was almost never any extra food, since most of the boys came from poor families who had arrived from war-ravaged Europe in the past five years with little more than the clothes on their backs. Many of them belonged to families that had been in the displaced persons camps and British detention camps that were suddenly emptied soon after Israel became a state. They were part of that wave of immigration that Mrs. Yedidah was telling them about. The new State of Israel may have been proud of its growth, but the price of that growth was a bleak austerity program coupled with social programs that made up an unhealthy portion of the state's annual budget.

When Thomas got home, he took Yigal along because it was Thursday. On Thursdays and Fridays, Myra, the teenager who babysat Yigal while Rebecca was at work, had to leave early. Yigal was now four years old, and Thomas doted on his little brother. Most of the other boys wouldn't dream of bringing a younger brother along; in fact, they considered it a punishment if their mothers said they had to take their siblings along for some reason or another. But it was different with Thomas and Yigal. For some reason, Thomas felt he had to protect and watch over Yigal.

Pista, Thomas's best friend, was from Hungary. His family had been rounded up at the end of 1944. He once told Thomas about how, just before the war ended, he, his brother, and his mother and father were left in a boxcar on a rail siding, some of the last being sent to Auschwitz. They had been locked in the railcar without food or water for days before being found by Russian soldiers. His brother died on that train. He was only four years old, the same age as Yigal. The subject only came up because Thomas was at Pista's apartment one day and noticed that his father was sick in bed. Thomas asked Pista what was wrong, and Pista said his father would still get sick from that time during the war, years before.

They rarely talked about such things, even though every boy in their "gang" had some kind of story to tell. Thomas started to realize at that time that his experience during the war was different, but he didn't quite know what had gone on. They certainly never talked about what had happened during the war at home. For his mother and father and grandmothers, it was as if there hadn't been any war. It was all just erased. There was nothing before they arrived in Israel, and all the time before began to seem like a dream to the little boy. Every now and again, though, he would have this memory come to mind about an older boy, a French boy named Virgil, and having to be quiet and stay hidden . . . Maybe it had just been a dream.

Thomas and his gang of friends would often play war games, and whenever the *bad guys* weren't the scary Arabs who had attacked when Israel became a state, then they would be the hated Germans. That was about the only time the boys ever discussed the war in Europe.

"I'm David Ben Gurion!"

"Ben Gurion? But he's so old! He's not even a general."

"Then who should I be?"

"Dayan. Here, make an eye patch out of this string and your sock."

"But it stinks!"

"Not my fault . . ."

"And your little brother is the Grand Mufti! No, no! He's *Nasser*!" Aaron shouted as he kicked sand at Yigal, and Yigal, who was just sitting peacefully building a sandcastle, began to cry.

"Hey!" Thomas shouted as he gave Aaron a firm shove and ran to help Yigal. "Leave him alone!"

Aaron, a malicious child, was always picking on someone. "What's the matter?" he said in a nasty, whiny voice as he regained his footing. "Can't your *baby* brother take care of himself? Do you have to change his diapers too?"

"Watch what you say, Aaron, or I'll give you such a beating that someone will have to change *your* diapers!"

"Oh, yeah?" Aaron said defiantly as he stepped closer to his playmate, making fists of his hands and raising his bony little arms while taking a proper pugilistic stance.

Although they were both twelve, Thomas was filling out and beginning to develop muscles. He stood about half a foot taller than Aaron and outweighed his antagonistic friend by almost twenty pounds.

Thomas was busy brushing the sand off Yigal and making sure none of it had gotten in his eyes while Aaron stood posturing behind him. "Shut up, Aaron!" he finally growled.

"Make me!"

Thomas just stood up and turned to face Aaron with a look in his eyes that said he was serious.

"Alright! Alright!" Aaron said as his resolve crumbled and he immediately backed down. "Let's not play war anymore. Whaddyawannado?"

"I wanna screw Myra Goldstein," Pista said with a laugh.

"The babysitter?" Aaron asked.

"What's that mean?" Yigal asked innocently.

"Shut up!" Thomas snarled at the two older boys

as he nodded toward Yigal.

"I'm hungry," Chaim piped in. "Let's get something to eat."

"Eat? Where?"

"I dunno."

"You got any money?"

"No."

"Then why did you say it?"

"I can't help it. I'm hungry."

"Let's go over to the market."

Thomas walked at the measured pace he always used when Yigal was with him, not so fast that his younger brother couldn't easily keep up as he tagged along in a zigzag pattern, always interested in everything going on around them. Thomas would occasionally tell Yigal to hurry up, but it was more coaxing than nagging. Sometimes the other boys wanted to go faster, but they had learned not to say anything because Thomas would tell them to just go on ahead. Thomas was very popular in their group, as close as they had to a leader, so they never took him up on it.

The market was a sprawling open-air affair typical of European cities from Avignon to Budapest. There were all manner of booths with fresh vegetables, fruits, spices and nuts, butchers and fish merchants, as well as occasional peddlers dealing in a wide range of odds and ends from kitchen utensils, sewing needles, and thread to used clothes and shoes. There were also booths with roasted chickens and other meats for families who didn't have ovens. And in those early days in Israel there were quite a few families whose "kitchen" consisted of a camp stove on a table in the corner of a one-room apartment and a couple of military "mess kits" with tin plates, silverware, and drinking cups.

It was a place of discovery and enchantment for a group of boys like Thomas and his friends. The enticing smells of cooking food, the colors of the fruits and vegetables, and the sight and sounds of people from so many different lands. Those first years saw tidal waves of humanity sweep upon the shores of the new Jewish homeland. After the "displaced persons" and the British detainees on Cyprus were released to Israel, many other groups began to emigrate. The War of Independence, or "the Palestine war," as the Arabs referred to it, fanned the flames of anti-Semitism in the Arab countries to the point where their Jewish populations were in danger. This brought a new tide of immigration that included the "Oriental Jews": the Jews of Iraq and Persia, of Yemen, Tunisia, Egypt, Syria, Jordan, and all the other Moslem countries. And as the "Iron Curtain" descended, the Jews of Poland, Romania, and the Soviet Union also tried to make their way to Israel.

Thomas and his friends stopped at a booth and watched, entranced, as a spit loaded with chickens slowly turned and the constant drip of juices splattered into the brilliant red glow of the hot coals. Each splatter erupted with a loud sizzle into seductive yellow tongues of flame that licked at the crisp, golden-brown skin of the birds. Aaron's stomach suddenly growled so loudly that all of the boys heard it, and they nearly fell over themselves laughing.

There were two men tending the booth, and the

one closest to the boys, a rather round-faced Arab in a dirty white apron, smiled at them. The other, a nasty-looking man with a pinched brow and a sharp nose that sat atop a coarse, bushy, jet-black moustache, yelled at the boys in some Arabic tongue to get away. The boys recoiled and started to run, but as Aaron took a quick look back, he saw the man with the round face throw something his way. Aaron stopped just in time to catch a small roasted chicken wing. He smiled and gave a quick wave before turning back to catch up with his friends, but not so fast that he couldn't finish off the wing before rejoining the group.

Thomas stopped at home for a moment to drop off Yigal, now that his mother was home, and then the boys continued on their way, eventually ending up in Pista's garage. It wasn't really Pista's, or even his parent's. The garage was just a beaten-up, old block building that had been abandoned years before. There was only the suggestion of what was once a roof. The windows were all broken out, the doors were gone, and even the wall where the doors had once hung had long since fallen apart. Pista had found this place when he was younger and knew in an instant that it would be a wonderful hiding place, a clubhouse to which he introduced his friends, and so it became his by right of discovery.

The boys sat in the corner of Pista's garage talking. Over the time they had known each other, they had gathered whatever they could to make it more like a clubhouse. A couple of old blankets and a mattress against the wall became their couch, and they found a couple of rickety wood chairs and a small table, and even a dented old kerosene lamp for those rare occasions when they stayed out after dark.

"Anna likes you . . ."

"I don't like her."

"Why not?"

"She smells funny."

"Funny?"

"Like my grandmother's kitchen . . . like boiled cabbage. I like Chava."

"Me too. She's really pretty."

"Chava likes you too."

"She does? Did she say so?"

"No. It's just the way she acts. She always laughs a lot when she's around you."

"That's 'cause I'm funny."

"Funny looking."

"I bet she wants you to kiss her."

"I'll bet she wants him to lay on top of her and pound her like a jackhammer."

"Hey," Thomas said, "don't say that stuff in front of Yigal!"

"What are you talking about? Yigal isn't here."

"I don't mean now. I mean what you said earlier about Myra! Jeez, Pista! Don't talk like that around my kid brother. You know he'll tell my mother."

"He's so dumb. He doesn't even know what I'm talking about."

"That's how he gets me in trouble! He'll ask my mother what it means!"

"How come you always bring him with, if he gets you in trouble all the time?"

"He's my brother. Where I go, he goes . . . so just

shut up about it."

"I got a kid brother, too, but you don't see me letting him run after us all the time."

"We gotta take care of each other. That's what brothers are for. You can't count on anybody else."

"Whaddya mean? What about your mother and father?"

"He might not stick around."

"Your father? Where's he going?"

"I don't know. I never know for sure. Sometimes it scares me . . ."

"Scares you?"

"If he leaves, I don't know what we'd do. We'd just have to find some way to get by. We got by before when he wasn't around, Momma and me, but now we've got Yigal too . . ."

Thomas looked like he was going to cry for an instant, but he caught himself and just drifted into silence, lost in his thoughts. Pista and the others were also quiet as they thought about their own stories. They were all wounded little boys, and they didn't know how to help each other. Lost in their thoughts . . . lost.

Eventually the conversation started up again, returning to girls and who liked who and the required vulgar sexual references boys that age only dare to use among their friends, language that is required as proof of masculinity in their macho posturing within the "gang."

They called it quits as the sun started to shoot bright yellow rays through the broken windows, signaling the impending sunset. By the time they got to Thomas's, Pista was the only one of the group left, since he lived nearby. When they walked in, the apartment was warm and welcoming as Rebecca peeled carrots in the kitchen while a chicken baked in the oven and a pan of boiling water awaited the spaetzle dumplings. It was a conventional scene of domestic bliss, except that Jakob still wasn't home. He was always late getting home.

"When is Tateh coming home?" Yigal asked as Thomas went to the bedroom he and Yigal shared.

"Soon, Sweetheart," Rebecca answered with a smile before turning to Pista. "And how are you?"

"I'm fine," Pista said as he stood next to Rebecca, leaning against the counter so close that he was almost touching her as he watched her work. She had known for a long time that Thomas's friend had a crush on her.

"And how is your family?"

"Everyone is good." There was a slight pause before the exchange took an odd turn. "Is Mr. Stein ever coming home?" Pista asked in a quiet voice without looking her in the eye.

"What? Of course he is! Why would you ask such a question?"

"Uh. . . I don't know," he said shyly as he tried to tell Rebecca what had been bothering his friend, but then he finally looked up. "Thomas said he might not come home someday."

"Thomas said that?"

"Uh huh . . ."

"Well, you don't need to worry about that, Sweetheart. Mr. Stein will always come home."

"It made him sad."

"He told you that?"

"No . . . He was. . . he was almost crying."

"He was crying?" Rebecca asked, surprised since Thomas never cried. She couldn't remember the last time he had. Even when he got a cut or bruise, the sort of thing that most little boys would cry about, he held it in.

"Almost."

Her first thought was to call Thomas out and tell him it was ridiculous, that his father would never leave them. Maybe she could make him believe it, even if she wasn't completely sure herself. But she couldn't embarrass him in front of Pista. He'd probably get mad at him for having told her. After thinking about it for a moment, she decided it would be best if she didn't mention it to him.

"Don't tell him I told you," Pista continued.

"I won't," she said, brushing back his hair with her hand. "Looks like you could use a haircut."

"That's what my mother says. That means she'll be getting out the scissors . . ."

They talked a bit more until Thomas came out and the two boys went to play until Pista had to go home for dinner. Just as Pista left, Jakob came in.

Later that night, after the boys were asleep and Jakob and Rebecca were getting ready for bed, she told him about her conversation with Pista.

Jakob was caught completely off guard by this revelation. He thought everything was going fine, and he couldn't imagine why Thomas would say such a thing, but he kept calm as he asked, "What did Thomas say when you asked him about it?"

"I didn't say anything to him."

"You didn't say anything?" Jakob asked accusingly,

as though her silence was concurrence.

"I think you need to ask him about it. You weren't there for so long and then . . ."

"It was the war! I didn't even know about—"

"I'm not accusing you of anything," Rebecca said, cutting him off. "You and I know about war and life and how things happen, but Thomas is just a little boy. All he knows is there was all that time when you weren't with us. He's afraid."

Jakob let out a big sigh and then climbed into bed. He knew she was right, but still he felt as though he was being accused of something and wasn't completely sure that Rebecca had forgiven him for the past. "I'll talk to him."

"When?"

"When? When I get a chance. Tomorrow or the next day. Saturday for certain."

"Don't forget. This is important."

"You're telling me this is important? My son thinks someday I just won't come home and you think I don't know this is important?"

"Now go to sleep," Rebecca said as she rolled over.

He turned off the light and got into bed. "I love him," he said in the darkness. "He must know I love him. How could he think such a thing?"

"He knows you love him," she finally said as she rolled over to face him. "That's why it scares him that you might go away. He loves you and is afraid he might lose you. Remember, some little boys just have imaginary monsters in their closets. Thomas had to deal with real monsters. I think he just needs to be reassured."

He forced a smile as he looked into her eyes. She

pulled him close and kissed him as they cuddled together, falling asleep in each other's arms.

The next morning was a beautiful morning, but Jakob didn't notice. The family breakfast was rushed, and he was soon on his way to work. His job with the intelligence agency had become a routine of sorting through vast amounts of paper in an effort to sift out any information that could be useful to the Mossad for predicting belligerent actions from their Arab neighbors or any other possible threat to the security of the country.

It wasn't the sort of thing Jakob had in mind when he had started working for the Mossad. He had fully expected to be a field agent, but they kept putting him off, saying they needed him where he was for now. He felt like an office clerk, and the wages didn't do much to alter his opinion. He had accepted the job with a sense of duty, but he thought he would be a spy . . . traveling, living with danger. The most dangerous part of his job was the ever-present threat of a gaping paper cut. As hard as he tried to keep his mind on the task at hand, reading a report on the amount of coffee shipped through the Suez canal during the preceding twelve months, his thoughts kept drifting back to how his job had turned out much different than he had expected.

As the workday came to an end, he found himself thinking about what Thomas had said. Maybe his disaffection with his work was showing. Maybe his boredom was obvious and Thomas thought it included his family too. Maybe it did. Family life had become routine. He was now an old married man with two boys and a job as a clerk. But he had never thought about leaving. He accepted his life . . . maybe with some regrets, but accepted it nonetheless.

He found himself passing by his mother's apartment on his way home and decided to stop in.

"Thomas came up with something strange the other day . . ."

"Really? What?"

"He told his friend that he had to take care of Yigal because some day I would go away and leave them alone."

"Oh . . . that's terrible!"

"That's what *I* thought."

"I didn't mean that way," she corrected. "I mean it's terrible that he feels that way, not that he said it. It sounds like you think he should feel bad for hurting your feelings."

"Well . . . it was uncalled for. I've been a good father. I keep them fed and clothed . . . a roof over their heads."

"It sounds like you've forgotten what it's like to be a little boy. All of those things are taken for granted. A little boy lives in a world of monsters and heroes. Something is either right or wrong, and when they're hurt . . . they fear the hurt may come again. He remembers how long you were gone."

"That's not fair! You and Rebecca keep bringing it up as though I—"

"We're not talking about *you*. We're talking about Thomas. That's what it means to have a child. Thomas is your son, and you have to put him first. You don't have the luxury of hurt feelings. You're the father. You have to be bigger than that. Stop talking about how he's hurting you or insulting you. He feels what he feels, and you need to address that without asking if it's true or not. You can't change the past. You can only help him now."

"Now? I'm not going anywhere. All I can do now is keep doing what I'm doing. The time will come when he sees he was wrong. That I never left."

Amalie took a deep breath and ran her hand through her hair, something she never did, but now she combed her fingers through her hair as though trying to massage her brain. It was a strange gesture, and Jakob could tell she was deeply upset and trying to keep her cool. "Don't you love him?" she finally asked as she looked her son dead in the eye.

"Love him? Now you don't think I love him? Of course I do! Thomas and Yigal . . . and Rebecca . . . they mean everything to me."

"If he means so much to you, then why does it sound like a contest between you two to prove who's right and who's wrong?"

"Don't be ridiculous, Mother," Jakob countered as an angry last resort.

"*Love* him, Jakob. When was the last time you held him . . . the last time you kissed him?"

"Kissed him? He's twelve years old. He doesn't want his father to kiss him."

"Men!" Amalie huffed with contempt at her son's ignorance.

"His friends would . . ."

"I'm not saying you should embarrass him in front of his friends. Twelve years old is not so old that a boy doesn't want . . . ," Amalie started to explain, but then she changed her tack. "You have to understand.

Even though he says he's too old, he still wants that
kind of love. He has to say he doesn't because he's
growing up and he wants to be independent, but
there's a part of him that's still a little boy, that needs
his parents' love and acceptance and, yes, even their
kisses. He just wants you to spend time with him. He
wants to know that he's important to you. Don't you
remember when you were Thomas's age? That was
when you started doing well in sports and you and
your father became much closer."

That last sentence stopped Jakob cold. "When
Honig was killed . . . ," he said thoughtfully as he
remembered.

"Honig? Oh yes. That terrible day at the lake.
You're right. That must have been quite an awakening for Gunther, that day when you were hurt.
Maybe that was it. Maybe this is your rude awakening, Jakob. Your son thinks you're going to disappear. This is your chance to let him know that he
means too much to you for you to leave. Maybe
that's what he's saying . . . that he doesn't think you
care enough to stay."

"I care."

"Then *show* him. These days are . . . ," Amalie tried
to explain, but once again halted as she let out a big,
gasping sigh. Tears started to form, but she didn't
cry. "I don't suppose you want to hear your old
mother go on, but these days are so special. When
we're young our days are all in front of us, as though
we had held out our hands and God filled them with
all these glittering gold coins, so many that we could-
n't hold them all. Some slip from our fingers care-
lessly, but we think we've got so many that it doesn't

matter if we let a few slip away. And then a few more slip away and we begin to think maybe we should have spent them more wisely. When you get older you'll be amazed at how quickly it's all gone. Don't let this time slip through your fingers, Jakob. Your boys will grow up so fast."

"I'll talk to him," Jakob said with a note of finality, as if to say the topic was closed. "So . . . what else is new?"

"Have you heard about this trial going on in Jerusalem?"

"What trial?"

"A libel trial. A man named Grunewald . . ."

"Grunewald? Like Klaus Grunewald?"

"Well, *Green*wald . . . but close enough. This Greenwald accused another man of collaborating with the Nazis."

"A Jew?"

"Yes. A man named Kastner. He was with a Jewish rescue committee in Hungary, and this Greenwald says Kastner took money from the Nazis and collaborated with them to get his own family out of Hungary to Switzerland."

Jakob looked at her blankly. He didn't know quite what to make of what she was saying, especially in the *way* she was saying it. Her tone was . . . defiant. Defiant and angry. As though this Kastner shouldn't be questioned. It was starting to sound exactly like what they had been through, the way Amalie had blackmailed her way out of Theresienstadt. Then Jakob finally understood. His mother was saying that any person would do, *should do,* whatever they could to save their family above all else. It might as well be her on trial.

"What are you looking at me like that for?" she asked intensely.

"Well, if he was working with . . ."

"So you think he was wrong?"

"I don't know all the facts, but . . ."

"It wasn't the same for us!" she said animatedly. "If Kastner took advantage of the circumstances, that was one thing, but we *made* the circumstances. It's not the same thing."

"I didn't say it was, Mother. I never said any such thing."

"Do you think I was wrong?"

"No, of course not. You saved a lot of lives. I did things that . . ."

"Let's not talk about it anymore," she said as she sat down. It was too much to think about now. She would not have done it any other way, but sometimes she wondered about it. They said that when Kastner saved his friends, other people took their places in the gas chambers. If that was true, then she had done the same thing. Had people died who wouldn't have if she hadn't had those few pieces of paper?

"Well . . . ," Jakob started in a clumsy attempt to change the subject back, "I suppose I'd better start paying more attention to Thomas."

"That sounds like a good idea," she agreed quietly. "It doesn't have to be anything special. Just spend some time with him."

Jakob thought about his father as he walked home. He thought back to the time when he and his father were close. Looking back, it was really a very short time, three or four years at the most, and then suddenly he was gone. Fifteen years ago . . . no, it was twenty years now since his father had been killed. He wondered for a moment what Gunther might be like now. He had been the same age as Jakob was now when he was killed. He was a young man when he died, but Jakob had always thought of him as so much older.

"How about you and me go see a movie?"

"What?" Thomas asked as he looked up at his father.

"Just you and me. We'll go on Sunday."

"What about Mother and Yigal?"

"We never go anywhere alone. Let's just you and me go out for a movie and a sandwich somewhere."

"Okay . . . ," Thomas said with a fair amount of suspicion in his voice as he wondered to himself what it was that had brought this about.

Three days later, as Thomas and his father started out the door late in the afternoon, Yigal began to cry because he wanted to go along. Jakob picked up his youngest son and hugged him, explaining that this time it was just going to be Thomas going along and promising that next time it could be just he and Yigal.

"But I don't want to go without Thomas . . . ," Yigal cried. Thomas smiled at that, and Jakob gave Yigal a last hug before handing him off to his mother. As he looked on, it occurred to Thomas that Jakob would always hug and kiss Yigal, but rarely did he touch him.

"There's an American movie showing on Dizengoff. It's called 'Shane,'" Jakob said as they walked.

"Pista saw it . . . said it was great. I like American westerns."

"You do? So do I. When I was about your age, I used to read books about the old west. I don't know if you remember Otto . . . he came out of the concentration camp with you and the others. Otto wrote books about cowboys and Indians."

"Otto? Otto Maus? Grandma gave me some books by him."

"My old books? No, she couldn't have. She couldn't have saved them through the war."

"No, she found some here . . . in an old bookstore. She told me you had them when you were young."

"Did you like them?"

"I read them. They were okay . . ."

"Maybe I liked them more because I knew Otto."

"Why are we going to the movies alone?" Thomas asked, as though ready to put an end to the small talk and get down to the business at hand.

Jakob looked at him, at the serious expression on Thomas's face, and smiled and shook his head. "You're always so serious. You're such a thinker. You take everything and turn it over and over, trying to figure it all out."

"Is that bad?"

"How old are you?"

"You know!"

"I asked how old you are."

"Twelve."

"Twelve years old. So serious at twelve. When I was twelve I . . ."

"Is that why you like Yigal better?"

Jakob stopped in his tracks in the middle of the sidewalk and looked at Thomas. The expression on Thomas's face was accusing but was quickly melting into a sad, hurt look.

Jakob sighed and smiled a half smile. "Come here," he said as he moved to Thomas and put an arm around his shoulder and then led him over to a nearby bench. He sat down and pulled Thomas close to his side.

"I guess you're pretty mad at me," Jakob said after a moment.

"No . . ."

"Yes you are. You can say it."

Thomas sniffed and looked up at his father with piercing, tearful brown eyes, and Jakob had to look away. He couldn't look at him. It hurt too much to see Thomas so sad and to know that he was the cause.

"My father never told me that he loved me," Jakob said quietly. "I think he did. I'm sure he did, in his way, but he never said it. He never held me. He never kissed me. I'm sure that's the way his father was with him, and his father's father. With Yigal, when he was born and being little . . . it just seems easier."

Jakob turned back to Thomas, looking him straight in the eye. "I love you, Thomas," he said wistfully. "I didn't know how to say it. Some things just seem so difficult. After I found you and your mother . . . after everything had happened with the war, I didn't want to be away from you. But I didn't know how to be with you . . . I wasn't sure how to love you. I thought you didn't want me to—"

"I was afraid you would leave again. I . . . ," Thomas interrupted as he began crying.

Jakob held his son close, in an embrace so tight he thought he might hurt him, but he couldn't let go. Thomas managed to stop crying, but he didn't pull away. They just sat there for a while. "I'm not going anywhere, Thomas," Jakob finally said. "I love you . . . always will . . . My work will take me away from time to time, but I'll always come home."

Thomas sniffed and Jakob pulled out a handkerchief. Thomas blew his nose, and Jakob used the corner of the handkerchief to dab away the remaining tears from his son's face. "Now," he said as he pulled himself together, "let's go get a sandwich and see that movie."

As they walked along the sidewalk, Jakob was surprised as he felt Thomas's hand slip into his. He looked over at him and smiled, pulling Thomas closer to his side, bumping into him. Thomas reciprocated by bumping into his father, almost knocking him off balance and laughing.

Jakob knew it was only a beginning, but he thought at least there was hope. Once not long after that he picked Thomas up and hugged him, wrestling him around the room when Pista was there, and suddenly that thought about embarrassing Thomas in front of his friends popped into his head. But when he looked at Pista, it wasn't ridicule he saw in Pista's eyes. Perhaps Jakob read too much into it, but he thought Pista wished his father might hold him like that.

Things were getting easier, better at home. It was

getting to a time when he stopped thinking so much about what he didn't have, the places he couldn't go, and started to like the place where he was. An outside observer might ask if he was content, and that would be one way of looking at it, but a more accurate explanation was that he was finally coming to see the value of his life, the value of this family of his.

Even the mundane nature of his job—checking information at the intelligence agency—was bearable.

Then one day Jakob looked up from the stacks of paper on the table where he worked as Chanoch Zimra, the head of his department, walked up with a handful of folders, reading the top one. Jakob respected Chanoch for his intelligence, but his boss was something of a bookworm. Sometimes he would get so caught up in his work that he wouldn't notice those around him. This was just another example, as he stopped in front of Jakob, reading the file without acknowledging him at all.

"More work?" he finally asked after waiting for Chanoch to say something.

"What?" Chanoch asked, realizing that Jakob was talking to him. "Oh, Yakov. We need someone to go to Egypt."

"Egypt? Are you asking me?" Jakob asked with surprise.

"You have the background they're looking for. German-born . . . knowledge of the Czech language."

"For what?"

"They need a new face, someone to send in as an

East German businessman involved in a Czech arms deal. They want you to talk with the interrogators and see if they can work with you."

"Work with me?"

"They'll tell you about the Egyptian police and their intelligence agents . . . just in case you were to get picked up. But more important, they'll see if you've got the temperament. This isn't like being a partisan. You have to fit in, be part of the scenery. Not too handsome, not too ugly. The sort of person who just comes and goes and you can't even recall what they looked like."

"Not too flattering."

"You'll think it's flattering enough when it saves you from getting stopped by the police. Are you interested?"

"Yes."

"Then let's go and meet the boys."

"I already know them."

"Not like this, you don't. Their job is to push you to the edge and find out who you are. It's not like when you go out to lunch with them. It's night and day. They're all business."

"The boys," as Chanoch referred to them, were a special division within the Mossad that assessed agents. They were a group consisting of a strange mix of field agents, psychiatrists, and military personnel. This group comprised a sort of "think tank" that debriefed agents after missions, as well assessing the abilities and potential of new agents and the continuing status of existing field agents. The first day's interviews were routine questions about his past, such as where he had lived and what his military experience had been like. From there the questioning took on the distinct feel of a psychological examination as two men asked him about everything from his relationship with his parents to his sex life.

Jakob felt wrung out by the time he went home that evening. He had worked very hard at avoiding key bits of information throughout the questioning, about the events surrounding how Amalie had blackmailed her way out of Theresienstadt.

That evening he told Rebecca he might be going into the field. She wasn't happy about it, but even as she protested, she knew it was a controlled response to his wanderlust. She knew he hadn't been happy with his job and that he did it as a concession to her and the boys.

The next day's questioning began on a more esoteric note. "Do you believe in good and evil?"

"Good and evil?" Jakob asked, almost laughing as he repeated the question. "What do you mean? Angels and devils?"

His interrogator showed no reaction to Jakob's jibe. Instead he just pressed on to another question. "Do you believe in right and wrong?"

"What are you? A Rabbi?" Jakob asked, arching his eyebrows.

"Do you do things you consider to be wrong?" the man pressed.

"Don't you?"

"Why do you want to be an agent?"

"They asked *me* to do this."

"So you *don't* want to be an agent? We could all save a lot of time."

"No, I want to do it."

"Why?"

"I think it's important."

"Why? Why is it important?"

"It's us against them. We need whatever edge we can get."

"Them?"

"Them . . . the Arabs, the Nazis, the Poles . . . them."

"The Poles?"

"You know . . . Kielce."

"Oh . . . Do you hate them?"

"Of course I hate them. What they did to the Jews coming back home from the death camps, surviving all that only to be killed by those Polish pigs when they tried to claim their homes and property."

"All Poles?"

"What?"

"Do you hate all the Poles?"

"Let's just say I don't trust them. Auschwitz was in Poland . . . Treblinka, Sobibor . . . No, I don't trust them. I don't think it's all just a coincidence."

"What about the Russians?"

"The Russians? I guess that's an interesting question. There's Stalin . . . He's as big a killer as Hitler ever was. And then there were the Cossacks. The Protocol of the Elders of Zion came from Russia, the Czar's secret police. And then there's the fact that Egypt is getting arms from Czechoslovakia . . . t380hat's the Russians too. No, I guess I don't trust them either. When you get right down to it, I can't think of a lot of people I trust anymore. Is that a bad thing for an agent?"

"No. And you're not alone on that count," the

interrogator added, as though changing speed. "You were a partisan?"

"Yes."

"In Czechoslovakia?"

"Yes."

"Would you go back there?"

"To live? No."

"On missions?"

"Yes. On a mission . . . of course."

"Why wouldn't you want to go back there to live?"

"This is my home."

"You've had a lot of homes."

"No . . . I've lived a lot of places, but this is home. My wife and sons are here."

"So your family means a lot to you?"

"Of course."

"Then why would you think about being an agent? It could be dangerous."

"I think I'd be good at it. I think it's important work."

"So you said. Us against them. What does that mean?"

"Oh, come on! It's a war!" Jakob said in exasperation. "I know you're supposed to feel me out and see what I believe, but let's not be ridiculous. The Mediterranean on one side and Arabs on all the others."

"Have you ever killed a man?"

"Of course!" Jakob replied.

"In battle?"

"Yes."

"Have you ever killed a man up close?"

"Yes."

"Tell me about it."

"He was a traitor," Jakob continued as he thought about the murder of Cecil Baker. "I was told to kill him and make it look like an accident."

"What did you do?"

"I followed him. I ended up next to him on a crowded train platform and pushed him onto the tracks."

"How did you get away?"

"I just walked away. Blended into the crowd. There was so much excitement nobody even realized he had been pushed. I just kept calm and walked away."

"That takes a lot of nerve."

"There wasn't much choice. If I hadn't kept calm I would've gotten caught."

"Do you think you could do that now?"

"I'm not signing on as an assassin."

"No, of course not, but if you had to do something like that, if the circumstances left you no other choice, do you think you could?"

"If there's one thing I learned from the war, it's that a man can do almost anything to survive. I heard of a man in one of the camps who removed a gold tooth from the mouth of his own brother after the Nazis killed him . . . because that was his job. I heard about another man who shaved the head of his own sister-in-law just before she went to the gas and never told her what was going to happen." Jakob paused for a moment. He was not unaffected by those stories. "So, to answer your question, yes, I think I could do it again if my life depended on it, but I wouldn't go in specifically to kill a man."

"Tell me about Sasha Petrov."

"Sasha?"

"Sasha Petrov. You remember . . . He was a Czech, a boy who went along with you into Hungary."

"How the hell did you—"

"He didn't come back."

"A lot of people didn't come back."

"We've heard some rather disturbing things."

"What kind of things?"

"Someone has suggested that you were involved in . . . Well, there is talk that somehow you were involved with Reinhard Heydrich and then Wilhelm Canaris. It's not the sort of thing one wants following them around. How would you explain it?"

Jakob was stunned. His first thought was wondering who could possibly have betrayed him. Who could have known about Heydrich, Canaris, *and* Sasha? He hadn't known Sasha until after his return from Switzerland. It must be a bluff. Just rumor and innuendo.

"I don't explain it. It's absurd. I didn't even join the partisans until after Heydrich was dead, and I don't even know this other man you're talking about. As far as Sasha . . . we were with a group of Hungarian partisans. We had to get out of Prague because the SS knew about us. We ended up with these Hungarians, and they were betrayed as they were about to attack a German column. Only two of us survived. Lorencz and me. I tried to get Sasha out when he was shot, but he died there at my side, and then I was shot. This Lorencz got me out of there and left me with a farm family while my wounds healed."

"Some say you were the traitor."

"That's stupid! It's ridiculous. They'd only say that because I survived. That's the sort of shit people always say. If their brother or son or father died in an ambush, then anyone who survived must have betrayed them, or why else would they be alive and their man dead. My only crime was living. Besides, if I had betrayed them, believe me, Lorencz would have killed me. He could easily have done it with his bare hands. He could have just left me for dead and the Germans would have finished me off."

"Do you have anything else you want to tell us before we end this interview?"

"No," Jakob said confidently, despite his uneasy feeling that they knew everything about Heydrich and Canaris. Maybe he shouldn't have told them about Cecil Baker. Maybe they had some pieces of that puzzle and he had just filled it all in for them. But there was no going back now. "No," he repeated, "I don't have anything to hide. Will there be another interview tomorrow?"

"Yes, and you're to stay here tonight."

"Stay here? No one said anything about that."

"They weren't supposed to tell you. It's one of our little surprises."

"Surprises?

"Yes. You'll stay with us tonight, and tomorrow we'll tell you the rest."

"Can I call my wife?"

"We've already informed her. I'm afraid the night won't be terribly comfortable for you.

The interrogator was right. Jakob was escorted to a small room, a mock-up of a prison cell with just a cot, and he wondered how far they were going to take this. *Is this a test they put all their agents through,* he wondered to himself as he sat on the edge of the cot while the door to his little cell was closed and locked, *or do they know what I did for Canaris during the war?*

No, he told himself, *it couldn't be that.* If they thought he had been a Nazi collaborator, they wouldn't waste their time on him. He had to keep his head. That was exactly why they were doing this, to see if he could keep his wits about him.

Suddenly he wondered . . . a fleeting thought passing through his consciousness. If there were a physical manifestation, it would be like a butterfly floating into the room, rising and falling and then suddenly disappearing. He thought about the question they had asked him on that first day. Did he believe in God? It was strange, since he didn't believe in God, that he now wondered if God would forgive him. Could God forgive the things he had done, the things he had been sure were absolutely necessary. Could God forgive him for that?

He finally managed to fall asleep, wondering as he drifted what they had in store for tomorrow.

Tomorrow came quickly. They stormed into his cell at two o'clock in the morning, two strong young men who gave an excellent impression of prison guards employing brute force as they dragged him from his cell and back to the interrogation room.

He was thrown into a chair in that small room. It was classic. A bright light in his face, a shadowy, indistinguishable figure hovering about somewhere in front of him. A voice beyond the light barking out

"What is your name?"

Jakob was about to say his own name as he looked up, but he realized it was just a test and he was supposed to give his cover story.

"Karl Loescher."

"Loescher? German?"

"Yes, I'm a German businessman from Dresden."

"Why are you here?"

"Business. I represent the Czechs."

"The Czechs? Why would a German represent the Czechs? I didn't think the Czechs were very fond of the Germans."

"They're fond of our technology. We supply—"

"Who are you here to see?"

"I'm not sure. I was told to come to Cairo so I would be available . . . My office said they would give me instructions when I arrived here."

This was the tenuous link of the Israeli background. They had someone set up in an office in Dresden to back up the story, but it was just a façade, and if the story were investigated in detail, they would quickly find out it was a ruse. The interrogation went on for about twenty more minutes before Jakob was returned to his room, but then he was pulled out again some two hours later. They wanted to see how he would hold up under sleep deprivation, which was a very common technique employed by the Egyptians.

Jakob found it easy enough to stick to the cover story, interweaving elements of his experiences in Prague and Dresden to give the story flavor.

He realized as he went through the interrogation that the truth didn't matter, not to these people.

That's why they had asked if he believed in God and in right and wrong. They just wanted to see his reaction. They needed to know how well he could convince others of *their* truth—how well he could convince others of what the Institute wanted them to believe. Truth was to be a very small part of the job; it was something their agents had to keep inside themselves, tucked safely away like a compass hidden in a secret coat pocket, so that someday they could find their way home after it was over.

He made it through the interrogation with flying colors, but he knew it was only a simulation. They hadn't tortured him, and he knew after all that his interrogators were not Egyptians, and that he was safely tucked away in an Israeli intelligence building in Tel Aviv. It would be different in Cairo. If he were caught, just the thought of being trapped on his own in a foreign country would change his view. Would he be able to hold up there? *Best not to get caught in the first place,* he thought to himself.

He was allowed to go home for a day after that. When he returned, they went over the cover story again, showing him where he had made a mistake but commenting that he had covered up the mistake very well.

Then they went on to the specifics of his mission.

"It's a relatively simple mission, just passing on information and a small package to a group that's already been put together in the Cairo area. But just because the mission is simple doesn't mean it isn't dangerous. The irony is that you have to keep your guard up at all times without ever looking like your guard is up. Don't give anyone reason to notice you.

I've heard it myself before when questioning people. 'There was a nervous-looking fellow standing by the platform,' they'll say, 'and that's when we knew we had our man.'"

Jakob nodded in agreement as his instructor continued.

"The project is code-named 'Operation Susannah.'"

"How long will it take?"

"From what we know at this point, you should be in and out in a week. We have to send you round-about to get into Cairo. You'll be going by way of Italy. Once there, you'll go to an address we'll give you and tell them that the operation is a go. You'll be taking in some supplies, but they're small and well hidden."

"Guns? Explosives?"

"Small incendiaries. It's more for show than anything else. We're not trying to blow up military installations or anything. We just want to put on a show to suggest that the area is unstable. If everything goes off as planned, there shouldn't be any casualties."

"So that's it. In and out with a quick delivery?"

"Yes. Well, if you should happen on something you think we should know about . . . don't go out of your way, but if you hear something."

Jakob just arched an eyebrow in response. It seemed ridiculous to tell him he should report any rumor he might hear on the street, but he didn't come out and say it. It just sounded so amateurish. But they must know what they're doing. They are the state intelligence agency.

Less than two weeks later Jakob found himself in

Port Said, at the head of the Suez Canal. It was a bit more than a hundred and fifty kilometers to Cairo.

Jakob exchanged some of his German currency for Egyptian pounds and piasters and located a bus bound for Cairo. The bus was crowded and hot. Even though it was early May, the temperatures were already close to a hundred degrees Fahrenheit.

The bus driver was an ugly little man who drove like a drunken sailor on leave. His face was humorless and somber as he pulled and pushed at the steering wheel with the abandon of a skilled circus acrobat flying from rope to rope, oblivious to the fate of his passengers as they were tossed about from side to side on every turn.

It was the combination of being tossed around and the smell of some of his fellow passengers that made Jakob increasingly ill as the trip came to an end. He thought to himself that he must be getting soft. After all he had been through in the war, to now be brought down by a shaky bus ride and a few noticeably unwashed fellow travelers . . . The truth, however, was that he was unused to the relentless heat, and he was also tired and nervous. This wasn't quite like the war. He felt very alone. He had told himself that he was riding into familiar territory, some kind of link to his past, but this was different after all.

The plan was to meet with an agent and give her the plastic explosives he had smuggled into the country in the lining of his suitcase. The plastic explosives were harmless without the blasting caps attached, blasting caps that were disguised as a dozen fountain pens.

The goal of the agents working for the Israelis was merely to set off a few small explosive devices in public places, incidents that were not intended to cause any casualties, but designed to make the British reconsider their plans to withdraw from Egypt.

He went to the little hotel on the west side of Cairo as he had been instructed. This was the modern part of Cairo. The eastern part was the old city, mostly Muslim and poor. He spent the next two days in his hotel room. He shouldn't have, but he wasn't feeling well, and somehow he couldn't bring himself to go out yet. He couldn't even acknowledge that he was scared. He just told himself that he was sick. The water, the heat . . . for whatever reason, he was sick. He had a week to make contact, so it wasn't as if he was neglecting his duty. He just had to get a little rest.

The woman he was to contact was Jewish, from a family that had been in Egypt for generations. Maybe this was why he felt uncomfortable. They had given him this information at the Mossad as though it was merely incidental. Jakob wasn't exactly what you would call a "good Jew," someone deeply in touch with his Jewish identity and heritage, but still he couldn't help thinking that if this mission somehow went wrong, all the Jews in Egypt—all the Jews in all the Arab countries for that matter—would be persecuted because of it.

He left his hotel early in the morning and made his way to a restaurant, where he was supposed to make contact with Anat Scholem. She made a habit of visiting the Café deux Sœur that overlooked the Nile, and so she had suggested this would be a good place to make first contact with the agent who would be smuggling in the explosives.

The sky was a clear, bright blue as Jakob made his way through the streets of Cairo. The shops and cafés had a familiar look. He began to notice that Cairo looked a lot like Tel Aviv, at least that part of Cairo where he was to meet Anat. He only had a vague description of her, a description that could match a dozen young women he had already seen that morning, but when he reached the café she was just where he had been told she would be, sitting at the farthest sidewalk table. Anat could easily have been Egyptian, with her dark Semitic beauty, jet-black hair, bronze complexion, and engaging, big brown eyes.

"Pardon e moi, Mademoiselle . . . Parlez vous Française?

"Seulement un peu, mais Je parle Allemand."

"Allemand? I speak German, but it's not very popular these days . . ."

"It's not a problem," she assured the stranger. "There are many East German businessmen in Cairo now."

These were the passwords for contact. Once assured of who he was, Anat told Jakob where he should bring the suitcase. Jakob glanced around as they talked, scanning the street and sidewalk for any signs of trouble. He noticed that Anat never glanced away. Either she was supremely cool and confident, or she was naïve.

Jakob felt a bit more at ease after he was a few blocks away. He had gotten through it without walking into a trap, at least not yet. It also clarified things a bit more for him. His fear, which had virtually over-whelmed him for those first two days, came from the fact that he had been sent on this mission by strangers. He realized that in Prague, when he went on a mission, other people's lives depended on him as much as his life depended on them. That was all removed in this situation. Some supervisor at the Mossad office back in Tel Aviv who decided that Jakob should go to Cairo wasn't risking his own life . . . Jakob knew that if he failed, they would simply send another agent. It was much more remote than life with the partisans had been. He realized he was much more disposable. He was beginning to under-stand the true nature of this spy business.

That night he made his way to a rather fashion-able apartment building and rang at the door for Anat, who told him to come right up. When he was invited into the apartment, Jakob was amazed to find that there were half a dozen other people there. It looked like he had just walked into a dinner party.

"This is the rest of the group," Anat announced to Jakob as he stood before them, and she then went on to name everyone, introducing them as though Jakob were a visiting cousin meeting her college friends.

Jakob was stunned. He tried to be polite but couldn't manage a smile or even a handshake. He just handed Anat the suitcase and was greatly relieved when she said that they had already been instructed how to use the explosives by another agent. That meant Jakob didn't have to stay around for anything, and he quickly left. He actually laughed to himself when he had put a little distance between himself and the apartment, imagining Anat and the others commenting on how rude he was to leave like that. He couldn't believe that a group of operatives actually met that way. In the world of partisans, they were always careful to make sure that no one knew too many people. They kept people separate so that if anyone got caught, there was only so much the person would know about anyone else and couldn't turn in others if they were tortured. They had also told him this when he was training at the Mossad. So how could this group of people be working like this? Jakob knew it was trouble, and he didn't want to be around when something went wrong. They may have been committed, they may even have been talented, but they were clearly *playing* at the game of being spies, and that sort of game always ends badly.

He was glad to be on the ship out of Port Said the next day, having gotten his feet wet in this spy business and survived. His thoughts were with Anat as the ship lost sight of the Egyptian coast. His revelation about being dispensable was very clear when he thought about her. Whoever recruited this young woman, perhaps by telling her that Israel needed her, never told her how to do the job or what the consequences might be—consequences that could go far beyond her, even beyond her family. She and her friends were being used in a very shortsighted and cynical way. Jakob knew he had to say something when he got back home, but who could he talk to?

The route home was even longer than the route to Egypt. The difference was that nobody would have known he was coming when he arrived in Cairo, but once he had been there, it was conceivable that someone might have spotted him. Especially after having contact with Anat, if her less-than-professional conduct had drawn attention. The point was that Jakob couldn't just travel to Italy and then to Israel. He now had to go to Germany and make some kind of appearance at the office that had been set up as a cover story for him. It was like a diver coming up from a deep-water dive. He had to decompress gradually, leaving his cover story slowly and carefully so that he wasn't spotted. Three days later he was given approval through contacts to return to Israel.

Once he was back in Tel Aviv, he tried to warn Chanoch Zimra about the slipshod organization of Anat's friends and how he was almost certain they would get caught. Chanoch told him that the people who had arranged everything knew what they were doing and it wasn't Jakob's place, as an agent on his first mission, to tell them how to do their job. Jakob then contacted Martin and told him what he had seen, but Martin agreed with Chanoch. It wasn't long after Jakob returned home that "Operation Susannah" blew up . . . literally.

Two of the young men from Anat's group were waiting outside a movie theater to set off one of the small explosive devices, but no matter how well a plan is laid out, there is always the unexpected. Somehow the device went off prematurely in the pants pocket of one of the young men. A policeman in the area rushed in to see what had happened and, making the connection between the other "bombings," arrested both of the young men. The wounded "agent" had severe burns on his leg, but after being treated at a nearby hospital, both men were interrogated. The two of them only held out for a day before giving up the names of the others in the group.

And then the operation blew up in Israel. Moshe Sharett, the prime minister of Israel at the time, began to issue stern, indignant denials as the Egyptians accused the Israelis of sending saboteurs to try to destabilize their government. Sharett knew there was no connection between these saboteurs and the Israeli government because the defense minister, Pinhas Lavon, assured him of it.

Lavon knew there were no Israeli operatives setting off bombs in Egypt because he, as defense minister, would be the only one in the government to give approval for such an operation. It would have to go through him. Then came that terrible moment when an army officer went to Lavon and explained that the people who had been arrested in Egypt were, in fact, Israeli operatives. The major didn't, however, tell the defense minister that the operation had specifically been planned and executed without his knowledge. This incident would crop up on the Israeli political scene many times in different forms over the next three decades and would become known as the "Lavon Affair."

As events unfolded, Jakob began to realize why Anat had been used for this mission. If the object had been to keep the defense minister out of the loop, then it only made sense to use amateur agents. The people setting up the operation wanted to recruit agents outside of the Mossad because they were, in essence, creating their own intelligence group so that no one would know what they were up to. But not only hadn't they considered what would happen to their untrained operatives if they were caught, they hadn't gauged the backlash of world opinion or the reaction of Arab countries to the Jewish populations within their borders.

Nasser used this incident as pretext to pursue the arms trade agreement with the Soviets that allowed him to purchase millions of dollars worth of state-of-the-art military weapons from Czechoslovakia. Thus the road was paved for what seemed to be an unavoidable war with Israel.

CHAPTER 8

The question of Palestinian refugees would haunt Israel from the earliest days of statehood.

When Syria, Lebanon, Transjordan, Egypt, Saudi Arabia, Iraq, and the Arabs of Palestine all came together to destroy Israel as the British withdrew in 1948, there was no help forthcoming from the UN or any other nation individually. As such, once Israel survived the Arab assault, the borders and divisions prescribed by the United Nations were suddenly up for reevaluation in the face of the new reality of an existing state with defensible borders. When any country is in a fight for its very existence, it seems obvious that they shouldn't leave belligerents behind their front lines. Many Arabs fled their homes and moved toward the Arab armies thinking they would be protected until Israel was annihilated, at which time they could return. Other Arabs who were willing to stay in their homes in Israel were forced out. The city of Haifa, for example, had been divided fairly evenly among Arabs and Jews until the war. During the war, however, Israeli troops and policemen evacuated whole neighborhoods of Arabs, forcing them out with nothing but the clothes on their backs. Soon afterward their abandoned homes were taken over by their Jewish neighbors.

From the moment the Palestinian Arabs became refugees, they also became political capital. One would be hard pressed to find another population that labeled themselves as "refugees" for half a century. But none of the surrounding Arab nations that sought to destroy Israel would accept the

Palestinian refugees—for whom they were allegedly fighting—into their own countries.

Even though there was no room for the them in Egypt after the war, Nasser did offer weapons to the Palestinian refugees in the area surrounding the city of Gaza, on the Mediterranean, so they could attack Israeli outposts. By 1956 the refugees in the Gaza Strip, who called themselves "fedayeen," a term meaning "those who sacrifice themselves," were making constant incursions into Israel to attack a kibbutz here and there, sometimes even going as far as Tel Aviv, and the death toll kept rising.

From the beginning, the people of Israel knew that they must be on constant alert for such attacks and that such vigilance meant a standing army. In September of 1949, the Knesset, Israel's parliament, enacted legislation that required all citizens to perform an active tour of duty in what became known as the IDF, the Israeli Defense Force. Men were required to serve twenty-six months of active duty when they turned eighteen, and women, twenty months. After their active duty, men were required to serve in the military reserve force until they were forty-five, while women were obligated to reserve duty until they were thirty-five or they got married, whichever came first.

A light breeze ruffled Thomas's hair as he stood at the lion's shoulder, looking into the valley below where the Kfar Giladi kibbutz, with its green fields and pastures, seemed to spill out from the foot of the hill.

Thomas was about to turn eighteen in a few

months, the age of mandatory military service in Israel, and Jakob's friend Martin wanted to show him the kibbutz where he had grown up. He took him up to the monument on the hill, the sculpted lion monument that kept watch over Kfar Giladi. Martin knew that Thomas had always lived in Tel Aviv, and he thought "the boy" might benefit from seeing how people lived on the borders of Israel.

"I suppose you don't know anything about Joseph Trumpeldor."

"A little . . . ," Thomas replied. "They told us about Trumpeldor in school."

"That he only had one arm?"

"Yes, of course. Every Jewish schoolboy knows that. He lost it in the war, right?"

"Which war?" Martin quizzed.

"World War I?"

"No, before that. The Sino-Russian war. In 1905, when the Russians and Japanese were fighting in the East. He even got a medal. Ten years after that he was trying to organize an army in Russia to take Palestine from the Turks."

Thomas looked at Martin with surprise. "During the war?" he asked. "He was trying to raise a Jewish army in Russia *during* the First World War?"

"That's right. It took a lot of courage."

"It sounds like he might have been a little crazy."

The initial look on Martin's face was one of alarm. How could this boy be so cavalier about Joseph Trumpeldor? But as Martin looked at the teenager, his face quickly melted into a patient smile. "Passionate," was all he said in reply, letting the word hang in the air for a moment.

Thomas expected him to say more and waited for the rest of the thought, but then before Martin could break the silence, he spoke up. "I remember now . . . 'If we cannot be an army, let us be pioneers.' How many times have I heard that? 'Let us be pioneers.' But I never put it together before, that he was really trying to build an army. I thought it was just a way of talking."

"This is where he died," Martin said as he gestured to a rocky patch on the hill. "He and a few others were trying to hold back a band of Arab raiders. Back then, in 1920, Palestine was divided up among British and French areas of influence.

"This area, up toward the town of Metulla," Martin continued as he pointed north, "was where different French and British zones met. There was some confusion about jurisdiction, and the Arab raiders took advantage of it. Since neither the French nor the British sent troops into this area, the settlers put together militias to protect themselves. And that's how Trumpeldor was killed, trying to protect my home. I was down there then, living in Kfar Giladi, a baby just five months old. Soon after that there were riots in Jerusalem. When it was over, the Arabs who had been arrested were sentenced to a few months in jail. The Jews who had fought back, including my father's brother Nuri, were given fifteen-year prison sentences by a British military court."

"Didn't you join the British army?"

"His Majesty's Jewish Brigade," Martin affirmed with pride.

"Why?"

"I had to do something. Did you know that

Trumpeldor was in the British army too? The Zion Mule Corps. The only thing they would let the Jews from Palestine do was lead their mules across the battlegrounds. But he did it," Martin continued emphatically as he turned to face Thomas. "He went. Why? I think there were a number of reasons. To show that the Jews weren't afraid to fight, and to gain some military training that would be helpful back in Palestine. I suppose each man had his own reasons. I joined because I couldn't just stand by. The rumors about the killing started early here. I think people were more able to believe it than in other countries. After all, what Jew doesn't know about *Pogroms?* But I think the other countries, the Allies, refused to believe it even when proof kept showing up again and again. Witness after witness with the same story. Either they didn't give a damn or they just couldn't believe it. I don't know. But I believed the stories, and I had to do something about it."

"Martin . . . why did you bring me here?"

"I wanted you to see all this."

"But I've been here before. Remember? Mother, father, and me and Yigal. We all came up here when I was . . . thirteen? Or was it fourteen?"

"That was different. You're just about to turn eighteen. You'll be called up for military service."

"Everyone has to go into the army."

"I know. I just wanted to show you why it was so important. You're not going into the army just because a group of old men think it's a good idea. Do you ever think about the War of Independence? Do you ever wonder why we won that war when we were so outnumbered? How did we hold off the Egyptians and Syrians and all the rest?"

"I guess we just had to," Thomas offered with a schoolboy's shrug of the shoulders.

Martin arched his eyebrows. Thomas had stumbled on the answer, but Martin was sure the boy didn't understand the full meaning of it. "That's it . . . we *had* to. Look at the World War . . . when the Nazis invaded France, for example. They occupied the country and made things difficult. That's the way most wars go. One country wants some land, or something like that, and so they attack the other and things are terrible for a while, but then eventually things get back to normal. When the Arabs attacked, they didn't just want the land. They wanted to kill every Jew. Every man, woman, and child."

Thomas listened intently as Martin went on. He listened because Martin had never talked to him like this before—like Thomas was a man who had to be told about these things, not like he was a boy who had to be instructed.

"That's why we fought them back the way we did. It was a fight for our lives and the lives of our families. How could you ever surrender in a war like that, knowing that not only would you be killed if you surrendered, but so would everyone you loved?"

Martin's words just hung in the air when he had finished. The two of them stood there in silence, looking over the valley below.

"Have you thought about what you're going to do?" Martin asked after a moment or two.

"I like radios. I thought maybe I could work with radios."

"In the field? Or do you mean behind the lines?"

"Wherever they need me."

"Let me show you something," Martin said as he headed for the car with Thomas right behind.

They drove for a few kilometers until Martin pointed and said, "There it is."

Thomas couldn't really tell what "it" was as they began to wind around a twisting road that brought them up to the top of another hill. All he saw was a signpost with the name METULLA on it.

"This is the border with Lebanon, right here," Martin said as they pulled off to the side of the road. "And that," he continued as he pointed at a concrete block building at the very top of the highest hill in the area, "is our ears."

"Ears?" Thomas repeated, thinking he had misunderstood.

"That's a listening post. From there the IDF listens to radio transmissions from Lebanon and Syria, and they also have radar to track planes."

Martin and Thomas talked a while longer, and Martin, due to his rank and the fact that the officer on duty knew him personally, was able to arrange for Thomas to get a quick tour of the listening station.

Martin never told Thomas the whole truth as to why he had brought him on the impromptu visit to Israel's northern border. It was true that he wanted to talk to Thomas about his impending military obligation, but Martin never told him that Rebecca had asked Martin to find some way to keep her son safe. The other reason was a conversation Martin had had with Jakob.

"I had the strangest thought . . . ," Jakob had said

to Martin one day when they were meeting for lunch a week or so before the trip with Thomas.

"What's that?" Martin asked between large bites from a sandwich.

"I was thinking of leaving."

"Leaving?" Martin asked loudly, caught off guard with his mouth full. "What do you mean? Leaving Rebecca and the boys?"

"No. Not leaving them. I mean all of us."

"Moving out of Tel Aviv? Where do you want to go?"

"I actually thought of moving back to Munich."

"Munich? Are you mad? How could you even think of moving back to Germany?"

"Both Rebecca and I grew up in Munich. Thomas was born there."

"And the Germans killed six million of us. Have you told Rebecca about your asinine plan?"

"No. I didn't say I was planning to do it. I just said I was thinking about it."

"Why? Why would you even consider it?"

"The boys . . . I've seen too much war. Do you know that my mother and father brought me to Munich just as the Communist revolution broke out? Thomas and Yigal wouldn't have to carry a gun in Munich."

"There's no guarantee of that."

"No . . . no guarantee, but a better chance there than here. The fedayeen rebels down by Gaza are killing more than a dozen people a month. Every month! And we're not even at war. Somebody's son or daughter is coming home in a box every week. I don't know what I'd do if that were Thomas. I think about that. I think about my . . . ," he fumbled as he tried to find the words, " . . . my beautiful son being killed and I think I'd go insane. I don't think I'd be able to go on living."

The conversation stopped cold. Martin looked at his friend. It was so out of character for Jakob. Martin had never before heard him say anything to show how profoundly devoted he was to his son.

That was the genesis of Martin and Thomas's journey to Metulla.

Martin wanted to see what Thomas was thinking and whether he could help the situation. Thomas's interest in radios helped. He had gotten good grades throughout school, and a technical position could keep him out of the front lines while still being vitally important to the country's defense. Thomas wouldn't have to feel that he had been carefully placed out of harm's way.

When Thomas returned home and told his parents that he wanted to go into communications, he was so excited about it that Jakob never even mentioned his thoughts about leaving. Maybe everything would be all right. Thomas wouldn't have to be on the front lines facing Arab guerrillas.

THAT NIGHT AS JAKOB and his family slept with the comforting belief that some of the fear and uncertainty of the future had been cleared away, squads of armed men were executing a secret mission some four hundred kilometers to the southwest in Cairo. But this wasn't just another bit of Israeli intrigue like the failed "Operation Susannah" in which Jakob had participated a few years earlier. This was the culmination of Gamal Abdel Nasser's plan to wrest control of the Suez Canal from the French and English.

The Suez Canal had been constructed between 1859 and 1869 by the Suez Canal Company, which was made up of investors from France and the Ottoman Empire. The British only came into the picture years later when they bought out Egyptian interests after the canal was built.

When Nasser announced the nationalization of the canal, he used the exploitation of the Egyptian laborers a hundred years before as justification for his actions. It wasn't hard to sell this logic in the Arab and third-world countries where anti-colonial sentiments were clearly against the French and British interests.

Nasser blamed the Western powers, personified by the World Bank, for the takeover of the canal, saying that they had left him no choice when they unjustly denied him funds to build the Aswan High Dam, but a cynical mind might believe he was playing both ends against the middle. It was only after Nasser had surprised the Western democracies by making a deal for military arms through the Soviet Union and soon thereafter recognizing Communist China that American and British financiers reconsidered the loan for building the Aswan Dam.

On the night of July 25, Nasser's armed agents took the canal offices and control centers by surprise, forcing out the British and French workers.

World reaction was split along political lines. The Arab nations hailed it as a victory against imperialist colonialism, while the Western democracies condemned it as a violation of international law—the blatant theft of private property.

The French and British governments adopted a wait-and-see attitude. In their arrogance, they assumed that the canal would be shut down without their technical guidance and support, and that the Egyptian president would soon have to come groveling at their feet for help. They had, however, underestimated world opinion and the support of Communist countries. Engineers and pilots were soon coming from East Germany and other Communist bloc countries to work the canal.

A few weeks later, British and French officials came up with a strange plan. It had only been eight years since the British had not only left Israel defenseless, but had even provided information to help Arab countries in their war against the Jews. And now they proposed an alliance with the Israelis.

The story of Israel's political alliances in its first decade was a constantly changing chess game between the Soviets and the Western democracies. British oil leases were expiring at about the same time that Arab states were declaring independence from their former colonial masters, one after the other, and suddenly Arab oil became a critical concern for Western Europe. This fact gave Israel strategic importance. The British, for example, believed that Israel could provide important air and naval bases in the region, but as soon as Anthony Eden became prime minister in 1952, relations with Israel cooled, since Eden had always favored diplomatic relations with the Arab countries.

It was the age of the cold war, however, so when British–Israeli relations cooled, the Israelis turned to the Soviets. Israeli relations with the Soviets, however, were also strained, since the Soviet government was concerned about the effect Israel was having on Soviet Jews. The Soviets felt that Jews in their country should be grateful to live in the classless society of their Communist state, which by definition was propagandized to be free of anti-Semitism and other racist attitudes. Soviet officials were thus genuinely concerned when visits by the Israeli ambassador, Golda Meir, were met by cheering crowds wherever she spoke.

Israel's relationship with the United States had been a rocky affair for much the same reasons that strained British–Israeli relations. America had major oil holdings in the Middle East, most notably in Saudi Arabia, but there was also a large Jewish minority in America that politicians courted with each election. The problem with the Americans was that they believed their own press! The common opinion among American foreign relations experts was that a tiny nation like Israel should be grateful for any American support and should therefore do as they were told. But Israel hardly ever did as they were told. Sometimes to its detriment, but that was just the nature of the Israeli people and their government.

The Israelis had an amicable relationship with France, which allowed Israel to acquire modern military aircraft when France agreed to sell them a number of Mirage jet fighters, planes that compared very favorably to the MiG-17 fighters that Nasser had purchased from the Soviets.

And so that was the state of Israeli international

relations in a nutshell. Then came the takeover of the Suez Canal. Suddenly the British were disposed to a new alliance with Israel, although they insisted that it be kept secret!

British and French representatives hatched a ridiculous scheme to try to regain control of the canal. The British and French had begun military preparations within days of the nationalization of the canal with the intention of invading Egypt and removing Nasser from power. The Americans, however, warned the British and French that they would condemn such an assault. That was when the British and French decided to involve the Israelis in their plan. It was the Israelis who were to provide the pretext for an invasion of Egypt.

Basically, the plan was for Israel to attack the Egyptians across the Sinai Desert in response to the constant fedayeen attacks from the Gaza Strip. When the Israelis arrived at the Suez Canal, the British and French would step in as peacemakers, sending in troops to protect the canal from both the Egyptians and the Israelis.

The idea that the Israelis would launch a preemptive strike was not out of the question. There was rumor of such an attack even before the Suez crisis. Prior to the proposed attack on Egypt, Israel had already made incursions into Syria, Jordan, and the Gaza Strip in response to attacks by the fedayeen rebels, although these attacks were small-scale military responses, each of which was greeted with international criticism and even censure from the United Nations.

Even faced with United Nations censure, there

were three specific reasons why the Israelis were willing to move against the Egyptians. First, Nasser had been stockpiling weapons for years by that time, and he made no secret of his intentions to move against Israel at some time to redress the humiliating defeat suffered by Egypt during "the Palestinian war." Second, the Israelis wanted to establish a military buffer zone by driving the fedayeen rebels away from the Gaza Strip, where they were within easy striking distance of Tel Aviv, not to mention the farming collectives along the border. And finally, the Israelis wanted to end the Egyptian blockade of the Gulf of Aqaba.

From the time of independence, the Egyptians had denied the Israelis access to the Suez Canal. To add insult to injury, they also blockaded the Gulf of Aqaba where the Israeli port of Eilat would have given Israel access to the Red Sea, albeit at the southern tip of the Negev Desert.

And so the stage was set for "Operation Kadesh," although most citizens of Israel weren't aware that there was an "operation" in the planning. They only knew that border skirmishes with guerrillas had been increasing along the Jordanian border. There was tension in the air. If one had listened carefully to the press conferences and other interviews, it was clear that Israeli military leaders had long espoused a policy of preemptive strikes as necessary for the survival of the Israeli state. With the constant threat of guerrilla attacks, military units in one part of the country or another always seemed to be on alert or practice alert, and so it was hard to tell when there was a major troop movement. That, of course, was the point. It was apparent to the troops, however, that there had recently been a significant influx of new weapons, French military supplies that had been part of the unpublicized alliance agreement.

It was now months after that day when Martin had shown Thomas the listening post in the north, and Thomas's eighteenth birthday had come and gone. Thomas took a slow drag from the cigarette that Avram had just passed to him. He pinched the cigarette awkwardly between his index finger and thumb, extending his other fingers out so they wouldn't get burned. He never actually took the smoke into his lungs. He just drew some in and then let it out slowly, trying to make a smoke ring. Just as he was about to make the best ring of the afternoon, he began to cough. Avram smiled and took back the cigarette as Thomas continued his coughing spasm.

"It's okay, kid. It happens to the best of us."

"Kid?" Thomas repeated in protest. "I'm only two years younger than you."

"I'd call you *kid* even if we were the same age."

"What do you mean by that?"

"You're innocent. You haven't seen anything."

"And you have?"

"Yeah. I learned to shoot a gun when I was six years old."

"So? I wasn't much older when my father taught me how to shoot."

"When I was twelve, I was shooting at raiders who would attack the kibbutz. What were you shooting at?"

Thomas just made a grunting noise, knowing he couldn't keep up with Avram's game of one-upsmanship. During the War of Independence, Thomas and his father had only driven a few miles out of Tel Aviv when Jakob showed him how to shoot a rifle. Thomas was only ten years old, and they were only shooting at empty vegetable cans. They had two rifles, a .22 caliber and a British Enfield .303 SMLE. Thomas was good enough with the .22, but his attempt at firing the Enfield proved to be traumatizing. Jakob told him it would kick back hard and that he should hold it tight to his shoulder, but even with these warnings, Thomas was unprepared for the cannonlike explosion and the recoil that knocked him backward, flat on his back. And worse than that, he wound up with a bright purple bruise that covered his entire shoulder for more than a week, until it finally started to fade into other strange hues of green and then yellow. His mother would wince every time she saw it, although he did enjoy showing it off to his school friends as a sign of his courage, assuring them that he hadn't even cried when it happened.

"Stein! Lazear!" Lieutenant Dvorcyk called out as he entered the barracks. "We're mobilizing. Both of you are being temporarily reassigned."

"Mobilizing?" Avram asked. "What's happening?"

"They'll fill you in when you get there. Here are your orders. You've got an hour to pack. Bus to Haifa, train to Tel Aviv. They'll tell you what to do from there."

Later that afternoon Thomas and Avram reported to the large, nondescript two-story building in Tel Aviv that served as the communications center for the small country. There were numerous redundant monitoring stations and hubs around Israel, but this was the administration center for all of those stations under military control. When they found the right office, they were told to take a seat in a long hallway. Thomas found himself staring at the two-toned institutional green walls as wave after wave of soldiers hurried up and down the hall. It was clear that something was up. The mobilization they had been told about was obviously a large-scale operation.

Eventually the soldier who had told them to wait appeared at the doorway and, without a word, waved for them to follow. When they went into the office, the secretary, still without a word, pointed at one of the doors past the reception area.

When they entered the office, Thomas followed Avram's lead and they came to attention with a crisp salute. Avram, as the more senior of the two, announced, "Lazear and Stein reporting as ordered from Metulla, sir."

The officer behind the desk glanced up for an instant, curtly returning the salute, and then once again buried his face in the folder he had been reading when Avram and Thomas entered.

They stood there at attention for what seemed like another ten minutes until the officer looked up again, noticing that they were still at attention. "Sit," he said, as though they should have known that they were allowed to take advantage of the chairs drawn up in front of the desk.

"We need you to go south," the officer continued, making direct eye contact for the first time.

"South?" Avram asked.

"Yes. You're to monitor radio communications in

Gaza."

"Gaza?" Thomas asked nervously.

"Outside of Gaza City. Before we go on, it's important you know this is all top secret. Don't discuss it with anyone, not even your family. There will be plenty of time for that later. Now, having said all that . . . everything goes off in a couple of days. You're on your own tonight, tomorrow you'll get your equipment ready, and the next day you'll be traveling. After that everything will break loose."

"It's something big," said Thomas. It was a statement rather than a question, because he knew by the feel of it, by the sense of urgency and tension that filled the air, that it was going to be a big operation.

"That's right," the officer answered. "We're going to clear out the rebels in Gaza. All of them."

"But what about the Egyptians? Won't they attack?"

"That's where you come in. We've set up mobile monitoring posts to go in with the troops, but we don't expect much from the Egyptians in Gaza."

"Why not?"

"You'll just have to trust me on that one, son," the officer said with a smile.

The information had quite an impact on Thomas, as he realized this was going to be a real shooting war, not just raids and counterraids. He told his mother that he was on a short pass when he unexpectedly showed up at home that night. When he said he couldn't talk about it, he realized it was ridiculous, since his father would obviously know even more than Thomas from his role in intelligence. But neither father nor son said anything that night about the military actions in which they were about to participate.

Thomas found himself looking at Yigal across the dinner table that night. His brother was seven years old now. Would Yigal have a war when he was eighteen? It suddenly occurred to Thomas that this might be the future of Israel. Every generation with another war—another war that would really be nothing more than a continuing battle extending all the way back to the beginning of the Zionist dream of a country for the Jews. An endless war . . .

Dinner was quiet.

Thomas was up by 5:30 the next morning and gone by 6:00, as was Jakob. Jakob even shook Thomas's hand as they left. "Good luck." Those were the parting words, perhaps the last words father and son would ever share, a thought that was not lost on either of them as Jakob pulled Thomas into an embrace.

When Thomas met up with Avram at their departure point, they found a large panel truck filled with equipment and a very young, freshly scrubbed driver named Ravid. Ravid looked to be about thirteen or fourteen years old, but he was a very serious young man who considered virtually everyone his superior. They were astounded as they looked over the interior of the truck. Brand-new state-of-the-art equipment, the likes of which they had only seen at the Haifa training center—equipment so scarce that thirty men trained on a single set. All of the controls had been hastily labeled with their Hebrew names written on tape that covered the French-language nameplates. They spent the entire day checking the equipment and familiarizing themselves with the lay-out of the truck.

That night the three of them slept in a nearby barracks until three o'clock in the morning, when they were called to get into convoy position, and eventually a line of trucks moved out of Tel Aviv into the Negev Desert toward the Gaza Strip. Unknown to them was that at about the same time, Israeli para-troopers were beginning their flight toward the Mitla Pass, less than forty miles from the Suez Canal.

Thomas had never been to Gaza City before, even though it was only seventy kilometers from Tel Aviv.

On the eve of the attack toward the Suez Canal, the Israeli leadership decided that the push into Sinai would be an excellent opportunity to clear the rebels out of Gaza once and for all. They had sent intelligence agents into Gaza in advance to compile lists of rebels and rebel supporters, and now it was time to close the trap.

"Pay close attention to that air traffic since we're close to the ocean," an officer told them just before they pulled out of Tel Aviv. "We don't want to get caught by surprise."

KARIF IBN UMAR had lived in Gaza, just three kilome-ters outside of Gaza City, since he and his family had been forced out of their home in Jaffa in 1948. He and his wife had thought that they, along with their son Yacoub, could make their way to Cairo, where his wife had a cousin, but they were stopped by Egyptian troops in Gaza. The Egyptians stopped the flow of refugees there before they could move across

Sinai into Egypt proper. Granted, some aid was given by the Egyptian troops—food and water along with some tents and other temporary housing—but their main purpose was to keep the refugees from moving toward Egypt.

Karif and his family lived in a little house of clay blocks, where they had a small orange grove that required intensive cultivation, but it was enough for them to live on. He was awakened in the night by the sound of Israeli trucks coming down the rough, two-lane highway. He quickly threw on a dusty linen caftan and cautiously made his way out into the night. The memory of the day when the Israelis had forced him and his neighbors out of Jaffa was still fresh in his mind. The Israelis had not been angry or excited. It was clear some of the men moving them out with their rifles and bayonets didn't even like what they were doing, but still they did it. It wasn't an angry mob running them out. The Israelis were just . . . relentless.

Karif's eyes soon adjusted to the darkness, and he could see the dots of lights, the headlights, bouncing up and down as they navigated the dirt highway. He rushed back into the house and woke up his son. Yacoub was now fifteen years old.

"Wake up!" Karif ordered. "You must go. Now!"

"Go? Go where?" Yacoub asked as he squinted his eyes and tried to shake himself awake.

"The Jews are coming. You have to go and tell them in the city. Go tell Najjar. He will tell the others. Quickly! Get up!"

Once he realized what his father was saying, Yacoub was up in an instant. He dressed in half a minute and was out the door. Stored in the tool shed was an old motorcycle that Najjar had given to Yacoub three years earlier, when Yacoub was only twelve, just for this reason—so that Yacoub could give warning if they saw Israeli troops about to enter the city. Yacoub spent hours every week maintaining the twenty-year-old motorcycle. It was his pride and joy. He took off like a shot into the darkness. He had practiced riding in the dark many times, so he didn't even need to turn on the headlight. He had the advantage of youth on his side, and his night vision was still keen. There was no question that he would arrive in Gaza well ahead of the lumbering trucks on the highway as he took his cross-country shortcut.

Najjar didn't waste a minute, once Yacoub had woken up the household with a desperate pounding on the door. Amid the hysterical barking of dogs in the neighborhood, Yacoub told him about the trucks, and he went back into the house just to say something to his wife and then brushed past Yacoub, telling him to go and alert Dabir and Fahd. Within five minutes, half of the rebels in Gaza City knew of the impending arrival of the Israeli troops. They all assumed it was just another raid on the city to look for weapons and perhaps make a few arrests as an example to the others. This was the way it had always gone before. There would be no battle here with their wives and children caught in the crossfire. The men who were obvious targets would go into hiding until the troops pulled out, a couple of days at most, while the others would deny even knowing the wanted men, much less knowing where they might be. The rebels knew how to play the game.

The Israelis knew the game, too, but this time they were using it to their advantage. They knew the rebels would be alerted, but the Israeli agents had been infiltrating the rebels in Gaza for months in preparation for this operation. When intelligence had planned the raid, they hadn't known about Operation Kadesh. When the Anglo–French alliance and the impending all-out attack on Sinai had been revealed to the intelligence group, they expanded the raid on Gaza City to a full-scale roundup of every rebel in the city.

The Israelis had carefully prepared lists of rebels' names, photographs, and even information on the underground hiding places throughout the city.

Kafir couldn't believe the size of the military convoy as it stretched off into the desert while passing by his little farm, but he had no way of communicating this revelation to the rebels. Once the column had reached his farm, two men in a jeep had stopped and entered his home, cutting the telephone lines and searching for any radios. They didn't find anything suggesting that Kafir himself was a rebel, and his name was not on the list, but nonetheless they suspected he would get word to the rebels. The high-pitched whine of a small motorcycle had been heard a few moments before their arrival—but that was part of the plan, that the rebels would be alerted. That way the rebels would think it was just another raid and would react the same way they always did, without mounting an armed resistance, running to the hiding places that the Israelis already knew about.

Just like Kafir, people watching the approach of

the column were surprised by the number of troops. The size of the invading column was considerable, because these were the troops that would move into Sinai in a few hours, after participating in the roundup of the rebels. The troops spread out into a broad line, calmly and quietly sweeping into the city just as daylight broke and the muezzin began the day's call to first prayer from the minarets, the towers in the mosques.

The squads consisted of one soldier from the intelligence group with his list and a dozen regular soldiers who would round up about four or five men. They would then return to the base camp on the edge of the city, where the rebels would be held under guard.

Thomas and Avram worked quickly to set up the truck on a clear rise about two city blocks from the camp. They soon had everything up and running and were monitoring all the radio traffic, although at that point there was very little to hear. They did get some of the Hebrew transmissions from the planes returning from the paratroop drop in Sinai, but they were very brief and cryptic.

Avram volunteered to take the first watch and told Thomas to go stretch his legs for a bit. By this time, about 9:00 A.M., the blitz of the city was already completed. It took less than four hours to gather up ninety-five percent of the men on the master list. The rest was just "mopping up" as they checked out the various hiding places.

Thomas looked down over the camp, taking notice of the Palestinians. Even from that distance he could see the hatred and rage written on the faces of these men. Their body language, the way they talked to each other, the way they looked at their captors . . .

He turned away, gazing out over the city just below his position. He was looking for a secluded place where he could urinate as he pulled out a cigarette. He lit it up and took a deep drag, something unusual for him, and was just about to let it out as he heard the sharp crackle of gunfire. He assumed the rebels must be putting up a fight at the last minute, and he dropped to the ground. He realized he must make a good target standing out on that hill above the city. When he heard more gunshots, he looked around, trying to see where they were coming from. That was when he realized the shots had been fired in volley, a number of rifles firing all at once. He scanned the skyline until his eyes finally came to the camp again, just as another volley was fired. It was the Israelis! They were executing the rebels by firing squad! All of them. Without a trial, or even a military hearing.

He couldn't believe it. He rose up slowly, transfixed as he watched stretcher bearers move the bodies of the victims out of the way so that six more men could be brought up for execution. As he stood there, something caught his eye a few yards away at a brick wall that fenced in the small courtyards of a dozen homes.

A head had popped up from behind the courtyard wall. It was a handsome Arab boy about twelve or thirteen years old. The boy looked around with quick, jerking motions as his eyes carefully scanned the area. He looked like a mouse popping out of his hole, checking before venturing into a room.

Thomas waved at him to get down and told him, in Arabic, to run away.

The boy stared at Thomas for a moment, and Thomas thought he didn't hear him or understand, so he repeated himself, telling the boy to get down and go back into his house.

This was where Thomas made his mistake. He thought he was still in the real world, the world of his childhood and his family. If someone warns you of danger, you take that advice and hide. That was why he never even saw the rifle.

The troops down in the camp fired another volley just as the boy pulled the trigger. Thomas was caught completely by surprise as the bullet burned into his thigh. His legs fell out from under him, and he found himself choking in a cloud of dust as he rolled down the hill. His body came to rest just short of the wall as he passed out, completely out of sight of the camp and the communications truck. The boy had long since run away.

After a few minutes, Thomas came to. He couldn't believe the pain. He couldn't believe he was shot, and on top of all that he had peed his pants. What should he do now? If he yelled out, would other Palestinians find him first and finish him off? He was so close to the communications truck that he could have hit it with the good throw of a stone. He felt someone was watching him, and he twisted around as best he could to face this new attacker.

The sudden move frightened Bahira, who was peeking around the corner of the wall after hearing the gunshot that felled Thomas. She was a small woman in her midthirties who had overcome her fear enough to dare to check if the death squad was moving toward her home. She was prepared to run, leaving everything behind, but she needed to see first, just to be sure. She had been told the Israelis were executing men close by, but when she saw Thomas, she knew what had happened. She also knew it would go very badly for the people in these houses if he was found there.

She rushed over to Thomas and tried to look at the wound, but he pushed her away, thinking she was attacking him. She looked into his eyes plaintively, and he realized she was trying to help. When he relented and let her look at it, she saw that the bullet had gone completely through without hitting the bone. Nonetheless, it was a messy, bloody wound. She told Thomas she would be right back and ran to her house to find something to use as a bandage. Moments later, she returned with a bottle of some kind of alcohol, a pair of scissors, and a bedsheet. She quickly cut the bedsheet into strips and used a piece of it as a rag to wipe away the blood. Thomas was not only fortunate that the bullet had missed bone, it had also missed a major artery by only a fraction of an inch. Bahira could actually see the artery pulse with each beat of Thomas's heart as she tried to clean away the excess blood. Thomas was barely conscious, and when the splash of alcohol hit the open wound, he passed out again. Bahira did her best to clean out the dirt and then used the rest of the bedsheet to tightly bind the wound.

Another few minutes passed, and Thomas came to once again. Bahira was determined to get him away from her house at that point. She tried to get him to stand up, and after a couple of tries, Thomas made it up on his good leg. Bahira told him in Arabic that she would help him get to the camp, but that they must not see her, so she would get him as close as she could. She told him she didn't know who shot him and begged him not to send troops to her house, where her parents and daughter were hiding. Thomas just nodded in agreement, and the two of them slowly made their way along the wall toward the camp. He believed her even though she had lied. The boy who had shot Thomas was her son.

The whole incident hadn't taken much more than forty-five minutes, and so Avram hadn't even noticed Thomas was gone. Bahira left Thomas as he leaned against a tree just around the corner from the camp, about a hundred meters away. "Thank you," he said in Arabic, "and don't fear . . . I won't send anyone to your house."

Bahira took his hand and thanked him profusely.

Thomas then hobbled into view of the camp as Bahira ran back to her home. Just then one of the Israeli soldiers saw Thomas and called out to a captain, who told the stretcher bearers to go help him— coincidentally, the same stretcher bearers who had been carrying the bodies of the recently executed rebels.

Thomas was quickly taken to the medics, where he was told that he was the first casualty of the action. He asked them to get word to Avram back at the communications truck.

That was the end of the war for Thomas. It was a

clean wound, one that would heal in a couple of months with virtually no residual effects. It was the kind of wound that American GIs in World War II had come to call "a million-dollar wound"—a wound that would take you out of the fighting without crippling you for life. Thomas had time to think on his way back to Tel Aviv. He told himself that everything had been his fault, that he shouldn't have been standing on that hill in plain view, that he should have known the boy might have a gun. He had been naïve and stupid. He started to cry. After all, he was barely more than a boy, and he felt he had failed on his first time out, letting down his friend Avram and the rest of the people counting on him.

WHILE THOMAS WAS WALLOWING in shame and defeat on his way home in that ambulance, his father was in Syria. Jakob had been sent there on a particularly dangerous mission. The Israelis weren't sure what the Syrian reaction to the attack on Egypt would be, even though their intelligence told them that Syria was not in a position to mount an attack against them. The Golan Heights, however, was a particularly vulnerable area for northern Israel, and so military intelligence decided it would be best to have someone monitoring the situation from within Syria.

Jakob was thirty-nine years old, not exactly the peak age for a covert military infiltration behind enemy lines, but his experience recommended him. He led a group of four other soldiers, the oldest of whom was twenty-one. In civilian clothes, they were to move past al-Qunaytirah to a place where they could observe Syrian troop movements into the

Heights. It would have been easier to send jets over on reconnaissance missions, but military headquarters didn't want to give the Syrians any reason to attack, including the pretext of calling a reconnaissance mission an aerial attack formation. The risks were very high for Jakob's squad, since they would certainly be executed as spies if they were caught, but it seemed the lesser of evils.

The young men under Jakob moved with an incredible skill and precision that came from months and months of intensive training. It was the ultimate game of hide and seek, with the ultimate penalty if they lost. They crossed the Golan Heights in the dark, careful not to run into any hidden Syrian camps. Two other similar squads were dispatched at the same time, and the orders for all three of them were to lay low and watch the highways that the Syrians would use to bring up an attack force.

The other risk, along with being discovered by accident, was that if they did see troop movements and used their radio to report it, the Syrians could track the signal right back to them.

While Jakob and his group were monitoring the Syrians, the first stage of Operation Kadesh was a complete success for the Israelis. They had destroyed the threat of guerrilla attacks from Gaza and had moved quickly across the Sinai Desert toward the canal, as well as moving south toward Dahab, Nabek, and Sharm es-Sheikh, which controlled the Gulf of Aqaba and the Strait of Tiran.

The Syrians didn't try to mount an attack, even though Nasser had called on them to do so, along with Jordan, Lebanon, and all the other Arab countries in the region.

As they days wore on, however, it was becoming apparent that perhaps their success was too complete.

The Israeli advance had been a virtual blitzkrieg across the Sinai. In spite of the Egyptian blockade of the Gulf of Aqaba and the guerrilla attacks that Israel had been fending off for years, attacks that clearly had Egyptian support, the Israelis were being condemned by the world at large as the aggressors. The next few days unfolded rather unpleasantly for the Israeli government as the French and British clumsily tried to play out their scheme for reclaiming the Suez Canal. No one believed that the French and British were innocent bystanders trying to play the role of peacekeepers, and when they finally resorted to bombing raids on the area around the canal, they, along with Israel, were soundly censured by the United Nations. Or at least they would have been officially censured had the British and French UN representatives sitting on the Security Council not used their veto to override the motion for censure.

America played an interesting role at that point, as President Eisenhower thought he could step in and tell the Israeli government to back down under threat of withholding foreign aid and blocking money sent by Jewish-American citizens through charity donations. But the Israelis had the audacity to ignore his proclamation, thus infuriating the American President.

After two days, Jakob and his squad returned

from their mission in Syria without incident when military intelligence determined that the Syrians wouldn't attack and recalled them. He ran into Martin after being debriefed at headquarters, and they decided to grab something to eat.

"Well . . . ," Martin said with a sigh as the waiter left the table, "this has turned into a hell of a mess."

"I think it's kind of funny," Jakob replied.

"Funny?"

"We're being called imperialists. England, France, and Israel. The colonialist oppressors of the freedom-loving peoples of Egypt. Don't tell me that you can't see the humor in that."

"When you say it, it's a joke," Martin answered harshly. "When they say it, we'll lose a lot of foreign aid. That's no joke. If we lose American money . . . well, let's just say the British and the French won't help us."

"We need the money, but does that mean they can always call the tune?"

"Yes. That's what it means."

"Well, they can go to hell too! They're no different than the God-damned Russians. Or the God-damned Nazis, for that matter."

"The Nazis?" Martin asked with mock surprise, pretending Jakob had shocked him.

"It's all conquest. Just because there aren't troops marching down Dizengoff doesn't mean that we aren't conquered. Look at Iran. The Shah is overthrown. The Americans don't like it. The Shah is suddenly back on the throne. So what happens if they don't approve of our prime minister or president?"

"What are we? Whores to be bought and sold?" Martin roared with a smile as he played the role of indignant foil.

"It's the game," Jakob continued as he lit up a cigarette, pausing for effect as he issued his great pronouncements. "Haven't you heard? The balance of power. Maybe this Suez nonsense is all for the best. Maybe it's best that we break the rules now and again."

World attention was soon diverted from the Suez crisis by events taking place in Hungary. One of the concerns expressed by the Israelis during the planning of the Sinai campaign was the possibility that the Soviets would resupply the Egyptians and possibly even send in Soviet troops, but the uprising in Budapest changed all that. The Soviets had their hands full, with newsreel cameras sending images of Hungarian civilians armed with rocks and Molotov cocktails facing down Russian tanks. Soviet relations with Egypt had been going sour for some time, as Nasser insisted that his acceptance of Soviet aid gave them no say in the policies of his government. When Nasser came shouting for help as the Suez crisis developed, he was privately told that he was on his own, but publicly the Soviets made threats against Israel and the United States.

The Anglo–French vetoes at the United Nations were eventually overturned as events in the Middle East were taken up in the General Assembly. Israeli leaders expected that Gamal Abdel Nasser would lose all credibility as a result of the Suez crisis. They assumed that he would soon be overthrown. They had completely misread the situation. Instead, the crises had made Nasser a hero in the Arab and third-world nations. He had stood up to the imperialist West and, with the aid of the UN General Assembly, had won. The Israelis had been painted with the same brush as the British and French: the Western colonial imperialists.

In the aftermath of the General Assembly votes, British and French troops were forced to withdraw from the canal zone within the next few weeks, and the Israelis were forced to withdraw from Sinai and Gaza after a few months. The United Nations did at least concede that the threat to Israel's security from Gaza was real and that the Egyptian blockade of the Gulf of Aqaba was unjust. The result was that a United Nations Emergency Force was sent to administer Gaza in place of the former Egyptian authorities, and UN peacekeepers were also sent to ensure that the Gulf of Aqaba was kept open to international shipping.

It was all a matter of process. The crisis had subsided, and the world made it past that tense moment when it thought Israel and Egypt would strike the match that would light the fuse that would set off the bomb that would end the world. The Americans backing Israel, the Soviets backing the Egyptians, and suddenly the pawns would checkmate the kings. The moment passed, and things were getting back to normal.

Jakob was back home with Rebecca and Yigal, back at his job with the Mossad, and Thomas was back in Mettula at the listening station to finish out his service in peace. Time was passing quietly and quickly once again, like a sparrow's wing, come and gone before you even realize it. Jakob and Amalie debated at length the rights and wrongs of the crisis over those next months. He was surprised to find that his mother had become quite the committed Zionist—a very pragmatic Zionist at that. She insisted that Israel's highest moral duty was to exist, that the country—the government—must do whatever it deemed necessary to protect itself and survive.

"Do whatever it must?"

"Yes," Amalie answered emphatically.

"Do you know what that means?"

"Of course I do. I'm not a child. Nor am I naïve."

"Neither am I. I know what goes on. We rarely are what we hope to be. That's never more true than in politics. But if we don't even aspire to a higher morality, what chance do we have?"

"Are you saying we should pay lip service to an unachievable moral purpose? What kind of government would that be? I'll tell you. An ineffectual one. We have to live in the real world."

"That's funny. When you asked what kind of state would ascribe to an unachievable moral purpose, the answer that came to my mind was a Jewish state. That's what being a Jew is supposed to be. To perfect the world under God."

"Don't mix religion and politics."

Jakob just threw up his hands and laughed. She was so serious and uncompromising.

Conversations like this and the one he had had with Martin were occurring all over Israel, indeed, all over the world, as Jews tried to figure out what this State of Israel was going to turn out to be.

A few months later Jakob was talking with

Chanoch Zimra back at his Mossad office in Tel Aviv.

"There were times when I didn't think I was going to make it. I can't believe the trouble I had crossing the Golan Heights. Those kids didn't even break a sweat, and I was struggling like a hundred-year-old man."

"Comparing yourself to teenagers?" Chanoch asked. "No wonder you feel old. You're in pretty good shape for forty."

"I'm just saying that last field mission was too much."

"You made it, didn't you? You pushed yourself and did what you had to do. That's all that matters. The rest is just talk."

"I honestly don't know if I could do it again," Jakob announced quietly with a shake of his head.

"Well . . . I do have something else for you."

"What?"

"We need someone in South America."

"Move to South America? I don't like the sound of that."

"No, we don't need you to move there. We have men there now, but they may have been spotted, so we need a new face. We need someone who can go in, quietly track down some leads, and report back."

"Is it dangerous?"

"We've already lost a couple of men."

"Lost? I love a good euphemism. How many bullets are involved in 'lost'?"

"They were asking questions. The two of them were found in a cinema in Paraguay, both of them shot in the head."

"I guess they're right when they say discretion is

the better part of valor. Who are we looking for?"

"Well, there are three names that keep coming up. Martin Bormann, Josef Mengele, and Adolf Eichmann."

"I thought Bormann was dead."

"There are all sorts of rumors. They say he escaped Berlin and made it to Buenos Aires. I don't know . . . it's something we'd like to check out. It could be a wild-goose chase, but we're fairly sure Mengele is in Paraguay, and we've just had a report on Eichmann sent to us from Germany by a prosecutor who thinks the German government might just sweep it under the rug. They think Eichmann is in Buenos Aires."

The assignment in South America intrigued Jakob. This was something that he could really get his teeth into. It wasn't like the field assignment in Cairo years before. There was no moral ambiguity to hunting Nazis. He would be an avenging Jew who would bring a murdering Nazi to justice!

When Jakob told Rebecca that he had a new assignment that would take him out of the country, he didn't tell her any of the specifics because he didn't want her to worry that he might get hurt.

A few days later he stopped in to let Amalie know that he would be gone for a while.

"Did you hear the news today?" she asked after he had told her he would be leaving.

"What news?"

"Kastner. They killed him."

She was talking about Rudolf Kastner, the man who had lost his libel case against Malkiel Greenwald a few years earlier. Greenwald had accused Kastner of trading with the enemy because Kastner had chosen to save friends and family among the 1,685 Jews freed as a sign of good faith when he was bargaining with the Nazis to save the Jews of Hungary in 1944.

Amalie had identified strongly with Kastner. She felt he had done what anyone would have done—in fact, what she had done—to save his family and friends by any means possible.

"What happened?"

"Three men waited for him at his house and shot him."

Jakob shook his head. He wasn't sure how to reply. He knew that to his mother it was as though they had passed sentence against her. He finally put his arms around her, something he rarely did.

"They weren't there," he said, referring to the people Amalie felt had passed judgment on her. "They wouldn't have stood by and let their families go to the gas if they could have stopped it. They have no right to judge all these years later."

CHAPTER 9

The life of Holocaust survivors in Israel was a strange existence.

When Zionists argued for an independent Jewish state, they glorified Holocaust survivors as proof of the indomitable spirit of Judaism and insisted that they had earned their own state through suffering. The Zionists were adamant that only through a Jewish state could people such as the survivors be protected, as part of a sovereign nation rather than existing as a minority of some "host" state where they were subject to the whim of changing political ideologies.

Soon afterward, however, Holocaust survivors were silenced—silenced in the sense that it became apparent to most survivors that people didn't want to hear their stories. In general, they were looked down upon by Jews who had lived in Palestine during the war. In an incredibly egocentric perception, victims and survivors of the Holocaust were seen as sheep who had gone willingly to slaughter. The Jews in Palestine had no idea how carefully and effectively the trap that had caught European Jewry had been built and sprung. Yet as completely ludicrous as it was, the idea of victims going passively to their deaths became a shameful persona adopted by many survivors who would not talk about their past, even to wives or husbands they had married after the war. They would later have children who had no idea what their parents had gone through.

Years later, when anti-Semitism was on the rise throughout the world once again, David Ben

Gurion was informed that Adolf Eichmann had been spotted in South America. He decided then that a way to combat the rise in anti-Semitism would be to have a show trial of a German war criminal held in Israel.

There had been many sightings of Nazi war criminals around the world, ranging from Alois Brunner in Syria to Josef Mengele in Brazil, but when and how could they be found, and how could they be brought to Israel?

On a stiflingly hot afternoon in July of 1947, Albert Waldhramm was sitting in a restaurant in Encarnación, Paraguay, sweating profusely as he worked his way through a bowl of Puchero, a Paraguayan beef stew. Albert was a short, heavyset man in his late forties with sad eyes, pronounced jowls, and an unkempt mop of hair that was receding almost as quickly as his fortunes.

Albert's luck had run out a few weeks earlier when his plan to sell an *estancia* in the Mesopotamia region of Argentina to a German émigré fell apart. It seems the fellow found out that Albert didn't own the ranch. That was Albert's cue to leave Buenos Aires and head north to Paraguay.

Ah, well, Albert thought to himself as he paused between noisy spoonfuls of stew, *something will turn up soon. It always does.*

It was when he was digging through his pockets for money to pay the check that he noticed the young man at the other table across the room. They made eye contact for an instant, but Albert thought nothing of it as he quickly looked away to count the coins he had fished out. He tossed a few coins on the table, made a vague attempt to straighten his rumpled linen suit, and walked out of the restaurant without looking back.

He kept turning it over in his mind again and again as he walked down the street, asking himself how he could get some money. Paraguay may not have been his best choice of destinations after Buenos Aires. There wasn't much of a tourist trade, and the wealthy were usually either part of the military dictatorship that ran the country or were well connected to the military. In other words, they were not the sort you wanted to take advantage of, because you could end up disappearing in the middle of the night. He had some smaller routines that he would run just to get a little spending money, but Paraguay was a land of extremes. You were either rich or poor, and his particular brand of legerdemain was best directed at a middle-class audience, people who could afford to take a little hit but weren't able to strike back with any significant reprisal. He wasn't the kind to resort to common theft or burglary, but he was beginning to feel that his options were limited.

He stopped at a newsstand, bought a paper, and sat on a park bench along the boulevard as he further considered his options. He began reading the paper, but soon got the strange feeling that he was being watched. He glanced around casually as he lowered the newspaper to turn a page and was startled to see the man from the restaurant looking his way. He rose up, but as he did, the fellow watching him crossed the street. Albert's first thought was to run, but then he thought he should confront the man, since he obviously couldn't outrun him. He rustled the newspaper about as he folded it up, using it to cover the fact that he was pulling a pistol from under his coat.

The man who approached him seemed to be in his midtwenties. He was slender with a sharp, thin nose and dark patches under his eyes that gave him a sinister look.

"Good afternoon, sir," he said very politely. "Are you waiting for the train?"

The question seemed very strange to Albert since the train station was six blocks away. He just looked at the young man.

It seemed like he stared at him for a long time before he realized he had heard about this before . . . "Are you waiting for the train?" That was the password. He had been talking to his friend Diego in Buenos Aires, a rather disreputable friend plying the same trade as Albert, and Diego had told him about Germans who had been coming into Argentina, rich Germans, top Nazis escaping from Europe. But now he couldn't remember what the response was, and he ran the phrase over and over in his head trying to come up with it. He fingered the Walther pistol nervously under the newspaper.

The man who had approached him, Erich Scharber, was waiting patiently. In his experience, this wasn't an unusual response. The men he contacted had to decide in a split second if Erich was a valid contact for the Odessa or some international agent trying to trick them and arrest them for extradition back to Germany. They were a very suspicious and edgy lot.

"Not now," Albert said slowly as the reply came back to him. "I'm waiting for the night train to La Paz."

"Very well," Erich replied with a vague attempt at a smile as he gave a slight nod and a very subdued imitation of coming to attention and bringing together the heels of his boots. "If you'll come with me, we have some supplies for your trip, Herr Reichsleit—"

Erich stopped, realizing he had made the mistake of addressing the man by rank, and waited for the man to fill in the blank, letting Erich know how he should be addressed.

Once again, Albert just stood silently, not realizing what was expected of him, but then it came to him that all these Nazis must be traveling under aliases, and being called by rank in public would be a grave error on the part of this young man.

"Never . . . ," Albert growled as he began to get into character, "never let that happen again. You will call me Bauer, Señor Ricardo Bauer."

Albert had used the name Bauer before in some of his dealings, but only for setting up background for one of his cons, not in any criminal activity. It was his "safe name," an alias that he kept clean so no one could trace it back to him, in case he was investigated by the police.

He realized he was putting himself in a dangerous situation. When he and Diego had been laughing about the world of Nazi cloak and dagger and how far the mighty had fallen, they also traded stories about what happened to people who ran afoul of these Nazis on the run. At this point, the Nazi leaders had little to lose, and since a number of these South American countries were ruled by military dictatorships that had been sympathetic to the Nazis, these men could act with impunity. They could even get away with murder, as long as they paid off the right official and the victim wasn't part of the ruling elite. But still, Albert and Diego had wondered if it wouldn't be better to have nothing than to have held the world in your hand one moment and then be forced to live the rest of your life on the run.

"Ja wohl, Herr Bauer," Erich replied as he motioned for Albert to follow.

They walked about four blocks through the quiet city streets until they came to a three-story stucco apartment building, indistinguishable from all the others on that block.

Erich flew up the stairs to the second floor with Albert laboring on behind him. Once Albert arrived at the apartment door, Erich told him to wait a moment while he went in to make sure everything was all right.

Albert didn't say anything, but suddenly he felt ill at ease. Could this all be some kind of confidence game they were playing on him? *No,* he thought to himself, *no one would mistake me for someone with money.*

A moment later Erich came to the door and called Albert into the apartment. There was another man there, this one a little older than Erich. Short-cropped blond hair and the classic Aryan looks that the Nazis so loved.

"My God, we thought you were dead," he said as Albert entered the room.

"No. It was close, but I made it out," Albert said, trying to play along so that he could find out more of what was going on.

"Red Cross papers?"

"Yes. Yes, of course."

"Do you have the passport?"

"No, no . . . ," Albert sputtered out with hesitation. "I lost it. Stolen. I must have missed a contact. I ended up sleeping in a park. They made off with my bag. I got a shot off, but I missed."

"No matter. We can get you new papers, Herr Reichsleiter. What name?"

"Ricardo Bauer," Erich piped in to show that he knew what was going on.

"That's right," Albert confirmed.

"Did you get a chance to see your wife? We heard she had taken the children to Bolzano."

"No, I didn't. We . . ."

"We were sorry to hear about her death. We had always heard such good things about Frau Bormann, and then to hear about the cancer. It's a terrible shame. To survive the war and then . . ."

Bormann! Albert thought to himself. *That's who they think I am.* He was glad to hear that Frau Bormann was not in the country, or she would have made short work of his impersonation plot.

"Yes . . . ," he said as he feigned the grieving husband. "We were to meet here when things were settled. She would bring the children and . . ." Albert actually managed to improvise a single, anguished tear and then composed himself. "But we must go on."

"Yes, yes . . . We have some funds here for you.

There is a contact in La Paz, and they will have a place for you to stay for a while until you can decide what to do next."

Albert knew that the first thing he would have to do was dig up some information on Bormann. He had to do some research if he was going to go any further in this charade. He didn't even know the wife's name, but luckily his host hadn't asked. How many children did this Bormann have, and what were their names? How was he supposed to have been killed, and how could he have escaped? Yes, there were a lot of answers he would have to research. This was only the first contact. They would start asking him specific questions later. And then he wondered if he looked enough like this Bormann to pull it off. Just because these two thought he looked like Bormann . . . What if he ran into someone who knew Bormann personally?

When he left the two men in the apartment, they gave him some money and directions to an out-of-the-way hotel whose owners, he was assured, were sympathetic to his plight. He was told to come back in two days to pick up the promised identification papers, but otherwise to keep a low profile. Then he would be free to continue his journey.

Over the next few days, Albert was careful to watch for anyone who might be tailing him. He found a couple of bookstores that had some material on the Nazi leadership, which wasn't unusual, considering the pro-Axis leanings of the South American countries and that Encarnación had a significant German population. The books and magazines he found were all German propaganda pieces, but they provided Albert with some of the important information he needed. He was surprised to find some old American magazines too. One of them had an article about the Nuremburg trials. From that he found that Martin Bormann was thought to have died in Berlin as he tried to escape from the Führer's bunker when the Russians moved in for the kill in those final days of the war in Europe. But his body was not found, and so he was convicted of war crimes in absentia and sentenced to hanging.

There were few pictures of Bormann, but from what Albert could find, the resemblance was uncanny. The biggest difference was the haircut, but otherwise, from what he could tell from the black-and-white photographs, they were the same height and weight and had the same facial features. Albert worked to memorize what details he could find as far as Bormann's career, the names of family members, and any other bits of personal information. He knew he didn't have to know everything. From what he read, suddenly the approach of the two men at the apartment made sense. They were in awe of him. He, or rather Bormann, was the highest ranking Nazi. He wondered what would happen if Bormann, the real Bormann, suddenly appeared on the scene, but then that was Albert's business. He lived by his wits and took calculated risks, knowing that someday he would make a big score. Someday it would all pay off and he would be able to live the high life. Or he would be killed in the process.

He sat there among the pile of books and magazines and decided he would take the chance. He had heard about Nazi loot coming into South

America, rumors of gold and diamonds and art masterpieces being sent to Argentina, Bolivia, Chile, and Paraguay, as the Nazis feathered their postwar, postdefeat nest. He knew he could get a piece of that. He could play the role of Bormann. He knew what these Nazis were like. If anyone questioned him, he would just fly into a rage and make them cower at his name. After all, he had been Adolf Hitler's right hand. Who would dare question him?

Albert was actually born to play the role. He was an educated man, a man whose family in Germany had broken ties with him after he disgraced them by squandering his portion of the family fortune. He only had one brother, who had died in Hamburg during the war. His father had died before the war. He didn't know about his mother. If she was still alive, she wanted nothing to do with him, so for all intents and purposes, they were dead to each other too. Albert had made it through the University of Mannheim, graduating in 1922 with a law degree, but then he decided that he didn't want to become a lawyer. In fact, he decided he didn't want to work at all. For a few years during the twenties he managed to live off the extravagance of some wealthy friends. But then he determined to make a good marriage and became engaged to the daughter of a wealthy industrialist. The problem, though, was that he didn't love her, and when he ended up getting another girl pregnant, the engagement was broken off and his old friends no longer found him amusing. Nor did his family. That was when he decided to travel.

And so he ended up in Encarnación in the hottest part of the summer of 1947, preparing for a theatrical role as the leader of a fourth German Reich, a Nazi underground in South America.

The years passed and he passed hurdle after hurdle. With every success, there was less chance of him getting caught. It was a case of the old adage: Nothing succeeds like success. The more he was accepted, the less there was of anyone daring to challenge him. And he owed some of his success to the Nazi hunters. Men like Simon Wiesenthal, who tried to tell the world that these Nazi war criminals were out there and should be brought to justice. The fact that they suggested Bormann was living in South America gave further credence to Albert's role.

It was eleven years later that Jakob Stein arrived in Buenos Aires on his mission as a Mossad agent looking for Martin Bormann et al. His first stop was to meet with Ephraim Ilani, the Israel intelligence agent stationed in Buenos Aires.

It was incredibly hot and humid when they met late one afternoon in a Buenos Aires coffee house. Jakob could feel the sweat spontaneously forming on his neck and face just as quickly as he wiped it away with a handkerchief.

"It's like living in a land of ghosts," Ephraim told him with a wry smile. "I've even heard that Hitler himself made it out of that bunker and was brought here by submarine, and he now lives the life of a country gentlemen, coming and going as he pleases."

"What do you think about these others? Bormann, Mengele, and Eichmann."

"Well . . . we looked into the Eichmann sighting last year. He was supposed to be living under the name Schmidt, but when we got a look at the man, there was no way that it could have been Eichmann. I've had some very strong leads about Mengele. I believe without a doubt that he's in South America. There was something about a medical operation gone bad in Paraguay, an abortion or something he had performed, and he left that country. He seems to keep moving. He has a brother up in Encarnación in Paraguay. I've heard Mengele visits him there occasionally, but we never know when. To me, that seems like the only way we would catch him. If we set a trap and he came to us . . . but he's a very cautious man."

"What have you heard about Bormann?"

"Rumors . . . lot's of rumors. It's as though Bormann is a tourist trade for Nazi hunters. For a few thousand dollars someone will offer to take you to an *estancia* on the border in the Chaca region, where he supposedly lives surrounded by armed guards. Of course, you might disappear once you pay them the money, but that's the way this game is played."

"Well . . . I'll be careful. Do you have some background for me?"

"A few files in the briefcase," Ephraim said with a subtle nod at the case he had left by Jakob's side of the table. "Like I said, mostly rumors and unsubstantiated reports."

"Anything on the two who were killed in Paraguay?"

"As much as we have. They were cocky. They underestimated these people. Remember, some of these men were SS and Gestapo. They wrote the book on counter-espionage. Our agents thought they were after some two-bit gangsters on the run, but they were actually chasing a lion into its den."

"A lion?" Jakob smirked.

"You know what I mean. A wounded animal backed into a corner is the most dangerous."

"I'll buy the 'animal' part. Well, I suppose I'd better get going. Catch up on my reading. If I have to contact you, I'll call and ask for Uncle Peter. If you can't talk, or if there's a problem, just say it's a wrong number."

"Uncle Peter? What the hell is that?"

"I'm using the name Peter Mueller."

Jakob left first, exiting the coffee shop just as it started to rain. He went straight to his hotel room, sat down at the rickety little table in the corner, and started going through the reports Ephraim had given him.

The first file was the report that Adolf Hitler himself had been smuggled into Paraguay. Jakob was sure Ephraim had put that file on top as comic relief. He read through the report, which detailed a clandestine submarine landing in a secluded bay a few weeks after the war had ended. At the end of the report, Ephraim had made a note that the report had been made by the two agents who were subsequently killed. It occurred to Jakob that this might have been why the agents let down their guard. It sounded like a comic opera or a confidence game.

The hotel room was small and stiflingly hot, but he had been so eager to get a look at the files that he hadn't taken the time to open the French doors that looked out onto the piazza in front of the hotel.

When he took a break and swung the doors open, the room suddenly filled with the refreshing, cool air that had been ushered in with the rain. As Jakob sat back down at the little table with his stack of papers, there was an earth-shaking explosion and brilliant flash as the skies opened up with the heaviest rain he had ever seen. It came down in steady sheets for half an hour, accompanied by a fantastic thunder and lightning show.

He read the reports of Mengele's travels and the Eichmann investigation carefully as each page was punctuated with flashes of lightning and rolling thunder.

The next day Jakob prepared to start talking to some people recommended by Ephraim.

Back in Israel, Chanoch had told him that many of the Mossad agents preferred the Beretta .22 caliber semiautomatic pistol as their weapon of choice because it was relatively inconspicuous, yet its substantial heft made it easy to handle. It was a close-quarters weapon whose report could easily be mistaken for a firecracker or the backfire of a car. A disadvantage was that the small caliber didn't have much penetrating power if you had to shoot your way out of a bad situation. Many agents, however, thought the lack of power was a benefit, since a stray bullet would be less likely to penetrate a wall and accidentally kill an innocent bystander.

This mission was different than anything Jakob had done before. He had been in the field a few times after Cairo in 1952, but they were just missions to gather information, like the trip to Syria. He didn't have to make contact with other agents on those missions. It was just a matter of getting in, finding what he needed, and getting out. Now, of course, he was to be the hunter, and his prey could easily turn and suddenly *he* would become the hunted. It was exciting and terrifying all at once. He remembered the mission in Cairo and how he had hesitated, hiding out in his hotel room. He forgave himself for that and decided it was just a matter of self-preservation. It wasn't cowardice; it was his way of getting his bearings. Better to take a day off than to rush headlong into the unknown. Most important, he hadn't compromised the mission. And besides, the aftermath of that mission spoke for itself. It had been poorly conceived and executed, and in the end it had failed miserably through no fault of his. He had been right to be concerned.

He had decided when he heard about the other two agents who had been killed that he would be well armed. He wasn't going to lose *his* life over this. None of these Nazis were worth it. He would do his best, but he was going to take care of himself. He carried the Beretta in a shoulder holster, but he had also picked up a snub-nosed .38 revolver, which he carried in an ankle holster. Besides that, he had bought a little .380 semiautomatic pistol. This gun was small enough to fit in the palm of his hand. The .380 caliber was a short version of the 9-mm bullet and actually had less range than the .22 caliber, because the .380 bullet was heavier than the .22 and there was proportionately less powder in the cartridge. In fact, there were stories about people being shot in the head with a .380 at close range and the bullet not even penetrating the skull. When Jakob talked to Martin before he left Israel, Martin said that if he wanted to carry an extra gun, he should have Rebecca sew up a little pouch with a belt that he could wear in his underwear.

"Wear the gun right over your Schwanz," Martin instructed as he nodded downward and held his hand at his crotch. "They never search you there. Especially if they've already found a gun."

And last, but not least, Jakob had an American paratrooper knife that he had picked up at a military surplus store. The blade retracted into the handle by means of a spring. When you wanted the blade out, you just flipped the knife out and inertia locked the blade into place. This was something else Rebecca helped him with, making a cloth holster with elastic straps that he wore on his right forearm under his sleeve. It was somewhat conspicuous under just a shirt, but not when he wore a jacket. Of course, the same was true for the shoulder holster, so he assumed he would always have to wear a suit, sport coat, or some kind of jacket. He told Rebecca that the holsters were for hiding his money and papers. She knew better, but didn't question him.

He stood in front of the mirror in his hotel room, checking to see if any of these weapons would be obvious to the casual observer. After a few moments of posing and checking from every angle, he was convinced everything fit the way it should, and he headed out for the day.

It was much cooler that morning after the rain. At first he felt confident as he walked down the street, as though he could now take care of himself. Maybe a little invincible. That thought disturbed him. He had known young men who fought with the partisans during the war who had felt invincible because they held a homemade Sten machine gun in their hands. They often tended to become foolhardy, and as a result, they didn't live long.

He wasn't used to wearing a shoulder holster, and it was a little uncomfortable as he walked. It just didn't seem to move the same way he did. And then there was the ankle holster, which felt as though he had a rock tied to his leg. But worst of all was the little .380. After about a block, he realized he hadn't tightened the strap enough on the pouch, and the gun that was hanging over his genitals was starting to sink. Yes, the little .380 was heading south, and it was getting worse as he walked because it started to hit his legs, so that every step began to push it from side to side and make it slip down even faster.

He broke stride for an instant as he thought what to do, then walked down a nearby alley. He found a secluded nook in the alley and started to reach down into his pants.

"Señor . . . ," came a voice from a little ways down the alley.

Jakob froze. This was certainly a compromising position, but he did have his hand on the pistol, since he was trying to reposition the pouch. The question appeared to be could he actually use it? Or more appropriately, did he *need* to use it? No, of course not! He was overreacting.

"Señor, we have a toilet inside that you can use."

Jakob's head drooped a little as he inhaled and mumbled a curse under his breath. He turned slightly and saw that the building was a restaurant and the voice was that of a waiter, a thin young man with curly black hair. Apparently he had walked right past the waiter, who had been standing in the kitchen doorway, without noticing him.

"Gracias," Jakob replied tersely, deciding to take advantage of the offer. He had never been much of one for breakfast, but it seemed like a good idea. It would give him time to compose himself. He found the restroom and readjusted himself as needed, tightening a strap here and there before going out to the dining room.

It was midmorning, and he found himself alone in the dining room. As soon as he sat down at a nearby table, the waiter appeared.

"What would you like, Señor?" the waiter asked with a smile.

"Eggs . . ."

"How would you like them?"

"Surprise me," Jakob said casually as he looked out the window at the gray sky and the people passing along on the sidewalks. "And coffee."

"Is Señor new to Buenos Aires?" the waiter asked as he returned to the table with a cup of coffee.

"Ah . . . yes," Jakob answered hesitantly. "Is it that obvious?"

The waiter just shrugged his shoulders. "There are so many tourists in Buenos Aires . . . Things that are obvious to me, other people don't notice."

"Oh, I see," Jakob said with a smile. "You're some kind of detective."

"No, no, Señor," the waiter replied quickly. "It's just. . . It's my job. It helps if I can tell something about people."

"Gets you better tips!" Jakob added.

"Yes. Yes, that's it."

"I see. So what can you tell about me?"

"Oh, I don't know, Señor . . . It's like a magician. I don't like to tell how the magic works."

"Come now, you've got me intrigued. You can't stop like that."

"Are you sure you won't be offended?"

"On the contrary," Jakob said with a sweep of his hand, a gesture inviting the young man's comments.

The waiter smiled. "Well, I would say you are from Germany. Not now, but you probably lived there as a child. Southern Germany. I think you still have a trace of the Bavarian accent."

"Very good."

"But now you live somewhere else . . ."

Jakob just smiled vaguely, knowing this kid would never guess.

"Israel. You're an Israeli. And I'm sorry to tell you that the knife up your sleeve is very obvious."

Jakob raised his eyebrows. He was really impressed. "You're right to be concerned about saying too much."

Suddenly something flashed in the waiter's eyes. It was fear. But only for an instant.

"I'm a writer," Jakob continued. "A reporter. My name's Peter Mueller. I'm writing a story on anti-Semitism in South America."

"You're Jewish?"

Jakob just raised his eyebrows and looked at the young man, as if to say "you're getting too personal," but then he thought better of it and answered, "Yes, I'm from Israel."

"What's it like? I've always wanted to go."

"It's a place. Nothing special."

"Nothing special?"

Jakob recognized the tone of indignant youth. "Let me guess . . . you're Jewish."

The waiter nodded.

"Every Passover," Jakob continued, "you hear that line 'Next year in Jerusalem' and you have some kind of fantasy about this wonderful place."

The waiter grimaced and shrugged his shoulders.

"Well, I'm sorry to tell you that a Jew can't even get into Jerusalem. The Arabs control the city. There are too many people. They came too fast, and there's not enough money. It's not the paradise for Jews that they say it is."

"If you don't like it, why don't you leave?"

"My family is there. There wasn't any other place for us to go after the war."

"That's how I got here," the waiter countered. "My sister and I came to live with our aunt and uncle. They were the only ones left. I was ten years old. My parents were killed in the war. Auschwitz."

"Were *you* in Auschwitz?"

"No, my parents managed to hide us with friends. Gentiles. They saved our lives."

"I've heard stories like that. You're the first one I've met. I thought it was like a fairy tale or a myth. I thought someone just made it all up because they wanted to convince us that somewhere in a world filled with danger and evil there was still kindness and compassion. Somewhere out there."

"Well, it's true. They were a Catholic family. They had two children of their own, and they took in three Jewish children. They saved our lives."

"For the whole war? How did they do it?"

"It was just the last year of the war. The family who saved me were farmers, so they managed to feed us without ration cards."

"Istvan!" came a call from the back of the restaurant, which drew the waiter's attention.

"That's your breakfast. I'll be right back," Istvan said to Jakob just before disappearing in the back of the restaurant.

"So . . . what should I know about Argentina?" Jakob asked when Istvan returned.

"Don't talk politics."

"That's a pretty good rule in any country . . ."

"Especially here. You say you're writing a story on anti-Semitism in South America?"

"Yes," Jakob replied with a nod.

"Then you must have heard the stories."

"Stories?"

"Nazis. Nazis who came to Argentina, Paraguay . . . Bolivia . . . Chile."

"Newspaper men hear all sorts of rumors."

"And yet you came all this way."

"It sounds like you have something to say to me."

"Señor, I'm just a waiter."

"Just a waiter . . ."

"Just like you're a newspaper reporter," Istvan said dryly.

"Why would you say something like that, Istvan?" Jakob said as he tried to nonchalantly eat his breakfast. "Why would you say something like that to someone you don't even know?"

"Maybe we should get to know each other, Señor.

Maybe I could help you with your . . . with your story."

"Sure, Istvan. Sure," Jakob said as he got up and tossed a couple of bills onto the table.

His first appointment of the day was to talk to a Buenos Aires police officer recommended by Ephraim, but as he left, he stopped outside for a moment and took note of the restaurant's address. The waiter was probably a crackpot with a big mouth, one of the con men Ephraim had warned him about, but he couldn't help feeling there was something unusual about Istvan. He didn't have that hungry look that hid behind the eyes of liars and thieves. His was the look of eager youth, even if it was somehow misguided.

"Encarnación. That's where you should start. There's a large German colony there. It's a contact point for the Odessa. Escape route for top Nazis."

"What about the authorities?"

"Authorities? In Paraguay? You must be joking! All it takes is money and you can get whatever you want. I even heard a story where they delivered a box with fifty pounds of gold dental work to General Stroesser's office. They didn't even try to disguise it!"

The reference made Jakob uneasy, considering the gold he had taken from Gertie Haas's apartment at the end of the war. He thanked the policeman and moved on to his next contact.

It was a long day without any significant discoveries. He made his way back to the hotel and went to bed early, not sure what he would do the next day.

He was startled the next morning by a loud knock on the door. He reached for the gun under his pillow just as a woman's voice called out, "Señor, may I clean the room?"

He went to the door and cautiously opened it just enough to see who was there, and sure enough, it was just one of the cleaning women. "Just a few minutes," he said. "I've overslept. I'll be gone in twenty minutes. You can clean then."

That day he had decided he would talk to a newspaper reporter who was on Ephraim's list, but as he walked down the street, he passed by the same restaurant he had visited the day before. It was almost lunchtime by then, so he decided to stop.

"Señor Mueller!" came a greeting as he walked in. "How nice to see you again."

"Buenos dias, Istvan."

It was 11:00 in the morning, and the restaurant had a few customers for lunch, but Istvan stopped what he was doing to show Jakob to a table.

"How are you ?"

"Today? I'm afraid I overslept."

"No, I mean yesterday."

"You certainly have a big nose for a waiter."

"A big nose, Señor?"

"Yeah, you're putting it where it doesn't belong."

"No, Señor. I'm just curious."

"Well, to be honest, I didn't get very far."

"That is most often the case with the police."

Jakob slowly looked up at Istvan. He didn't say anything, but he wanted to know how this boy knew he had been talking to the police.

"Do you know what you want?" Istvan continued.

"I'm just looking for information."

No, Señor. I mean, what do you want for lunch?"

"Oh . . . just bring me a sandwich and a beer."

"Very good, Señor. I think I can also help you with that other request. But not here."

Jakob realized that this was it. Now Istvan was going to start his game. Should he go along with it for a while? What could Istvan possibly know?

"Where? When?" Jakob found himself asking.

"What hotel are you staying at? We could meet there."

"No. That wouldn't be good."

"How about a movie theatre?"

"No . . . ," Jakob said with a laugh as he remembered the murdered agents in Paraguay. "How about one of those sidewalk cafés in Los Bocas?"

"When?"

"When are you done with work?"

"Five o'clock."

"I was at a place last night called La Bella Luna. Let's make it seven o'clock there."

Jakob spent the rest of the day down at the harbor, trying to chase down the stories of phantom submarine landings, but the only leads were those with a very high price tag. He had no intention of paying for information like that. Not that he couldn't get some money if there was a promising bit of information, but this certainly wasn't the time.

The afternoon passed quickly, and he soon found himself getting ready for his meeting with Istvan. He thought it was probably just another wild-goose chase, but decided to go through with it anyway.

Istvan was also preparing for their meeting. "You take this," he said to his sister as he handed her a military smoke canister and a pistol.

"You're kidding!"

"No, I'm not kidding. If something goes wrong, you create a distraction. You just pull the pin and throw it."

"And the gun?"

"Just in case. You don't have to shoot anybody. Just fire into the air to make a diversion so we can get away."

"Do you know anything about him?"

"I've talked to him a couple of times. Me and Eli will meet him at the restaurant to see what he knows."

"And you think he's a Nazi?"

"No. I think he's a Nazi hunter. He could be an Israeli agent."

"An Israeli agent . . . and he just happened to run into you?"

"Why not?"

"Did you stop to think that maybe he's an Argentine? Maybe he's looking for you?"

"That's where you come in. If something goes wrong, you create a diversion and we all disappear."

She just shook her head, thinking the whole idea was crazy, but she agreed to do it because she knew her brother believed in what he was doing.

The evening was hot again after the previous day's respite. Istvan and Eli arrived a few minutes early to look everything over, and Istvan made sure his sister was where she was supposed to be. They chose a table close to the street and waited.

Jakob was about fifteen minutes late. He walked casually down the sidewalk and quickly caught sight of Istvan, joining them at their table.

"And who is this?" he asked with a nod toward Eli.

"This is Eli. He's a friend of mine," Istvan answered. "I thought he should come along."

"Peter Mueller," Jakob said as he extended his hand to Eli before turning back to Istvan. "You're expecting trouble?"

"No. I just thought we could talk."

"About what?"

"I think we have something in common."

"What would that be?"

"Oh, c'mon, stop playing around. I think you're looking for something, somebody. And I think we can help. I think we can help each other."

"How?"

Istvan took a deep breath before replying. "Eli and I are part of a group here in Argentina. There are a lot of Jews here in Buenos Aires. There's been a Jewish community in Buenos Aires for a long time. I'm from Hungary. My parents were killed in the war."

Istvan paused for a moment and looked around as he took a drink.

He leaned back in close to Jakob as he continued, speaking quietly. "When it became apparent that certain people . . . Nazis . . . were making their way to South America, a group was formed called 'Commando Isaac.' We are trying to find these people and—"

"And what? You want to kill them?" Jakob interrupted.

Neither Istvan nor Eli answered. In fact, Eli, who hadn't said a word, actually looked away.

"Do you have any idea what that really means?

Have you ever . . . ," Jakob continued, but then stopped dead when he caught sight of Istvan's sister as she walked up behind Istvan.

Istvan saw that Jakob was looking at something that surprised him, to the point of leaving the man speechless. Istvan turned around. "What are you doing?" he asked his sister as she approached the table, finally standing between Istvan and Eli, watching Jakob as she drew close.

"So . . . what has he told you?"

"I . . . I . . . ," Jakob stuttered.

"Get out of here!" Istvan cut in, unable to comprehend what she was up to.

"How are you, Jakob?" she asked.

"You know him?" Istvan asked incredulously.

"Galia . . . ," Jakob said softly, with disbelief in his voice.

"I never dreamed I'd see *you* again," Galia said as she nervously lit a cigarette, belying her attempt to maintain a calm exterior.

"What the hell is going on?" Istvan growled, trying not to make a scene, but desperate to find out what was happening.

"I told you about the partisan we took care of, the wounded man they brought to the farm, and how we hid him and fed him, and then one day he left . . . without a word. He just rode off."

"You?" Istvan accused Jakob.

"I had to leave . . . The war was still going on. I had to go back. How could I say good-bye? They would have tried to keep me there. It was all I could do to leave. I couldn't have faced them after all they had done."

"Poor Jakob!" Galia mocked. "What pain you must have gone through!"

Galia hadn't changed. Of course, you hear that about people and it's never really true. She had put on a few pounds, but she looked better for it. Her big brown eyes hadn't changed, and the passion was just as obvious in her anger as it had been with her love. Jakob imagined he could still see the naïveté of the nineteen-year-old girl she had been back then.

"That's enough," he said in a granite voice, the sort of tone a schoolteacher might use to make it clear that he's the one in charge and that the students are still merely on the cusp of adulthood.

"You say it's enough," Galia challenged, "but I don't think it even begins to cover it."

"What do you want, Galia? It was a long time ago. A different world. You can't hold onto it forever."

"You can go to hell!" she spat out.

"Galia, we've got other things to talk about," Istvan interrupted.

"So talk!" she said as she defiantly pulled up a chair.

"We have some good background information," Istvan went on as Galia glared at Jakob. "Have you heard of Otto Skorzeny? We've found out that Skorzeny was the top man in setting up the escape route for Nazis trying to get out of Europe after the war. They call it 'The Spider.' When Juan Perón came to power here, he was very fond of the Nazis and let his sympathies be known. We don't have proof, but it seems that in the last year or so of the war, when certain Nazis saw that things were going badly, they were looking for a safe haven. They contacted Perón and sent him boats full of loot that they had taken from the countries they occupied."

"And from the Jews," Galia interjected.

"Yes. From the Jews. We have a friend who works in a bank who told us he actually *saw* crates full of *gold teeth*! Not to mention boxes with gold ingots stamped with Nazi markings."

Jakob flashed back to his adventure in Sardinia when Istvan mentioned the gold bars. Could that be what happened to the rest of the gold that had been taken by Klaus and the others?

"So we tried to get someone else in the bank after we heard that, and eventually we had three men working there. Whenever they got a chance, they would try to find out which accounts the gold was going into. They found out names, withdrawals, and addresses. I have actually seen Mengele."

"What?" Jakob asked, suddenly hearing something that he didn't already know from Ephraim Ilani's files and those of the Mossad back in Israel.

"I saw him. I was just watching the bank one day because someone had seen a note about one of the customers coming in to make a withdrawal . . . and there he was! Mengele. He just walked up to a teller as though he owned the bank, made a withdrawal, and that was all there was to it. Just like any businessman on any day. He didn't look around. He wasn't nervous. He just walked in, made the withdrawal, and left. I didn't know what to do. I guess I didn't really believe it would be him. Everything up to then was just guesswork and speculation. And he didn't look like a monster . . . not the 'Angel of Death.' I—"

"It's all right, Istvan," Jakob said, cutting him off.

"No one expected you to bring him in all by yourself. These things take planning. And what's more, he probably wasn't alone. Just because you didn't see anyone with him doesn't mean he didn't have a bodyguard close at hand. You probably would have been killed if you had tried to take him."

"He's right, Istvan," Galia agreed. "It was enough that you saw him, that you identified him. That's a place to start."

"So, who are you?" Istvan asked Jakob.

Jakob pursed his lips and let out a sigh. He thought to himself that he could trust Galia. And if this was her brother . . . "I've been sent to see if Mengele and Martin Bormann are really here."

"I told you!" Istvan said to his sister, then turned his attention back to Jakob. "By who?"

"Israeli intelligence."

"I knew it!" Istvan exclaimed.

"Could you please quiet down?" Jakob continued. "There are people who would gladly kill me if they found out."

"I might be one of them," Galia interjected.

"I'm serious."

"You don't know how much you hurt me, do you? You don't care. You just think everything is fine because it was years ago."

Eli, who had been silent through the entire meeting, just shook his head and smiled at Jakob.

"Galia, this isn't the time for . . . ," Istvan began.

"Oh, shut up, Istvan!" she snapped.

Istvan stopped short, looking as though his sister had slapped him in the face, but the fire in Galia's eyes didn't subside. She wasn't sorry for what she had said.

"Well," Istvan continued as he stood up, "apparently we're not going to get a chance to talk now. It seems Galia has a few words for you. Can we meet tomorrow? I think we could help each other."

"Go to hell, Istvan," Galia countered as she also stood up. "I'll leave. You and your new friend can play your secret agent games."

The three of them just watched in silence as Galia stormed off down the sidewalk, the staccato beat of her footsteps providing a dramatic finale to her performance.

Istvan sat back down, and the remaining three began to talk as though Galia's outburst had never taken place. Suddenly they were as thick as thieves. Eli finally spoke, starting by telling Jakob about Juan Perón's ascension to power and his admiration and support for the Third Reich during the war. Eli and some of his anti-Perón friends did their best to keep tabs on Perón and his actress wife, Evita. When they heard through their Commando Isaac friends about the Nazi gold coming into the country, they were sure it was directly connected to Perón. Nothing like that could happen without Perón's knowledge, and if he knew about it, he was sure to take a percentage. Then they had spotted Skorzeny and everything became certain.

It wasn't long after that when Istvan identified Mengele at the bank, and from there they knew who they were looking for. It was about that time that the stories of Nazi war criminals surfacing in Argentina and neighboring countries began to proliferate, along with the footnote that sympathetic South

American dictators not only allowed the fugitives entrance to their countries, but even protected them once there.

The next day Jakob called Ephraim Ilani and asked him to meet him for lunch.

"Who are these people?" Jakob asked. "What is this Commando Isaac group about?"

"It's a group of young men and women, mostly university age . . . students. They're a vigilante organization. They could be dangerous, but fortunately they lack the organization to get into too much trouble."

"What do you mean?"

"Well . . . for example, there was the time they actually found a Nazi, a leader of one of the Einsaztzgruppen."

"What happened?"

"They killed him. They shot him outside a department store, right in front of his wife and daughter."

"Christ!"

"That's right. And the two who actually committed the crime were arrested on the spot. All their little friends thought there would be a big trial and then everyone would know what was going on."

"And?" Jakob prodded impatiently.

"And they were never heard from again. They were taken away, and there was no trial. No bodies were ever found, no word from the government whatsoever. And worst of all was that they went after the family of one of the boys, his mother and younger brother. They disappeared too."

"What kind of place is this?" Jakob asked incredulously.

"The kind of place where people with money are safe and people without money who cause problems can easily disappear."

That night Jakob met with Istvan and Eli again.

"Have you heard of Martin Bormann?" Jakob asked. "There are rumors that he . . ."

"This is where you'll find him," Istvan declared as he pointed at a spot on the map in front of him with the degree of absolute certainty that youth so consistently possesses.

Jakob, who had been carefully looking over the map, raised his eyes. He noted the cocksureness and went back to the map. "Paraguay?"

"There is a place. They call it Waldner . . . Waldner 555. It's a special little district with armed guards. The river is on one side, and raw jungle surrounds the rest of it. You can get to it by the river, but you'd be seen before you got there. You have to leave the river and make your way through the jungle to get in."

"How would I get there?"

"I have some friends. We could put together a hit squad."

"Hit squad? Christ, I just want to see if he's there. I'm not here to assassinate him. If Bormann is here, they want him back in Israel alive."

"Why?"

"I don't think you understand, Istvan. I represent the government. A government doesn't look for that kind of revenge. My guess is they would try to extradite him for trial. It wouldn't look very good for a government to send out assassins."

"You've got to be joking," Istvan said with a laugh.

"Perón is famous for sending out death squads. What about Trotsky back in forty?"

"I guess my government is trying to operate on a higher moral plane than Stalin."

Istvan laughed again. "So you want to risk your life to see if Bormann is really here and then just go back home."

"How much would it cost me?"

"I'm not doing it for money."

"Then why?"

"For the same reason you are."

"The same reason I am? You don't know why I'm doing it."

"Because it's important. Because they've committed terrible crimes and need to be . . . ."

"I'm doing it because it's my job," Jakob said as a matter of fact. "Someone that I work for told me to do it."

"So you don't care what they've done."

"No."

"I say you're a liar," Istvan proclaimed.

"And you're very young. You believe in what you're doing. I guess I'm just older. Some would say practical."

"Practical? It sounds more like moral cowardice to me."

"Cowardice . . . ," Jakob said quietly under his breath. He was clearly angry, but controlled. "We'll go," he continued, "but we do things my way. I give the orders. We'll just identify him and leave unless . . ."

"Unless what?" Istvan asked.

"Let's just leave it at that for now."

Istvan was as good as his word. It only took three days for him to get everything ready for a trip to Paraguay. He introduced Jakob to three of his friends: Eli, Neil, and Ruben. They were all quiet and intense young men, about the same age as Istvan. Jakob couldn't tell them apart. Not that they looked alike, but there just didn't seem to be anything distinct about any of their personalities. Eli, with his curly black hair and dark eyes, was the only one of the four whose features could be described as Semitic. Neil's family, on the other hand, was originally from Denmark, and with his light complexion, light brown hair, and round face, there was nothing about his appearance that would've led anyone to guess he was Jewish. It became a running joke when they were alone and one of the boys would use the old "Funny, you don't look Jewish" line. Ruben's family had lived in Argentina for four generations, and his very handsome face was clearly a blend of nationalities.

Once they were on their way, Jakob was dismayed to find that the bus ride to the Argentine border by itself was a major obstacle. There was no toilet on the bus, and there were long distances without any bus station where they could stop. It was slow going because of the need to conserve gas over the long distances. And on top of all that, the weather during the four-day journey was a mix of horribly uncomfortable extremes—hot and dusty one day and then suddenly rainy and muddy the next. No less than four different times the passengers were called on to get out of the bus and push it out of muddy ruts where it had gotten stuck.

They crossed the border into Paraguay on foot to avoid immigration checks from both countries. It took fourteen hours to cover the five miles of jungle that lay on either side of the border.

Jakob sat down near a tree, landing with a thud and an exhausted sigh. "Now what?" he asked Istvan as he took off his hat and wiped his forehead and neck with the rag he had been wearing as a bandanna.

"We travel east to the city of Encarnación."

"What's in Encarnación?"

"I have to contact someone there. That's where we can get whatever we need."

"Guns?"

"Guns . . . up-to-date information . . . whatever we need to get Bormann."

"I told you we're just going to look first."

"Right, right . . . we're just going to look."

They found a place where they could catch a bus, although they had to wait until the next day, since only one bus ran along the deserted road, going east at seven in the morning and returning west at eight o'clock at night. They didn't stay up much later that day, since they had all been worn out by the journey.

Eli took the first watch.

They arrived in Encarnación in the early evening of the next day. Jakob was impressed when Istvan took them to a "safe house." It showed that there was some real degree of planning and organization beyond just Istvan and his friends in Buenos Aires.

"Tomorrow we go shopping," Istvan announced as they settled into the house. "We can use the house for two weeks. That will give us time to find our friend and get him out."

Jakob was tired of correcting him, so he just let it pass.

Ruben and Eli stayed at the house while Jakob, Istvan, and Neil went to meet Istvan's contact, who would get them guns and whatever special supplies they would need. They took Neil along because they wanted a lookout while Istvan and Jakob talked to Istvan's contact. "He's a storekeeper," Istvan said as they walked along. "He left Germany when the Nazis took over."

"Jewish?"

"No. Just anti-Nazi."

"Does he have a name?"

"Franz Harimann. He's given us a lot of information from Encarnación."

"Is he your only source of information here?"

"Yeah, why?"

"It's not a good idea to rely on just one source. Believe me, I know. I was in Lebanon once and we—"

"It'll work out!" Istvan interrupted, annoyed at Jakob's constant criticism.

"Fine, fine . . . I'm just saying it pays to be careful. This isn't a game. A mistake here, and I mean *especially* here, could cost us our lives."

"This is the place," Istvan said as he pointed at a dry goods store across the street. "Let me go in first and make sure everything is right. You wait here and I'll come and get you."

Jakob nodded, and Istvan crossed the street, looking extremely obvious as he surveyed the area around the store before going in. Jakob knew Istvan was in over his head, no matter how much the young man protested that he knew what to do, and so Jakob decided to check things out himself. He told Neil to stay put and walked about a half block up the street before crossing and then walking back in front of the store. He took a casual glance as he passed the store and saw that there were about a half dozen people inside. Obviously, they hadn't considered that. It would draw attention if this storekeeper suddenly told everyone to leave and closed up while he talked to Istvan. Maybe there was another clerk.

Jakob went in and pretended to shop, looking over the canned goods. He realized he stood out, since he was the only man in the store besides Istvan and the store clerk, so he tried to keep out of sight. He noticed Istvan waiting patiently at the counter as the clerk rang up the sale for the lady in front of him on an ancient cash register. It looked like a bad way to make contact. What would he say? "Excuse me, Mr. Harimann, do you have any guns today? We're going Nazi hunting."

On the other hand, it didn't seem dangerous in the store, so Jakob decided to retreat and wait for Istvan to call him. Just then, the store clerk, who had been hunched over as he inventoried his customer's purchases and rang them up, stood up and smiled at the housewife as he gave her the total.

Jakob quickly turned away. He couldn't believe his eyes! He moved down the aisle a ways to get a closer look, watching as the clerk thanked "Senora Ruiz" in a booming voice with a smile and a little nod of his head. Jakob could almost hear the man click his heels. Now certain of the man's identity, Jakob beat a hasty retreat out of the store and waited for Istvan to come out.

It was twenty minutes before Istvan appeared at the door and waved for Jakob to come over. Jakob just shook his head and waved at Istvan to come to him. Istvan had no idea what Jakob was doing, and so he waved him over again, this time with more animation. Jakob just leaned against the building and shook his head again, then stood up and started to walk away, thinking the storekeeper might soon come out to see what was keeping Istvan. And Jakob had no doubt that if the storekeeper saw him he would recognize him. After all, it hadn't been that long since Klaus Grunewald and Jakob had last seen each other.

Istvan was furious! He couldn't imagine what Jakob was up to, and he ran across the street to catch up with him.

"What are you doing?" Istvan demanded.

"It's a trap," Jakob answered calmly.

"A trap? What the hell are you talking about? How could you know from standing here that it's a trap?"

By that time Neil had joined them out of sight of the store.

"I went into the store. You didn't even notice me, did you?"

"You didn't go in the store!" Istvan declared.

Jakob's eyes flashed. "You know, Istvan, if you keep insinuating that I'm a liar and a coward, one of these times I'll surprise you by breaking your nose."

"You go ahead and try," Istvan replied as he took a step back and put his hands up, ready to fight.

"It's true," Neil interrupted. "He did go in the

store. He was in there for at least ten minutes." Neil wasn't happy to contradict Istvan, but he couldn't understand why Istvan was being so stupid about it.

There was an awkward pause as Istvan glared at his friend, as though Neil had betrayed him, but Istvan soon recovered his belligerence and countered, "So what?"

"So I saw your Herr Harimann," Jakob answered. "I recognized him. He's a former SS man."

"You're wrong. We checked him out. We talked to a lot of people. There's no way—"

"I know that man personally. I know—"

"What? Are you one of those who saw an SS guard in a concentration camp a dozen years ago and now you know him on sight? Isn't it possible you're wrong?"

"No, I'm not wrong. He was my prisoner ten years ago. I spent time with him in close quarters. I even knew him before the war. There is absolutely no doubt that the clerk in that store is Klaus Grunewald. He was an Einsatzgruppen leader and then an officer in Theresienstadt. They're setting you up! Don't you understand?"

Istvan looked like he had been punched in the face. "Suppose you're right . . . what do we do now? I told him I was bringing you right back."

"Were you going somewhere with him?"

"Just into the back room. We're supposed to tell him what we want and then he'll get it for us."

"How long would it take him?"

"Someone told me that we should expect to come back in two days, but I'm not sure what Harimann will say."

"Then you and Neil go in. You do the talking and Neil can just nod. I'll stay here. You let me know what happens, and we'll decide what to do from there."

Istvan and Neil tried to appear casual as they walked back into the store, but they only succeeded in looking nervous and out of place. Jakob didn't worry about it, though, since he assumed their awkward manner would lull Klaus into a false sense of security. Klaus would assume that he had these two neophytes right where he wanted them.

The doorway where Jakob had taken refuge was that of an empty store, so he made himself comfortable in the shaded portico, a welcome refuge from the blazing sun. But it was still stiflingly hot, even in the shade—a humid, sweltering heat that can put you to sleep if you get too comfortable and let your mind wander. Just as Jakob started to nod off, a car with a very loud muffler rolled past. He woke with a start, then shook himself and tried to get his bearings. When he looked at his watch, he was alarmed to see that almost forty-five minutes had slipped away. He got up and cautiously looked over at the store in a controlled panic. Had something happened? Had Klaus or someone else taken the boys out and killed them? It wasn't a pleasant thought. Not that it meant a lot to him. He could just walk away from it and no one would ever even know he was there except for Ruben and Eli. And what did that matter? They didn't even know who he was or where he came from. But then there was Galia. He didn't love her, but . . . well, he owed her something. At least not to walk away without even letting her know that Istvan was . .

Just then Istvan and Neil came out of the store.

Jakob retreated to the doorway and waited for them. "What happened?" he asked as they came around the corner.

"We talked about guns and cars. He said he could get us British Sten machine guns, lugers, ammunition, hand grenades, and two cars. But he said we had to give him money up front. I told him we would give him half the money tomorrow morning and the rest when we got the guns."

"I think we should do it."

"But you said he was an SS man!"

"I think he'll come through with the guns. My guess is that they want you to make an attack on Bormann so they can justify it when they kill you. That would also serve as a warning to others who might try it."

"So you think he'll actually get the guns?"

"Yes. And that's when I'll have a little talk with Uncle Klaus."

That afternoon Jakob went to a bank, where he had Ephraim wire him money from Buenos Aires. Istvan returned to give Klaus half the money as promised, and Klaus told him he would have everything two days later, on Thursday.

Those days of waiting were hard on Jakob because he had determined from the start that he would not get to know any of these young men. He didn't want to get caught up in their reckless ideas of justice, which might lead them to do something stupid. He still felt that if he could get a good look at Bormann, that would be enough. He didn't need to put himself and these boys in danger. But of course, he did want to have a talk with Klaus Grunewald. The memory of how Klaus had shot him and left him for dead in that bay off Sardinia ten years before was still fresh in his mind.

Jakob had chosen Eli as his partner when they were planning the attack on the store because he knew that Eli had served in the Argentine military. The two of them spent the intervening days going over a few combat moves.

Eli went out by himself on Tuesday and, with money Jakob had given him, managed to buy some pistols. They weren't pretty, just old revolvers made sometime before the turn of the century, but they were functional and would easily kill a man if necessary.

Jakob was nervous as they started out for the store on Thursday morning. His only thought since he had first seen Klaus was to kill him. Now he was having doubts. Klaus had killed his father, and there was no question in Jakob's mind that he should die. But what if Klaus could lead them to Bormann? Could Klaus be trusted? Probably not . . . but when he had been cornered, he had led them to the gold in Sardinia. Maybe if there was enough in it for him, he could be trusted to save his own neck.

"I'm going in the back door with Eli," Jakob said as they went over the plan one last time. "You and Neil go in the front. Ruben stands guard. Ruben, make sure you let us know if anything, *anything*, looks wrong. We could easily be walking into a trap here. They want to kill us. That's the only thing we know for sure. The big question is, will they try to kill us here once they have the money, or do they want to kill us out in the jungle?"

"Why don't we just kill him?" Istvan asked, referring to Klaus.

"I told you. He might be able to lead us to Bormann. This might not be a complete lie. They may be the first line of defense for Bormann. We want to take him alive and see if he knows anything. Give me and Eli time to get in through the back, and then Neil keeps his gun ready, following close behind you so they can't see it as you come in the store. If it is a trap, everybody dies except Klaus."

"Unless we have to . . ."

"Unless you *must* kill him. I don't want any of us to die over this. Protect yourselves at all cost."

Jakob let out a deep sigh. "Well, that's it," he said with finality. "Let's go."

When Jakob and Eli were behind the store, Eli pulled out a silenced semiautomatic pistol and handed it to him. "Where the hell did you get that?" Jakob asked with surprise.

"It's American. They call it a 'hush puppy' because they used it for killing guard dogs on commando raids."

"I know. I just can't believe you found one. This will come in handy."

"I thought it might," Eli said with a smile.

The door at the back of the store was unlocked when Jakob tried it. Either there was no ambush, or these people were incredibly sloppy. But then, Jakob reasoned to himself, they assumed that these boys were complete amateurs.

They drew their guns as Eli stood next to the door

and Jakob opened it just enough so that he could slip in quickly. Jakob crouched down, his heart beating furiously as he waited for his eyes to adjust to the darkened room. He then moved aside and waved for Eli to follow. They didn't say a word as they quietly moved toward the doorway that led from the storeroom to the front of the store. Jakob stopped suddenly as he heard a whisper.

"Wann kommt sie?"

"Soon," came an answering whisper from somewhere near the first. "Now be quiet. They might hear you."

Jakob pointed to a pair of boots, barely visible in the dimly lit room, which hung slightly over the edge of a shelf above the door leading to the front of the store.

Just as Eli focused on what Jakob was pointing at, the boots moved almost imperceptibly.

"Da!" whispered the first voice.

Jakob knew this meant that Istvan and Neil must have entered the store. He motioned for Eli to move up to the wall just beneath the two would-be ambushers. He then signaled for Eli to get down so that he could use him as a stepstool, climbing up to get at the assailants.

In the front of the store, Klaus saw Istvan and Neil coming toward the door. A young woman was browsing along one of the shelves, and just as Istvan walked in, Klaus told her that the store would be closing soon. Istvan and Neil walked up to the counter and waited. They saw no reason to be subtle or pretend that they had other business. They just waited for the young woman to leave. She looked at them askance, knowing instinctively that this was no place for her, and then left without saying a word. Klaus followed her to the door, locking it and pulling the window shades.

"Well, gentlemen," he said casually as he sauntered toward the counter. "Do you have the money?"

"Yes," Istvan said as he felt Neil's gun hand twitch involuntarily against his back. "Did the . . . did the merchandise come in?"

"The merchandise is here," Klaus said with a smile as he moved behind the counter. "May I see the money?"

"Certainly," Istvan answered, tossing a dirty military rucksack onto the counter.

Klaus slowly, calmly, reached for the flap of the bag and flipped it open, putting his other hand on the counter as if to steady himself. When he saw the money, he picked up the bag and put his hand on the shelf below the counter, reaching for the pistol that he kept there. The move was so subtle that Istvan didn't even see it, but Neil did.

"Should I count it?" Klaus asked mischievously, but he only said it to distract their attention as he pulled the pistol from its hiding place. But Neil saw it coming, and before Klaus's hand even cleared the shelf, he had his Webley revolver pointed squarely at Klaus's nose.

"Let's not get carried away here," Klaus said nervously. "And I should warn you that there are guns pointed at you right now, and if you don't put down that gun—"

Before Klaus had a chance to finish, the door behind the counter opened and Jakob stepped in with a look of immense satisfaction on his face.

Klaus was speechless. He actually blinked to try to make this hallucination go away. He couldn't believe what he was seeing.

Finally, after what seemed like an eternity, he whispered, "Oh, my God . . . ," just as Jakob connected with a blistering right uppercut.

Klaus flew backward against a shelf, bringing down a noisy avalanche of cigarette cartons and miscellaneous items as the shelf gave way.

"Well, now . . . ," Jakob said as he stood over the fallen man, "what have you been up to lately, Uncle Klaus?"

"Just a simple storekeeper, Jakob," Klaus gasped out as he recovered from the blow and wiped at the corner of his mouth, holding up his hand and looking at the smear of blood on his fingers.

"That's strange. For some reason, these boys think you know the whereabouts of some important men. Some very bad men."

"I can't . . . ," Klaus stuttered nervously. "I can't help what other people think."

"Well, I believe them. I think you can help us find someone we're looking for."

"Help you find . . . Why would I do that?"

"To save your life. I haven't forgotten that bullet in Sardinia. I—"

"But everyone was shooting!" Klaus interrupted. "You can't blame me for trying to get out of there."

"I'm afraid I can. There's something about being shot that changes your whole perspective. I'll tell you, I wanted to kill you right off. But then I thought I should keep my personal feelings to myself."

"You might just as well kill me. If I lead you to any of these men, I won't live out the week."

"Is that your final word?" Jakob asked as he raised his pistol.

"What about Konrad?"

"Konrad? Who's Konrad?"

"My son Konrad, in the back room . . ."

"Which one was Konrad?"

"*Was* Konrad?" Klaus asked soberly. "What do you mean *was*?"

"There were two of them. One was killed."

Klaus then surprised all of them as he leapt up and ran to the back room. Jakob was right behind as Klaus stopped dead in his tracks.

When Jakob and Eli had crept into the back room and discovered the two men, they knew they had to overpower them. It was when Klaus went to pull the shades at the front of the store that they decided to strike. Jakob vaulted up onto the shelf and shot the first man in the head with the silenced pistol, killing him instantly. But the second man was on Jakob immediately, and Jakob rolled over on top of him, knocking the gun out of his hand and losing his own gun. By that time, however, Eli had pulled himself up onto the shelf, too, and managed to launch a hard, solid punch to the side of the other man's head, just in front of the ear, instantly rendering him unconscious. Jakob recovered his gun, and he and Eli quickly jumped down to the floor, pulling the unconscious man down off the shelf after them, then using the man's belt to restrain him. The scuffle had only taken moments, but Jakob was sure that they had made enough noise to be heard, and that was when he had burst through the door and interrupted Klaus, leaving Eli to watch over their prisoner and the back door.

When Klaus came flying through the door, Eli shouted very distinctly for him to halt as he pointed his revolver at his head. Klaus stopped, slightly raising his hands, but then sank to the floor beside his son. "Is he alive?" he asked.

"Yes," Eli answered cautiously as he looked at Jakob with a bewildered expression. "He's just unconscious."

"Let him go and I'll do what you say," Klaus suddenly said to Jakob.

"That doesn't sound like a good idea. It would make more sense to keep you both with us. I'll let both of you go if you help us find Bormann."

"Bormann?" Klaus repeated loudly. He looked anxious and unsettled as he thought for an instant. "Can we talk alone?"

"First let's make sure you don't have any more surprises," Jakob answered as he handed his pistol to Istvan and patted Klaus down.

"There's my office," Klaus directed as he and Jakob left the others to wonder what this could possibly be about.

"Jakob . . . ," Klaus began as he closed the door, but then he stopped talking and sank into the chair behind the old desk in the little office as Jakob sat down in front of him. Klaus was clearly shaken.

"Konrad . . . he was born during the war. Konrad is only seventeen. He's the only one of my sons who survived the war," Klaus finally announced somberly.

"I see he didn't learn much . . ."

Klaus glared at Jakob. "We have to watch ourselves all the time!" he barked. "We live like hunted animals..."

"If this is all you have to say to me, then save your breath," Jakob barked right back. "You brought this on yourself and your family. You thought you were gods. You thought you could murder and never have to pay for it."

"Murder?! I was ordered to do what I did. If I had refused, I would have been shot for treason!"

"Klaus, I'm not stupid. I remember you from when I was a boy. You volunteered because you wanted to be there. You knew what they intended to do. You were the loudest voice in the Horst Wessel chorus! I'm not here to debate this. I don't give a damn about your orders. Right now I've got orders, and you have a choice. Either help me or I kill you and Konrad. That's it. That's the choice. And don't make the mistake of thinking I won't do it. You must have figured out by now that I'm not my father. This is my war, and I won't give you a chance to cross me again."

Klaus took a deep breath and then asked in a quiet voice, "What happens to us when this is all over?"

"We get our man and we let you go."

"Just like Sardinia . . ."

"I was going to let you go. Just like I said."

"What about the others?'

"They would have done what I said. Just like now. I'm in charge here, and they'll do what I say."

"That's not good enough."

"Not good enough? I should kill you just because you killed my father. I should kill you for Sardinia!

I'm offering you your life . . . your life and your son's life . . . and you say that isn't enough?"

"Let's not get carried away. If I lead you to Bormann, if I go even farther and tell you how best to take him, my son, my wife, and I would all be killed. We would have to leave South America. We'd need money and a way out."

"Money? For the love of God, you took off with about a million deutsche marks worth of gold from Sardinia. What about the money we just gave you?"

"There were expenses."

"Expenses?"

"I don't know what you know about the German colonies here, but basically those who bring something with them are expected to turn most of it over to . . . well, let's just call it the corporation. It's like a company. You invest some capital and they make you a lifelong employee."

"Isn't *that* ironic," Jakob replied. "It sounds like Communism."

"We live comfortably," Klaus went on, ignoring Jakob's comment, "but we don't have the kind of money it would take to leave the country and start a new life."

"Suppose I agree to any of this. Do you have access to any of the materials that you promised my friends out there?"

"Yes, I can get the cars and guns."

"Do you have them now?"

"No."

"You were just going to shoot my friends out there and dump their bodies out in the country?"

"Like you said, it's war."

"Well, I'm not going to let you wander around looking for guns and cars and then bring back some friends."

"You can come with me. We've done it that way before."

"I'll send Eli. And we keep Konrad. If anything goes wrong, you die first and Konrad is next."

Jakob had thought the guns and cars would be there because he had been sure they were going to let them get into the jungle before trying to kill them. Now the schedule was all off because they had to wait for the guns. It worried him that Klaus and Konrad would be missing for all that time, not knowing who might come looking for them. He thought Klaus might be stalling for time and setting them up, but then Klaus insisted that they bring his wife Katrina to the safe house so that they could leave immediately after the operation.

"Are you sure you want to do that?" Jakob asked. "What if you or Konrad, or both of you, for that matter, get killed?"

"Then you have to get her out."

Jakob paused for a moment before agreeing.

Katrina had followed Klaus to Paraguay when he had sent for her six years earlier. They had separated during the war because Katrina blamed Klaus for the deaths of their three oldest sons, but eventually they got back together. It was a strange relationship, but somehow they felt they belonged together. And when Klaus left Europe, he promised he would send for her when he settled.

While they were waiting for "equipment," Jakob wondered how often Klaus had contact with his

friends in the German colony who were in contact
with Bormann. He suspected that if someone like
Klaus, someone at the fringes of their operation, disappeared without explanation, security would tight-
en around people like Bormann. But there was no
way he could go after Bormann sooner. He hoped
that two days wouldn't be long enough for anyone to
get nervous.

Klaus drew a map of Waldner 55, saying that he
and Konrad had been there a number of times.
There were eight armed guards patrolling the
grounds at any given time and three or four others
in a barracks. According to Klaus, the guards rotated
shifts every two hours, like clockwork.

"If it were me, I would go in just before the
guards change. The ones on duty would be waiting
for their replacements, and their minds wouldn't be
on the fence. They're locals, not Germans, so their
loyalties are up for grabs. If you could get into the
compound quickly, you could take the others while
they're still in the barracks, and the others might
just run. Can you use knives?"

"Three of us have training."

"What about them?" Ruben asked, referring to
Klaus and Konrad.

"They're going in through the front gate."

"What?" Klaus asked.

"You said you've been there before. They know
you. You're going to create a diversion by telling
them that you've heard there's going to be trouble.
But don't try anything, because Ruben will be in the
seat behind you with a gun pointed at your head. If
anything even *feels* wrong, he'll shoot. As soon as

they clear the gate, I'll toss a couple of sticks of dynamite at—"

"Dynamite?"

"We managed to pick up three sticks. It's just for
show. If I can throw one at the gate and a couple at
the barracks, we should create enough confusion to
put the fear of God into the guards and get into the
house."

"You would do better to take out the generators."

Jakob almost smiled. Here was the Uncle Klaus he
knew. Once he decided where he stood, he could
change alliances in a heartbeat.

"But what about the gate?"

"They have a signal. You flash the headlights . . .
two long and two short. That's the only way you get
close enough to talk to the guards. Otherwise they
open fire on any cars coming up the road."

"That's good to know."

"Since I'll be driving the car . . ."

"Ruben will take the silencer. You slow down at
the gate, he takes care of the guard, and then you
pull up to the generators. We'll move in when
Ruben dynamites the generators. The lights will be
out, and we can take care of the guards in the barracks and then move on the house."

They finished up making their plans, and then
Jakob called Neil, Eli, and Ruben together. He had
talked to Istvan alone before and knew where *he*
stood, but he wanted to make sure the others knew
what they were in for.

"So you're going to have to kill a man before the
day's over. Can you do it? Are you all prepared for
this."

"I've killed before," Eli announced.

"This is different. It's different than when you're part of an army. If things go wrong, either the government or the Nazis will execute us. We all have to be certain in our own minds. Once we leave this house we're committed. Any one of you can call off this operation right now. I'm going to let you talk this over for a few minutes, and you let me know whether we go or not."

A few minutes later Neil came out and found Jakob. Jakob was sure that Neil would be the one to back out if any of them did, so he assumed the others had sent him to break the bad news. Jakob was actually relieved, though. He didn't feel good about playing on the misguided loyalties of these boys. He had tried to figure out why they followed Istvan, and he decided it was some kind of guilt over the war or some ridiculous romantic notion of avenging six million dead. Whatever the reason, he was glad Neil had come to his senses, since he had serious doubts about taking untrained young men on a commando raid.

He smiled at Neil, ready to tell him that his decision to quit was a good one—that if he had doubts, it was better to call the whole thing off now.

"We're going," Neil said as he put out his hand.

Jakob's smile disappeared as he shook Neil's hand.

The first leg of their trip was a twenty-mile drive into the jungle on rugged dirt roads. They left at ten o'clock Saturday night so that they could arrive in plenty of time to move into the camp on foot and await the arrival of Klaus, Konrad, and Ruben for the diversion. They quickly unloaded the guns, ammunition, flashlights, and canteens for their hike. They had a couple of semiautomatic carbines, which Neil and Eli carried, each of them using electrical tape to attach a flashlight to the barrel, and they also had a Thompson machine gun and a homemade version of the British Sten machine gun. Jakob took the Sten because he knew a homemade version might jam, and he didn't trust one of the "boys" to stay calm and keep it working. He also carried an Argentine-made version of the Colt .45 semiautomatic pistol.

The moon was a pale, glowing ivory, the color of old piano keys, but Jakob and the others soon lost sight of it as they left the road to snake their way through the dense rain forest. Once their eyes adjusted to the darkness, since they had to move quickly and quietly, and since it was only the four of them, they tried to get by without using machetes to cut through the dense undergrowth. Instead, they tried to weave their way through the forest, only cutting when it was absolutely necessary.

The jungle was like another world for Jakob. He may as well have landed on another planet. It was smothering. The humidity and dense foliage seemed like an enemy in itself, constantly pulling at and reaching for him, always seeming to hold him back. There was a smell and feel to it, the soft, moss-covered ground that never seemed completely firm, as though it could fall away at any moment and send him tumbling into a bottomless pit. And the sweat. The sweat poured from his body in rivers. It was completely different from the dry heat of the desert that he had come to know. They only had three miles to travel as they approached the compound, but it began to seem impossible. Istvan had underestimated the jungle—or overestimated his comrades. Riding along the broken, rutted clay road gave them a false impression of it, as though it could be tamed. The truth is that it can be destroyed, but never tamed. One must either take it as it is or burn it to the ground, because there is no compromise with the jungle.

It was Istvan who first spotted the compound just a few minutes after two o'clock in the morning. He was ahead of the others, the point man as it were, and he realized the jungle ended abruptly in a clearing ahead of them. As he slowly crept along, he noticed a guard was walking toward him only a hundred yards or so ahead. He didn't actually hear the guard, who managed to move silently through the coarse grasses, but rather "felt" him—sensing the movement in the darkness—and stopped before the guard could see him.

He managed to crawl back far enough so that he could signal Jakob and the others behind him to stop without the guard noticing them. They waited for the guard to go by, and then Jakob checked his watch.

"We're on time. We've got twenty minutes before the car arrives. Do you see any lights or anything?"

"I saw the fence Grunewald told us about. Open field for a couple hundred yards, and then the fence. There are lights, but they're just floodlights. There aren't any searchlights or towers. We could get within twenty yards of that fence before they had any idea we were there."

"You can take the guard?" Jakob asked.

"Yeah," Istvan answered confidently. "The guard should be back past here in a couple of minutes on his way to change the watch. I'll get back up to the tree line and wait, take him when he goes by, and then we all move up and wait for the car to come."

"Right," Jakob said as the others nodded in agreement. Istvan started back, and Jakob communicated to the others with hand signals that they were to spread out on either side of Istvan so they would be in position to take the guard if Istvan failed.

They watched intently as Istvan moved out of the jungle and into the sea of heavy, coarse grass before them, moving so quickly and gracefully that it looked like he was floating on top of it. He moved outward and tried to anticipate the path the new guard would take on his patrol, finally finding the rut that the guards had worn on their nightly parades. Once he found the path, he moved off a bit and seemed to be swallowed up by the grass as he waited for his prey.

I. wasn't long before the replacement made his way toward them. They couldn't see him very well in the pale moonlight, just enough to know that he was of average height and weight. He moved like a hunter trying to flush birds, walking a ways and then stopping, waiting to see if a nervous quail might take wing. But Istvan, his heart pounding loudly, was going to wait him out.

The guard had a flashlight, and when he stopped he would wave it along the tree line, trying to catch the glow of a pair of eyeballs, whether human or not. Jakob couldn't decide whether the guard was just unnerved by the darkness or a veteran who knew a few tricks. The guard kept moving closer and closer until it seemed that any second he would step on Istvan. He stopped again and cast his flashlight in toward the trees. He was so close that Istvan could smell him, the scent of his dirty fatigues and sweat. He could hear him breathing.

Suddenly the guard was engulfed in a shadow. The beam of the flashlight danced up and down frantically and from side to side until it suddenly disappeared into a little glowing spot in the grass.

Jakob and the others rushed toward Istvan on their way to the fence. When they got there, Istvan had the dying guard in a choke-hold with one hand over his mouth so that he couldn't cry out as he died. They were both covered in blood. Istvan must have cut an artery when he used his knife. Jakob's first thought was of a photo he had once seen of a jaguar caught as it killed a young antelope and held its neck in its jaws, staring passively at the camera as it strangled the last fleeting breaths of life from its victim.

No one said a word. They all moved on toward the fence, dropping into the grass as they got close. Only a few of the lights strung along the fence were on, since the electricity in the compound came from generators, and they only turned on all the lights if someone sounded the alarm. Jakob checked his watch. They only had ten minutes before the car was supposed to arrive at the gate.

Back on the road, everything was on schedule as Ruben sat in the back with two guns, one pointed at

Klaus and the other at Konrad. Ruben was calm and quiet. He had let them know at the beginning that he was ready and willing to kill. He wasn't too worried about Klaus, because the old man seemed to understand that he and his son could make it out alive. But Konrad worried him. Konrad was young and nervous.

"You're thinking too hard," Ruben said to Konrad as they started driving to their rendezvous with the others at the compound.

Konrad just grunted.

"We don't need to make this hard," Ruben continued in a calm, low voice as he lit a cigar. "All you have to do is get me up to the gate and then stay out of the way. That's all there is to it. Keep down and let us do what we need to do, and then we all part company as friends."

Neither Konrad nor his father said a word.

"Then I take it we understand each other. We should be there in a few minutes. Slow down for the gate, give them the signal, and I'll take care of the guard. Then head straight for the generator shack and wait for everyone else to catch up."

Ruben crouched as low as he could when he felt the car slowing as the engine wound down. He could hear the switch clicking as Klaus turned the headlights off and on—two long, two short—and then the brakes. They must be at the gate.

"Halt . . . halt," a voice called out. Not a frantic voice. Just the way any guard would instruct a motorist before inspecting the car.

As the guard came up to the driver's window, Ruben fired two silenced bullets into his face. Klaus then sped up, just as planned, and headed for the generator shack. But the arrival of an unscheduled vehicle brought another guard out of the field to see what was happening. He opened fire on the car with an automatic rifle, sending two rounds through the windshield. Klaus floored the accelerator and turned toward the man. The guard tried to fire as he was running, but he missed and Klaus ran him down. He bounced up onto the hood, his rifle shattering the windshield right in Klaus's field of vision, and then just as quickly slid off the side of the car. Klaus pulled up about a hundred meters short of the generator shack, abruptly putting on the brakes.

Ruben had made sure the three sticks of dynamite were held firmly in the pocket of his jacket before they had started, and he was off and running as soon as the car stopped. Klaus thought about asking Ruben for one of the guns, but knew he wouldn't get it, so he concentrated his energy on getting out of the car and under cover.

Ruben used the silenced pistol as another guard came out to see what was happening. He emptied the pistol to be sure he brought the man down and then threw the gun aside, grabbing two sticks of dynamite. The fuses on the dynamite were set to burn for five seconds, so he ran to the door of the generator shack, kicked it in with a running jump, and landed on his back with the two sticks of dynamite in one hand and his cigar in the other. He quickly lit the fuses and rolled one of them under the nearest generator. Then he saw a couple of barrels of petrol and threw the other stick in that direction. He didn't know who might be waiting for him outside the door, so he crouched down, grabbed the Webley pistol from his other pocket, and took off out of the shed.

When Jakob and the others heard the automatic rifle fire, they decided to take the fence right away, even though the lights were still on, rather than wait for the dynamite. Istvan and Neil had the wire cutters and began cutting the fence while Jakob and Eli stood watch. Just as Istvan pulled away enough of the fence for them crawl through, someone came rushing toward them from the barracks with gun blazing. Neil took a careful stance and dropped the man with one shot from his carbine. At that same instant the dynamite went off. The first blast took out the generator, cutting off the lights, and then the other sent up a huge fireball from the drums of petrol. Istvan hurried everyone through the fence, and the four of them ran for the barracks, splitting into two squads. Neil and Eli had turned on the flashlights attached to their guns, and Istvan followed Neil with his machine gun while Jakob followed Eli with the Sten.

By the time they arrived at the heart of the compound, the fire from the generator shack had spread to the barracks and all the guards were running for their lives. Jakob had told everyone that they couldn't take prisoners and couldn't let anyone escape, so they shot each one as they came out of the barracks, half of them unarmed. It was all done in less than five minutes. Then they moved on to the house.

Jakob was worried about the house more than anything. Bormann could be anywhere. He might not even be there at all. The first thing Jakob wanted to do was to surround the house. Ruben was already in front with the car, where Klaus and Konrad were hiding, so he only needed to send Eli and Neil to watch the sides and back. As Eli ran off, Jakob asked where Istvan had gone.

"He's already at the door," Eli shouted back, and Jakob rushed over to join him, but Istvan had apparently gone in by himself.

Jakob got out his flashlight and crouched down at the entrance, readying his gun and then quickly slipping inside and off to the side of the doorway. He held his flashlight as far from his body as possible, in case someone decided to shoot at the light, and flashed it around the room quickly to orient himself to the house. His finger was hot on the trigger of the Sten as he forced the stock up tightly under his arm to hold it steady.

"Istvan!" he called out in a loud whisper. No sooner had he spoken than a burst of gunfire erupted in an adjoining room, followed by a single shot. Jakob ran to the hallway and peeked around the corner into the room. All he could see was the beam of Istvan's flashlight stretching along the floor.

"Istvan," he called out again.

"Jakob . . . ," a voice called out weakly. "He went upstairs. Get him. Get . . ."

Jakob rushed over and found Istvan sprawled out on the floor behind a an overturned table in a pool of blood.

"It's him," Istvan gasped. "Don't let him get away."

"Where are you hit?" Jakob asked.

"Don't let him . . . ," Istvan continued as Jakob put

an arm around his back and brought him up to a sitting position.

"Shut up, damn it! Just tell me where . . . ," Jakob started, but Istvan passed out. Jakob then heard glass breaking upstairs, and a heartbeat later there was shouting outside the house and an exchange of rifle and pistol fire. Jakob kept his mind on Istvan and laid him back down, looking him over with the flashlight to find the wound, but it wasn't easy, since he was still covered with blood from the guard he had killed earlier. Jakob found the source at Istvan's upper right leg, where the blood seemed heaviest. He cut his pants open, and blood began spurting out with every weakening beat of Istvan's heart. He had seen wounds like this before. The pistol shot had struck the femoral artery, and the only hope was to put a tourniquet on the leg. He knew it meant Istvan would lose the leg by the time they got him to help, but it was his only chance to survive. He pulled a tablecloth off the table in the adjoining dining room and cut it with his knife, tearing off a long strip for a bandage. Then he broke up an end table and used the leg to tighten the tourniquet. He worked quickly and silently, finishing up as Neil rushed into the house.

"He tried to get out the window. I told him to stop, but he shot at me and I shot back. He fell off the roof."

"Bormann?"

"Yes, Bormann. He fell off the roof."

"Dead?"

"No, he's still breathing. Got him in the arm and shoulder. He doesn't look too good, though. The fall didn't help, but he's not dead."

"Help me with Istvan."

"How is he?"

"Not too good. I had to use a tourniquet. Make sure it doesn't come loose. He's lost a lot of blood."

They carried Istvan out the door and laid him in the grass, trying to make him as comfortable as possible. Jakob then ran over to where Ruben and Eli were kneeling next to Bormann.

"Still alive?" Jakob asked.

"Still breathing. Out cold," Eli replied.

Bormann was curled up on his side, and Jakob rolled him flat on his back and began going through his pockets. He didn't find anything significant in his pockets, no identification at all. Jakob then reached into his own pocket and pulled out some papers, which he tried to unfold with one hand as he held the flashlight with the other. One paper was a photostat of an old black-and-white photograph. The man certainly looked like Bormann. The other papers had to do with identifying marks.

"Tilt his head back," Jakob ordered Eli. "Get his mouth open."

Eli quickly followed the instructions, and Jakob shined the flashlight into the man's mouth and then back to the papers, going back and forth several times. "Hard to tell . . . This guy has a lot more dental work, but it could have happened in the last few years."

Ruben moved over beside Jakob and took a look. "Not likely. This much dental work would more likely be done over a long period of time. This guy had good teeth," Ruben said as he tapped the paper in

Jakob's hand. "He was already in his late forties?"

"That's right."

"This kind of deterioration in the next . . . what . . . ten years?"

"Yeah, about ten years."

"I don't think so."

"Pull down his pants," Jakob ordered.

"What?" Eli asked with a smile as he began sliding the pants down. "He's got some sort of Nazi super-Schwanz?"

"Shut up," Jakob answered. "He's supposed to have a scar on the inside of his right leg from some riding accident."

"Nothing," Ruben said as he shined the flashlight slowly down the man's inner thigh.

"It's not him!" Eli announced with shock as he looked up at Jakob.

"No, it's not him."

"Then who the hell is he?"

"An impostor? A double?"

"What do we do with him?"

"We're going to leave him."

"Leave him? What if he knows where Bormann really is? We could bandage him up, take him with and question him later."

"It's not worth it. Istvan is already going to lose a leg. Let's get him to a doctor so he doesn't lose his life."

"And this one?" Ruben asked as he gestured to the impostor. "Do we kill him?"

"No. If he dies, fine. If he lives, they know we can get to them. We didn't get Bormann, but we let them know they can't hide forever. We don't win this time, but we didn't lose either, not if we keep Istvan alive. It's time to cut our losses. Let's get out of here."

"What about Klaus?"

"Don't tell him the guy's an impostor."

"Won't he figure it out if we leave him here?"

"Tell him Bormann's dead. If our friend here pulls through, they'll just think we didn't check closely enough. We'll pack everything up into one of their cars," Jakob said as he gestured over to a jeep and sedan parked nearby. "Let's get going. I'll go tell Klaus to take that car. Where is he?"

"They took cover behind the car just before I blew the generators," Ruben answered. "I guess they're still there."

Jakob nodded and headed over to the car. "It's over, Klaus," he said as he came around the car. "You can . . . ," he continued almost jovially, but then he stopped in his tracks as he brought up his flashlight to reveal yet another bloody scene. Klaus was holding Konrad to his chest, rocking slowly back and forth, and there was blood all over both of them.

"A bullet in the neck," Klaus said quietly, plaintively as he stopped rocking. "I couldn't stop it . . . I couldn't . . ."

Jakob knelt down to make sure there was nothing they could do. Klaus looked at him as though hoping he might perform a miracle, but Jakob just shook his head, and Klaus began to sob. Jakob forgot for an instant that he was supposed to hate Klaus.

"What am I going to tell his mother? What am I . .

. ," Klaus choked out between sobs, "You should have just shot me back at the store! Kill me! Kill me now, Jakob!"

"I'm sorry," was all Jakob could say as he backed away and started toward the others as Klaus kept shouting, "Kill me! Shoot me!"

They loaded Istvan into the jeep they had found and took off, leaving Klaus and the burning compound fading in the distance behind them.

Dawn was breaking as they finally reached a small village outside of Encarnación. Istvan had told them before they started out on their mission that they might find help in this little village if anything went wrong. Ruben went into the village on foot to try to find a doctor. Istvan had slipped in and out of consciousness during the jarring ride from the compound, trying to talk when he could, but he was in a delusional state brought on by shock. Eli and Neil just tried to keep him quiet while Jakob stood watch. Ruben came back after twenty minutes with an old woman in tow, still in her nightclothes.

The woman leaned into the jeep, quickly examining Istvan's wound and then pointing at a nearby house. Jakob drove up to the front door, where Neil and Eli quickly unloaded their friend before Jakob went off to find a place to hide the jeep.

Ruben explained that the old woman was a midwife who also took care of the occasional farm accident victim. The woman motioned for Neil and Eli to put Istvan on the table. He was unconscious again, so the woman directed everyone to hold him down and quickly went to work. It was horrible to watch, as she used a sewing needle and thread to close off the torn arteries and then got out a meat saw. Jakob had seen many things, but never anything like this. Neil started to get wobbly, and Jakob called out to Ruben to catch him as he fainted. "Just let him lay there. Hold Istvan down in case he comes to."

The old woman never wavered in her work. She kept going until Istvan's leg finally separated and fell off the table, landing next to Neil on the floor. Neil started to come to, saw the leg beside him, and went right back out again. No one was laughing, though. The others were doing all they could to keep from joining Neil on the floor. Mercifully, it wasn't long before the old lady had the leg tightly bandaged into a stump.

The midwife told Ruben that she didn't know if Istvan would make it or not because he had lost so much blood. "Take him to the sick house in Encarnación. They say they can put blood into people there," she said, "but go slow. If the boy is thrown around too much in your car, the wound will open up again and he will die before you get to the city."

Ruben interpreted the message for Jakob, who immediately went for the jeep.

As they loaded Istvan into the back, the old woman put her hand on Jakob's shoulder and looked up at him with a tender smile. "Go with God in your heart and he will keep your son safe," she said in Spanish as she patted his shoulder and then turned back to her house.

"What did she say?" he asked Ruben.

"Nothing . . . she just said she hopes he'll make

it."

They drove for a short distance to a spot on the outskirts of Encarnación, where they had stashed the other car that Klaus had gotten for them. It was a rusty old Ford sedan that would be less conspicuous than the jeep.

"There is doctor here who they say will help you and keep his mouth shut, but you have to pay him off."

"How much?" Jakob asked.

"He likes American money. One hundred dollars American just to see you. Then he'll want more."

"Okay . . . let's go."

"Not you," Ruben said emphatically. "If he sees you . . . he'll charge a foreigner ten or twenty times more. He might not even do it if he thinks he could get into big trouble. Believe me, it's better if just Eli and I take him in. We'll tell him it was an accident, and he'll think we're just petty thieves who got caught robbing some *estancia*. You go back to the house."

Jakob and Neil did just that, watching carefully to make sure they weren't followed. They had no idea what the repercussions of their raid might be. They didn't know how organized these Nazis were in Encarnación.

Jakob's imagination began to run wild. Was the word already out? Did everyone know Bormann was dead, or at least the man they thought was Bormann? Suddenly he felt everyone was watching them, looking for them. Maybe the impostor had lived. Maybe Klaus patched him up and now they were about to walk into an all-out war. Damn it! Why hadn't he killed Klaus when Klaus begged him to? Now it was going to come back to haunt him.

A whole day had gone by when they finally made it back to the safe house in the darkness, slowly pulling into the short driveway lined with overgrown bushes, which nicely concealed the car.

"You've got your pistol?" Jakob asked.

"Right here," Neil answered as he patted his pocket. He had been holding the pistol inside his pocket the whole time they were driving. Obviously Jakob wasn't the only one who was worried.

"Do you want the front door or the back?"

Neil didn't understand at first, but then realizing Jakob meant they should both go in from different directions, he said, "Front."

"Take it slow. We're not in any hurry. Keep down and get out of the doorway as quick as you can. Oh, yeah . . . and make sure you don't shoot *me*."

Neil smiled for the first time since they had left the night before. "Only if you promise the same."

"Promise," Jakob said as he put out his hand and Neil shook it. "Wait a minute! I forgot about Katrina. She could be hiding in the house."

They got out of the car, and Jakob told Neil to wait a couple of minutes before trying the front door so he could get around back.

When Neil tried the door it was unlocked. Crouching down and off to the side, he opened it and gave it a gentle push, so softly that it seemed to take forever to open all the way. Neil moved in slowly, peeking around the corner as he went, crouching all the way. In a moment he was in the living room, and he quietly closed the door behind him. He made his way across the room toward the back of the house and saw Jakob moving into the kitchen. As he stood up to check the hallway, suddenly he heard a voice say, "If you move, I'll kill you."

Neil froze. He tried to see who it was with his peripheral vision, but he couldn't tell. He wondered why they didn't just shoot him.

"God damn it, Klaus!" Jakob's voice came roaring from the kitchen. "You nearly scared us to death! That's Neil. Put the gun down."

"I scared *you* to death? How do you think I feel? Katrina is up hiding under the bed."

"What are you doing here?"

"What am I doing? You said you would get us out."

"But you don't need to go. They'll never . . ."

"They'll know. Maybe not today or tomorrow, but they'll know. We have to get out."

Jakob looked at Klaus as his words sunk in, and then the other reality hit Jakob. "How did Katrina . . . How did she take it?"

"Konrad? Not well. She keeps asking what we'll do with him."

"Do with him?"

"Burial. She's afraid she'll never be able to visit his grave."

"What did you do with him?"

"He's in the car. I didn't know what to do with him."

"He's in the car right now?"

"Yes! I couldn't just leave him there. Not only would they have come for me, they would have desecrated his body."

"So you're saying we're not just getting you and Katrina out of the country, but Konrad goes with..."

"He has to."

Jakob thought about it for a moment. Before he had been worried that Klaus had resurrected the Bormann impostor and mounted a Nazi army to hunt them down. Now he realized the old man just didn't want to leave his son's body in a distant, unmarked grave.

"We'll take him back to Argentina and get you out from there."

"Argentina?"

"If we cross the border at some small town as part of a funeral procession, they probably won't ask any questions. I have contacts in Argentina."

Ruben didn't arrive back at the house until after midnight. He told Jakob that Istvan was awake and talking when he left him. Eli had stayed at the hospital.

"We have another problem," Jakob told Reuben.

"What problem?"

"We need a mortician."

"A mortician? Why?"

"Klaus's son. Klaus brought the body here. He insists we take it with us."

"Are you crazy? It will be hard enough for us to get home with Istvan in the state he's in."

"If we can get Konrad embalmed, we can use a funeral procession to get us across the border."

Ruben stopped to think that over for a moment. "It could work," he finally said. "We'll have to move fast."

Once again it involved a bribe, the rest of Jakob's

"discretionary funds" from Ephraim in Buenos Aires, but Ruben found a mortician, had Konrad embalmed, and bought a cheap wooden coffin.

They got Istvan out of the hospital on that same day, even though the doctor warned them it was too soon, but at the same time the doctor was glad to be rid of them. "Watch for any signs of infection," he cautioned as they lifted Istvan into the old sedan.

Istvan didn't say anything as they drove. He didn't say anything when they got to the house, either. And no one tried to get him to talk. They cleared out one of the rooms so he could have it to himself on that night before they were to leave for home. Just before Jakob went to bed, he stepped into Istvan's room and stood watching as Istvan lay there with his eyes closed, breathing evenly. When he was convinced Istvan was all right, he started to close the door.

"You should have let me die," Istvan said without opening his eyes.

Jakob froze for an instant and then sighed heavily. "What am I, the angel of death? You want me to let you die, Klaus wanted me to kill him. For God's sake, do you think I knew it was going to turn out like this? I was the one who said we shouldn't go through with it, and you called me a coward. I could say I told you so, but that wouldn't help matters. This is a rotten, horrible outcome. Nobody wins here. We didn't accomplish much at all, and you're maimed for life. This is just the kind of thing I was worried about. Now you get to see what I meant when I said there are worse things than dying. Now you have to see what you're made of . . . and nobody else can help you get through this, not in the way that counts the most. You've got your sister and you can get by, but now you'll really have to fight every day in your head just to keep going . . ."

Istvan didn't say anything. He just started crying. Jakob felt like he should go over and comfort him, but he couldn't. It was just too much. What the hell was this all about? He just closed the door gently and walked away. He needed air.

He went outside and sat on the grass. Then he lay back and looked up at the sky, taking in the stars and the moon with its pale gold hue. *'The inconstant moon,'* he thought to himself. The line from Romeo and Juliet. The same color moon he remembered back in Hungary when he and Galia would run off to the little lake on the farm where he was recovering from his wounds. Would this have happened if he hadn't met Galia? It's so strange the way things come together. Strange connections that can bring such terrible results. He had tried so hard not to like Istvan, not to get to know him, but . . . That time in Hungary, he was lucky he didn't lose his leg. The wound was almost as bad . . . the same artery. There was nothing else he could have done for Istvan. It was time to remember that Istvan was alive. When it comes down to it, we all fight to stay alive.

The next day they started out early on their way back to Argentina. This time they would drive all the way instead of taking the bus.

They had taken the chance of returning to Klaus's store to get an old pickup truck that Klaus had used for his business, and they loaded Konrad's coffin into the back, covering it with a canvas tarp.

They didn't have any trouble getting across the

border, once the border guards opened the coffin and verified that it really was a corpse and that nothing was being smuggled.

Jakob had called Ephraim back in Buenos Aires and told him what had happened. He told him about Klaus and Katrina, and about how they would need a place for Konrad as soon as they arrived. By then it would be about four days since he . . .

"You told them you could relocate them?"

"It was part of the price."

"But we don't have that kind of an operation here."

"I know, but I thought you might be able to help me put something together."

"Like what?"

"*I don't know!*"

"Alright, alright . . . we're not getting anywhere like this. Let's look at it another way. What does this former SS man have that would make him valuable enough to help him out?"

"Well, he was in Czechoslovakia during the war. He. . ."

"That's it!"

"What?"

"The Americans. I've heard of them paying former SS for information. They've even resettled some. This Czech connection might do it."

"But who?"

"I know an American CIA man in town. He's fairly new here. My guess is they want to destabilize the government down here. They keep trying to play these games. If he thought your friend had something on the Communists, they'd get him out."

"Can you send him over? We can set up a meeting. Klaus could do it. He's good at playing both sides of the fence at the same time."

When Jakob brought up the prospect to Klaus, he agreed immediately. "Katrina has cousins in America. In the city of Chicago. With the help of your agent, we could settle there."

"And you have something to tell him?"

"I think I could come up with something."

"Like what," Jakob asked coyly.

"I suppose I could give them some names. Eichmann, Mengele . . . Barbie?"

"They're here?"

"Of course they're here."

"Where?"

"You could drive to Eichmann's house from here in an hour. Mengele has an apartment not twenty minutes way. Barbie's in Chile."

"And you'd give them up?"

"Jakob, let me tell you a secret," Klaus said as he leaned toward him. "The war is over. We lost. I've had enough. Konrad is the last straw, and it was inevitable. They told him he should become a Nazi here, that there would be another chance. A fourth Reich. Well, as the years go by . . . an old man like me sees things differently. Nothing would come of it."

"So now what? Are you telling me you're a different man?"

"A different man? Oh, I see. You think I'm the devil. You know, I've read a lot about the party leaders. Do you know they did a psychiatric profile on the top men in the Nazi party? The Allies . . . the

Americans thought they could show that they were insane. The premise was that they had to be insane to do the things they did, this killing of the Jews. But it didn't come out that way. They weren't insane. They were ordinary men in a strange time, a strange world. Who knows exactly how and why it happened. Maybe it was a divine experiment. I think maybe God scared himself when he found out what these beings he created were capable of doing to each other. I do know this, though. All of those we killed . . . killed us. No one survived. Now our children cannot even speak our names out loud. To be German is to be a criminal, and it will take generations to erase that stigma. My generation, in fact, all the generations who lived through those years, must be gone and buried before a future Germany can get past what we have done."

"Is that some kind of apology!?"

"Apology? From me? I might as well apologize for the rain. I was only a drop in the storm. I don't know where the storm came from or where it went. You can kill me if you want, but I'll tell you now that I know it won't erase the crime. It won't ease anyone's pain. Justice is an illusion. I've lost as much as anyone. I lost my family, my life. I'll tell you this, Jakob. If you cling hard to your absolute sense of right and wrong, it will destroy you in the end. It's time to let the past go."

"Let the past go . . . Klaus, you are such an ass. How dare you say that. You are the murderer."

"I'm trying to tell you, Jakob. It's as trite as the ages. Absolute power corrupts absolutely . . . Wasn't it the Romans who came up with that one? That's thousands of years ago. Germany was desperate for a voice, and when that voice came, they didn't refuse it anything. Fanaticism is the enemy. The absolutes. If you give your soul over to anyone, how can you be surprised when you suddenly find it's lost?"

Jakob shook his head. Klaus was trying to convince him that he was the victim, and the frightening thing was that it sounded plausible. But then Jakob's thoughts flashed back to that time when he had been in Theresienstadt. He remembered what his son looked like, drawn and gaunt, sleeping on a bed of dirty hay like an animal, with a yellow star sewn to his coat. And he remembered seeing Klaus there in his neatly done uniform like the superhuman Aryan he imagined himself to be. That was Jakob's truth. The truth of his own experience, not somebody else's propaganda or revised history. He knew he wasn't going to be Klaus's executioner. That would be up to someone stronger than he.

"THAT'S THE THING with you crazy Israelis," the CIA agent in Buenos Aires said in a slow, condescending way as he leaned back in his chair after Jakob had brought Klaus in to talk to him. "You don't seem to know the war is over. Been over a long time, as a matter of fact."

Jakob saw Galia one more time before he left Argentina. He was surprised that she didn't blame him for what had happened to Istvan. She even had a kind word as Jakob left. It seemed that having the chance to tell him off allowed her to let him go. She wasn't mad at him anymore.

Jakob had done what he had come to do, and the mission was considered a success when he returned to Israel.

A few months later, a group of Israeli agents arrived in Argentina again. This time their mission was to carefully orchestrate a raid using all the information they had gathered. They knew the whereabouts of Adolf Eichmann, and they were going to bring him to trial in Israel.

CHAPTER 10

The 1960s in Israel were a period of consolidation and growth. Major events that shaped the young country politically were the Eichmann trial, ongoing developments in the Lavon Affair that caused the fall of David Ben Gurion's government and led to his resignation, and the biggest event, the three-day war of 1967. But it was the three-day war that had the farthest-reaching effects, consequences few could have imagined.

When Arab armies were once again defeated by the Israelis, many citizens of Israel began to believe that they couldn't be beaten. This attitude had a devastating effect on Israeli preparations in 1973 when Egypt attacked again, this time with a successful surprise attack during the High Holy Days. But the farthest-reaching consequence of the three-day war was the formation of Arab terrorist groups soon afterward.

It was during the period immediately after the three-day war that Yasir Arafat started a group called the Palestine Liberation Organization. Many such groups were formed during that time, including the Popular Front for the Liberation of Palestine led by George Habash and "Black September," among others. These people realized that a small group with a political agenda could publicize and in many cases garner support for itself through dramatic acts of random violence that were outside the actual arena of conflict.

Within months of the end of the three-day war, Arab guerrillas began hijacking international airliners from other countries. Soon thereafter, certain airline companies began paying money to terrorist groups so that their planes wouldn't be hijacked. That money was then used to fund even more terrorist acts as other international terrorist groups, such as Germany's Baader-Meinhof Gang and the Red Brigade, began to ally with them to carry out even more horrific acts of violence.

Arab terrorism became a depraved riddle. People around the world would ask, "Why did three Japanese terrorists pull automatic rifles and hand grenades out of their bags in a crowded airport and start firing into crowds of innocent tourists?" And the answer would be, "Because they visit Israel, thus supporting the Zionist murderers who have oppressed the people of Palestine."

They found him in a poor working-class suburb of Buenos Aires. He was such an ordinary, average-looking man—middle-aged with a receding hairline and black horn-rimmed glasses. They watched him go to work and they watched him come home at night on the bus. They watched as he played with his young son and laughed. He worked as a foreman at the Mercedes Benz plant using the name Ricardo Klement. But his real name was Adolf Eichmann.

Then one night they waited for him to come home from work. A man stood in front of him, blocking his way, and thinking he was about to be robbed, he reached into his pocket. He was wrestled to the ground and then forced into a waiting automobile. They took him away and questioned him in a house they had rented. Once he had acknowledged that he was, indeed, Adolf Eichmann, they continued with their plan to take him to Israel for trial.

There was even a moment when the head of the Mossad thought they would also get Josef Mengele, the "Angel of Death," who had stood at the head of the lines of incoming Jews at Auschwitz, pointing either left or right—to the gas chambers or the work camp. Mengele, however, had moved just a few weeks before the Israelis visited his former apartment in Buenos Aires.

After Eichmann had been smuggled aboard an El Al flight that had brought the Israeli ambassador to Argentina for an anniversary celebration, there was a moment of worldwide condemnation. Other nations railed at the idea of the Israelis kidnapping an Argentine citizen to put him on trial in their own country. But their objections were soon overcome with an apology to Argentina and a statement that said there were none better qualified nor more deserving of the opportunity to sit in judgment of Eichmann's crimes than the nation of Israel.

The United Nations voted on the issue and agreed. Eichmann was officially a prisoner of the Israelis, awaiting trial in Jerusalem. The trial was to be held in a former theater that had been turned into a courtroom, a fitting venue for the drama about to unfold before the world. And they even built a glass booth, a cage to protect the defendant.

Thomas Stein stared at the man behind the glass in the same way one might stare at a strange animal in a zoo. "What was God thinking when he made that?"

Like an animal in a zoo . . . what a perfect metaphor! It was exactly what David Ben Gurion and the rest of the Israeli leaders had in mind. They wanted the world to look at this terribly ordinary little man and ask themselves if this wasn't what anti-Semitism was all about. Was it possible that *any* ordinary man could fall into the darkest recesses of existence as they sought to destroy what they didn't understand or what was simply different from themselves?

Thomas was sitting some six rows back in the gallery as he gazed at the man on trial. Adolf Eichmann was of average size, but the proceedings seemed to make him appear smaller, like a cockroach about to scurry away as the lights come on. But he couldn't run. He was caught. He huffed and squirmed indignantly, twisting his mouth from side to side as witness after witness recounted the crimes committed by the Third Reich and, among the most heinous, those committed by Eichmann himself.

"I was only following orders. I had no real authority," he would say when confronted with orders he had issued and signed. One moment he would insist that his signature was only perfunctory, but then when it came to things that he had supposedly done to reduce the suffering of Jews—slowing down deportations and the like—he claimed he had issued those orders courageously and at great personal risk. Overall, however, he tried to convey the image that he was nothing more than a cog—an insignificant little cog—in the horrible, ravenous gears that had ground up millions of Jews.

But then they asked him about the Wannsee conference in January of 1942. He had been there sipping cognac and smoking cigars with no less than

Reinhard Heydrich. That was where the phrase "the final solution" had been coined in reference to the impending genocide. That was when it was decided how the Jews were to be rounded up and executed. The details were sorted out: bullets or carbon monoxide, trucks or boxcars, women and children? One officer brought up the problem of finding soldiers who could take the emotional strain of the job.

All the questions were discussed and the plans made. It was the final step on the road to six million dead. Most of the concentration camps were to be passive killing centers. That is to say that whereas camps like Theresienstadt or Dachau were not set up with gas chambers, conditions were geared to high "attrition" resulting from insufficient food and medical care combined with backbreaking work. Then there were the actual killing centers—Treblinka, Sobibor, Lublin, Belzec, Maidanek—set up specifically to murder large numbers of Jews. A few months after the Wannsee conference, an insecticide called Xyklon-B was introduced to the Auschwitz-Birkenau complex where gassing was considered to be the most efficient way of killing.

The testimony for the prosecution was carefully orchestrated to produce the ultimate effect. That is not to imply that it was in any way fabricated or inappropriate, but that the prosecutors laid out their case for ultimate impact. This court case wasn't just about trying to convict a criminal; it was about educating the world.

Certain phrases would stay with Thomas for the rest of his life. When Israel Gutman was on the stand describing his experience, he said the

Germans "were drunk with blood." And when Eliahu Rosenberg gave testimony about one of the death camps, he said "not even ravens left Treblinka alive." He went on to explain that if a raven picked up some piece of bone or flesh and took flight, the guards would open up with sustained machine-gun fire until the bird was felled so that no evidence of their crimes would leave the camp.

Thomas was having a hard time as the trial went on. He had only the vaguest memories of his time at Theresienstadt, and he couldn't reconcile the fact that somehow he and his family had gotten out. He had to ask, but he didn't want to. He wasn't entirely sure he wanted to know the answer.

And as Thomas sat there listening to Eichmann and his lawyer insisting that Eichmann had only done what he was ordered to do, he heard the laughter of ghosts. Not the ghosts of six million Jews, but those of the men he had seen shot in Gaza in 1956.

He had done a lot of thinking about that day in Gaza. He couldn't pick out any of the faces from the dozens of bodies. In fact, the only face he remembered, or at least thought he remembered, from that day was that of the boy who had shot him. What unnerved him most were the descriptions the survivors were giving during the trial, descriptions of how the Germans would line up their victims and shoot them, bringing up more victims and shooting them so that they all fell into a pile. That was just the way it had been done at Gaza—even though, of course, it was different. In Gaza the people they rounded up had been identified as rebels. One couldn't equate the murder of innocent, unarmed men, women, and children with the execution of known rebels . . . And then Thomas came back to that horribly familiar reasoning: "But it was war."

He had to get out of there. People gave him strange looks as he made his way down the row, as if to ask, "What's the matter? Can't you take it?"

Once he got out the door of the theater-turned-courtroom, he stopped and leaned against the wall, rubbed his eyes, and took a deep breath.

"You okay?" someone next to him asked in English.

He turned as the man offered him a cigarette. He took the cigarette and nodded.

"You a survivor? Were you in the camps?"

Thomas just looked at the stranger. He was obviously an American.

"Reporter?" Thomas asked after a pause.

"Yeah. *Los Angeles Times.* There's a big Jewish community there. Lots of interest in this Eichmann guy."

This Eichmann guy . . . , Thomas thought to himself. All this was obviously just a story to the reporter.

"What do you know about the camps?" Thomas challenged, an edge to his voice as he confronted the reporter.

"The camps? I was with Patton. Rode a tank. Saw Dachau just after they liberated it. Those poor bastards."

Thomas straightened himself up. "Those 'poor bastards' were people," he announced. "I've heard from people like you before. You pity the survivors, but you never understand that they're just like you and your family. You talk about them like they were poorly treated animals."

The reporter had no response, and Thomas just turned and walked away.

"Good for you," came a voice came from close behind him as he walked purposefully down the street. "Americans are so arrogant."

Thomas glanced to his left to find a young woman about his age, perhaps younger, catching up with him. Thomas stopped and looked at her. She had wavy jet-black hair and sparkling brown eyes.

"I said Americans are arrogant," she repeated.

Thomas was embarrassed when he realized that he was staring at her.

"My name is Chaya," she went on when he still said nothing.

"Ignorant," Thomas finally said.

"What?"

"They just don't know. They can't understand. It's like they said in the courtroom. You can never fully understand if you weren't there."

"I wasn't there, but I think can understand some of it."

"Are you Sabra?"

"Yes. My parents left Germany for Palestine just before they took over Austria."

"Germany? I came from Germany. Where did they live in Germany?"

"Kiel."

"Oh . . . my parents came from Munich."

"I've heard Munich was a lovely city."

"Would you . . . ," Thomas stammered. "Have you had lunch yet?"

"No, but that sounds like a good idea."

"There's a nice little place just down this way," Thomas said as he started walking, motioning for Chaya to come along.

"Have you been to the trial?" Thomas continued.

"Yes."

"Why?"

"I . . . I'm not sure. I just had to go."

"Had to go?"

"I wanted to see for myself. I had relatives who were all killed in the camps. Some lived in Kiel, some in Czechoslovakia. Do you know what they call the survivors? Sabonim. Pieces of soap. That's how they talk about the people who made it out of the camps."

"It's a funny thing, but my father told me that this would end the war for him."

"End the war?"

"The trial. He hasn't even seen the courtroom, but he says this must be the end of it. He says we can't go off kidnapping people to try to exact some kind of revenge. There could never be justice to match what happened."

"Don't you think they should have done it?"

"I didn't say that. The world is watching this trial. They're hearing the stories. I think that's important. If nothing else, they'll hear how it was done. Maybe they need to hear how it happened so that it doesn't happen again.

"So you think he's the last Nazi out there?"

Thomas laughed and shook his head. "I never said that. I just mean the whole incident with Argentina put us in a bad light. This can't happen again. We can't be a rogue nation kidnapping people from other countries and bringing them to Jerusalem for trial."

Thomas stopped and opened the door for Chaya when they came to the restaurant. There was an awkward pause once they had gotten their sandwiches.

"So . . . ," Chaya began, "what do you do? I mean, for a living."

"I have a radio repair shop."

"Your own shop? You seem young to already have your own business."

"Well, my father gave me the money to get started, but I've been running it for a year now, ever since I got out of the army."

"What did you do in the army?"

"The same thing . . . I worked as a radioman."

"How are things going at your shop?"

"It's picking up. I've started selling televisions and stereo FM radios. It's going to be really popular."

"*What* kind of radios?"

"FM. Frequency modulation. It's been around for years, but now they have a way of broadcasting in stereo. When you listen to an orchestra, it sounds just like you're in the audience, because with two speakers, the music is all around you."

They went on talking for hours. It had been an unusual meeting for Chaya. She wasn't the sort to strike up a conversation with a stranger, but there was something about Thomas. He seemed strong and steady. Something she was looking for. And for Thomas's part, he wasn't exactly a ladies' man. He was good looking enough, but he was shy. It was easier for him to understand mathematics and technology than people, so when Chaya showed interest, he was flattered. And when she persisted in the following days and weeks, even though his shyness would have put off other women, Thomas began to open up. Chaya wasn't disappointed. The more they got to know each other, the more he proved to be just what she had thought he was in the beginning.

It was months later when Thomas and Chaya were having breakfast at a sidewalk café that they heard the report on the radio announcing that "Adolph Eichmann was executed at midnight after the denial of a last-minute appeal of his case before the Israeli Supreme Court. His body was cremated and the ashes committed to the sea just beyond Israel's territorial waters."

They paused for a moment, as did others around them, when the radio went on to play "Hatikvah," Israel's national anthem, in a recording made by a children's choir. The children's voices raised in song about the hope of the Jewish people brought tears to Thomas's eyes.

ACROSS TEL AVIV, his father was experiencing the same thing. Jakob was listening to that same reporter on that first day of June in 1962. He hadn't attended the trial. His trip to South America had changed him. The death of Eichmann wasn't a victory to him. It only showed that it would never end. He thought about Istvan Bartalan and his missing leg. He thought about Klaus Grunewald. He realized that he no longer wanted Klaus dead. It wasn't that he had forgiven him; it was just that Klaus's death wouldn't change anything. He felt as though he had spent the last years chasing ghosts. The Bormann

incident convinced him of it. He came to the conclusion that it was the paranoia of Holocaust survivors, and Israel in particular, that had allowed the
impostor to take advantage of the Bormann myth
and live like an exiled potentate in the jungles of
South America. He knew all the arguments—about
how justice should be timeless and how he would
feel different if it had been his family who had died
in one of the camps—but now he was just tired of it
all.

"I want to move," Jakob announced when he
came home from work one day.

"What do you mean? You want to buy a house?"
Rebecca asked.

Jakob sat down at the kitchen table as Rebecca
went on cutting up a small pile of carrots for dinner.
"I want to move. I'm tired of all this. I want try some-
place new. I want to leave Tel Aviv."

"Where then? Haifa."

"I was thinking about America . . ."

Rebecca left the carrots and sat across from him
at the table. "America?" she said with awe. Not so
much for America, but at the thought of making
such a major move. "But we don't even know anyone
in America," she said, punctuating her comment
with a carrot she still held in her hand.

"Yes we do. Don't you remember David Frieder's
friend, Joseph Hubert? He'd remember me and my
mother. I'm sure he'd sponsor us after what my
mother did for him."

"But what about the boys? Take Yigal out of
school and put him in an American school? His
work will suffer if he suddenly has to learn English."

"He knows English!"

"He knows *some* English. Not everyday English."

"But he's smart. He would pick it up."

"Yes, I know he would pick it up, but it would be a major setback in his education. He'll have to work twice as hard just to keep up the grades he has now."

"I still say he could do it. And what's to say he wouldn't get a *better* education in America? When he gets past the language, he has a chance at some of the best schools in the world."

"But what about Thomas?"

Jakob raised his eyebrows and pursed his lips.

"He wouldn't come with us, you know," Rebecca continued. "How could we leave him behind? And what about your mother and mine? And our friends?"

"I know it's a big move, but think about it. Why did we come here in the first place? Fear. We thought if we came together we would be safer. And now here we are, surrounded by enemies. Everywhere you look there are soldiers carrying guns. We're living in a prison of our own making. I want out."

"What would you do there?"

"There are lots of opportunities. I've got my law degree . . ."

"But you've never practiced."

"I can go to school in America. I was thinking of international business law."

"At your age?"

"My age? Thanks for the vote of confidence. Rebecca, we've got enough money to get by for quite a while without either of us working if we live conservatively. And my background in intelligence wouldn't hurt. There are a lot of people who would be willing to pay for my expertise . . ."

"Expertise? You'd sell informa—"

"My God, Rebecca, you know me better than that! I'm not talking about being a traitor to Israel. I'm talking about information on other countries. America runs on Arab oil. What American oil company wouldn't want information that could help them in their negotiations?

"So it's all about money?"

"No. It's not about money. I told you, I've just had enough. I . . . I haven't told you what I've done in my work. Not that I would have done anything different, but I've just had enough. I've got some connections in the intelligence community. I could find work with international companies interested in doing business in the Middle East. If I take a couple of years to learn American law . . ."

"A couple of years? Living in America? I had no idea we had that much money."

"Well . . . I got a couple of rewards for the work I did out of the country, and I just hid it away thinking that some day we might need it."

"America . . . ," Rebecca said thoughtfully. It conjured up all sorts of images for her. Big cities and open prairies. Hollywood movies and New York City all lit up at night, with the Broadway theaters, the Empire State building, and the Statue of Liberty welcoming people to the land of opportunity.

Jakob knew that Rebecca might be won over, but leaving his mother . . . He wasn't sure how to approach her. If she wanted to go, he thought he could take her along.

A few days later he was at her apartment. He explained it all to her and she sat silently, patiently listening until he finally asked, "So, what do you think?"

"What do I think . . . ? It makes me sad. That's what I think. Your grandfather was a religious man. Every year at Pesach he would end his Haggadah reading with that old phrase, 'Next year in Jerusalem.' Everybody said it. For twenty centuries every devoted Jew who had been forced from this land kept saying, 'Next year in Jerusalem.' And now you're telling me that you want to leave. How do you think I feel? What do you think I think?"

"I didn't expect you to be happy, but I thought you might understand. Hell, I thought you might even consider coming with!"

This brought a smile to Amalie's face. Only a son could think such a thing, that a mother would be so completely wrapped up in his life that she would have no life of her own and gladly leave everything behind to be with him.

It was magnificently manipulative. She brought up religion as though she had always been a pious Jew, which couldn't be further from the truth, and the incredibly ironic twist was that Jakob thought he was doing a noble thing by saying that she should come along, because she always appeared to be wrapped up in his life.

"Then it's all decided?"

"Yes."

"And when are you leaving?"

"It won't be for a while. It will take two or three

months to wrap everything up."

"New York?"

"New York? No, Washington. We'll be moving near Washington, D.C."

"How far is that from New York?"

"Why? What's so important about New York?"

"Nothing. It's just the only place I know in America."

"Well, I'll be calling Joseph Hubert in New York. I'm counting on him to help. But I think I can brush up on my law degree in America and get work in Washington helping out companies doing business here."

"Then why not live here?"

"I'm tired of my work. I'm tired of being afraid of another war. I need to start a new life."

Amalie smiled slightly. She remembered arriving in Munich all those years ago to start her new life. "A new life . . . I'm afraid it isn't that easy, but I doubt I can convince you of that. You're right. You should go. I can't lead your life for you and you can't lead mine for me. We've finally grown so far apart that . . ."

"It's not about us growing apart. I'm not doing this to hurt you. This is just what I have to do."

"Yes, Jakob, I understand. That's just what I said to my father a long time ago. I'm not happy about it, but I don't suggest that you shouldn't go."

"And you?"

"Me? Do you mean will I come with? No, of course not! I took my life in my hands to come here."

That was the end of the discussion. Jakob decided

later that it was the difference in their ages. His mother was now in her sixties and he in his forties. He could still make a change like this, but she was probably afraid. She was set in her ways and just couldn't make such a huge change in her life. But then he thought again about his own motives. Was it fair to make Rebecca and Yigal leave everything behind? He just thought there would be more for him, and them, in America. Israeli intelligence was not the sort of place where one became rich. He still had a significant amount of money from the Swiss account he had opened with the proceeds from Friedrich Haas's loot. He had made investments discreetly and done well. As far as he knew, at least, no one suspected that he was worth almost a quarter of a million dollars.

America would be a new life. No one would know him. He was sure he could be even more successful there. Out of the Mossad, he could even spend some of his money without drawing attention. But he knew he had to wait a while for that. They would have to live modestly for the first few years, but then he would be free of his past. And there wouldn't be Arab raiders killing children on school buses. They could be safe there.

The more he thought about it, the more he was convinced it was the thing to do. He got in contact with Joseph Hubert, who agreed to sponsor the family for immigration.

Soon after Jakob began making preparations to emigrate, Thomas brought Chaya to dinner. Chaya struck Jakob as rather plain looking. Not that she was ugly, but she certainly couldn't be called beautiful. He thought her face was too long and narrow and her mouth too wide, as though God had tried to put too much into that limited space.

Rebecca thought Chaya was beautiful. She thought the young woman's face had character and warmth. And she noticed how Chaya's whole face lit up when she smiled, and that she smiled a lot with Thomas. And she noticed how Thomas was more . . . well, it was hard to describe. More relaxed? That sounds like a strange thing to say about a member of your family. You should be able to be whoever you are when you're with your family, but Chaya seemed to somehow bring that out in Thomas.

About two months later, Thomas told his parents he was going to marry her. Jakob was happy for his son, but he wondered if Thomas had rushed into it because he felt he would be alone when the rest of his family went to America.

Chaya's parents loved Thomas. She had two younger sisters and a brother, who at fourteen was the youngest of the children, just a year older than Yigal.

Thomas and Chaya had a traditional Jewish wedding. As he watched the ceremony unfold, Jakob wore a kippa for one of the few times in his life. His son stood under a white canopy with his bride, and the Rabbi wrapped a wine glass in a napkin and set it on the floor in front of him. Then there was a cheer as Thomas broke the glass.

Rebecca held tightly to Jakob's arms as the tears came. This was what *she* had wanted. This was what Rebecca had imagined her life would be like before the war changed everything. But she wasn't sad. She was so happy that her dream had come true for Thomas. And that night they danced and ate and drank until the sky became streaked with magnificently colored rays of sunlight.

Chaya's parents had paid for the wedding celebration, so Jakob gave the newlyweds a gift of a honeymoon at a resort in Greece. When they returned, there were only six weeks left until Jakob, Rebecca, and Yigal were to leave.

And then suddenly the day arrived. It was a dark and rainy morning when Thomas and Chaya drove them all from Tel Aviv to the airport about forty-five minutes away. Jakob had shipped most of their things to New York in care of Joseph Hubert, so the family only had a few suitcases to take with them. It was hard to say good-bye. Chaya and Rebecca were both crying, and everyone was hugging everyone else. Yigal tried to put on a brave front, but when Thomas picked him up in a bear hug, that was all he could take. The two brothers had been so close, with Thomas as the protector and Yigal the idolizing follower. It was bad enough that Thomas had moved out and married, but now they would be on opposite sides of the world. Jakob felt terrible at being the cause of such heartbreak, but he told himself that it was for the best in the long run.

Jakob had to promise right then and there that they would come back to visit as often as they could. Rebecca insisted that they return for Passover. Jakob didn't know if they could actually do it, but he agreed anyway, thinking that he would cross that bridge when he came to it.

For Yigal, the flight was the one high point of the

expedition into the unknown, but Rebecca, on top of all the emotional upset, was terrified at the thought of flying. Jakob told her everything would be fine as they found their seats and buckled themselves in, but she didn't believe him. When Jakob got up and started to fight his way up the aisle, she actually thought he had changed his mind about the whole thing and also started to get up, but he told her to sit down, and that he would be right back. He made his way toward the front of the plane, against the current of other passengers making their way toward their seats, and finally found a stewardess. Explaining that he knew they wouldn't normally serve drinks at this point, he told her he was afraid his wife might become hysterical, and that some wine or brandy now might save them a lot of trouble later. The stewardess said she couldn't possibly do that, but Jakob did his best to charm her, and in a moment he had a plastic cup, a can of Coca-Cola, and three tiny bottles of rum that the stewardess told him to keep secret from the other passengers. He slipped her a few bills and assured her that he was very good at keeping secrets.

Rebecca drank on occasion, having a glass of wine or beer, but rarely more than one, and she was even less likely to drink liquor. So when Jakob insisted she try the rum and Coke to calm her down for the flight, she had no idea how that sweet beverage would catch up with her. It went down so easily that she quickly drank two of the little bottles with the can of soda pop, and by the time the jet started to pick up speed for takeoff some twenty minutes later, she was fast asleep. It worked so well that they did the same thing when the time came to change planes in the Netherlands.

Arriving in New York was like landing on a different planet. Joseph Hubert greeted them at the airport with open arms. But this was not the Joseph Hubert that Rebecca had known in Theresienstadt. He was in his early sixties now, had put on fifty or sixty pounds, and his hair had gone a respectable silvery gray. And she noticed something in his manner that . . . it occurred to her that he might be . . . a homosexual. Not that she knew any homosexuals, or so she thought, until it occurred to her that Joseph and David Frieder had been . . . She decided not to say anything to Jakob about her suspicions.

Joseph had become quite a success since returning to the United States after the war. He had been in America before the war, but that was during the depression, and the factory that he had started with some of his parent's money had gone bankrupt. When that happened, he decided to return to Germany, on the eve of Adolf Hitler's ascension to power.

Joseph had been a friend of David Frieder's, having met Amalie through David before the war, and was part of the group that Amalie had gotten out of Theresienstadt. When they arrived in Switzerland, he was able to gain access to enough money in a Swiss account to return to America under the good graces of friends he had made there before the war. He had given some money to Amalie and David to help them get the others out, but it had always bothered him that he had left them there. And now he was going to make up for it by helping her son and his family.

When Joseph had come to America before the war, he only knew that he wanted to invest his money, so he took the advice of a friend and bought a factory that was already operating. The problem was that he didn't understand America. The factory he bought produced old-fashioned wooden icebox-type refrigerators. His friend, who was also a German émigré, said that he should buy an existing factory so he wouldn't have all the start-up costs of a new factory. And with a typical German bent toward conservatism, he believed that with the depression, people would rather buy cheap old-fashioned ice-boxes than spend a lot more money to buy a new-fangled electric or gas refrigerator. And that was the flaw in their logic. They didn't know that the people who would buy an old-fashioned icebox were too poor to afford one at all, and the people who could afford one chose to make time payments on new-fangled refrigerators. That was all the education Joseph needed. When he came back to America with a few thousand dollars, good credit, and friends willing to invest, he knew that he would never build something that was made for the previous generation. He would build for the next generation. And so he started building television sets and high-fidelity phonographs. "Technology," he told Jakob as they walked through the airport, "America loves new technology. Build it fast. Build it better. They break down my doors to buy my televisions and phonographs and radios!"

"Is this *your* car?" Yigal asked in disbelief as Joseph unlocked the trunk of his big black Cadillac.

Joseph smiled and nodded as he took the suitcase from Yigal and tousled his hair.

"I'm so tired," Rebecca said once they were in the car.

"It's a long flight," Joseph sympathized.

"We'll get to the hotel and get some sleep," Jakob stated.

"You'll sleep for a whole day!" Joseph said with a laugh.

"How far is the hotel?" Yigal asked.

"Like they say here in America, 'I've got some good news and some bad news . . .'"

"What does that mean?"

"It's a kind of a joke they tell here. It goes something like this. A man goes to a fortune teller, and she says, 'I've got some good news and some bad news,' and the man asks, 'What's the good news?' The fortune teller says, 'Your wife will be coming into a lot of money!' And the man says, 'That's wonderful! What's the bad news?' The fortune teller says, 'It's from your life insurance policy!'"

Jakob smiled politely at the joke, but he was more interested in where they were going to stay that night. "So what's our bad news?"

"I didn't get you a hotel room."

"What?" Jakob asked with surprise. "Where are we going to stay?"

"I got you better than a hotel. I got you a Manhattan apartment."

"An apartment?" Now it was Rebecca's turn to express surprise.

"A Manhattan apartment. A year's lease."

"A year?" Rebecca asked. "But what about

Washington?"

"This is just a place to stay while you get settled. A year is a short lease here."

"But we can't afford—" Jakob started.

"What afford? I owe your mother my life. This is a gift. You stay here, make telephone calls to Washington so you can find a house or apartment there, and then when you're ready to move, you just sublet."

"Sublet?"

"You rent the apartment out to someone else. It's done all the time. Your name is on the lease, and you collect rent from someone else."

"This is too much, Mr. Hubert," Rebecca blushed.

"Nothing is too much. And you should call me Joe. I should warn you now that in America, they like nothing more than to shorten people's names. Jakob, believe me, before a month is out you'll be Jake or Jack."

"What?"

"It's true! It's not an insult. That's just the way America is. Rebecca here will be Becky, and your little boy's friends will all call him something like Yiggy or Gally. You mark my words."

Jakob just looked at Rebecca and shook his head.

"Oh, and the food . . . They cover everything in cheese."

"Cheese?" Yigal asked. "Like what?"

"They have something here they call a 'cheeseburger.' It's a chopped beef sandwich, and they melt cheese on it."

Yigal just made a face and looked at his mother as if to ask, "Could this be true?" Rebecca didn't keep a kosher kitchen, separating dairy dishes from meat dishes, but the food was distinctly Jewish or German in nature, and all the restaurants in Tel Aviv were kosher. The thought of cheese on beef was sickening for Yigal.

"They have something they call a Reuben sandwich," Joseph continued, "and it's supposed to be Jewish! They melt Swiss cheese on corned beef and call it Jewish! Not that I keep kosher . . . But back to the apartment. It's a couple of hours on the train to Washington. You can make phone calls from here and then stay at a motel in Washington for a few days while following up on your plans."

"Motel?"

"It's like a hotel," Joseph started with a smile, "only smaller. It's because of all the cars. One or two stories and lots of places where you can park. They don't cost as much as a hotel."

Joseph was their guardian angel in those first weeks. Jakob was amazed at the size of the factories that Joseph owned and even more impressed when he considered that it had all been built up in only seventeen years. He had partners in these businesses, but he was the majority owner. It just confirmed Jakob's belief that there was money to be made in America.

Everything came together just as he hoped it would in those first years. He attended Georgetown University for almost three years so that he could begin practicing international business law in America. They didn't make it back to Israel until the second year, but it was just in time for Rebecca to be there for the birth of Chaya and Thomas's first child, a girl they named Ruth in honor of Amalie's mother.

Everybody was so happy to see them again, but Jakob warned that it was terribly expensive for three people to fly round-trip from America, and so he didn't know when they would be back again. It was as though he had said they would never return.

When he finished his courses at Georgetown, they moved from the apartment in Washington to a small house in New Carrollton, Maryland.

Once again Joseph Hubert lent a hand as he pressed his friends and business associates for contacts in the oil companies. Eventually, through this "friend of a friend" process, Jakob made his way into the negotiating rooms. And since those negotiations were by and large with Arab nations, he once again became a gentile.

"So I don't think we should mention it if someone I work with should come over for dinner."

"Don't mention it?"

"This is America. Lot's of people with the name Stein aren't Jewish. I'm just saying it wouldn't be a good idea. We're dealing with Arabs, and it would make it impossible for me to do business if I were Jewish."

"*If* you were Jewish?"

"You know what I mean."

"And what do we tell Yigal? Do we tell him he has to change his name?"

He didn't have any response to that. He certainly wasn't going to tell Yigal to . . . He couldn't . . . wouldn't put his son in the same position he himself had been caught in when he was a boy.

And suddenly it all became painfully clear. He was the Nazi. He was looking at Rebecca just like his father had looked at his mother. Suddenly he was back in a Chinese restaurant in Munich in 1932, and his mother was saying, "But I'm Jewish," and Jakob was saying, "It's all right mother. *We didn't tell them.*"

He asked her not to mention it to Yigal and never brought it up again. But he never mentioned it in his professional life. It was the great divider between his work and his home life.

That was just one of the changes Jakob went through in those years. The first to go were his illusions about America. A year after he arrived, the President was shot dead in a place called Dallas, Texas. And then the man who shot him was shot right on TV as the police were moving him to a different jail. And then there was the racial unrest. He watched on television with his wife and son each night as the bluish-gray pictures flashed past of black children running from police dogs and being swept down streets by the powerful spray of fire hoses.

And then there were the riots in Harlem in '64.

And then there were the riots in Watts in '65

And then there were the riots in Chicago in '66

In 1967, Jakob and Rebecca were eligible to become American citizens. Rebecca was torn by the thought of giving up her Israeli citizenship, and yet she had adapted very well to America. Just as Joseph had warned them, Yigal became "Iggy" to his friends, also known as "Jack and Becky's boy." But Rebecca liked these Americans. She liked the big grocery stores full of food and the used Plymouth station wagon that Jakob had bought for her. And she liked how Yigal's friends thought so highly of them that they treated her house like their second home, even though it meant things were relatively noisy most of the time and there was always a shortage of cookies and Popsicles.

And it became a time for her to explore herself as Yigal got older and she had more time to herself. Her life had been taken up with so many other things, all the things she needed to do just to survive, and now she had time. She had become a classic American persona of the late sixties and seventies; she was trying to "find herself." While Jakob had been studying the law, she began taking classes in English. Her first goal was to learn the American colloquialisms that confused her so in their first year in America. And then she wanted to lose her accent, but that was much harder. By the time Yigal was in high school, he spent more time with his friends away from the house, and Rebecca, finding herself with time on her hands, decided to take some college courses.

Yigal was just about to graduate from high school, and since he was still under eighteen, he would become a citizen when his parents were naturalized. And so they went ahead. The one thing that frightened Rebecca about America was that when they became citizens—when Yigal became a citizen—it meant he would be eligible to serve in the American army and could be sent to Southeast Asia to fight in the American war against the North Vietnamese. But Jakob told her not to worry, since Yigal had done well in school, just as Jakob had predicted, and now he would go to the same university where Jakob had studied law: Georgetown. Their son wouldn't get caught up in this war.

But while they were worrying about Yigal's future, Gamal Abdel Nasser was giving a radio speech in Egypt. "We swear to God that we shall not rest until we restore the Arab nation to Palestine and Palestine to the Arab nation. There is no room for imperialism and there is no room for Israel within the Arab nation. We shall not enter Palestine with its soil covered in sand, we shall enter it with its soil saturated in blood."

Nasser then ordered the United Nations peacekeeping forces out of Gaza and the Sinai desert, and once again, just as he had before the Suez crisis ten years earlier, blockaded the Strait of Tiran.

But this time it wasn't just Egypt making threats against Israel. The Syrians were also ready to move against Israel because of an Israeli irrigation project that began pumping water from the Sea of Galilee. Since the Sea of Galilee, also known as Lake Tiran, was on the Syrian border, the Syrians objected to the Israelis' unilateral decision to use the resource for a major water supply project. As a result, the Syrians diverted the waters of the River Jordan to stop the Israeli water project. Israel then bombed the diversion project.

Tensions between Israel and Syria became even more strained in April of 1967 when Israeli jets, responding to an incursion of Syrian jets, downed six Russian-made Syrian MiGs and then, to add insult to injury, continued on to the Syrian capital of Damascus to flaunt their victory. Shortly after that, the Russians, who were courting the Syrians in an effort to strengthen their foothold in the Middle East, cautioned Israeli leaders that their actions were "endangering the very fate of their state."

By the end of May, Israel was in a state of total mobilization, expecting an attack by Arab nations at any moment. The United Nations commitment to upholding the peace in the Middle East crumbled in the face of Nasser's demands that UNEF soldiers leave the area.

When Israel began desperately looking for foreign support in the face of another all-out war with the Arab nations, France, Britain, and America made it clear that they were not willing to provide assistance. Three years earlier, when he became chief of staff, General Yitzhak Rabin had reported to the Knesset security and foreign affairs committee that Israel would never be able to sustain a prolonged military effort. Therefore, any future war would have to be won in four days. That was the deciding factor. Without foreign support, the military leaders decided they had no choice but to strike at the Egyptians before they attacked Israel.

The Israelis had substantial intelligence on the Egyptian military and various outposts, but the far greater concern was that a first strike, if not dramatically successful, would give Nasser all the cause he needed for an all-out attack against Israel with his substantial stock of Soviet-supplied armor, aircraft, and rockets.

Thomas's radio shop had done well in the six years since he started it, expanding from radio repair into television repair and eventually into sales of new sets. He and Chaya had bought a house in

Tel Aviv, and in the midst of all the turmoil of the impending war, they were boarding up windows in preparation for bombings. It wasn't much protection, but it was something to do—to keep busy so they didn't think about what might happen. They now had two children. A year after Ruth was born, they had a son they named Aaron. The children were now four and three years old, and because both Thomas and Chaya were in the military reserve, they would have to leave them with Amalie and Abby while they went off to war.

The pressure of those days was so intense that General Rabin actually had what could best be described as a mild nervous breakdown.

After all of the debate as to whether or not they could actually succeed with a surprise attack, it was finally decided that they had no other options. And so on the first Monday of June in 1967, Israeli jets took off for Egypt. Israeli agents had reported that the Egyptian air force flew patrols of the Sinai on a regular schedule, and there was a brief window of opportunity in the morning when the patrols returned and all of the jets were lined up neatly on the runways. The Israeli jet squadrons came in low off the Mediterranean and caught the Egyptians completely off guard. Within a couple of hours they had destroyed 300 of Egypt's 340 planes on the ground. Israeli squadrons also moved on Syria, destroying two-thirds of the Syrian air force, and then went on to wipe out Jordan's small air force. Spurred on by these successes, Israeli jets even flew missions into Iraq.

Once Israeli ground force commanders heard of

the successes of their air force, they quickly began an aggressive assault in Sinai. The commanders knew that they had to push hard to press that advantage, assuming that word of the destruction of the Egyptian air force would demoralize the Egyptian ground forces.

But what the ground force commanders didn't know was that Egyptian radio was reporting just the opposite—that the Israelis were being destroyed on all fronts. This was Nasser's plan to prevent the demoralization of his troops. Israeli intelligence had expected as much, and so before the attack even began, orders had been issued for complete Israeli radio silence.

While Egypt and Syria had been threatening to attack for weeks, Jordan's King Hussein had refused to be a part of their war. That refusal earned him death threats from his fellow Arabs, who encouraged the people of Jordan to rise up and assassinate their king. Eventually Hussein agreed to join the alliance against Israel, but he stated that his country would only maintain a defensive posture.

When it was clear to Israel's military leaders that the battle was going their way on the Egyptian and Syrian fronts, they reevaluated the situation and approached government leaders with a new plan. According to the first UN partition plan, Jerusalem was to be an international zone open to everyone. But when the Arabs attacked after the Israeli state was declared, the Jordanian army held the old city of Jerusalem, splitting the city and denying Jews access to that part of the city. Now Israeli leaders were told that there was a chance Jordan could be drawn into the war, and then Israeli forces would counterattack and take over the entire city.

Jerusalem was an ancient capital of the Jews, and so the thought of regaining the city was irresistible. The crux of the plan was simple. They would only have to transmit the radio broadcasts coming out of Egypt, which were reporting that Israel was on the brink of collapse, and see if the Jordanians would take the bait.

But there was a fly in the ointment. Three days after the war began, an Israeli jet spotted an American ship in the Gulf of Aqaba. The *U.S.S. Liberty* appeared to be an American freighter that had gotten caught in the wrong place at the wrong time. Later that day, however, Israeli communications officers intercepted radio transmissions directed to the Arabs from an unknown source.

"There's something going on in the Saudi sector," one of the radiomen in the crowded intelligence operations room said as he flagged down an officer.

"What have you got?" the officer, Gedeon Ravid, asked as he cocked an ear to the monitor.

"It sounds like American radio traffic. Very close. Maybe an American base?"

"What are they talking about?"

"Egyptian broadcasts. They're trying to find out why the signal is so strong," the radio operator said as he offered his headphones to the officer. "I think they're trying to locate our signal-boosting stations."

"Damn!" Captain Ravid said after listening for a minute. He tossed the headphones back to the radioman and rushed out of the room.

Less than twenty minutes later, Captain Ravid was

at air force headquarters. "We've got a problem . . ."

"We've got a lot of problems," the major replied. "Which one are you talking about?"

"There's an American listening post out there transmitting information to the Saudis. It could compromise the Jordanian action."

"Have they been warned about foreign broadcasting in a combat zone?"

"Yes, sir, we issued all the standard warnings."

"And . . . ?"

"No response. We know they must be receiving. They've got some very sophisticated equipment out there, but they're ignoring us."

"Do you know where they are?"

"We've got it narrowed down."

"So you want a flyby?"

"Yes, sir, but we need a communications expert to know what we're looking for."

"I can supply a pilot."

"I have someone in mind to go along, but he's a reservist."

"We'll find him."

"He runs a small electronics factory and supplies parts to the air force. He was just in France and Germany looking at new technology. I think he would know just what to look for."

"He's the best?"

"Yes, sir, I would say he's the best."

It was less than an hour later that, after making a few calls, Captain Ravid found Thomas Stein at a military communications center outside Jerusalem.

"Can you fly?"

"Fly? What are you talking about?"

"I mean, are you afraid of flying or do you have any physical problems?"

"I don't think so ... Why?"

"I need you to do some spotting work out there. We're looking for an American bug."

"Bug?"

"They've got a listening post out there, and we need to identify it. We know the area. We just have to pinpoint it."

"When do we go?"

"Right now. I'll send a car to take you to the airstrip."

"I'VE NEVER BEEN in a jet before," Thomas said with a nervous laugh.

"Don't worry," the pilot said as he helped Thomas into the cockpit. "I'll take it easy. Just don't touch anything."

When the jet took off and started to ascend, Jakob began feeling queasy as his stomach did a little dance under the g forces. Within minutes the Gulf of Aqaba was in sight. The pilot's voice soon came over Thomas's headset. "They told me to take a look at a freighter out here first. If that isn't what we're looking for, we'll work our way up the coast."

"How far is the ship?"

"We should see it any minute now. They weren't traveling very fast."

Thomas tried to spot the ship, but everything looked so different from a jet. When the pilot called out that the ship was just off to their right, he still had trouble spotting it.

"I'll go in low and slow. Tell me if you recognize

anything unusual."

When the pilot came around for his run, Thomas finally found the ship. As they flew by, the American sailors on deck waved at them. He almost waved back, but then concentrated on the ship's communications array.

"Go around again," he said to the pilot.

"We'll come from the other direction. That's about as slow as I can go."

When they flew over again, they got the same waves from the sailors on board, but this time Thomas got an even better view of the antenna array.

"That's it."

"You're sure?"

"No doubt about it. That's specialized equipment. Intelligence. That's an American CIA ship." Thomas paused and the pilot said nothing.

"So what do we do now?" Thomas continued.

"We take it out."

"Take it out?" Thomas exclaimed. "You mean attack? That's an American ship! We can't fire on an American ship!"

"I have my orders."

"But all those men!"

"We're just going after the communications array," the pilot said, and then called back to the base to confirm that the *Liberty* was a target. He then banked sharply and headed back toward the ship. "Where is the most effective place to hit the array to knock it out?"

Thomas swallowed hard.

"I said where's the best place to hit that array?

We'll be there in a minute."

"I . . . I guess . . . ," Thomas stammered, "the dish would be the first. Hit the parabolic dish and that will take out the longest-range communications ability. After that you would try for the base of the main mast. That's where all the sensitive wiring runs."

"I hope you've got your seat belt buckled. We're going in hot."

Thomas grabbed the side of the seat tightly as the jet climbed and then dove in on the ship, firing two rockets at the antenna mast. Thomas heard the swoosh of the rockets, but he didn't see what happened to the ship as the jet climbed up and banked sharply. It seemed like an eternity before the plane leveled out and came in low to assess the damage. Then Thomas saw the ship. The pilot had taken out the parabolic dish, but the angle of attack had been too steep, and the deck of the ship had also been hit. Thomas could see that there were injured men on the deck.

"Oh, my God," Thomas said in a shaky voice, "they've got men hurt."

"Damn . . . ," the pilot muttered to himself. "That's it for us. We're heading back."

Thomas was greatly relieved to hear that, since he would rather have been almost anyplace than in the plane that had just fired on an American vessel. He thought that was all there was to it, but just as they turned back for home, they spotted several more jets moving in toward the ship.

"What are they doing?"

"We must not have done the job. They're the second wave."

Thomas felt sick. He was sure that by the time they got back to the base, the Americans would have declared war on Israel.

Once they had returned to the air base, he didn't say anything to anyone. He climbed out of the plane and went looking for the car and driver that had brought him from Tel Aviv. The pilot of the plane was debriefed on his mission. When asked about Thomas, he said that the communications expert had done what was needed, identifying the communications array and telling the pilot how best to destroy it. When the officer debriefing him asked why Thomas wasn't there to be debriefed, the pilot explained that Thomas probably didn't even know what a debriefing was. "He was just there to give technical advice. He got out of here pretty fast. He was pretty shaken up."

"Shaken up?"

"He didn't seem to understand what the mission was all about. He must have thought it was just reconnaissance. He was really surprised when we fired on them."

"You don't think he'll talk to anyone about it?"

"No. He was just scared."

"Well, we'll send someone to talk to him . . . ," the officer said as he buried his face in a file folder and started writing.

The officer had nothing to worry about, since Thomas was more than happy to keep his role in the attack on the *U.S.S. Liberty* confidential. He was horrified that his expertise had resulted in the attack.

He reported back to his post at communications headquarters for the Israeli forces that were moving to take Jordanian territory on the West Bank of the Jordan as King Hussein fell into the trap that had been set for him. Thomas didn't know he had played a role in the events unfolding before him by helping to stop the Americans from passing on information that would have precluded King Hussein's decision to attack. In short, if the Americans had passed on information through the covert CIA listening post on the *U.S.S. Liberty* that Egyptian radio broadcasts were complete lies designed to cover up a staggering Egyptian defeat, King Hussein would not have attacked Israel.

In the next few days, as the scope of the Israeli victory in the face of overwhelming odds was realized, Israel was transformed. Just as with the Suez crisis in 1956, the United Nations once again censured Israel's actions, completely ignoring the provocation of the Arab nations. It's interesting to note that in spite of the attack on the *U.S.S. Liberty,* which the Israelis claimed was an accident, President Johnson sent in the American fleet as a warning to the Russians, who were threatening to intervene as it became clear that Nasser would be defeated.

In America, it was days before Rebecca and Jakob could get a telephone call through to make sure that everyone was safe. That was when Rebecca insisted that they had to make a trip back to Israel by the end of the year. They made it for the High Holy Days, arriving for Rosh Hashanah and staying through Yom Kippur.

They all went as a family to Jerusalem to see the wailing wall in the old city. When Israeli troops moved into the area after the war, the first thing they did was to confiscate houses in the area, clearing space for an open square in front of the wall. Rebecca was deeply moved as she walked up to the wall and felt the stones, and she tried to explain what it meant to Yigal, but she knew it was just a stale history lesson to him. Yigal wanted to feel the connection, but it just wasn't there. Jakob walked up to the wall with them and also put his hand on the stones, but it was just something he did for the sake of appearance. But they were happy to see Amalie and Thomas and everyone else again.

Jakob fell in love with his grandchildren, just as Rebecca had. It was a very warm reunion. Everyone commented on how Yigal had grown, and he told them all about how he wanted to be a psychologist, and that he was going to attend a university in Baltimore called Johns Hopkins.

Jakob had a few moments alone with Thomas and told him that they were doing well in America. He went on to say that he hoped Thomas and Chaya would come and join them, and that he would pay for the move. Thomas was touched. It meant so much to him that his father asked. But in the end he said he was going to stay. This was where he belonged

Jakob, on the other hand, as hard as it was to leave part of his family, was just as sure that he had done the right thing in moving. But he couldn't have known what life in America would be like in the next year. It marked the assassination of Martin Luther King Jr. and the riots that accompanied his death, along with the assassination of Robert Kennedy by a Jordanian national named Sirhan

Sirhan. It was also a year of growing opposition to the war in Vietnam.

The next year found Jakob on his way to Iraq to try to negotiate with leaders of the new Bath party, which had recently overthrown the government. Iraq's socialist government had ties to Russia, so it was obvious from the outset that the negotiations would be difficult. As it turned out, the talks failed, but the experienced men on the team were impressed with Jakob's style. He definitely had an ability to read his Iraqi counterparts and offered helpful suggestions throughout the negotiations, including his assertion that they would be invited back later to talk again, once the new government had consolidated its hold on the country.

Jakob's associates weren't the only ones who took note of his performance in Iraq. Two weeks after Jakob returned home, he was at work when he got a phone call.

"Mr. Stein?"

"Yes?"

"Jack Stein?"

"Yes, this is Jack Stein."

"Mr. Stein, I'm with the government, and we understand you just made a trip to Iraq."

"Yes . . . ," Jakob answered slowly, wondering what the call could be about.

"Well, this is an unusual request for our office, but we—"

"Your office? What office is that?"

"I'm not at liberty to say just now. I was hoping we could meet and then I could explain what we're looking for."

"Let me get this straight. You're working with the government, but you won't tell me where, and you want me to meet you. I suppose you have some dark alley picked out where we could meet at midnight?"

"I'm sorry for the cloak and dagger, but we want to keep a low profile. Could you meet us for lunch? There's a nice Italian restaurant about four blocks from your office called Mattiacci's. It's at—"

"I know where it is."

"Good. Can you make it at one o'clock?"

"And you'll be wearing a white carnation?"

"No, just ask for Mike Kronforst. I'll leave my name at the door."

"Kronforst?"

"Right. With a 'K.'"

It all sounded absurd, but Jakob couldn't think of any enemies who would go to all the trouble of finding him in Washington. Certainly no one from Iraq. He had been briefed on the situation in Iraq before he went, but it was nothing new for him. He knew about the various Muslim factions from his days in the Mossad. He didn't know what this was all about, but it was enough to make him paranoid.

He went to meet the mystery man early, arriving at the restaurant by 12:15. He stopped at the maître d's station and asked if his wife had made a reservation for lunch, and when the maître d' looked down the list, he saw the name Kronforst. He then asked for a table and ordered lunch. He waited until the maître d' was escorting a slow-moving elderly couple to a table at the back of the room and then strolled up casually, as though he were going to the restroom, and stopped at the desk to see which table

Kronforst would be at.

He then returned to his table and enjoyed an excellent lunch of veal scaloppine. About forty minutes later he noticed a couple of gentlemen being led to Kronforst's table. They certainly looked like American agents—CIA or FBI. One looked young, probably in his midtwenties, and the other in looked to be in his late forties. They both wore dark suits, ties that were a couple of years out of date, and white socks.

And there was something familiar about the older man. Jakob spent a few minutes watching them as he drank a cup of coffee. He decided it wasn't an ambush, and curiosity got the best of him, so he wandered over to the table.

"Mr. Kronforst?"

"Stein?" the young man answered.

"You haven't changed much," the older man added.

"Changed?"

"That's right. Don't tell me you don't remember me."

"Uh, you look familiar, but I can't quite . . ."

"The last time you saw me was in a bunk on some damn Israeli steamship."

"Sardinia?"

"Bingo!" Bill Hanlon said as he extended his hand.

Jakob shook his hand and then Mike's as he sat down. "I don't mind telling you that you've got my nerves up. What's this all about?"

"I'll tell you, Jack," Hanlon started, "we don't want to go into everything here. We just wanted to feel you out. We keep tabs on people going into Communist countries, and when your name came up . . . You probably figured we've got a file on you."

"A file? I'm impressed."

"We know you worked for the Institute. That just sparks our interest. This here is just a get-acquainted meeting. I was hoping you might meet with us somewhere a little more private where we could talk."

"What do you want?"

"Are you still employed at the Institute?"

"No."

"Why'd you leave?"

Jakob just looked at them for a moment. Was that some kind of accusation? "To tell you the truth, I left because it doesn't pay well. I like the work, but I can make more money this way."

"Fair enough," Bill said with a nod. "You're not the first one to go into . . . the private sector. Especially considering what they pay. You can make more being a postman here than you do as . . . well, you know."

"So I came to seek my fortune. It's working out well."

"If you're looking for compensation, that's part of the deal."

"When should we meet?"

"Sunday. Sunday would be good. Very casual. There's a nice house out in Arlington. You're just coming over to watch football."

Jakob took the note Bill offered with the address and other information. A few days later he told Rebecca he had to go to a meeting, and thus he was on his way to becoming an operative for the CIA.

"Back in the thirties they thought that queer friend of yours from New York was a Commie," Bill Hanlon announced as they began their discussion, "but it was just the company he kept."

"What are you talking about?" Jakob asked.

"That old queer who sponsored you in New York."

"You mean Joseph Hubert?"

"Don't tell me you didn't know."

"I . . . I never thought about it."

"Well, don't worry about that Commie thing. He's cleared of all that. Hell, more than one man's gone to a Commie meeting for a piece of ass. It's just that most of 'em are looking for wimmen!"

"Wimmen?"

"Girls! Chicks! You know . . ."

"Oh! Women."

"That's what I said."

"Before we get into details here, I want you to know we're not talking about information about Israel. For one thing, we wouldn't be able to trust you if you did give us any information. You've got to understand that our relationship, the contact between America and Israel, is at best a love–hate relationship. There are a lot of people in the American government who hate Jews just as much as the Arabs do. And there're a lot of people in government who say that we shouldn't have anything to do with the Jews 'cause it'll piss off the Arabs and that's where the oil is. Now Lyndon Johnson was a friend to Israel."

"Johnson?"

"Not because he loves Jews. No, sir, not because he loves Jews. It's because the Jews in Israel are such a royal, God-damned pain in the ass to the Russians. They're the underdogs, and they're fighting the same bad guys as Lyndon. Lyndon knows what it's like to be the underdog. He knows what it means to have to fight dirty while professing the highest ideals. And now there's Nixon. He'll be good to Israel too."

"Why?"

"Because the boys in Israeli intelligence have got a lot of dirt on Nixon. Hell, in Israel they wanted Nixon to win in 1960. They didn't know anything about Kennedy, but they had dirt on Nixon. He was part of the whole project dealing with Nazi war criminals right after the war. Yeah, Nixon will be good to Israel."

"So, what are you looking for? What do you want from me?"

"I've seen the file on you. You probably don't know I'm the one who finally got your friend Klaus Grunewald settled in."

"Klaus Grunewald? No, I didn't know that. He's not my friend."

"You let him go. You sent him to us. Working for the Israelis, I'd think you would have just killed him and left him in that jungle."

"Can we please get to the point?

"Well, this kinda is the point, Jack. I'm trying to tell you that all these different things come together in strange ways. *Spy* is a funny word. That's why we always use the word *intelligence* now. Not that it has anything to do with being smart . . . Sure, it's all pretty slick when it works, but spies are just human. And the situation with the Palestinians and all the other Arabs . . . It's kind of like Kennedy. When he was killed—"

"You don't mean the Palestinians had a hand in assassinating Kennedy?!" Jakob asked incredulously.

"The Arabs?" Bill shouted with a laugh. "Hell no! The A-rabs is the only motherfuckers who *weren't* in on the Kennedy termination. What I'm saying is, we're supposed to be so damned smart and five years later we still can't say who killed the President. They worked so hard selling that Oswald chump, and I know there're people somewhere who know exactly what went on, but that's not us."

"So, it's the same here," Jakob said.

"That's the point. That's what I'm trying to tell you. It's the same all over," Hanlon said with a smirk and a wave of his hand. "We tried to make things work, but it's just not that easy. We'd like to have you on board, but you've got to know there's risk. If you're in Iraq or Iran and someone points a finger at you saying you work for the CIA, they're just as likely to cut your head off as put you in some dark hell of a prison. And that's no bullshit. I've seen them pull out a big sword and chop a man's head off. It's not pretty."

"I know all that, but I'm not talking about James Bond or commando raids. I'm too old for that. I just thought you might be in the market for information if anything came up."

Bill looked Jakob in the eye, considering what he was offering, and then they finally started to talk.

CHAPTER 11

One step forward, two steps back.

The Yom Kippur War of 1973 seemed to be the culmination of the years of terrorist activities that followed the Six-Day War in 1967. Plane hijackings and terrorist attacks all over Europe came to a head when the Black Septembrists, a faction of the PLO, broke into the Olympic village in Munich in 1972 and took the Israeli athletes hostage. The world watched on television as the standoff between the terrorists and West German police went bad and all the Israeli athletes were killed.

The next year, the Yom Kippur War caught the Israelis by surprise just as Anwar Sadat had planned. Allied with the Syrians once again, this time it was to be the Arab nations that launched a surprise attack. Golda Meir, the Israeli prime minister, was reticent to put the country on full alert because it was the High Holy Days, and also because it cost millions of dollars for a small country that could ill afford to spend that much if it wasn't necessary. The result was a war that pushed Israel to the very edge of survival, so close, in fact, that at one point Israeli leaders were considering using the atomic weapons arsenal which they had kept a closely guarded secret.

Israel won that war, but an important outcome was that Anwar Sadat's near success gained him great credibility in the Arab world, so much so that he dared do something no other Arab leader had done. He agreed to go to Jerusalem in 1977 and negotiate directly with the Israelis for return of the

Sinai Peninsula.

Four years later Sadat was assassinated by Muslim fundamentalists, but his death did not diminish that first dramatic step taken between the Egyptian leader and Israel's Prime Minister Menachem Begin and their subsequent peace talks held under the auspices of President Jimmy Carter in America.

While Sadat and Begin were talking peace, the PLO guerrillas were following their own agenda. Throughout the '70s the PLO had made itself at home in Jordan to the point where King Hussein feared they would attempt to overthrow his government. That was when he asked for help from the Americans to drive the guerrillas from his country. In an ironic twist of fate, the Americans suggested, and Hussein agreed to, an Israeli show of strength that supported his plan. Eventually he succeeded in forcing the guerrillas out of the area, and the PLO moved into southern Lebanon.

Menachem Begin, the former partisan fighter from Poland, former Irgun leader who had ordered the bombing of the King David Hotel, was now in the wrong place at the wrong time. It seems he believed that the world viewed Israel—perhaps the Jewish people in general—as victims. The Holocaust, the War of Independence, even the Six-Day War when they were desperately looking for support from the British, French, and Americans, all seemed to say that Israel would never be able to stand up for itself. He wanted to show that Israel was now a military power in the Middle East, and so in 1978 he sent troops into Lebanon to end the PLO threat. This became Israel's war of attrition, a war like the one America had recently ended in

Vietnam and the Russians were involved with in Afghanistan. It would eventually break Menachem Begin as Israeli citizens protested the war, demanding to know why their sons were being sacrificed in a war that couldn't be won. And then came the lowest point. In 1982, after the death of Lebanon's President Bashir Gemayel in a bomb blast, Christian Phalangist Lebanese militiamen were allowed to enter the Palestinian refugee camps of Sabra and Shatila, ostensibly to gather up weapons left behind and to eliminate any guerrilla fighters who might be hiding in the camps. But when the night was over, more than 2,000 unarmed women, children, and old people had been slaughtered and world opinion held Israel responsible and condemned them for it.

After years of fighting, the PLO forces left Lebanon, relocating to Libya, where they were welcomed by General Muammar al-Qaddafi, but the cost to Israel had been high.

And then came the Intefadeh, which more than anything else paved the way for an independently governed Palestinian state. The Intefadeh was the general uprising of Palestinians within Israel's borders. The uprising was characterized by boys and young men throwing stones at armed Israeli soldiers. It was the Palestinian version of nonviolent disobedience. In the age of instantaneous global communications, the Intefadeh brought attention to the Palestinian situation in a much different way than PLO hijackings and murders of innocent people had in the previous two decades. It's a strange twist that once talks began about holding elections for an Arab Palestine, Yasir Arafat had to quickly make his way to Gaza lest

*the revolution start without him. But his was the
face that Palestinian Arabs knew and the name
they called, because he had been waging a battle in
their name for decades. He was the one who had
appeared before the United Nations in their name.
To most of the world he was Palestine.*

*And perhaps strangest of all was the develop-
ment that once Arafat was elected president and
became responsible for keeping the peace in Gaza,
many Palestinians noted with alarm that his methods of keeping order were just as bad as the Israelis.*

Klaus sat up on the edge of the bed as he fought
to wake up. He reached for a pack of cigarettes
on the nightstand, and his face was soon obscured
by a silvery gray cloud of smoke as he let out a deep
breath.

He hurt.

Nothing unusual, just the same sorts of aches and
pains that everyone gets by the time they're in their
eighties.

He had dreamt that old dream again. It was slightly different, but it was still pretty much that same old
dream.

He was back in that pit of bodies, the body of one
of his sons laying beside him while another son
warned him to act as though he were dead, but
instead of looking up to see himself aiming a pistol
at pitiful survivors as he readied for the coup de
grâce, there was a shadowy figure . . . Well, it wasn't
shadowy in the sense that one might expect the
form to be malevolent; in fact, it was paradoxically a

bright visage full of light wrapped in shadows. Klaus couldn't put a name to the being. Was it man? Woman? A beast standing like a human? It reached for him and pulled him from the pit. And then somehow he knew that it was also him, just like the figure of the Nazi officer who was shooting at people. He was all of them. He wondered if he wasn't everything in that dream. Murderer, a victim dying thousands of deaths, a savior, a child and a man.

The remnants of the dream slipped away from him, and he dismissed it when he got up to take a shower and shave. He was eighty-six years old. He put on an old pair of khaki work pants and a paint-spattered gray shirt. He had taken to working with wood as a hobby and enjoyed these early summer days. He would go out to his garage with the intention of finishing off an Adirondack chair or a porch swing, but invariably a couple of the neighborhood children would come by and ask for help with their bicycles. Or David would ask if he could help build a swing, or Nathan might ask if Klaus would help him build something for his mother for Christmas six months away. Klaus was always busy. He made a little money on the side selling yard and porch furniture, but he did it because he liked working with his hands. He didn't work too fast, but he always kept busy.

It wasn't unusual for someone to come up to the garage and ask him to make something for them, so he didn't think too much of it when the black Ford stopped in the street and a young man got out.

"Hello," the young man called out loud enough to be heard over Klaus's electric sander as he smoothed out a corner of the chair he was finishing.

"Hello," Klaus said with a smile in his very notice-able German accent.

"How are you today?" the young man continued as Klaus turned off the sander.

"Fine . . . fine. It's a beautiful day, ja?"

"Yes it is."

"What can I do for you?"

"Are you Carl Dekker?"

"Yes. Are you looking for some chairs?" Klaus said as he nodded toward the chair he was working on.

"No. No, sir. I was hoping to talk to you," the young man continued as Klaus noticed another man getting out of another car across the street. Klaus immediately knew something was wrong. Not that he had such incredible instincts. In fact, he had felt that way hundreds of times, maybe thousands of times, since he had gone into hiding after the war. He had been in America outside Chicago since 1960, when Jakob had made arrangements with the American CIA to provide him a new identity in exchange for information. He and Katrina had lived in peace and quiet for over twenty years, despite a few paranoid episodes when Klaus was sure he had been discovered.

"Is your real name Klaus Grunewald?" the young man continued as his friend came up beside him.

Klaus's legs almost went out from under him. He had to sit down in the chair he had been building.

"Are you all right, sir?" the immigration agent asked loudly as he knelt beside Klaus, afraid that he was having a heart attack.

Katrina happened to look out the window and see

the two men as Klaus stepped back into the garage. She grabbed her cane and made her way out to him as quickly as she could.

"What is it?" she called out anxiously, the cane flailing desperately in one hand as she tried to maintain her balance with the other while propelling herself outside and toward her husband. Her eyes filled with panic as she came to the garage door and looked accusingly at the two young men. "What have you done? What have you done to my man?"

"Mrs. Dekker?" the second man asked as he reached for Katrina's arm to steady her, but Katrina pulled away indignantly.

"Ja! What is it? What have you done?"

"Calm down, Sweetheart," Klaus said gently. "They just want to talk to me."

"Sir, are you Klaus Grunewald?" the first agent insisted again.

Klaus looked up at Katrina, and she could see how tired and old he looked. "No . . . my name is Carl Dekker. You must be mistaken."

No one in the neighborhood could believe it when they heard that "old Carl" had been arrested. And then when they heard that he was to be deported for trial in Israel because he was a former Nazi who had committed "crimes against humanity," their disbelief turned to outrage. Obviously the state department had the wrong man.

In Israel, however, they knew they were right. Word of Klaus's presence in America, in that neatly trimmed, white Chicago suburb, had reached Israel years before.

Klaus, sitting in his cell awaiting extradition, was

certain it had been Jakob Stein who had betrayed him, but he couldn't figure out why it had taken all these years for Jakob to turn him in. Klaus hadn't done anything while living in America that would have drawn attention, much less angered some old enemy. The truth, however, was that Jakob had nothing to do with Klaus's predicament.

A small local newspaper had run a story about "Grandpa Carl" and how he always had time for the neighborhood children. Klaus didn't even know there was a story until a smiling, blond high school student came bouncing into his garage one afternoon chirping and babbling about how they had published her first "newspaper story." He was surprised and shocked, but he kept calm. He thought about it for a while and decided that it wasn't a problem. It was such a small newspaper and such an innocuous little story that he just put it out of his mind.

But the story wasn't small enough. The picture was seen by someone Klaus had known years before in South America. Their relationship had always had a distinct measure of animosity. Micah Eerdmann had reappeared briefly in Klaus's life in South America as part of the "Fourth Reich" network. When the rumor circulated that Klaus had helped the Israeli squad that had attacked the Waldner compound and killed Martin Bormann, Micah believed it, embellished it, and spread it further and faster. He saw to it that Klaus was marked for death.

By that time, Eerdmann felt safe in making occasional visits outside of Argentina. After all, he wasn't a major war criminal. His body count wasn't high enough. He had been visiting friends in Chicago, and he was using their bathroom when he just happened to pick up a copy of the local newspaper from the little magazine rack on the wall, and there was the picture and article on the front page. Eerdmann laughed to himself. Klaus Grunewald's fate was sealed. Eerdmann wasn't even sure it was Klaus, but he had enough suspicion to pass on his accusation anonymously to both American and Israeli authorities, who after a brief investigation found enough cause to continue looking at the kindly old grandfather. It was a little over two years later that the two agents appeared at Carl Dekker's garage.

Katrina hired a lawyer, who immediately filed papers to block the extradition. Klaus suddenly found himself the center of media attention. He had been hiding for so long that the sudden herd of reporters, photographers, and newspeople with video cameras that surrounded him whenever he appeared in public horrified him. He remembered the trial of Eichmann and knew that he would never make it out alive if he were extradited to Israel. His lawyer was not very encouraging. He told Klaus he had made a terrible mistake by admitting his name in the first place, but that was water under the bridge.

"If they do extradite you and there is a trial, we'll concentrate our defense on the fact that you were just a soldier who was ordered to—"

Klaus didn't let him finish. "That," he said, "was the same defense Eichmann used. His ashes ended up in the stomach of some sea bass foraging the bottom of the Mediterranean."

A few days later, as Klaus was being transported from a courtroom back to his cell from another minor hearing in the deportation process—one that his lawyer had delayed—one of the reporters caught his eye. "Carl, did you do it?" the young man yelled.

"Come visit me," Klaus called back.

The reporter, a young man in his early thirties named Matt Christopher who worked for a California newspaper, showed up at the jail at ten o'clock the next morning. He wasn't completely sure if Dekker had meant it, but he wasn't going to take the chance.

"You said I should come talk to you . . ."

"Ja."

"Why me?"

"To tell you the truth, you look like my youngest son, Konrad."

"And where is he?"

"He was killed."

"In the war?"

"No. After that. He died in South America. It shouldn't have happened like that."

There was an awkward pause as Matt flipped through a notebook he had brought, trying to find the right question. But he really wasn't sure where to start. "Why did you ask me to come here?"

"As I said . . . you remind me of Konrad. And I . . . I wanted to say . . . I regret it. I thought it was right back then. I believed it all."

"You regret it?" Matt asked, surprised that Klaus was apparently admitting that he was Klaus Grunewald.

"I can only tell you that if I hadn't been in the

army, I would have gone my whole life without harming another human being. Just like you, I never would have killed anybody. I'm an old man who has seen a lot, and I can tell you there's good and bad in everyone. You shouldn't be so blind that you think the Americans never committed any so-called atrocities. But they won the war, so they write the history. Look at what the Jews have done to the Arabs of Palestine."

"You don't mean to suggest . . ."

"I'm not saying they're doing what the Nazis did. But look at the time when they killed all those Egyptians without even declaring war. Look at what happened in those refugee camps in Lebanon just a year ago when they allowed thousands of innocents to be murdered."

"Are you comparing Israel to the Nazis?"

"I'm only saying there is a danger. Things are done by a state, done in the name of its citizens that . . . Like the philosopher said, beware when you fight monsters that you might become a monster yourself. There are circumstances in history when one is caught up . . . I wish I had not been there. I wish I could have done differently, but I see it all as fate. There were no other roads."

"Are you saying you're a victim?"

"I know it will upset the Jews, but yes. I lost everything. I lost my sons, three of them during the war. My youngest died from the war even after it was over.

Matt let the cryptic remark pass. "Would you then describe yourself as a repentant Nazi?"

"A repentant Nazi? I would say that I was caught up in the times . . . ," Klaus repeated.

"Should you be punished?"

"I have been punished."

"Should you be punished by a court of law?"

"That is now up to them."

"But what's your opinion?"

"I am an old man. Almost ninety years old. Anything they do to me now in the courts would only be symbolic."

"Are you sorry for what you did?"

"Yes."

"Yes?"

"Does that surprise you?"

"Frankly, it does. Other Nazis who have given interviews usually say their only regret is that they didn't succeed in killing *all* the Jews."

"I've heard that. I don't know what to make of it. The idea of eliminating the Jews was to make Germany a great nation. Germany was supposed to become a utopian society, once freed of Jewish control. If that were the case, then Germany should have won the war. Instead, Germany was destroyed and divided.

"So you changed your mind?"

"Changed my mind?" Klaus asked, shaking his head. "No, you miss the point. I never imagined killing the Jews. When it all started, the talk was that Jews controlled the banks and the newspapers and the businesses. They taught in the schools and made the movies. They were like a cancer eating at—"

"I've heard all that before, Mr. Grunewald," Matt said, cutting him off and taking a chance at using his real name. "What's your point?"

Klaus hesitated for a moment, and Matt thought

maybe he had gone too far, that Klaus might end the interview right then and there, but Klaus was just collecting his thoughts.

"As I said, we only thought that the Jews were to be removed from government. They would no longer control the banks."

"If that was all the German people wanted, then how do you explain the killing?"

"We had people in Germany that we called 'super-Nazis.' Those were the people who believed everything they were told by Hitler and Goebbels. Even when they saw something with their own eyes, they would believe the complete opposite if Hitler said it was so. I wasn't a super-Nazi."

"And so it was just these . . . these *super-Nazis* who killed millions of people?"

"Yes, that's it. People like Reinhard Heydrich and Adolf Eichmann. They saw it as the road to power. They took what the Führer said and—"

"Don't tell me they misunderstood!"

"It took on a life of its own. They took him literally when he said destroy the Jews . . ."

"You can't really believe that!"

"It was Heydrich who came up with the phrase 'final solution.'"

"You mean at the Wannsee conference?"

"Ja."

"In 1942?"

"That is correct."

"Then how do you explain that a story was published in a Munich newspaper in 1938 detailing Hitler's 'final solution' for the Jewish problem?"

"I . . ."

"Weren't you yourself involved in war crimes?"

"I followed orders."

"Followed orders . . . it always comes back to that."

"Yes, it does. If I hadn't followed those orders, I would have been shot then and there. They would have called me a 'Jew lover,' and my dead body would have been thrown in right on top of the others. I saw it happen. You sit here all these years later . . . you probably have a comfortable home in an American suburb, probably never served in an army, and you pass judgment on me. I'll tell you this, when your life is in the balance, you make different choices. When it's the choice between dying or killing someone else, it's not so easy. Or maybe it's too easy. Most people choose their own life above everything else."

"How can you justify murder like that?"

"How can I justify it? It happens in all wars. Look at your Vietnam war. What was the name of the man who went to jail for killing people in that small village?"

"William Calley. You mean the My Lai massacre."

"Yes, My Lai. He was the lieutenant. He was the only one tried."

"And convicted," Matt stated, as though it disproved Klaus's contention.

"Convicted. That's right. But they didn't convict the soldiers. They said they were under orders."

"But you were an officer."

"Your Calley wasn't under orders. They didn't tell him to kill those people. My government told me to kill. And if I had not followed those orders, I would have been killed."

Matt shook his head. He was talking to the devil. He stopped and looked Klaus in the eye. He thought to himself that if he had any sense, he would press the conversation, get it all down and win a Pulitzer. But it occurred to him that this kind of thing could go wrong. Quoted out of context, he would be giving this man publicity, the sort of thing that group in California, the one that said the Holocaust was all a hoax, would use in their pamphlets. If he just let the courts take care of it, they would handle it better. Like the Eichmann trial. The Eichmann trial had shown what the Holocaust was like. He should have pressed the conversation and printed an exclusive story, but Matt just stood up and called for the guard.

"Where are you going?" Klaus asked incredulously.

"I've had all I can take," Matt said as the guard opened the door. "Sorry I wasted your time."

"You don't want the story?"

"No. I'll tell you what the problem is, Mr. Dekker. Sometimes people need to recognize when something is wrong and just walk away from it. I suppose I won't save any lives here, but it's right that I leave."

"Fine. I will just talk to someone else!"

"I suppose you will. I just hope they have the guts to walk out on you, too, you pathetic son of a bitch."

Klaus was authentically shocked. He never imagined he would get that kind of reaction. Matt never wrote up the interview, and Klaus didn't speak to anyone else until months later. The other reporter didn't have the same scruples as Matt, and so Klaus's interview was published almost two years later.

IN WASHINGTON, Jakob had retired in 1982. He had done well in his business, including his regular reports to the CIA whenever he did business in the Middle East. He was now officially a millionaire based on his income as a lawyer and the investments he had made along the way. He was worth about five million dollars when he retired, a figure that made him well off, but . . . like they say, a million dollars doesn't go as far as it used to.

His relationship with the CIA had gone as well as could be expected. Sometimes they asked him for things he wasn't willing to do, and he simply refused. Then they wouldn't use him for a while as punishment. He had tried to warn his contact about what was going on in Iran in 1978, but the new agent, the one who had replaced Bill Hanlon when he retired in 1974, didn't believe Jakob was reading the situation correctly. He put Jakob's comments in his report, but he made it clear that he didn't agree. Within months of Jakob's report, the Shah of Iran was deposed, and ten months after that the revolutionaries stormed the U.S. embassy and took the embassy officials hostage.

Besides being the year when Bill Hanlon retired, 1974 was also the year that Amalie died. She was seventy-nine, and she died peacefully in her sleep. By that time Yigal had gotten married, and they all went to Israel for the funeral. It was the first time Thomas and Yigal had seen their father cry, that is, *really* cry. He stopped at the coffin and sobbed. Rebecca led him away, and Thomas and Yigal came up too. Jakob tried to give a eulogy. He tried to tell about what she had been like in Munich before the Second World War, and he tried to explain how she had saved all those people, but it all came out jumbled and confused. What could he say and what couldn't he say? There were dozens of people there, and he just didn't know how to get around all the secrets.

Rebecca insisted that Jakob go through the Jewish rituals of death and grieving, sitting Shiva and saying Kaddish. After it was over he felt better because he had been surrounded by all of his family, and they prayed together for the first time. And they cried together and told the stories of Amalie. Thomas and Yigal learned about the escape from Theresienstadt for the first time and were amazed that their bubba, their sweet old grandmother, had been a spy. They started to ask Jakob question after question, but soon it got to be too much as they started to delve into the moral questions, and Jakob had to cut them off. "You had to be there to understand it," he told them. "You can't look at it today and judge it by what you know now. It's so easy to say what should have been done, but it's different when you're living in that moment and you don't know how things are going to turn out."

Ten years later Jakob and Rebecca were back in Israel for their annual visit, this time without Yigal, whose wife Rachel was expecting their fourth child. Thomas and Jakob were watching television while Rebecca and Chaya had taken the children over to see Rebecca's mother.

"And also in the news tonight," the TV anchorman said in his most poignant rendering, "Klaus Grunewald, the suspected Nazi war criminal under indictment by the Israeli courts for crimes against

humanity, has died in his jail cell of an apparent
heart attack. Grunewald was slated for extradition
from the United States after almost two years of legal
maneuvering. He was eighty-nine years old."

Jakob had been watching the developments in the
case since he first heard about it. For an instant he
thought about coming forward to testify, but of
course there wasn't anything he could say that
wouldn't put him in a bad light.

"That was the man that killed your grandfather..."
Jakob said as though he were just making casual conversation.

"What?" Thomas asked incredulously.

"He was the one who killed my father in 1934. I
told you he had been a Brownshirt when I was
telling you about your grandmother after she died."

"Yes . . ."

"Your grandfather was killed when Hitler had the
Sturmabteilung purged in thirty-four."

"And you're saying that was the man? Klaus
Grunewald?"

"He was the one."

"You know that? How?"

"He told me."

"Told you? When?"

"It's a long story."

"What did you do?"

Jakob moved to the edge of his seat, moving in
closer to Thomas and looking him square in the eye.
"I'm going to tell you something, son. Revenge is for
the young and the innocent. And I'm afraid I'm neither. I'll tell you this; I did things for my country that
. . . if I told you some of the things that we did, you

probably couldn't look me in the eye. You wouldn't think of me in the same way. I did it because I thought we had to do it. And I've got some bad news for you. I was sitting in my reclining rocking chair in my comfortable home outside of Washington, D.C., the other day reading a magazine story about Klaus Grunewald's confessions . . . and he said the exact same thing. He said the exact same thing that I just said to you. That's a terrible thing."

But Klaus certainly wasn't the last war criminal to be brought before the courts. In 1985, after a new government took control in Bolivia, the French government was allowed to extradite Klaus Barbie, known as the "Butcher of Lyon," for trial. One day Rebecca turned on the television and there was the face of Aubin Chanler. She hardly recognized him, but then his name appeared below the picture and there was no doubt. Now in his early fifties, he was slated to testify at the trial about how Barbie had deported Jewish children from an orphanage and had them sent to Auschwitz. The camera zoomed in as Aubin started to break down, but he kept going. Rebecca knew then that Aubin had never found his lost brother. She wished so much at that moment that she could be with him. She remembered back to that day when they boarded the ship in Marseilles and how she had held the fragile little boy in her arms, and she wondered if the pain would ever end. Would it end when a generation passed into memory? Or would it go on in a collective memory? But she knew it couldn't be that simple. Humanity had passed through a forbidden portal, nothing less then Adam and Eve taking a bite from that apple.

We had gone through a door that was now locked against us with no way back.

A few years later, having returned once again to Israel, Jakob would be driving down a road. A flat tire. A quiet winding road without any service stations. A few old concrete block homes set into the sand-colored hill. Another car driven too fast by a young Palestinian, but it could have been anyone.

Jakob was trying to change the tire by himself. He let loose a few well-chosen profanities as he knelt in front of the tire and then climbed wearily to his feet, returning to the trunk to look for more tools. When he couldn't find a hammer, he looked around for a rock. He found a good-sized stone and began pounding on the lug wrench with one hand while holding it in place with the other. The car shook with each resounding blow until suddenly it slipped off the jack and Jakob did his best to get out of the way, moving backward into the road. At that same instant a car came around the corner going much faster than the fifty-kilometer-per-hour speed limit for the treacherous winding road, and before the driver knew what was happening, Jakob was hit and thrown back against his own car, crumpling to the ground.

The young driver started to slow down but then panicked and sped away.

It happened so fast that Jakob wasn't even sure of what hit him. The trauma left him completely dazed as he tried to pull himself up and away from the roadway. It was just instinct, since there was nothing in sight that would help him if he did make it to the curb. He was a wounded animal trying to distance himself from the unknown predator that had felled him.

The pain was excruciating. His vision was blurred as he crawled to the side of the road and collapsed.

And his last thought was of a train station that still existed in a misty land of dreams and memory, and a tall man in uniform sweeping him, the little boy, up in his arms. "It seems about time that we should meet, my little soldier." And a warm embrace.

LIST OF CHARACTERS

The Jakob's Star Trilogy is a work of historical fiction that follows the Metzdorf family from the time of their relocation from Salzburg to Munich at the end of the First World War on through to the Intefadeh in Israel in the late 1980s. An "F" following a name on the list of characters below indicates a fictional character, while "N" indicates nonfictional characters.

Per Anger *(N)*—Swedish diplomat who helped Hungarian Jews obtain provisional passes exempting them from anti-Jewish measures.

Yasir Arafat *(N)*—Leader of the Palestine Liberation Organization; eventually president of Palestine.

Bahira *(F)*—Palestinian woman who helped Thomas Stein when he was shot outside Gaza.

Niklaus (Klaus) Barbie *(N)*—German head of the Gestapo in Lyon, France, during the Second World War.

Galia Bartalan *(F)*—Young Hungarian woman who cares for Jakob Stein-Metzdorf when he is wounded during a partisan mission.

Istvan Bartalan *(F)*—Galia Bartalan's younger brother.

Mikhalis Bartalan *(F)*—Galia Bartalan's father.

Erika Bauer *(F)*—Older of Hannah Bauer's two daughters.

Hannah Bauer *(F)*—Friend of Amalie Stein-Metzdorf from college; their friendship is renewed in Prague when Amalie and her father leave Austria just before the *Anschluss*.

Karin Bauer *(F)*—Younger of Hannah Bauer's two daughters.

Ricardo Bauer *(F)*—Pseudonym adopted by Albert Waldhramm in South America.

Rolf Bauer *(F)*—Hannah Bauer's late husband.

Franz Beckman *(F)*—German soldier attending a refueling station in Sardinia during the war.

Menachem Begin *(N)*—Polish intellectual who became a partisan during the war and then a leader of the Irgun during the last years of the British mandate, finally rising to the position of prime minister of Israel.

Edvard Beneš *(N)*—President of Czechoslovakia (1935–38 and 1940–48) and, during the Second World War, head of Czechoslovakia's government in exile in Britain.

Giovanni di Bernardone *(N)*—Italian man who would become St. Francis of Assisi.

Martin Bormann *(N)*—Adolf Hitler's top aide during the Second World War; thought to have escaped the final assault on Berlin and made his way to South America.

Edward Bortner *(F)*—Pseudonym used by Klaus Grunewald.

Luciano Brindisi *(F)*—Pseudonym adopted by Nicolai Ostrechnotov.

Father Bruncatti *(F)*—Priest involved with the "Vatican ratline" that helped Nazi war criminals get out of Europe.

Admiral William Canaris *(N)*—Head of German military intelligence.

Neville Chamberlain *(N)*—Prime minister of England from 1927 to 1939.

Arnou Chanler *(F)*—Father of Aubin and Etienne Chanler.

Aubin Chanler *(F)*—French national who, as a boy of twelve, escaped France with Amalie Stein-Metzdorf in 1944.

Claire Chanler *(F)*—Aunt of Aubin and Etienne Chanler.

Henrietta Chanler *(F)*—Mother of Aubin and Etienne Chanler.

Chaya *(F)*—Thomas Stein's wife.

Winston Churchill *(N)*—Prime minister of England during the Second World War.

Madeline Courtmanche *(F)*—Prisoner of the Gestapo in Marseilles.

Carl Dekker *(F)*—Pseudonym used by Klaus Grunewald in America.

Kolya Doboszemski *(F)*—Russian agent who infiltrated the Vatican escape route in its early stages.

Mirabelle Ducloux *(F)*—One of Klaus Barbie's victims.

Micah Eerdmann *(F)*—SS captain in charge of transporting ransom money from the Jews in Tunisia to Italy as the Afrika Korps was evacuating North Africa.

Adolf Eichmann *(N)*—Lieutenant colonel in the SS who directed the transport of Jews from across Europe to the death camps in Poland; Eichmann was taken by Israeli agents from Argentina and put on trial in an Israeli court in Jerusalem in 1960 for crimes against humanity.

Eli *(F)*—Friend of Istvan Bartalan recruited to help Jakob Stein-Metzdorf on his mission in South America.

Josef Fedorovich *(F)*—Former professor of languages from the Ukraine who accompanied Jakob Stein-Metzdorf to Sardinia.

Ferko *(F)*—Youngest of the Hungarian partisan group that picked up Jakob, Sasha, and Jan when they were on their way to Bratislava.

Count Folke-Bernadotte *(N)*—Swedish diplomat who, while part of the UN commission trying to bring peace to the Middle East during the Israeli War of Independence, was assassinated in Jerusalem by Jewish extremists.

David Frieder *(F)*—Munich book publisher, head of Frieder and Son Publishing, which his father, Sam, had started years before; Amalie Stein-Metzdorf began working for

David as an assistant copyright editor in February 1919.

Sam Frieder *(F)*—Father of David Frieder; founder of Frieder and Son Publishing who retired before the end of the war and made a hobby of following the tumultuous political scene in Germany.

Charles Garrick *(F)*—Rare coin dealer in Zurich who bought concentration camp gold from Jakob Stein-Metzdorf.

Aliz Gazsi *(F)*—Galia Bartalan's assumed name.

Elga Gazsi *(F)*—Ferko Gazsi's mother.

Ferko Gazsi *(F)*—See Ferko.

Joska Gazsi *(F)*—Ferko Gazsi's father.

Abagail Geschwind *(F)*—Rebecca Geschwind's mother.

Max Geschwind *(F)*—Rebecca Geschwind's younger brother.

Rebecca Geschwind *(F)*—Girlfriend of Jakob Stein-Metzdorf; her family lived in the same neighborhood in the Fürstenried district of Munich.

Joseph Goebbels *(N)*—Nazi party's minister of propaganda; was headquarted in Berlin long before the Nazi party received the majority votes under the Weimar elections that brought them to power.

Hermann Göring *(N)*—World War I flying ace who became a confederate of Adolf Hitler in the early days of the Nazi party and eventually head of the German Luftwaffe during the Second World War.

Katrina Grunewald *(F)*—Klaus Grunewald's wife.

Klaus Grunewald *(F)*—Gunther Metzdorf's front-line comrade during the First World War; a conserative, right-wing militarist.

Konrad Grunewald *(F)*—Klaus Grunewald's youngest son, born during the Second World War.

Jacques Guignard *(F)*—Captain of a grain barge on the Rhône river in France.

David Ben Gurion *(N)*—Born David Joseph Gruen in Russia, he was leader of the Yishuv, the Jewish community in Palestine during the British mandate, and became prime minister of Israel when statehood was declared.

Friedrich Haas *(F)*—Young German befriended by Gunther Metzdorf while the two are looking for work in postwar Munich; Friedrich had been an ambulance driver in the medical corps and so in Gunther's mind qualified as a member of "the brotherhood of front-line soldiers," which later became a qualifying phrase of the emerging Nazi party.

Gertrude Haas *(F)*—Mother of Friedrich Haas and good friend of Amalie Stein-Metzdorf, who became part of the Metzdorf family when she moved in with them after losing her home during the crippling inflation of the early Weimar years.

Manfred Haas *(F)*—Gertrude Haas's late husband; Friedrich Haas's father.

Frank Hanley *(F)*—British intelligence office stationed at the King David Hotel in 1946.

William Tyler Hanlon *(F)*—Captain serving with the American military intelligence service who eventually went on to become a member of the Central Intelligence Agency.

Franz Harimann *(F)*—Pseudonym used by Klaus Grunewald in South America.

Theodore Herzl *(N)*—Known as "the father of modern Zionism"; it was Herzl, along with Émile Zola, who came to the defense of Captain Alfred Dreyfus of the French army in a famous case of government-sanctioned anti-Semitism that came to be known as "the Dreyfus affair."

Rudolph Hess *(N)*—Deputy führer to Adolph Hitler who flew to England during the war in an attempt to present a plan for peace; he was arrested and eventually became the only surviving defendant of those found guilty during the Nuremburg trials, becoming the sole prisoner in Spandau prison until his death in the late 1980s.

SS Obersturmbannführer Reinhard Heydrich *(N)*—Head of the Sicherdienst in Munich before the Nazis came to power in Germany; eventually appointed as Reichsprotektor of Bohemia and Moravia.

Heinrich Himmler *(N)*—Head of the Nazi SS, which included the Gestapo and Totskopf or "death's head" divisions responsible for the actual murders of European Jews resulting from the Nazi policy of genocide.

Paul von Hindenburg *(N)*—Head of the German High Command during the First World War who became president of the Weimar Republic after the death of Friedrich Ebert in 1925.

Adolf Hitler *(N)*—Leader of the National Socialist German Workers' Party (Nationalsozialistische Deutsche Arbeiterpartei).

Eleonore Hoffman née Stein *(F)*—Amalie's sister.

Louis Arthur Hoffman *(F)*—Amalie's brother-in-law; married to her sister Eleonore.

Rachel Hoffman *(F)*—Louis and Eleonore's older daughter.

Sophie Hoffman *(F)*—Louis and Eleonore's younger daughter.

Admiral Miklós Horthy *(N)*—Regent of Hungary during the Second World War.

Petr Hrmeni *(F)*—Czech national who married Hannah Bauer in Prague; also a member of the Czech resistance.

Joseph Hubert *(F)*—Longtime friend of David Frieder, Amalie's boss.

Cardinal Hudal *(N)*—Catholic cardinal who was instrumental in coordinating an escape route for German war criminals after the Second World War.

Ephraim Ilani *(F)*—Israeli intelligence operative in Argentina in the 1950s.

Izsak *(F)*—Leader of the Hungarian partisan group that picked up Jakob, Sasha, and Jan when they were on their way to Bratislava.

Izzy *(F)*—Member of the Haganah who showed Jakob Stein-Metzdorf around Haifa when he first arrived in Palestine.

Rudolf Kastner *(N)*—Member of the Swedish rescue mission trying to rescue the Hungarian Jews in 1944.

Hans Kleidenveld *(F)*—Nazi war criminal caught by Martin Aarohnson and other members of His Majesty's Jewish Brigade.

Ricardo Klement *(N)*—Pseudonym adopted by Adolf Eichmann in Argentina.

Abba Kovner *(N)*—Poet who became leader of a Hungarian partisan group that sought revenge against German war criminals after the war and also organized the *Brich-ha* escape route.

Bruno Kress *(F)*—Nazi war criminal trying to get out of Europe in 1945.

Pinhas Lavon *(N)*—Israeli defense minister in the 1950s.

Avram Lazear *(F)*—Thomas Stein's "partner" in the army; they worked in a radio communications listening post.

Mme. Lemieux *(F)*—Teacher/administrator at the *Colonie Enfants* orphanage in eastern France.

Rabbi Loew *(F)*—Actual rabbi in Prague in the 16th century; the myth of the Golem said that Rabbi Loew had created a manlike creature out of clay that he could control with magic.

Lorencz *(F)*—A Hungarian partisan fighting with the group that picked up Jakob, Sasha, and Jan when they were on their way to Bratislava.

Mendel Lubinsky *(F)*—Twelve-year-old orphaned refugee who ends up on the *Exodus 1947.*

Martin (Aarohnson) *(F)*—Member of His Majesty's Jewish Brigade from Palestine who met Jakob Stein-Metzdorf in northern Italy and convinced him to eventually join the Haganah in Palestine.

Alain Mahieu *(F)*—Alias used by David Frieder in France.

Millicent Mahieu *(F)*—Alias used by Amalie Stein in France.

Otto Maus *(F)*—Middle-aged author of books of the American West; client of Frieder and Son Publishing who lived in Ried, Austria; Amalie, as an agent of Frieder and Son, worked with Otto on some of his books.

Josef Mengele *(N)*—Doctor at the Auschwitz concentration camp who performed sadistic experiments on the Jewish inmates; nicknamed "The Angel of Death"; escaped to South America after the war, living there until his death of natural causes in the 1970s.

Schlomo Meicelzinsky *(F)*—Israeli soldier who arrested Klaus Grunewald.

Mr. Mengershausen *(F)*—Owner of the factory in Tel Aviv where Amalie Stein works in 1948.

Amalie Stein-Metzdorf *(F)*—Born in Salzburg, Austria, in 1895 to Ruth and Ethan Stein; the Steins are reform Jews; Amalie is the wife of Gunther and mother of Jakob, her only child.

Gunther Metzdorf *(F)*—Husband of Amalie and father of Jakob; served in the Austrian infantry on the Russian front in the First World War; moved his family to Munich at the end of the war.

Jakob Stein-Metzdorf *(F)*—Amalie's son; born in 1916.

Jules Millard *(F)*—Angelette Preruet's fiancé.

Peter Mueller *(F)*—Pseudonym used by Jakob Stein-Metzdorf during his intelligence mission to South America.

Baruch Mummenstein *(F)*—Israeli intelligence officer originally from Brooklyn who came to Palestine right after being released from the American army in West Germany after the war.

Benito Mussolini *(N)*—Leader of the Italian Fascist party, which took over the Italian government in 1922. Adolf Hitler, as head of the German Nazi party, sought to emulate Mussolini's early successes.

Ben Nagan *(F)*—Native-born Israeli who accompanied Jakob Stein-Metzdorf to Sardinia.

Gamal Abdel Nasser *(N)*—President of the Republic of Egypt from 1956 to 1970.

Alfred Naujocks *(N)*—Subordinate of Reinhard Heydrich's who worked with him in a number of clandestine operations.

Neil *(F)*—One of Istvan Bartalan's friends recruited to help Jakob Stein-Metzdorf on his mission in South American.

Ondra *(F)*—Assumed name of a resistance leader in Prague who helped Jakob Stein-Metzdorf after his return in 1944.

Nicolai Ostrechnotov *(F)*—Russian agent who infiltrated the Vatican escape route in its early stages.

Eugenio Pacelli *(N)*—Monsignor in Munich during the First World War; became Pope Pius XII prior to the Second World War.

Marshall Philippe Pétain *(N)*—French general during the First World War; formed a collaborationist government in Vichy in southern France after the France surrendered to Germany in 1940.

Sasha Petrov *(F)*—Young Czech resistance fighter who traveled with Jakob Stein-Metzdorf.

Henri Pinchot *(F)*—French partisan in Marseilles.

Pista *(F)*—Boyhood friend of Thomas Stein in Israel.

Angelette Preruet *(F)*—French hostage held by the Germans in Marseilles after a partisan attack.

René *(F)*—Associate of Klaus Barbie who watched over Aubin Chanler.

Joachim von Ribbentrop *(N)*—German foreign minister under Adolf Hitler.

Erwin Rommel *(N)*—One of the most brilliant generals of the Second World War; German field marshal who led the Afrika Korps in North Africa; nicknamed "The Desert Fox."

Ruben *(F)*—One of Istvan Bartalan's friends recruited to help Jakob Stein-Metzdorf on his mission in South American.

Anwar as-Sadat *(N)*—President of Egypt after the death of Gamal Abdel Nasser.

Anat Scholem *(F)*—Young Jewish woman in Egypt working for the Israeli military in the early 1950s.

Konrad Schwister *(F)*—Gestapo agent in Marseilles during the war.

Hannah Senesh *(N)*—Hungarian national who emigrated to Palestine before the war; a poet who joined a Jewish paratroop commando group created within the British military to warn Hungarian Jews of impending deportation to German death camps after the German occupation of Hungary in 1944.

Moshe Sharett *(N)*—Prime minister of Israel in the 1950s.

Otto Skorzeny *(N)*—German commando leader who rescued Mussolini from an Italian prison after the Italian capitulation to the Allies in 1943; went on to establish Die Spinne, an escape route for top-ranking Nazis after the war; also worked with Juan Perón to set up a sanctuary for Nazi war criminals in Argentina after the war.

Eugen Spengler *(F)*—Friend of Ondra who helps Jakob, Sasha, and Jan get out of Prague.

Ethan Stein *(F)*—Amalie's father; owner of a publishing house in Austria.

Ruth Stein *(F)*—Amalie's mother who died of influenza when Amalie was twelve years old.

Josef Brodz Tito *(N)*—Leader of a large resistance group in Yugoslavia; eventually became Yugoslavia's Communist leader.

Tonda *(N)*—Assumed name used by Jakob Stein-Metzdorf in the Prague underground in 1944 along with the name "Anton."

Guri Ben Tzuriel *(F)*—Israeli general who approved Jakob Stein-Metzdorf's trip to Sardinia.

Karif Ibn Umar *(F)*—Palestinian refugee relocated to Gaza from Haifa during the War of Independence.

Virgil *(F)*—Guide who led Amalie Stein through France.

Kurt Waldheim *(N)*—Young lieutenant in the Austrian division of the Waffen SS assigned to track down Yugoslavian partisans; later became Secretary General of the United Nations and president of Austria.

Albert Waldhramm *(F)*—Man who impersonated Martin Bormann in South America.

Raoul Wallenberg *(N)*—First Secretary of the Swedish legation in Budapest, Hungary, charged with starting a rescue mission for the Jews of Hungary in 1944.

Horst Wessel *(N)*—Berlin pimp who was also a member of the Nazi party; after he was killed in a fight over a woman by a man who happened to be a member of the Communist party, Josef Goebbels created the myth that Wessel had died fighting for the Nazi party, and a song was soon written celebrating this myth, a song that included such sentiments as "when Jewish blood drips from the knife, then we will all be happy."

Theodore Witherspoon *(F)*—British soldier patroling the beach south of Haifa.

Mrs. Yedidah *(F)*—Thomas Stein's grammar school teacher.

Chanoch Zimra *(F)*—Jakob Stein-Metzdorf's supervisor in the Mossad.

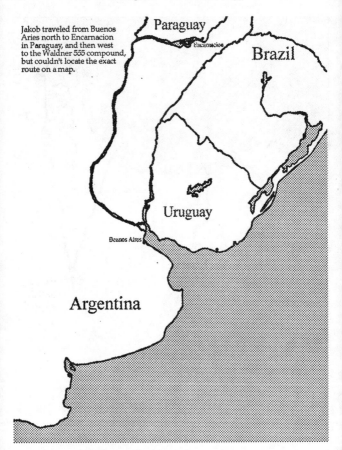

Jakob traveled from Buenos Aries north to Encarnacion in Paraguay, and then west to the Waldner 555 compound, but couldn't locate the exact route on a map.